THE DIGITAL MAGE

MAGE

BOOK FOUR OF THE LUCKY DEVIL SERIES

THE DIGITAL MAGE

BOOK FOUR OF THE LUCKY DEVIL SERIES

MEGAN MACKIE

Library of Congress Control Number: 2023945216

Paperback ISBN-13: 978-1-965097-16-8
Hardcover ISBN-13: 978-1-965097-17-5
Ebook ISBN-13: 978-1-965097-15-1

To Paul, my personal saint

CONTENTS

THE DIGITAL MAGE

ACKNOWLEDGMENT

Thank you to my husband Paul, my kids Byron and Alaina, and to my mom Connie, for supporting me while I work on my dreams.

Thank you to Beau, the best carebear in the whole carebear kingdom.

Thank you to Donn, for the literary tech support.

Thank you to Jen, my editor extraordinaire.

Thank you to Jake, the artist whose career has grown parallel to mine.

"Let it be. Because sometimes,
only time can answer your questions"

- Unknown

PROLOGUE

"We have to hurry," Maxx whispered harshly as he leaned in front of the door, covering it and the light in Compadre's mouth from any view from the street. His long, ragged-edged coat certainly was the right choice for their activities that night, despite Camela's protests about how it looked. A sound of laughing and shouting echoed up from the street down the alley, and both men froze for a second. "Yeah, definitely more hurry."

"I'm aware," Compadre said around the end of his flashlight, his nose ring flashing in the scant light. The hacker returned his focus on his task, lifting up his portable soldering iron to connect his *unlock jock pro.* The machine was of his own design, and Maxx really though he should have trademarked it. Compadre, however, was convinced that the corporate elites would find a way to break his trademark and believed the only way to keep it safe was for no one to know it existed. Maxx had never found a good argument against that.

Maxx eyed the cords snaking into the electrical circuits

of the lock through a maintenance port revealed on the side. He didn't know a whole lot about how the hacking machine worked; he didn't have to. That's why he had recruited Compadre—for those technical skills he just didn't have. It all seemed like magic to him.

Not fast enough magic. More people started to linger at the end of the alley. It just looked like office workers blowing off steam after work, but Maxx didn't want to linger himself to find out he was wrong.

"Two minutes. You said this would take two minutes," Maxx muttered, his hand checking for the gun he had tucked inside his coat. He didn't want to use it, but he would if he must.

"It's been one minute forty-five," Compadre intoned, "from when I plugged it in—"

A tiny beep sounded, and the screen of the lock started to blink red.

"We're in. We've got fifteen now," Compadre said, ripping his cord out and stuffing his hacking tools into the bag in front of him before slinging it back over his shoulder.

Fifteen minutes before the error loop Compadre had introduced into the lock's computer triggered the lock's automatic reboot function, which would send a silent alarm to the building's security of a problem. Possibly ten to thirty minutes until they responded to it, the human factor being what it was.

Maxx pressed down on the bar handle of the door and pushed his way in. The back door opened into an expected storage backroom complete with janitor's station that spilled down a short concrete hallway with doors at various intervals. The whole thing led into the main building.

Sliding down his sleeve, Maxx examined the map he had drawn on his skin in rave highlighter, specially designed to glow in dim light. "Third door on the right. Two more doors down," Maxx recited to himself.

He flipped out the set of copied janitor's keys he had made for this operation, each tagged with a color of the rainbow. The keys had been tricky to come by, but Camela had done

more for the cause than she ever should have needed to by dating that big slob of a janitor for three weeks just to acquire this asset. Maxx vowed to himself for the hundredth time to never question her dedication to the cause ever again, especially when the red key clicked open the lock of the third door on the right as smoothly as a silken caress.

The pair of men moved through, wasting no time on words. They had only a limited amount of it, and if they were caught, it could be all they had left.

"Two doors down, go right again," Maxx muttered, counting as he picked up the next key, an orange one. Second door unlocked. It opened into a room of cubicles, all separated by the gray and black dividers one would expect to see in an office for corporate serfs.

The lights were still on, but that was expected. Office lights never turned off for both security and cost effectiveness reasons. These lights in particular were outfitted with UV bulbs, which were supposed to be good for the workers and the office plants alike.

It also allowed the company to get away with not having windows. Those were only for the elites and their butt kissers.

Maxx narrowed his eyes at the offending lights. "Kill 'em," he stated, and Compadre stepped up to the door again, pulling out another device. Just like the floor plans said, an electrical box sat right above the door, feeding power both into the exit sign and the light grid system above. It was too high to actually reach, butted up against the ceiling like that, but Compadre's device sent a remote command through the wireless system that the company hadn't bothered using since they left the lights on all the time. Whoever installed it hadn't taken the extra steps to disconnect the feature, allowing Compadre to simply remote turn the lights off.

The second they were plunged into darkness, Maxx bolted forward, heading for the far end of the room. The Branch Manager's office opened with the yellow key. Smoothly, they bypassed the BM's desk with its computer set in the middle of the opulently decorated room. This room had a wide bay window to the outside world, albeit only of the street and the building on the other side. If it wouldn't have screwed up the mission, Maxx would have smashed them out of spite.

"We're doing good, boss," Compadre reported, checking his watch. He moved around the desk to face the computer.

That computer wasn't the one they wanted, though.

This was where things got tricky.

From behind the desk, Compadre shifted his weight around, using a third device that he said detected where all signals were coming from. It pointed him to a set of walnut bookcases that lined the left side of the office.

There was no color-coded key for this entryway. According to the plans they saw, there wasn't an office on the other side of the wall. Yet Maxx could tell at a glance that the branch manager's office was indeed a lot smaller than what the plans indicated. There was no sophisticated way to do this better, but to find which book wasn't a book. They proceeded to yank and tug everything off the shelves. Each volume made satisfying slapping sounds as they hit the floor. And sure enough, they found the right one. Pulling it forward, a mechanism released, like every bad spy thriller ever made, and the door made to look like a shelf popped open.

"What a poser," Compadre sniffed derisively. "I bet he drives an Aston Martin, too."

"Thank god for Hollywood movies and their psychological effects on the weak-minded," Maxx countered.

Compadre sniffed at that but said nothing more as he seized the edge of the shelf to pull it open farther. A light came on inside a small room, illuminating a computer at a lonely desk. A monitor with a hot-rod car screensaver greeted the two men, who stared at the find.

"You think this is it?" Maxx asked, doubt now invading his confident mind. They were so close to achieving their objective. This was when something would go wrong.

"It better be," Compadre dismissed, already moving to sit

in the wooden chair before the desk. He looked to the side at the computer CPU itself, ignoring the monitor for now. "Yeah, they are being cautious. It's wired to burn itself if someone tries to disconnect it from a power source."

"So, we have to copy it," Maxx said, leaning against the exit to keep an eye on the office door. Still no sounds of anyone having detected their intrusion.

Compadre was already moving, pulling out a spare hard drive that he had re-enforced to take any internal attacks the computer might have booby-trapped within. With supreme confidence, he plugged it in and shifted the mouse to wake the whole thing up.

"What the hell?" the hacker muttered as he stared at the screen.

"What? What is it?" Maxx asked, already turning around to face the next disaster, whatever it might be. He knew this was all going too smoothly.

"It's..." Compadre said, but it was all he could get out.

On the desktop inside the computer, a series of icons lined up along the right. It looked like fairly normal interfacing software to Maxx.

"What?" the revolutionary leader demanded, pointing at the upper right icon that represented the hard drive. "There it is. Get to work."

"You're not seeing this?" Compadre asked and gestured at the screen.

"See what?!" Maxx demanded, but then he did. He stopped focusing so hard on the prize and took in the whole picture, including the background wallpaper. It was a gray brick wall, like one would see in an alley, and across it someone had spray painted the words, "I've already got the Masterson Files."

The two men stared at the message, dumbfounded. No amount of planning had prepared them for this turn.

"Check," Maxx ordered, the first to react. "Check it now!"

Compadre spurred forward to seize the mouse when another voice cut them off.

"I wouldn't bother. You're not going to find it in there."

Maxx spun around, pulling the gun he carried out from inside his coat in an awkward motion, his nerves rattling his grip on the gun. It didn't matter because his nose met another gun, far more steady and far more ready. The barrel looked larger than life, the size of a cannon in Maxx's vision, and he froze, his hands automatically raising, the gun in one of them forgotten.

"Whoa, whoa, whoa, man," Maxx said, trying to catch his brain up to the situation. "There... There is no need for this."

He felt more than saw Compadre half rise out of the seat before freezing himself.

The man holding the gun on him smiled. It was a wicked smile that made his eyes seem crazy, twinkling demonically bright. Then those eyes triple blinked. The pupil and iris disappeared into a glow of blue that sheened over his eyeballs, making both men gasp in shock.

Compadre swore something in Spanish. "He's one of them. One of those... those Saints. Computer enhanced super soldiers."

"Ah, I see my reputation has proceeded me," the strange man replied, amused by the idea.

Maxx kept his hands up, trying to find a way to regain control of the situation. "Hey, hey, man. We don't want no trouble," he said.

"This isn't any trouble," the stranger said, both hands locked firmly around the grip, his trigger finger resting lightly, ready to pull. Everything about him bespoke easy confidence. His body stood turned slightly to minimize himself as a target while keeping his feet comfortably braced. He looked like he could hold that pose for hours.

"Okay," Maxx said, shifting his own feet. "Okay, then what do you want? What we got to do to resolve this?" He was just saying words, looking for any combination that might get them an opening to make a run for it. "You're the boss now. You tell us what you want, and we'll do it."

The Saint's eyebrow popped up when Maxx said the word "boss."

"Now, there's an interesting offer," he said. "You know I do have orders to simply kill you two, but—"

Before he could say anything more, Compadre rushed him.

For the half second it took for his partner to go, Maxx was certain the gun was going to go off in his face. The Saint didn't move his gun away from its original target, but his left hand snapped out to grab Compadre in a one-armed hug. Both men were bowled back into the main office. They created a loud, crashing chaos as the two bodies hit the desk. Compadre tried to throw a thousand punches at the guy with a primal roar.

Maxx drove himself forward to help, aiming to wrest the gun away from the Saint. Doing so forced him to drop his own forgotten weapon to the floor. He aborted his attack, scrabbling to retrieve it. *Oh crap, oh crap, oh crap, oh crap...* was all he could think.

Compadre screamed.

Blood slashed across Maxx kneeling on the floor. His partner bucked away, grabbing at his own face. Still lying on the desk, the Saint held up the hacker's nose ring, hooked around one finger like the guy had just pulled a grenade pin.

Their eyes met. The Saint grinned.

Maxx dove for the gun, but he fumbled it again. It slid instead across the floor.

When he looked up, the Saint's barrel was back pointing at his nose. The Saint still lay on the desk. Maxx's move had landed him right next to the desk. An easy target.

"Uh, uh, uh," the Saint tsked. "You're not a very good fighter for a revolutionary, are you?" He sounded amused, and he sat up without help, the core muscles exposed by his now torn shirt bunching like a washboard. The gun stayed steadily aimed. "Don't move, revolutionary."

Being called what he was, Maxx hardened his face. "So, you know who we are, huh?"

"Camela wasn't the only one doing the seducing," the

Saint said wryly. "How do you think she got the keys in the first place?"

Hot rage burned in Maxx's chest. "So, this is how I go down, huh?" he replied, his own brand of dark amusement coloring his words.

The Saint strolled over to Compadre mewling on the floor, still gripping his nose. "Eh, maybe. Let's see where this conversation goes," he said, then used the gun to cold cock the hacker across the face before he could react. Compadre dropped like a sack of stones.

"I'm not going down *that* easy," Maxx promised, unsure if he was lying or not.

"God, I hope not," the Saint said, then he did something odd. He bowed formally at the waist. "My name is St. Benedict. As you've probably already guessed, I was hired by this company's corporate powers-that-be to take care of your little infiltration project and stop you from getting their most prized asset."

"Look, man," Maxx dismissed, sounding bored, "just kill me already. I don't have any interest in standing here listening to your monologuing."

A pair of eyebrows shot up to the glowing-eyed man's hairline. "What they don't know is that I have in fact acquired that same program that they were hoping to protect, and you were hoping to steal."

Maxx narrowed his eyes to slits. "So, you're playing us all. You take what they want and blame us for taking it. Then kill us and walk off, unable to recover what they lost because it was destroyed in the attempt?" He nodded at the computer. "Blow up the source for good measure."

"Oh, yeah, I am totally blowing up the computer. No Chekov's gun about it."

"Then why are we talking? You sound like you got it all figured out."

"Because you gave me a really great idea just now," the Saint said. "I was going to do exactly as you said, but I've been working on a plan myself, and you and your little underground

revolution could fit very nicely into it."

"What do you know about us? You don't know *shit*," Maxx cursed, moving around the desk. Considering the whole situation, he should have still felt scared, but now it just made him angry.

The Saint countered, cocking his head to the side. "You do have some steel in that spine. That's increasing your value by the second."

"And you're still talking shit."

Then the Saint dropped his gun arm to his side, still holding it, but not aiming it at him anymore.

"Maxx, or Max X as you'd like everyone to call you, but nobody does. Wanted on several charges of hacking, conspiracy to commit fraud, and theft against several corporations. Human trafficking, conspiracy to commit human trafficking—"

"If that's what you call helping people escape corporate bondage, then yeah, guilty as charged," Maxx spat back.

"Would you be interested in doing something like that, but for me?" the Saint asked. Then he tapped his head. "In exchange, I'll give you what I stole from that computer."

"You want me to work for you?" Maxx sneered, making it clear that he would never go for that.

"Oh, no, of course not," St. Benedict said, smiling a big toothy grin. "I want to come work for you."

CHAPTER I

The Citadel building towered above Rune, but that wasn't unusual since all the buildings downtown more or less did that. The Loop was the heart of the city of Chicago, certainly its center. The collection of clustered skyscrapers was ringed by the train system that brought its workforce to and from it with constant regularity, both night and day.

Rune had never had much use for the downtown area, but it now had use for her.

Yippee.

Readjusting her coat so it sat better on her shoulders, Rune pushed her way through the revolving front door to the stone-faced lobby.

She knew how she looked to the three security guards in their nice suits at the desk to the left. Everyone else who passed her, and granted at 10am on Friday that wasn't many, were dressed in business casual, which required at least khakis and button ups or sweaters under black or grey coats.

Rune, by contrast, wore her long white coat, lined with red and gold brocade down the front edge and inside the large hood that she currently had off her head. The back of the coat was cinched with gold cord over a velvet, red kick-plate so everything was tightened around her otherwise curvy form, yet pleated in such a way as it didn't hamper her legs.

It screamed "magic person." The only way she could have been more magical was if she had carried a staff and wore a large-brim hat, but despite popular depictions of those from the magical community, most didn't actually wear "statement-making" hats. That practice went out about the same time as hats did for everyone else, but popular culture didn't give a damn.

As Rune approached the security desk, she reached into one of her many pockets to pull out her OmniSin, the universal ID that served as a person's identity card, public transport pass, and credit card all rolled into one. The way the security guards all reacted, you'd think she had offered them a magical talisman or a white, fluffy rabbit.

"Rune Leveau to see Ms. Rosenwald," she said politely. One of the guards took her OmniSin and ran it through a little machine connected to his computer while his partner behind the desk looked her up and down.

"You a wizard?" he asked in a tone of voice bordering on impolite.

"Yes," she answered simply.

"Where's your staff?" he asked.

Rune checked her sigh of exasperation and instead unbuttoned her coat's ornate buttons to show them her leather belt cinched around her waist. It was gorgeous, tooled with runic spells into the leather and set with pouches all around it. "I use this instead."

"One second," the third security guard interjected before

she could pull her coat closed. He whipped out a black wand then, not the magical kind, the looking-for-guns-and-bombs kind, and gestured at her to put her arms out.

"What are you going to do with that?" Rune asked, cocking a disbelieving eyebrow at it.

"Just put your hands out," he ordered with an overblown air of authority.

Rune thought about warning him but decided not to and held her arms out to comply with his command. A small cluster of businesspeople entered the building at that moment, their chatter hushed but not ceased in the echo-ey entranceway as they watched the little drama play out.

"One second, please," said the first guard. "I need to call this up."

Rune tried to ignore the group as they walked past, but all were openly staring as they flashed their OmniSins at the reader near the security gate that led to the elevators. Each passed through with green lights and none of the harassment.

Being magical in the corporate world sucked.

Taking a deep breath, Rune tried not to grimace as the security guard began passing the wand around her body, up under her coat. Predictably, the thing buzzed, and a spark snapped after the first pass.

"What the hell?" the security guard muttered. The second guard, who had been watching from behind the desk, came out around while the first one kept his eyes on them as he spoke softly to someone on the other end of the phone, holding Rune's OmniSin with the other hand.

"What's wrong?" the second one demanded as the third one fiddled with the now defunct device.

"I don't know. It fried or something." He shot her looks in between his fiddling, rightly putting blame for the problems on her, though it was nothing she had intended.

"That's because she's a magical being," a new voice said, coming up beside the group. To everyone's surprise, it was a talking frog. Dressed in a plaid, button-up shirt and khakis under a plain blue coat, the frog adjusted his out-of-fashion bow-tie as he approached, his web-footed-shaped dress shoes slapping the ground as he walked up.

"You're not going to be able to fix it. The magical energies she's giving off naturally overblew the buffer and fried the inside," he said, stopping beside her with a friendly nod.

"Ma'am, you said you're here for Ms. Rosenwald's office?" the first guardsman asked, setting the phone against his shoulder.

"Yes," Rune answered, wondering if she could put her arms down now.

He returned to his phone, continuing to talk softly.

"We're going to have to do a pat down," the third guard said, passing the busted instrument to the second one.

"I have an appointment," Rune said, setting her arms down without instructions. She'd had about enough of this.

The third guard's jaw gave a nice jut at her implied objection. *Yup, we are going to have a problem here.*

"Sorry, I can't wait much longer. I have to get to a meeting," the frog-person said, stepping away unsure toward the elevators.

"Thank you," Rune said, offering him a smile and permission to leave her. This was her problem, and she knew it.

He gave her a second even more apologetic smile, then turned to walk through the security gates, *his* OmniSin blinking green.

"Ma'am, please take off your coat and belt and any other talismans ... or whatever you may have on your person," the third guard said, crossing his arms as if he expected her to argue.

Which she completely intended on doing.

"Absolutely not," she challenged.

"Ma'am, are we going to have a problem here?" he asked, raising an eyebrow that wrinkled his bald head.

"Not if you let me get to my appointment," she said, crossing her own arms back at him.

Before his next move could escalate things, the first guard said in a very loud and poignant voice, "Yes, ma'am," and hung

up the phone. "She's free to go up."

"Excuse me?" the third guard shot back at his compatriot.

"She's free to go up," the first one repeated.

Rune let out a breath, then nodded at him. "Thank you," she said before turning toward the security gate.

"No, go up the service elevator," the third guard interjected, pointing at a pair of gray metal doors on the back wall that only had one handle between the two of them and a black box scanner to one side.

Before Rune could object, he added, "If she fried the scanner, she'll probably fry the security gate."

Glancing at the small clock sitting on the top lip of the security desk, Rune knew she was ten minutes late now, but she honestly hadn't expected to have this level of trouble getting into the building. "Fine. That's fine," she acquiesced.

"I'll show her," the second guard said, gesturing for her to precede him toward the double doors.

"Just another day in corporate Chicago," Rune muttered under her breath as she walked away.

The decadence of Ms. Rosenwald's office would have taken anyone's breath away. Ms. Director of Overseas Finance had done well by herself. The space was at least twice the average allotted to the rest of the office. Sumptuous carpet that made Rune feel like she needed to take her shoes off to walk on covered the floor. Mahogany shelves lined both sides of the room, leading the eye to a floor-to-ceiling window right behind the desk. The view overlooked the cloudy, late-winter world outside with its dabs of dirty snow on every edge of the buildings across the space. She even had a pair of standing lamps that looked like they were bronze cast and very heavy. There was so much space in the room that when Rune followed Ms. Rosenwald's secretary in, she saw the director in question standing on a wooden platform in the middle with plenty to spare.

As for the director, she was being fitted for an elegant midnight blue dress. The skirt sparkled with rhinestones in greater concentrations the closer they came to the bottom. More rhinestones flashed around the bodice in elaborate lines. Then, to Rune's surprise, some of the rhinestones began to blink and wink. The seamstress circled around the skirt with a remote, clicking it at the individual lights. Around Ms. Rosenwald's neck hung a single diamond-like stone the size of a chicken egg and cut with so many facets it added dramatic elegance to the dress.

The seamstress paused, holding her device at the skirt. "Ah, here's one. I see you, little bugger. Not going to shine for me, huh?" She knelt down, plucking a seam popper from her hair, where she had a bunch of other little sewing tools stashed, and proceeded to remove a tiny LED light.

"Oh, this is such a bother," Ms. Rosenwald complained while she stood there glancing between two mobile devices of differing makes, one in each hand. "I don't understand it. We keep having to replace these stupid lights. I thought LEDs were supposed to last."

The seamstress gave a pained smile. "I am sorry, ma'am. Usually, I don't have a problem with so many. I must have gotten a bad shipment. Don't worry. I'll get this sorted in a quick minute."

"You said that thirty minutes ago," Ms. Rosenwald snapped.

The secretary cleared her throat. "Ms. Rosenwald, the Talent you asked for is here—"

One of the Director's mobile phones went off. Instantly, her eyes lit up with delight. She held up one finger while answering the phone.

"Hi, Pookie!" she cooed, the cool, business-like demeanor drowning under a tidal wave of valley girl.

"My apologies," her secretary said, leaning into Rune. "She'll be with you in a minute. Can I get you something to drink?"

"Water would be great actually," Rune said, giving a

small smile.

Ms. Rosenwald scoffed loudly, cutting off the secretary's reply. "No, I'm having problems with my dress, and I swear I think I've got a Boggin infestation or something in this office. Boggin. It's those creatures, you know. They infest offices and make things stop working. Carol told me about them. From Accounting, yes. Oh, pookie, don't say *that*. I want you to like my friends." Ms. Rosenwald glanced over at Rune. Diplomatically, Rune gave her an indulgent smile, but it was hard to pretend she was perfectly fine with waiting. It must have been convincingly professional.

"Look, the wizard just got here to take care of it, so I gotta go. I'll see *you* soon!" She paused listening, the smile on her face absolutely radiant. "I love you too, pookie." She followed it by juvenile air kisses at her phone. At last, the call was over.

Like someone flipped a switch, the smile was replaced with a cool, professional exterior. "Sorry for making you wait."

"That's alright," Rune said, accepting the mini bottle of water the returning secretary handed to her. "My name is Rune Leveau, the consulting magic practitioner you asked for. What can I do for you?"

"Well, I'm sure you heard, but yes, apparently my office is infested with a Boggin, which is making everything electronic in the office stop working. Can you do something about it, or even confirm that this is true?" Ms. Rosenwald gestured at the space.

Rune cracked the water and took a drink to buy herself a second to think. "Okay, well, first off..." She glanced around the room. "I don't really think you've got a Boggin infestation. Usually, there are signs when a Boggin is present. They try to convert their environment into a swamp. Fresh vanilla scents just aren't their style."

Taking another quick sip, she cast an eye over the line of objects on the wall. Ms. Rosenwald had several art pieces on display. There were also religious objects from cultures that she was pretty sure Ms. Rosenwald was not a member of.

These too seemed to be treated as "art" pieces.

Rune continued her explanation, "Boggins tend to infest basements, garages, public park restrooms, that sort of thing. I've never heard of them getting into a brightly lit office in the middle of the Loop so high off the ground."

Ms. Rosenwald nodded, taking in the information, which was nice since it meant she wasn't dumb, just uninformed.

"I see. I didn't know that." She plucked one of her mobile devices and typed away at it as if the conversation no longer interested her. It was awkward.

"It's alright," Rune said, trying to ignore the rudeness. "No one can know everything. Just like I don't know much about overseas finance."

Ms. Rosenwald nodded, then looked at her other mobile while continuing to talk. "Well, then, what could be going on? I've had the techs up here a dozen times, and they insist that nothing is wrong. And if the cause is magical, there is nothing they can do about it anyway. But what else could it be? I'm not making up the electric—" Just then, one of the LED lights on the dress popped with a bright, dramatic little flash. The seamstress startled and hiccupped a yip.

"That... That shouldn't be possible..." the poor woman stuttered. "LEDs never... I'm mean, it's insanely rare... but there's not enough electrical power available in these batteries to..."

"Alright, that's it. I'm done!" Ms. Rosenwald declared, throwing her mobiles to her secretary so she could pull away at the spaghetti straps of the dress. "Get me out of this thing. I can't wear it! We're going to have to re-think the whole concept."

Rune furrowed her eyebrows at the small dress. Another of the lights popped.

"What is going on!?" her client whined, emerging from the voluminous skirt wearing only nude colored Spanx and a matching strapless bustier. She stumbled over to her desk in her nylon-stocking feet to drop inelegantly into her desk chair. Just then the lamp sitting on the corner popped its bulb as well,

making all three women in the room jump.

"Oh. My. God!" Ms. Rosenwald cried, pushing her chair away from the desk before leaning her head into her hands. "I feel like I'm going crazy."

"You're not," Rune assured her. "Something is definitely going on."

"Please, do something!" Ms. Rosenwald pleaded, genuinely freaked out.

"Okay, then," Rune mumbled to herself as she screwed on the top on her bottle of water. This was her job now. Time to make good.

Rune shared a glance with the seamstress, who looked worried bordering on devastated, but trying to keep it together. She didn't want to think about how much money the poor woman was probably losing on this dress faux pas. *Her* only hope was probably Rune proving it wasn't a fault with the LEDs.

"Okay, so what I'm going to do is a sort of scan," Rune explained before letting her eyes shift. There was an audible gasp from the room, but Rune expected it. She wasn't prepared to use her magical second sight just yet, but she found doing the eye shift thing beforehand got the inevitable gasps out of the way. Whenever she did this, her normal eyes disappeared behind a layer of glowing white. It could be disconcerting to those outside of the magical community. "Don't worry. We'll figure out what's going on."

Then the seamstress cleared her throat. "Um, sorry, but is it alright if I... I'll just take this out of here and..."

"Oh, actually, could you please leave that?" Rune said, gesturing for her to put the dress back on the floor. "I haven't ruled anything out yet."

The seamstress didn't like it. She obviously wanted to get out of there, but she complied, dropping the dress to pool on the ground.

Sighing, Rune turned away to regard the objects on the shelves.

They were her first guess at what could likely be causing the interference. Yet she didn't see anything that jumped out and shouted, "Magical Object! Magical Object!" Taking a deep breath, Rune stretched out a hand, calling up her own magic. "I wish to Find something magical," she said softly out loud.

Obeying her call, golden threads burst from Rune's palm. They were invisible to anyone who wasn't her. Most wouldn't even know what to look for, as no one but Rune had even been able to do this sort of magic.

Singing with intention, her threads shot out to comb over the objects as Rune slowly walked along the shelf, watching the tiny microcosm of images that flashed up them. Several of the objects *were* in fact magical, little whippets of fairly benign magics that only needed energy to activate. The small supply she provided didn't trigger any of the inlaid spells, so Rune dismissed those threads. They couldn't be the cause of any electrical interference on the scale they were observing.

While it was true that magic and tech didn't mix, it was by degrees. Rune's magical nature alone couldn't short out most tech. Honestly, most tech had magical dampeners, this strange hybrid material that looked like insulation. It protected everything from magic both ambient and most active. For example, her initiating a Finding like this wasn't interfering with any of her client's personal devices and only made a small hiccup buzz on Ms. Rosenwald's holodesk when Rune initiated the spell. As far as Rune could tell, she hadn't even noticed.

Glancing over at her client made Rune do a double take.

While everything on the shelf had one or two of her strings connecting to it, Ms. Rosenwald had so many strings coming out of her she looked like a sea anemone.

"Could I..." Ms. Rosenwald started, looking very unsure. "Could someone have cursed me?"

"Yeah," Rune said nodding. "Yeah, I'm going to go with that." She crossed to stand closer to the desk, staring through her mess of strings trying to focus on what they could be connected to. Rune wasn't prepared to rule out enchanted

underwear, but she thought it was more likely...

Much to her frustration, it got more difficult to confirm her hunch. The sea anemone metaphor turned out to be very apt, as she couldn't make out much past the strings of yellow light passing before her face, blocking her view. She finally grabbed a handful of them to twitch them to the side.

"What are you doing?!" Ms. Rosenwald cried in alarm, and it was only then that Rune gave a thought to what this looked like. Rune had leaned inward until she was barely a foot away, focusing her eerie white eyes on her client all while making weird gestures at her.

The woman, naturally, pulled away, clutching one of her phones before her like the tiny little shield it wasn't.

Rune straightened to a more comfortable, socially acceptable distance. "Apologies. I see a lot of..." she paused, then waved her hand through her threads again, each of them slipping over her skin strangely, "magical energies around you."

"What does that mean?" Ms. Rosenwald asked, looking around herself, but of course she didn't see anything.

"I don't know yet, but this at least explains your issue with technology. Something is shedding magic off of you. Therefore, wherever you go," the other lamp's bulb blew, "things go boom." Rune considered. Not everything had gone boom. "But not evenly so. Something seems to be stoking it at certain times." Rune thought quickly. "Could I have you come stand out from behind the desk, please? Just to make sure it's not something to do with the desk."

The client actually complied, though the expression in her eyes told Rune she didn't entirely buy the explanation yet. Rune supposed she had a lot of those sorts of looks in her future if she continued her new job as a consulting magic practitioner.

As Rune thought, the threads moved with Ms. Rosenwald away from the desk.

"Okay, it's not the desk," Rune dismissed. "There is definitely something attached to you." And it was probably the extravagant necklace, but Rune needed to actually *see* it to be sure. She'd hate to have to mess with something really freaking expensive only for it to turn out to be the chain or something.

"Is this going to take much longer? I would very much like to get dressed. This whole afternoon is shot now," Ms. Rosenwald snapped, returning to the safety and control symbolized by her device. More of the magical threads passed over Ms. Rosenwald, who was now practically engulfed in light. Predictably, the mobile phone fritzed.

The client yelped and dropped it to the ground.

Rune had enough of this and attempted to grab at the bunch of her threads again, how it looked be damned. She just couldn't get a grip on them like she normally would. This time they slipped away like wriggly fish.

"Okay, that's never happened before," Rune said out loud. She glanced over at the seamstress, who just stood there wide-eyed at the whole display. "You're not seeing this, right?"

"I-I don't see anything," the seamstress said, looking very uncomfortable.

"Okay, great," Rune said. "Let me know if you do." She had no idea what it would mean if the magic became visible, but it would be a change.

"Uh, sure," the seamstress agreed.

"Okay, I'm reaching my limit here," Ms. Rosenwald continued, picking up her useless device to tuck under her arm. Her other hand went up to cover up the necklace around her neck in a nervous gesture. When she did that, the threads dimmed and gathered to the sides, where her hand wasn't completely blocking the magic.

"Ah," Rune said, nodding. "Okay, it *is* the diamond."

At the mention of the necklace, something shifted in Ms. Rosenwald's stance. She gripped the gem, and the magical threads thickened into twine. They also all glowed an angry reddish hue. Her client's face twisted into something the nastiest valley girl would envy.

"You're trying to take him away from me," she accused.

"Oh crap," Rune said, now having a very good idea what she was dealing with.

"Ms. Rosenwald, I'm going to ask you to stay calm," Rune placated, holding her hands up to emphasize the request. "You're in your office in the middle of the workday."

"I know where the hell I am!" she shouted.

"Everyone can hear you out there," Rune said, not raising her own voice. The light in the room began to waver as the magic really began to pour out of the amulet disguised as a diamond necklace.

"Ms. Leveau..." the seamstress said, unsure. "I... I see something."

Rune saw it too, the magic throwing waves through her threads, echoed in the way the lights were flickering, like a pebble dropped in a pond.

"Ms. Rosenwald, try to calm down. This isn't you. You've been given a cursed item that's shedding all the magic."

"No, you can't have him. You can't take him away from me!" the possessed woman cried.

"Okay, there's no reaching her," Rune said and began going through the pockets on her belt.

"What's happening?" the office assistant asked, appearing in the doorway.

Rune waved a desperate hand at her. "Don't come in here! Shut the door and keep everybody else out!"

"Petunia!" Ms. Rosenwald cried, her beautiful face twisting into something profoundly ugly. "Get this degenerate out of here!"

The poor woman stood there torn between the two orders, obviously debating which she should obey. Unfortunately for the woman, the magic waves from her boss increased its spread. The smaller paintings on the wall danced on their hooks and then went flying. Other small objects not tied down also went, creating a whirlwind around Ms. Rosenwald.

Belatedly, Rune lifted her hand and called out "Shield," her other hand automatically grabbing for a crystal that was no longer there. For a split second, a yellow concave wall of energy appeared in front of her, only to blink out just in time for a painting to whap her in the face.

"Dammit!" Rune shouted, shoving the painting away. She was going to need more practice calling up her shield without the aid of her long-destroyed crystal. She hadn't gotten it to work once yet.

The secretary stared in terror at the maelstrom of magic before her, all centered on her boss. Then the device in her hand snapped, a bright spark with a little puff of smoke, probably killing it dead forever.

"I'm sorry, Ms. Rosenwald!" Petunia cried, retreating back into the main room and pulling the door shut behind her.

"I will end you! I will end all of you! Nothing..." the possessed woman then proceeded to utter some unintelligible words, followed by, "...get between me and my soulmate!"

She came at Rune then, releasing her hold on the amulet. Before her outstretched nails could get to Rune, the Talent flipped up the hood on her coat. While the coat protected from any of the malevolent magic now directed at her, it did nothing for the physical attack, and she found herself shoved back into the woman's desk.

As far as fights went, it was not pretty or elegant or sophisticated. Rune managed to throw the claws away from scratching, but momentum still put an elbow in her face, impacting the Finder under her eye. A piece of hair got caught, tearing the strands out painfully. The possessed woman switched tactics to rain down ineffectual blows onto Rune's head, but she ignored it, focusing instead on grabbing for the amulet. Magic poured off the thing, fueling its victim with unnatural strength and berserker rage. Its host simply lacked the ability to use either effectively. Which made perfect sense—she was a mathematician, not a soldier.

"Dammit, get off me!" Rune barked. Rune's coat pulsed, giving off its own repellent magic, and her attacker yelped at the reaction. The hostile red light dimmed, and Rune realized

something. The control magic had a limit on its victim.

So, she slapped her, open palm, straight to Ms. Rosenwald's face. It made a sharp snap sound and immediately the red light dimmed, her pain receptors shocking the poor woman out of her rage, at least for the moment. The magic in the amulet's only purpose was to protect itself, which meant driving its host to protect it. Yet the host still had the natural defenses every sentient creature had and a short, sharp, shock did the trick. Everything swirling around dropped to the ground. Ms. Rosenwald held her cheek, tears beading in her eyes as if it were the worst thing happening to her right now.

Not wasting the moment her bold move made for her, Rune seized the amulet from around Ms. Rosenwald's neck. It tore away, the delicate links of the chain snapping, but not easily. Her client yelped another cry, her head bucking forward by the momentary resistance of the chain. The tendrils of magic coming from the amulet flared red again briefly, then died immediately.

"Give…" Ms. Rosenwald said, now fearfully, as if Rune had just taken her newborn child hostage. "Give that to me!"

"Ms. Rosenwald," Rune said, judiciously moving around the desk, "this amulet is the cause of all your problems."

"No, please don't!" she begged, genuine tears spilling from her eyes as she held out a pleading hand. "If you destroy that, I won't love him anymore. I can't bear that."

It took every ounce of control Rune possessed to not roll her eyes. "Damn love curses."

Exhaling a breath, Rune lifted the amulet above her head and slammed it into the ground. There was an initial flash, and Ms. Rosenwald screamed as if she was being murdered. Still the crystal remained entirely intact since it *was* a crystal. Luckily, Rune grabbed the standing metal lamp, and that heavy thing did the trick. The cursed object cracked all the way through, disrupting the spell within which released another visible flash.

Finally, the crystal went black.

Breathing heavily, Rune set the lamp down. "Okay, I got it."

CHAPTER 2

Ms. Rosenwald stood there with a look of shock on her face, her hand resting where the amulet had been. Her beautiful hair hung in a mess, like she'd been in a cat fight, which, Rune guessed, technically she had been.

The seamstress cowered nearby, her arms wrapped around herself looking utterly terrified. "What... What just happened?" she asked.

Rune bent down and retrieved the ruined crystal necklace. "Someone put a love curse on you."

Ms. Rosenwald's perfect eyebrows arched higher. "A love *curse?*"

"Yeah." Rune nodded. "By legal definition, love *spells* only open the way for love that is already there. It takes a curse to force a feeling like love on someone. And it was a pretty expensive one too. Even more so because it had a protection component on it as well."

The executive numbly stumbled forward and seized one of the chairs before her desk that had been too heavy to knock over, only slid a bit. She sat down on the edge of it. "How... Why would someone do that?"

Rune gingerly touched the crystal but sensed no ambient magic within. It was a little warm from the burst of energy expenditure. "I mean... it's a love curse. I think the why is self-evident. What's more important is the who."

They all knew who, but Rune wasn't going to say it.

She held the broken crystal out to Ms. Rosenwald to take it.

The client reached for it automatically, then hesitated.

"It's safe now," Rune confirmed.

Ms. Rosenwald reluctantly took it, holding it like she found it disgusting.

"I can't believe this sort of thing is allowed," she said, wrinkling her nose. "I feel so ... violated."

"Oh, it's a highly illegal form of magic. This falls under a violation of mind-control laws. One this violent and dangerous, I would call this a felony, but I'm not a lawyer or an enforcement agent."

Ms. Rosenwald wrinkled her nose. "So, who would I take this up with?"

Rune sighed. "Well, what I would recommend is reaching out to your corporate police force and have them open a case with the Magic Guild. This would probably be tried in a Magic Guild court, but I can write up a report for you with all the details. I think I know the answer to this, but *do* you know who gave this to you?"

Ms. Rosenwald's face twisted. "Ugh, Bradford. Oh, God!" She dropped the offending necklace, wiping her fingers on her Spanx as if his slime was all over it. "That bastard."

"Ms. Rosenwald, I don't mean to be indelicate, but how involved was your relationship with this ... Bradford?" Rune asked, feeling sick as well.

The woman's face turned from pale to green. "Oh, God," she said again, her head leaning forward.

"Yes, use of this sort of magic is the same as a roofie. That's one of the reasons it's so highly regulated," Rune reported. "I'll

include that in my report too."

"Regulated? You mean there is a *legal* use for this sort of thing?" Ms. Rosenwald asked disgustedly.

"Yes, well, mind control magic can help greatly in treating mentally ill patients, that sort of thing, but those too are highly regulated." Rune bent down to retrieve the necklace. "Somehow whoever made this probably got ahold of one of those crystals and readjusted the spell within to make the curse."

Ms. Rosenwald took a deep breath, rolling her shoulders back before standing up into a power pose. "You can write a report for the police?"

While she had already said that, Rune nodded. "Absolutely."

"Petunia!" Ms. Rosenwald shouted, marching over to the door. She yanked it open and her poor assistant and half of the outer office fell into a comical pile at her feet. "Get my attorney on the phone as soon as you can." She snapped a finger to one of the other secretaries. "You, Kyle, get our police on the phone. I want them up here in no less than five minutes."

He nodded and dashed through the gathered group to obey. A third secretary who made eye contact with their boss's boss got orders to call for a cleaning crew, and several more people were sent off on various other errands. On the heels of that, a few more executives came into the room. The place became chaos as the story of what just happened was told and retold several times. Rune found herself relegated to a corner, next to the overwhelmed seamstress. She managed to rescue her dress creation from getting trampled, clutching it to her like her lost child or dog.

At last, a chime came from Ms. Rosenwald's desk, forcing all the execs to look back at it. Above the surface, a holographic clock appeared flashing a series of numbers. "Oh, crap! I'm going to be late!" Scanning the room, she located the seamstress and snapped at her. "Come on. Let's get this dress working."

The seamstress scurried over, and Ms. Rosenwald finally

noticed Rune still waiting politely. She crossed to grasp both of Rune's hands, her face a wash of relief. "Thank you. Thank you so much," which was when Rune found herself swept into an awkward hug, at least awkward on her part because she hadn't been prepared for it. Ms. Rosenwald fully committed. "Thank you so, so much. You've saved my life."

"I'm glad I could help," Rune said, trying to pat the woman's arm, but she had Rune's arms pinned down, making the gesture near impossible. And then she released Rune all at once to whirl back to her podium, stepping into the re-laid dress smoothly as her well-wishers escorted themselves out. Multitasking as ever, Ms. Rosenwald proceeded to slide the straps on as she waved good-bye and answered a call on her phone all at the same time.

"I'll see you out, Ms. Leveau," Petunia, the secretary said, appearing at her side.

"I guess I've been dismissed," Rune said under her breath as the Rosenwald circus continued without her.

"We're terribly behind. Please don't take offense. We are very grateful for what you've done for us," the secretary assured with a warmth that was probably the reason she had been hired. Despite herself, Rune smiled and nodded, following the woman out of the executive's office.

Once in the hall, Rune took a deep breath, steeling her nerve. "Actually, before I go," she said, pausing in the hall, "I should write up a report for her case while it's still fresh before I leave. Do you have an office I could use with a computer and printer?"

Petunia's eyebrows tweaked up a moment before she looked away thoughtfully. "Yes," she said softly. "Yes, I do think I know where I can put you. Follow me, please."

The secretary led Rune to a set of carpeted stairs that took her down to the floor below without using the elevators and off to a small side office. It was empty but had everything Rune needed: a desk, a computer, a printer, and a blind over the window.

"Will this work?" Petunia asked, coming around the computer to wiggle the mouse, waking it up before typing in a quick password to unlock it.

"That's perfect," Rune affirmed and politely took a seat once the secretary had cleared the way.

"Can I get you anything to drink?" the secretary asked automatically.

"No, thank you. This should just take me twenty minutes," Rune said, removing her coat so she could sit more comfortably.

Petunia hesitated another moment. "Do you know how to use a computer?" she asked.

Rune could feel her polite smile going stiff, but she held on to it. "I know enough to do a word processor," she said pleasantly at the discriminatory question. Everyone was taught computer basics in high school, but the perception that magically based people, or even those thought to be magically based like centaurs or the fae, didn't know how to use the devices persisted.

"Then I'll leave you to it," Petunia declared and left the office, shutting the door behind her.

Rune waited a count of five before she let her breath go.

Gods, she hoped this worked.

She dug the cell phone out of her pocket, along with a connecting cord from one of the pockets of her belt. Unwinding it in her shaking fingers, Rune tried to breathe slowly even as her heart raced. Sitting down, she connected the phone to the computer. A second later, the icon for the phone appeared in the corner of the computer's desktop. Immediately, the computer's network protections popped up, asking her for a password before allowing the cellphone access. Now began the dangerous part.

Rune turned to the surface of her phone and tapped the pre-installed program that she had been given. Her new employers had no idea she was using it for a personal reason, but she had recognized the opportunity the tool gave her. The program initiated, a small box of black with a million little white symbols filling it in with the language of computers that Rune could never hope to understand. The box was overlaid by a little animated icon of a friendly little mouse giving her a wink and a thumbs up before animating itself diving into the code and disappearing. On the computer screen, a long row of stars appeared in the little box asking for a password. The whole screen blinked and then the password box disappeared, permission granted.

Step one, complete.

Next, Rune opened the company's internal network page. An image showing a pair of smiling people working enthusiastically together filled most of the window, along with a list of announcements and the lunch menu. Rune ignored the list of food items, though the chicken pot pie sounded pretty good, and went instead to the row of other less food-based menus at the top. The second from the last was labeled "Human Resources." A menu dropped down and she found "Employee Lookup" at the bottom. Clicking that initiated another password request, but the hacking program didn't even wait for her to do anything. It filled in another row of stars, and she was granted access. The little mouse icon emerged from the box of code, burped, gave a thumbs up, and popped back into the codebox.

Step two, complete. This was working.

Taking a deep breath, Rune dug a note out of her pocket. It was worn at the edges and covered with the tiniest writing she had ever seen. Despite that, she had every word memorized. Still, the signature at the bottom was what concerned her and the name that scribble tried to convey. Staring down at it for the hundredth time, she knew the name started with a J and the last name started with a C. She had parsed out a few other letters from the penmanship, but she knew it was going to take a few tries to find the right one.

On her cellphone screen, she opened another program, this one with an eyeglass filled with an enormous eye that

blinked every few seconds. This program opened a white text box. The eyeball glanced back and forth as it waited for her to type something in. On the other end of the text box was a camera icon and a pen icon, but Rune ignored both of those. She had already scanned the signature into the program previously, so she tapped on the blank text box and a history menu appeared underneath, the picture of the signature the only one listed. Selecting that, she then tapped the eyeball. The little animation pulled out a second eyeglass from nowhere, and it began frantically examining the signature. On the computer screen, the lookup box began to fill with possible combinations of what was written there.

This was the part that would take the most time, so Rune clicked on the icon for the word processor. She *would* need to write the report, and she'd have to do it while the program hacked at the network. It was hard to focus on, however. Harder to not check the progress every few seconds.

A variety of names flashed in the box, the program going through every spelling combination it could figure out, many of them nonsensical.

She was partway through her first paragraph recap of the incident when the program stopped. The little eyeball returned to its place beside the box, glancing away ever so often on its pre-programmed loop. Beneath the box was a list of names, but at the top were the bold letters: "No exact matches in this network."

"Dammit," Rune muttered. Scanning the computer screen, she tried to find another answer. She couldn't give up yet.

The handwriting analysis program had identified some possibilities but no name matches above seventy percent. She looked over the list of names in the network that were below that, but of the five names there, none of them made her think they were the woman Rune searched for. Then something caught her eye on the computer's screen. In small blue letters, just under the search bar, she read, "Search Entire Kodiak Network?"

Rune glanced up at the single, utilitarian clock above the door. Half her allotted time was gone.

It was also now or never.

"Uh, yes please." She clicked the redirect link and was taken to another HR page, this one with the Kodiak's symbol in the corner and another password box.

"Gods, I wish I could just use magic," she muttered as she switched back to the hacking mouse to get past the newest hindrance. Once inside, she ran the program again.

Stepping out of her comfort zone and using all this tech to find someone had been tough. She was the Finder after all, but her magic relied on an object of personal connection to find someone, and they had to be in close range. The more people or things in an area, the closer they needed to be to find them. In a city of 8.8 million people, Finding her target with only a scrap of note she had touched for a few seconds was a near impossible task.

Rune had failed her so much already; she wasn't going to give up on her now.

Again, she ran the search through the phone, following the basic hacking etiquette she had been trained with by her new employers. Using the keyboard could allow for the possibility for someone to record her keystrokes if this corporation sprang for that kind of tech. Since you couldn't always know, better to be safe than sorry.

Quickly, Rune completed her report. It wasn't great, but it was good enough. Glancing up at the clock, she was already five minutes over the time she gave Petunia and could probably expect to be "checked up on" any minute.

"Come on, come on," Rune muttered as she watched the little eyeball continue its cartoonish search. She printed the report, making two copies so she'd have one to take with her. While the printer spat out her report, there was a ping from her phone.

87% match.

Rune stared down at the top of the list of names.

"Jasmeene Clarmont," highlighted in bold letters.

On the computer screen, she was listed there as well. Rune's hands began to shake again as she clicked on the name. A profile replaced it with a black woman's face that smiled, but the smile didn't reach her eyes. Her straightened hair was cut in a bob, and she wore a gray and white business suit, but the otherwise generic image gave very little information about her. Listed next to it was basic stats: her job title, salary, supervisor, associates in her immediate network, contact information ... and her home address.

"Yes," she whispered. She slid her fingers into a back pocket of her pouch, the largest one she had, and retrieved a handful of crystals. Opening her palm, the crystals winked at her with various colors. Only two of them were already cleared out, laying dully amongst the jewel tones. It took a second to hone in on a lavender one. Palming it, she tucked the others back into her pouch, closing the metal clasp with practiced fingers. Holding it before her, she breathed on its surface. The crystal ignited with active lavender light and wisps like smoke emerged.

"Corder," Rune whispered. Another tone echoed, signaling it was ready to record. In her soft voice, Rune carefully and clearly began reciting the address, not only saying but spelling out each word, so she could recall it perfectly later. The smoke made an imprint of what she said as she said it, then the words melted back into the crystal. As soon as she finished speaking, the door cracked open.

Her heart almost choked her as she jumped. Scrabbling, she grabbed for the connector to her phone, yanking it out unceremoniously. She shoved both into the pocket of her coat draped over the table. There was no way that whoever had opened the door had not seen what she was doing. She was caught.

Except, Petunia didn't come all the way into the room right away. She paused at the door, looking back into the main room. Having stowed the incriminating evidence, Rune moved to the printer and grabbed the two copies that she had printed, retrieved her coat, and went to the door, just in time for Petunia to finally turn in. Not expecting Rune to suddenly be standing next to her, she jumped a bit as the Talent held out one of the reports.

"Oh, I didn't see you," Petunia said, recovering quickly. She received the report. "Is this it?"

"Yes, please turn that over to whoever takes the case. I included my contact information for further questions."

She nodded as she scanned over it. "Ms. Rosenwald wanted to know if you would be interested in further magic security work?"

The question surprised Rune, though on further reflection, she didn't see why it wouldn't. "Of course. I can come on another, less dramatic day and do an assessment before writing up a proposal. Will that do?"

Petunia smiled. "Yes, thank you."

A laugh, merry and familiar caught Rune's attention. Turning to look in its direction, her heart caught in her throat.

"St. Benedict," she said out loud, spying him across the space.

"Oh? You know him?" Petunia asked when she heard Rune's muttered word.

Rune put her smile back on. "Yes, I know him. Do you mind if I go over and say hi?"

"Of course, I'm just going to run this up to Ms. Rosenwald," Petunia said, gesturing with the piece of paper. Once she was gone, Rune moved up to stand near the small group chattering animatedly with a handsome man who looked like he'd stepped out of the 1950s. Dressed in a gray, three-piece suit and matching fedora, he laughed animatedly as if he had just told an amazing joke. Judging from the faces around him, he probably had.

"So, what did you do?" one of the attending office women asked, twirling her hair between two fingers in an obvious show of attraction.

"Well, what every gentleman is supposed to do." He held out a hand to the woman, who blushed before taking it. Before she could respond, he twirled her in place, then dipped her to the delight of all. "You can never just leave a lady hanging."

The woman stared breathlessly up into his eyes, and he gave her a charming wink, then kissed her on the cheek. The noise she made wasn't appropriate for church, but then he set her back on her feet, letting her step back, gasping for excited breaths while one of her friends supported her. The rest of the group applauded. He turned around, basking in it, his green-blue eyes twinkling until they landed with surprise on Rune.

"What are you doing here?" she asked the second after he saw her. The whole group went silent, not only unsure by the sudden presence of the Talent but by the foreignness of her entirely. She didn't belong, and that energy resonated through them. It wasn't a magical sense, yet anyone could have felt it all the same.

She had invaded their world.

"Oh, Rune," he said, identifying her as someone he knew. "I didn't know you were here."

She *almost* believed that. St. Benedict was one of the most consummate liars she had ever met, but she also felt like she could read him better than anyone else in the world. He was obviously on a job, but she had come to not trust "coincidence." It wasn't that coincidence didn't happen, but they were as rare as real unicorns.

"I just finished a job upstairs." She flashed her piece of paper at him. "Wrote up a report."

"Yeah, okay. That's great," he said, glancing at the group. Rune got the sudden impression she was back in high school trying to talk to the quarterback in front of his way cooler friends. It still wasn't a great feeling, years later. Many in the group were now looking down their noses at her or checking out their cellphones. The woman he had been flirted with shot a murderous look at her that screamed, "Go away. You're not wanted."

Taking the hint that St. Benedict wasn't going to rescue her, include her, and smooth it over, Rune took a step back, slipping her coat on. "Well, I just saw you and thought I would say hi. See you around," she said impersonally.

"It was good to see you again," he returned about as impersonally. Rune nodded a polite smile and turned away from the group to head for the elevators as she pulled her brocade hood up and over her head. As far as retreats went, it wasn't that bad. So maybe some things had improved since high school.

"Who was that?" the woman of the group asked in a really pathetic attempt at a whisper.

So maybe not.

"Oh, just some Talent who works at my company. They've started this new Magic Securities division. I didn't realize she would be here today," St. Benedict said so dismissively that it almost hurt. Unfortunately for Rune, the elevator turned out to be only a few feet away. Not nearly far enough not to overhear, even if this group seemed to think so.

"So, she works under you?" one of the others asked.

"No, no, she's her own thing, but I do have to go. I will see more of you guys very soon," he said.

There was a collective moan of disappointment from the group, and Rune carefully turned to look at them sideways without being noticed. He had retrieved a briefcase from the ground and was taking his fedora off to do some sort of European bow to the smiling sycophants. They all waved bye and Rune turned back to the finally arriving elevator.

"Come on, come on, come on," she whispered under her breath to the door as it slowly opened. She entered, then began pounding the door close button to make it shut before he got there to join her. He strolled in the direction of the elevator, his focus still behind him so he didn't see what she was doing until the last second as the doors finally started to close. She got a great slice of his face as his eyes met hers, realizing what she had done. She smiled wickedly and hoped he saw it before the doors separated them.

Ha!

Did he think I would hold the elevator for him? What an ass, she thought triumphantly. It may have been a small revenge, but it was hers all the same.

A few seconds later, the doors traitorously popped back open.

"Oh, good. I thought you had left me," he said smugly as he got into the car. She noticed his right hand as the glow within the palm died away.

He had used his augmentations to halt the door.

Of course he did.

He turned and waved his hat one last time, though only a couple of the remaining group saw it as the doors re-closed on them both. As he did that, a coin slipped out of the brim to clink onto the metal floor. It was an enchanted coin with a crystal core in it that kept his fedoras from getting stained or damaged.

It had been a gift once, and he was still using it.

Once the door shut, he bent to retrieve it, bringing his body close to Rune's leg.

Rune kept her eyes staring straight ahead, studying her blurry reflection in the metallic wall of the elevator.

"I'm sorry," he said in a gentle voice, "for treating you like that."

"It's fine," she dismissed. "I interrupted your cover, didn't I? I get it. Savvy corporate pretty boy gets undercut by being friends with a magical co-worker. It's not hard to figure out. I'm at the same level as the data entry techs. I get it." She did too. Status was everything in this corporate world. It just sucked.

There was a long pause filled with affirmation. "Still…" But he didn't finish that thought. Instead, he shifted to another. "I should have thought of something else to say."

"Don't worry about it."

Another long pause as the elevator descended the sky-scraper, the floors ticking by on the digital screen.

"I only had microseconds to think of something. What

does that say about me that my instinct took me there?" he asked, his voice reflecting his pleading smile.

Since he wasn't listening to her dismissal of the incident, she didn't respond further. They weren't friends, and they weren't partners anymore, so she shouldn't have even tried.

Despite her attempts at a cold shoulder, his presence radiated next to her. He seemed to fill the space. Her entire awareness focused unbidden on his every breath, every shift, and that damn delicious smell of his whatever was fashionable cologne. She could sense him trying to will her to say something more.

Only three more floors to go. Was this really taking as long as it felt?

"Okay, so now tell me why you're really here?" St. Benedict asked, forcing even more joviality as if it were old times, but even then, she wasn't going to pretend with him now that they were alone.

The elevator stopped on the third floor.

"Dammit," she muttered under her breath.

The doors opened, letting on a pair of janitorial workers, their keychains jangling in time with their steps as they clambered on, chattering away in a combination of Polish, Spanish, and English. Their presence split Rune and St. Benedict apart and did wonders to counter St. Benedict's yummy smell with something closer to eau de gorilla. Just before the ground floor, they stopped again on what was designated the first floor and got off, leaving the same scent lingering in their wake.

At last, the elevator reached the ground floor. Rune marched out the second the doors opened enough for her to pass. She went straight to the front security desk, which was occupied by one guard now that the morning rush was over, to sign out. Not shockingly, St. Benedict followed her over, waving his hand over the reader there to do his check out. Just as she checked the clock to fill in her time out, the guard remaining piped up.

"Sorry about before," he said. Rune glanced up at him. He

was the one that had given her permission to enter after the confrontation, the one on the phone.

"Thanks," she said, dropping the pen on the desk and turning to get away.

"What happened before?" St. Benedict asked, and she prayed to whatever gods were listening that he would just bug off.

"I had a bit of an issue getting into the building," Rune answered, heading toward the rotating doors. Outside, the world gleamed, the brightness of the sun hitting what was left of the snow, amplified by the reflection from the towering buildings of Chicago's Downtown Loop. It had been a patchy winter with snow and thaw alternating with regularity, which never quite completely cleared the snow. In a few weeks, spring would be a present resident in the city, but it was hard to imagine as Rune pushed her way out to the street.

Her "shadow" followed her.

"Rune, my car is this way," St. Benedict said.

She spun on the street to see him following, standing in his suit without needing a coat even though the wind blew cold from the lake. She knew his augmentations were triggering his body to burn hotter so that he was comfortable, the prized, exclusive tech more valuable and costly than her entire self put together.

"I'm taking the train," she said, buttoning up her coat with already numbing fingers. Taking a deep breath of the sharp air, she focused on finding the core of heat within herself and bringing it forth, a minor bit of magic. Like hot water being poured through her arteries, warmth rolled out to her extremities, down her arms and legs and into her fingers and toes. She had her own tricks too.

"I said I was sorry," he repeated.

She furrowed her brows at him. "I said don't worry about it."

"But you won't come with me back to the office building we're both headed toward. You'll take the train that will take you twice as long, and I have a nice warm car with heated seats."

"Sounds like," she said and flipped up her deep hood. To

her relief, he didn't follow her. Walking down the cold-laced street, her stomach reminded her that it was late in the afternoon, and she had yet to eat anything other than one really dry cookie from a convenience store snack pack. Glancing around, she decided to duck into one of the downtown pubs to get some late lunch and maybe something hot to drink.

It felt eerily familiar to step into the pub with its long bar, but Rune had never been in there before. There was an atmosphere all bars of a certain age had. The decades sat in the air, even if the bar was clean to perfection. A pang slipped through Rune's heart, but she blinked back any errant tears and went to take up a stool at the bar. A handful of patrons were eating and talking at a scattering of tables, and a handful more sat at the bar nursing drinks, enjoying the dregs of lunches. Rune took up the stool at the farthest end.

The bartender was busy, so she waited, in no real hurry to get back to the office. "The office," a strange new concept that even after a month didn't feel natural yet. There wasn't much a woman like her, one imbued with magic, could do in a world where technology was replacing everything. Tech was easier and cheaper, sure, but for the longest time not nearly as powerful as magic. Now...

Thinking about her situation, Rune fingered the crystal in one of her pouches. She didn't activate it, but she turned it over in her hand. The lavender within had morphed into a sort of raspberry purple, indicating it had content inside it, securely kept until her command opened it again or a more powerful magic practitioner figured out how to dismantle the spell within. This particular crystal had been enchanted by Maddie, Rune's magical aunt. She had been one of the more powerful, wonderful people in their family. Dismantling one of her spells would be very difficult, and crystals preserved the spells within for a long time, so Rune had a great deal of faith that the information was secure.

"What can I get you?" a friendly looking bartender with floppy hair asked as he leaned against the bar. Rune felt an

instant affection for him, leaning there with a towel over one shoulder and sleeves rolled up to his elbows.

"Menu, please?" Rune asked.

He slid her one. "Can I get you something to drink?"

"She'll have a rum and coke. I'll take a gin and tonic," St. Benedict said, claiming the stool beside her. The friendly bartender's smile drooped a little, and he visually shifted modes to something more detached and professional.

Rune sighed as she skimmed over the specials on one side of the menu. "I suppose it was too much to ask," she said. As nonchalantly as she could, she slipped the crystal from one hand to the other hand underneath the menu. Unfortunately, though, there was a good chance he had already seen it, and if that was the case, if he became suspicious about what she was up to, she knew he could replay this encounter with his ocular recorder. Ah well, the onions were in the soup now. Too late to take them out.

"If you really want me to go, then let me ask a couple of questions, and I'll go," he said, turning with his back to the bar, three-quarters facing the door and seeing as much of the room as he could while still looking natural.

"Are you paying for lunch?" she asked.

He arched an eyebrow at her. "Technically, Corinthe is paying for lunch. It all comes from the same place, so what does it matter?" he countered.

"Yes, but you have a bigger budget than I do, so...?" She arched her own eyebrow back at him.

"Yes, I'm paying for lunch," he conceded and did something she rarely ever saw him do. He took off his fedora and set it on the bar. "Now, tell me what you were doing in there."

"I told you: I had a job. It's what I have to do now, just like everybody else in this damn city," Rune said. Their drinks arrived, and St. Benedict nodded to the bartender. As the bartender slid her glass over, he tapped the back of her hand with one finger, getting her to meet his gaze and mouthed silently, "Is this guy bothering you?"

She gave a little shake of her head and smiled to thank him. He didn't seem to like it but accepted it, took their lunch orders, and moved on down the bar. Rune was acutely aware that St. Benedict noticed the little non-verbal exchange too.

"Yeah, well that seems like too much of a coincidence," he said, his voice with an edge.

Rune finally looked at him. "Yeah, it does, doesn't it?"

He honest-to-god flinched, then refocused on his hands. He too fiddled with something in his long, piano-man fingers, a small device that Rune didn't recognize. It looked like a bean with a ring around it. "I'm going to guess this is St. Rachel's doing?" he asked, though whether it was to Rune or himself, she wasn't quite sure.

Rune rolled that idea around in her head, picturing the other cyberspy in their securities company, her classic femme fatale blonde hair covering one eye as the other looked coldly down her nose at Rune. It wasn't a secret to anyone that St. Rachel hated Rune, but...

"To what end?" Rune asked, scrunching her nose at the thought. "To get us to talk? She doesn't seem like the type. Besides, I'm pretty sure she's in love with you."

"No." He shook his head, the revelation of St. Rachel loving him sliding off his back like water if he was the duck. "More like she used whatever resources she saw fit and didn't tell the right hand what the left is doing."

"Which hand am I in this analogy?" Rune asked, the spark of their old rapport getting the best of her.

He didn't take the bait. Instead, her old partner seemed to be thinking hard. "So, you were the operative upstairs that took care of whatever the interference was?"

"Magic curse. Here, read for yourself," she said, fishing her report out of a pocket and handing him the folded piece of paper.

His eyes scanned her words, and he immediately handed it back. "Ah, okay, well that makes sense."

"Did you actually read it?" Rune challenged.

"Yeah. 'Upon smashing the errant crystal and dispelling the curse, Ms. Rosenwald immediately reclaimed her senses,'" he said, reciting word-for-word the last sentence of her report.

"Okay, well that's not fair if you've got augmented eyes," Rune said, slapping the traitorous report against her thigh.

"It's not my eyes. I've always been able to read like that. That's how my parents first knew I was a genius," the man with the handsome face bragged.

"Well, jolly for you," Rune countered.

Another long pause.

"Are you going to tell me what you were doing at the same time, or is this a one-sided interrogation?" Rune probed. Taking advantage of his inattention, she handed over her report, using it as cover to slip both itself and her crystal into the far pocket of her coat.

"Praetorium mission," he said, citing the joint secret about their company that they were forced to work for.

"And what did the underground want from Atropos Inc. today?"

"The same old," he said. He took a long draft from his gin and tonic.

"I have no idea what qualifies as same or old," Rune commented. "I'm just the corporate Talent, not the spy."

He chuckled in his throat. "I know that our past adventures will have skewed your view of what it is like being a spy, but I can assure you, it's mostly maintenance. Whatever magical do-hickey was messing with our programs also affected their internal security, and as this company's cyber security team, I got called in to check that the problems weren't the signs of an all-out attack."

"So, while you're there to help keep them secure, you're skimming data from them?"

"Yup."

"And you're not at all worried about talking about that here in the open where anyone can hear us?"

He held out the small device in his hands. "They can't.

Don't worry."

"Of course, Cybertech," she noted. "Interrupting sound or something."

He held the device out to her, letting it drop into her palm, which she opened to receive it. "You know how when you take pictures of me they come out all blurry and unclear, even if everything else around us is clear?"

"Yes," she said, sipping her drink. It had taken her a long time to realize that the problem had nothing to do with her spells or camera, and everything to do with the subject himself.

"This is like that, but extends it to all around itself. On cameras, we both appear blurry and vague, even in motion, and sound doesn't come out clear because it lays various frequencies over it that distorts it, and it can't really be cleared up because it's a part of the recording."

"It creates a field around us," Rune noted, figuring it out as he talked.

"Yes," he said, taking it back to leave it on the counter between them. "Feel free to talk about anything. We'll be fine."

"What about good, old-fashioned eavesdropping?"

"Well, don't talk too loudly," he said, just as their plates arrived.

Rune took a bite of the elaborate sandwich she had ordered, doing one better by saying nothing.

"How—" he started to ask, then stopped himself.

"I'm fine."

He remained still, not touching his own food. Considering how animated he usually was, the stillness unsettled her. "If you need any help, I'm still here for you, even if we..." But he let it trail there.

"Any more questions?" she asked, cutting off whatever speech he may have prepared. She wasn't interested, and the longer he sat there, the more of a chance she could give something away. She had no idea what could tip him off, but she wasn't going to give him the opportunity to figure out what she was up to.

"No," he said, standing up to get the bartender's attention. "Can I get this to go?"

Strangely, after he left, Rune didn't feel any better.

CHAPTER 3

By the time Rune got back to the Corinthe company head-quarters, she regretted not taking St. Benedict up on his offer for a ride. She had been correct. The CTA green line had brought her out as far as she needed to go. She had taken it several times before now, but there was still the cold walk from the nearest station to the building itself. The lone, long rectangle was surrounded by a double line of trees that ringed the entire property. At one time, the place had been a corporate prison. If it had been built for other purposes originally, Rune didn't know, nor did she truly care. What she did know was that the CEO of Corinthe Corp, Maxamillion Corinthe, loved the whole setup with its tree-lined barrier to the wide grounds leading up to the main entrance. It even had its own private driveway.

What it meant to Rune in that moment was that she had to trek her way over a field of lingering snow to get to the main door. She could have gone up the driveway, but that would have meant going around the whole tree perimeter to the start of it. She was tired and cold and just wanted to finish out her day so she could go take a hot shower. So across the field she went. She stepped along an existing tamped-down path through the snow, which made her trekking easier, but the thaw-freeze-thaw-freeze of Chicago winters had made the compacted snow icy slick. More than once, she had to pause to catch herself before she twisted an ankle and landed in the stuff.

Just when she thought she would never make the door, she reached it. Stamping her boots, she mounted the steps and pushed her way in. A heater had been installed just inside the doorway, bathing her face like a friendly dragon's breath. A guard sat at the marble desk just inside the foyer. The space was much smaller and more artificially lit than the building she had just come from, but this guard was far friendlier.

"And there she is," Trent, the security guard, said. "Did you break the curse?"

"Which curse?" Rune jibbed. "Hers or mine?"

Trent laughed, then gestured toward the far left elevator door facing him.

A hologram portal appeared in front of it, and he placed his head in the oval it formed. A scan went over his face, highlighting his eyes, then the elevator pinged at the top with a green light. He had to do this for her every time since the last time they had tried to program her face into the holo scanner, the magic buffers all blew with a fantastic and expensive pop.

"Alright, she's all yours," he said, gallantly gesturing to the opening doors.

Rune gave him a smile in return because he deserved one for his efforts, not because she really felt like smiling. "Thank you," she said politely and climbed in, giving a final wave as the doors closed.

The elevator dropped Rune down into the bowels of the building, lower than the ground itself by almost as many levels as she could go up. When at last the door opened, it was into a very different world than the one she had left downtown.

Instead of office cubicles filled with people in professional clothing, the doors parted into an enormous, cavernous room the size of two gymnasiums and about as open. All throughout the space were clustered desks and terminals with people working at them dressed in hoodies and jeans or whatever else made that individual worker comfortable. The monitors filled the semi-dark room with ambient light and motion. People worked away at the various setups, all part of the underground resistance movement against the corporate authority. Hackers and technicians and analysts worked side by side to forge a better future for everyone disenfranchised by the elites and their self-serving laws that never seemed to apply to themselves, only those beneath them. The underground resistance worked to undo it all from the inside.

And Rune was one of them. But also, *not* one of them.

At least, that was how Rune felt as she exited into the room, as much an invader here as she had been in any of the office buildings downtown.

The first cluster near the elevators all had their heads down typing away in a mysterious code, their overhead monitors showing their work. They didn't say a verbal word to each other but seemed to be in heated discussion in the clicking language of their keyboards full of intensity and focus. A couple of people came up behind them, making notes and talking quietly to each other as they watched what was happening on the monitors.

This setup was repeated a dozen times throughout the room. It made up the majority of the Praetorium, each cluster working on its own project. Occasionally, there would be cheers and high-fives, but Rune could never figure out why, even if she asked. You either got it or you didn't. The failures were often more subtle with groans and a general dispersal of the cluster. She'd only witnessed one tech completely demolish his monitor in rage early in her ... employment.

The largest difference between herself and most of the others in the room was the fact that she had no choice of being

a part of the underground movement at all. The corporate system had geared itself toward using those with skills but criminal records as a sort of indentured servant. The reason corporations got away with it was because she was still free to go outside before a certain curfew. She had a nice place to live, was cared for, and had meaningful work. But Rune could only see it for what it was. It was still a prison. And those around her knew it too, quietly treating her differently and with distance. At least this prison had a good catering service.

She headed over to the free-standing kitchen positioned in the right corner to grab some tea and a snack. Unlike the rest of the room, this section was better lit with a few old-fashioned lamps hanging over the gray and white checkered tile. A couple of other techs were talking softly beside the gray granite counters, toasting some sandwiches in a panini press. The techs immediately stopped their conversation to glance at her. Rune ignored them as she retrieved a cold iced tea from the black fridge.

She barely noticed the two techs scurrying away and didn't take it for the warning it was until it was too late. Turning all the way around, Rune came nose to nose with St. Rachel.

"Where the hell have you been?" the beautiful woman demanded, looming over Rune with her arms crossed over her perfect chest. The fierceness of her presence forced Rune to take a step back in retreat.

"Excuse me?" Rune asked, recovering enough to not back all the way into the fridge.

"The job ended two hours ago. Where have you been?" St. Rachel growled. She wasn't clenching her teeth because beautiful women didn't do that, but the words still ground out of her.

Rune narrowed her eyes, biting back the answer. Instead, she straightened and looked St. Rachel straight in the eye. "I don't answer to you."

St. Rachel stabbed her painted fingernail at Rune's chest. "You almost cost me my operation, so you *do* owe me an answer, Talent."

The Saint typically intimidated most people when she had a mind to. She had all the skills to snap Rune in two if she wanted, but that didn't worry the Finder. *Stay calm,* she told her face while she focused on keeping it as relaxed as possible. *You don't know what she knows yet. Don't give her the answers she isn't looking for.*

Instead, she chose to answer with her own question. "How?" Rune asked, sounding to her own ears genuinely perplexed by that statement.

"You almost blew St. Benedict's cover!" St. Rachel snapped, and Rune groaned internally. Why did everything have to always revolve around St. Benedict? Okay, so they knew she had been on the same floor as the other Saint. Still didn't mean they knew what she had done behind their backs. Right?

"I did my job. Get out of my face," Rune said, then winced internally. That did sound a bit guilty. To cover it, she pushed past St. Rachel. She could feel all the eyes in the room watching, but nobody was coming to her aid. Sans allies, the only move she really had was to just get out of there.

Crap. This makes me look like I'm running away, she thought.

Because she was.

"Maxamillion wants us upstairs now for an explanation," St. Rachel proclaimed, arresting Rune's retreat in its tracks with her words. With a sniff, the Saint confidently turned to saunter past the Finder, bumping Rune in passing. "You can answer to him then," St. Rachel threw over her shoulder as she flounced toward the elevator.

Crap.

The elevator doors parted again to reveal a textured glass wall with the Corinthe logo stenciled into frosted glass. At the top of the building, the executive floor of the Corinthe Corporation was everything it should be: a garden-like heaven

as opposed to the dark cavern beneath the building.

Rune exited and stepped to the left side, putting herself out of the way of the seething Saint she had shared the ride up with as she barreled her way to their boss's office. Obviously, St. Rachel was determined to get the first word in. Rune, on the other hand, would rather have taken the elevator back down and just avoided the whole conversation altogether. She had covered her tracks so carefully and seemed to have even managed to slip her antics past St. Benedict.

The doom and gloom feeling she wrestled with was in total contrast with the plants, sunlight, and elegance covering every inch of the large, impressive, main room. Having explored a handful of other such executive suites downtown when called to do gigs, Rune knew the current trend in office fashion seemed to be themed floors. This one's theme was island paradise getaway. The extravagance of all the greenery and ambience was all for show, but it was an effective show for those looking to do business with each other. The effect worked on Rune, who felt a wash of ionized air from the artificial waterwall dropping a sheen of crystal-clear water installed behind the reception desk.

The flutter of apprehension returned at the sound of a door slamming shut. It made the whole room flinch and paused any of the soft murmurs that had been going full tilt before. Rune sighed. There was no point in dithering.

Rune wove her way through the open concept floor plan with its little islands of clustered desks all facing a frondy tree in the middle. On the opposite wall were the separate offices of the executives. Glancing through their interior windows, Rune could see them all working away at their desks. Framed by greenery and behind their own glass barriers, they reminded her of exhibits at a zoo. Inside, each office was uniquely decorated as a reflection of that executive's personality, an introduction at a glance. It certainly told Rune more about the people within than the title plaques beside each door did.

No more so than Mr. Corinthe himself. Or rather his office.

Mr. Corinthe's office windows were tinted dark for privacy, a trick that all the executive offices could do. As Rune headed toward his door, another executive crossed in front of her to go into a fellow's office, causing the wall to dim into darkness when she slapped a switch by the door. Then the glass filled in with a hologram of a beach with animated palm trees and surf. There was even a small speaker projecting the sounds of water lapping and an occasional seagull protesting. The glass wall around Mr. Corinthe's doublewide office was literally the projection of a dark and forbidding castle, complete with flickering torches and a portcullis over the door.

"Who goes there?" a foreboding deep voice intoned as Rune approached.

"Ms. Leveau," Rune said, smirking a little at the strangely appropriate theatrics.

"Enter, if you dare," the same voice granted, and the digital portcullis rose up over the door, which opened itself inward like a normal door.

"Ah, there she is. We've been waiting," the princely man behind the mahogany desk said as she entered.

"Sorry. I came as soon as I could," Rune said, then realized it probably wasn't the best opener since St. Rachel had gotten to spit her side of whatever this was out first. It felt strange to call what was happening between them an argument since it seemed to mostly be St. Rachel's one-sided problem. But it had warranted a call to the "principal's" office, so maybe this was more serious than Rune was giving it credit.

Maxamillion accepted her statement with a bright smile, however, and gestured for the chair not already occupied by a seething, beautiful woman. "Come have a seat. I think we need to talk about the operation."

Rune had to admit she liked Maxamillion Corinthe well enough, but she just couldn't trust him for a minute. He was her jailer, after all. And if he knew what she was doing behind his back, he wouldn't be smiling so friendly-like. Unless he did know and was trying to lure her into a false sense of security?

Paranoia was exhausting.

Still, as Rune looked into his face, she didn't see any hint of a hidden agenda. He had a nice face actually, not handsome, but oozing with so much charisma he would have been thought of as handsome. His warm, dark-bronze skin glowed with health and vitality as he came around the desk to welcome Rune into his office with a bottle of artisanal fizzy water.

"You took longer than I expected," he said, glancing at the hologram clock ticking as it floated above the corner of his desk.

"I took the train, easier than trying to park downtown," she said as an excuse. It also happened to be true.

"She could have been here an hour ago," St. Rachel commented bitterly. "She refused to get a ride with St. Benedict."

"I see." He turned back to Rune.

"I also stopped for lunch. I hadn't eaten yet," Rune said, feeling more obligated to him to account for herself than to St. Rachel.

He nodded at that. "That's fine. Your time is at your discretion in general."

St. Rachel gave a feminine grunt at that, but he ignored it. He gestured to the leather chairs before his desk again before going back to his own seat on the other side. "Sit. Do you want a drink?" he offered.

Rune cocked an eyebrow, then lifted up the unopened water bottle. "You already gave me something."

He closed his eyes, shaking his head as he sat down. "Sorry. It has been one of those days." He laughed. "But if you would like something else, I can have something brought in? I also have something stronger if you prefer?" He gestured to an office sidebar against the left wall.

Rune settled into her assigned chair, definitely confused as to what was going on. Was she here to get scolded? It felt more like a school counselor trying too hard to be her friend. "No, thank you, Mr. Corinthe. I got—"

"Maxamillion is fine right now, if I can call you Rune?" he

asked, gesturing his hand to ask for her permission. "This is Praetorium business. And you're not in trouble if that's what you're thinking," Maxamillion said.

St. Rachel's face didn't agree with that, but she held her tongue while crossing her arms hard. She selected the chair farthest from the door, positioning her back to the corner so that she could observe most of the room. The unconscious paranoia of a Saint. Rune had dealt with it several times when out to eat with St. Benedict. When they were still partners, that was.

Not wanting to think further on *that* Saint, Rune cracked her bottle of fancy water, letting the effervescence rise to the top before completely removing the cap. It tasted good and she drank down a good portion before Maxamillion resettled behind his desk.

"So? How *is* it going?" he prompted, folding his hands on the desk. Again, he projected "trying to be cool and relatable principal."

St. Rachel shifted forward in her seat, taking charge of the conversation. "The operation has resumed with nominal parameters. St. Benedict was able to get in and make the repair to the code we needed. There was some exposure, but we limited it as best we could. No evidence yet that we were detected, but it'll be three days before I'm comfortable with that. While we have no evidence that the other entities monitoring them as well noticed us, we can't be a hundred percent sure," she said.

Maxamillion nodded. "So not an entire disaster?" he asked optimistically.

St. Rachel shook her head. "Depends on what happens. We know the other 'hunters' are there, but our only advantage was they thought *they* were tricking *us*. Now that we've had this exposure, the question becomes: did they see us see them? St. Benedict seems to have smoothed it over with his usual charm, and it helps that the issues seemed to have been caused by something outside the normal players."

"And what did happen to cause the interruption?" Maxamillion asked, looking now toward Rune.

"Something the Talent did," St. Rachel answered for her, but Maxamillion waited for Rune's answer.

She shifted a glance at St. Rachel, trying to decide where to start. She was going to have to be careful here about what she said, lest they discover her extracurricular activity, but so far, it was starting to look like they didn't know what she had done, and she already had her cover story for this scenario. She had worked it out on the train ride back.

"What have you been told?" Rune asked first, glancing over at St. Rachel.

"Don't worry about it. I want to hear your side," her boss said, which did nothing to reassure her of her position in this conversation.

Rune took another sip of her water. Prior to this convicted felon contract, Rune had only ever worked and been truly answerable for herself or her aunt Maddie. Having to be accountable to a boss felt ... weird and foreign to her.

"Not a whole lot to tell," Rune started. "The woman had an illegal love charm on her, one designed to protect itself from being dispelled or removed by weaponizing the host to protect it obsessively."

"How obsessively?" Maxamillion asked, his gaze already far away as he assimilated her information.

"Think mother with newborn child," Rune offered, if what she had witnessed was the best guide. "It was generating a magical field that seemed to be interrupting a lot of other equipment, including the office network."

He nodded. "So, how did you deal with it?"

Rune took another deep breath in, focusing on just the facts.

"Well, the charm was powerful but badly made. It made it easy to identify the source of the magic, but once I did, getting it off her was the bigger problem. So I had to use my magic, which added to the forces being literally thrown around. And the curse we were dealing with... It's one of those things that makes it so you can't reason with the one it's cast upon because it is actively usurping her will to make a reasonable choice."

"That sounds like something that should be illegal?" Maxamillion asked.

"Oh, it is a hella illegal," Rune agreed.

St. Rachel cocked her head to the side, actually engaging in the conversation instead of raging at it. "So, there is a case to be made against the person who gave it to her?"

Rune nodded. "Yes, absolutely. She seemed, I mean, the client seemed already set on doing just that through her corporate policing force when I left. I wrote up a report to that effect."

Maxamillion propped his head on his fist, thinking. "Yes, I understand that, but what did you *do* about it?" he pushed, finishing off his grapefruit juice.

Rune sighed and decided to rip the band-aid off. "I destroyed it. With a lamp."

His far away gaze shifted focus to her, his eyes going wide to lift his eyebrows. "A what?"

Rune glanced at St. Rachel, who had leaned in to hear her clarification. "I picked up a heavy standing lamp there and smashed the crystal with it. It was enough to crack it and disrupt the spell safely without causing further injury or property damage for that matter," Rune said.

"There was a burst of energy that rolled through the building at one point," St. Rachel said stiffly. "I'm presuming that was when you 'killed it with a lamp.'"

"Well, yeah," Rune said. It was almost like they were having an office gossip, and Rune realized the story might be more entertaining than she gave it credit for before.

St. Rachel straightened with an air of triumph. "*That* burst of energy endangered the whole operation. It's what caused the exposure. I told you it was the Talent's fault."

Bitch, Rune thought, but what she said was, "Right, but what did you want me to do about it? I was called on a gig, and

I did my job. I had no idea there was another operation going on at the same time."

"You're the magical person. You should have controlled the overflow. Absorbed it or something," St. Rachel stated as if it were perfectly obvious. It sounded to Rune like someone had been googling "magic practices."

"Okay, first, I had no idea what I was dealing with until I got there, and second, it doesn't work like that. That'd be like..." She reached for a relatable analogy. "Like asking a plumber not to spill a drop of water while they fix your plumbing. They can try, but it's not really going to happen. Destroying the crystal was going to have a backlash as the magic dispersed itself naturally."

"Plumbers shut off the water and hose out the pipes before they start working," St. Rachel countered.

"It doesn't get everything..."

"Okay, let's leave the metaphors aside," the charismatic leader interceded. He cocked his head curiously to the side. "Why wasn't she informed of the concurrent operation?" he asked, directing the question to St. Rachel.

That took St. Rachel aback. "We were working on a need-to-know basis and—"

"Okay, okay, so I think the source of the issue here is we are not having a enough interdepartmental communication. Am I hearing this right?"

St. Rachel pressed her fingertips against her forehead as if she could feel a headache coming. "What is the point of having a secret operation if we tell everybody about it?"

"I think we had a demonstration right here," Maxamillion observed. He tapped the desk with his hands like it was a bucket drum for a second. "Can you come up with a few ways we can increase communication with our Digital Wizard here while still keeping the anonymity of our various operations?"

St. Rachel's lips went very thin. "Yes, I can," she said.

The boss nodded, then turned to Rune. "Do you think you can try and figure out a way to ... cut down on how much water

might get blasted when you're trying to 'fix pipes,' as it were?" He air quoted his fingers over his metaphors.

"Maybe?" she hedged. "I'd have to research it, honestly."

"You see!" St. Rachel declared as if her point had just been vindicated. "She wasn't prepared for the job and endangered the whole operation."

"According to you, the operation is still viable," Maxamillion said, though it sounded more like a challenge. "Are you saying you were unprepared for this possibility, that the magic might interfere?"

Her mouth fished open and closed a moment before she said, "No, sir."

She glared at Maxamillion.

There was a test of wills for a moment that made Rune want to vacate the area, but then Maxamillion sighed and stood up again to pace around his desk. "Look, the plain simple truth is none of us have figured out all the ins and outs about having a magical component on the team. There are a lot of things we are going to need to figure out, and that is only going to take time and experience. These are growing pains."

"Yes, sir," Rune said softly.

St. Rachel echoed it a moment later, not willing to be outdone.

"Please, Rune. I'm only sir in front of the day office," he dismissed, stopping at the edge of his desk to lean on it casually with one hip. "St. Rachel, I'll talk to you further later. I'd like to speak to Rune a little bit more in private."

"Yes, sir," St. Rachel said, rising and promptly leaving.

The two remaining waited a beat.

"Mr. Corinthe—"

"Hold on," he said, holding up a hand, his eyes glued to the door.

CHAPTER 4

They sat in silence for a few moments more, then a bell rose under its own power to hover in the air in the corner and dinged. Rune jumped at the sharp sound. It reminded her of the elevator's ding.

"Okay, now it's safe." Maxamillion laughed, dropping his crossed arms and yanking on his tie. "Can't be too careful with that augmented Saint hearing."

"What is that thing?" Rune asked, laughing at her own startle as she got up to inspect the bell.

"Oh, got that at a flea market couple of years ago. It already had the spell inscribed in; they just needed to replace the name. I got someone to do the work for me and linked to the elevator to warn me when St. Rachel is coming and going," he said.

Rune glanced over her shoulder with a grin. "Really?"

"I am very secure in my manhood when I say that woman scares me to death," he said with a serious face that was anything but.

Picking up the bell, Rune turned the worn metal thing

around, looking at the rune scrolling all over it. "Ah, I see. It can only be tied to one person," she said.

"So you know that magic?" Maxamillion asked, gesturing at it.

"Well, I've had a lot time on my hands lately, finally got around to all that studying I promised Alf..." But she stopped, her throat closing up unexpectedly.

Maxamillion seemed to read correctly into her silence. "You miss them," he said, matter of factly, referring to her retainers, family, and friends.

Rune nodded, replacing the bell on its shelf.

"Rune..." Maxamillion stopped himself and licked his lips as he tried to find the right words. "I know how this is going to sound, but..." He hesitated and then opened a drawer in the desk. "I know how you are feeling."

He withdrew a folder from the drawer and came around the desk to hold it out to her. Cocking an eyebrow at it, Rune crossed the space and took the folder from him. Opening it, she looked down at a rough picture she had seen once before, in a digital file he had shown her when first trying to convince her that they meant her no harm. That they weren't a normal corporation.

The man in the picture had short braids sticking every which way out of his head, angry eyes, a rough face, and even rougher clothes. The picture was clipped to the folder, which also held printed sheets with stats behind it. All things she had seen before, but she looked up at Maxamillion for an explanation.

"I'm technically a convicted felon too," he said, sitting down in the chair St. Rachel had vacated. His gaze rested on the folder as if it were a tunnel into a past he could never reach again. Maxamillion's voice shifted, became less cultured and more affected. More honest. "Max X, the notorious street criminal and vigilante, or domestic terrorist, or sometimes just simply 'thug.' Whatever the corporations needed to tell themselves to justify what they were doing to me and my people.

That man there," he nodded at the picture, "seems a far cry away from the man I am now, don't you think?"

She nodded, taking her own seat across from him on the same side.

"Yeah, I was so full of fire, it's a wonder the whole city didn't burn down again. Right up to the day I got caught."

"You were a corporate convict?" Rune asked, putting the pieces together, looking back at the picture. "But that's not possible."

"You're right," he said as she sat back up again. "Max X was arrested and convicted on a dozen charges, most of them real, and disappeared into the corporate prison system until I, Maxamillion Corinthe, bought his convict contract to come work for me here at Corinthe Corp."

Rune nodded. "Like Maddie did with Anna Masterson," she said, adding her own original name before she had taken the one she had now: Rune Leveau.

"Very much so. We've used this same trick for half of the staff of the Praetorium down there. Countless times now for others we've helped place in our network. But we can't do it for everybody. The risk is pretty great, and if they can't help with the cause, we can't take the risk."

"And you took that risk for me," Rune said. "I know, sir. I do. I am grateful that I am not sitting in a real corporate prison right now. If you guys hadn't pulled me out of there and claimed jurisdiction over me, I would probably be dead now."

"Yes, but I want you to know, Rune, the system is imprisoning you—not us." He leaned forward, reaching out a hand to rest it over one of hers. "I'm in this with you. I don't have real freedom either, and I want you to know that you're not alone. You're as free as the rest of us can be, and if you want to, you could do like I did, shed your old self and become someone new again. It's your choice. Do you understand what I'm trying to say?" He looked at her pleadingly, and she could see for the first time how desperate he was for her to understand.

A spark of something, not magical, but emotional passed

between them through his touch. And Rune felt very confused. Apparently, her confusion came through her face because Maxamillion pulled back his hand and cleared his throat.

She decided to try to save the moment. "I understand what you're saying. I do. But I am still a prisoner, sir. Even if you give me all the freedom you can. You changed your name and now you're a corporate elite. I'm sorry, but I don't think I can do that." Rune closed the folder.

She expected him to be put off by her words, but instead, he leaned back and loosened his tie more. "'If you stand for nothing, what will you fall for?'" Maxamillion quoted, Rune recognizing the quote though not able to place its origins. Yet it kindled a fire in Maxamillion's eyes, and the ghost of the man she had only seen in pictures surfaced in his features.

"How's the apartment?" he asked, abruptly changing the subject.

"Nice," she answered. A pause grew between them as she struggled for something more to say. She decided the truth was probably best. "It's not my apartment, you know. Still going to need some getting used to."

"We can have some of your things retrieved if you'd like," Maxamillion offered. "I'm actually surprised you haven't gone over already?"

"It was offered. I just felt... I decided to leave everything there. Something to look forward to, you know, when this is over?" Rune answered, and she shifted in her seat to set the folder back on his desk. "Plus, the bar is far from safe to walk into yet. Alf... my retainers are still wrestling with insurance, and since my status with the Magic Guild is on indefinite probation, we don't qualify for a lot of sponsored grants or loans."

"You could always try for corporate ones," Maxamillion offered.

Rune shook her head. "That would mean giving up my Magic Guild membership entirely, and I can't do that."

"Even after everything they've done to you?"

She knew what he meant. After all, it had been the Magic

Guild who had the right to try and imprison her for her crimes, and they had sold those rights in contract through a back-channel deal with the Corinthe Corp.

"It would be understandable though if you harbored some resentment for how it all went down," Maxamillion continued.

"I can assure you, I don't harbor any resentments," Rune lied.

"I know with St. Benedict..."

"St. Benedict did the best he could with the cards he was dealt, just like I did," Rune snapped, the metaphorical fire she had been trying to hide flaring in her words. "I'm really getting tired of everyone assuming I don't understand that."

She could hear her tone was inappropriate to use with a boss, but she couldn't take it back. Maxamillion didn't seem upset by it though. Rather, he looked thoughtful, his eyes calculating like she was a problem to solve. He had treated her like an equal the whole time up to this point, coming around the desk, showing her his own criminal file, but something had shifted, and a wall she hadn't realized was down came back up.

The prince of the business world was back.

"Let's call it for today. Actually, no. Let's call it for this week." He straightened then and stood to go back around his desk, busying himself with tidying up the papers and relocating his file back into its drawer.

"Call it?" Rune asked, realizing too late she had made some sort of error and was flummoxed as to what to do about it, if anything.

"Take the rest of the week off. Boss's orders," he said as if that were a funny joke.

"I'm sorry. I don't understand?" Rune stood as well, taking her report, paralleling him as he came around the desk.

"Look, Rune. I'm not expecting you to get a hundred percent on board with everything already. It has only been... what—a month? Two months? Since you had your entire life upended?" He escorted her to the door of his office, then followed her out. Rune allowed herself to be swept along.

"Yeah, more or less," she said, refolding the report to stuff into her pocket.

"Exactly. Take an extra-long weekend, give yourself time to heal," he said, gesturing for her to walk with him through the maze of fancy, wood cubicles toward the elevators.

"But you wanted me to research on coming up with a 'bucket' spell," she argued.

"Oh, yes, well, I mostly said that so as to seem impartial in front of St. Rachel. I mean, don't get me wrong—that does sound like something we should have in the toolbox, but there is no time limit on it. In the future we're going to need your skills outside the 9 to 5 zone, so take the extra time off now."

"So, take Friday off?" Rune asked, making sure she understood this clearly. "But I have two gigs scheduled already..."

"Sheryl," he called out to the receptionist at the front desk.

She looked up serenely at him before rising with the elegance of a geisha. "Yes, Mr. Corinthe?"

"Clear Ms. Leveau's schedule for Friday. Move everyone to next week. Tell them we overbooked or something that makes us sound good."

She nodded with a smile as if it were her favorite thing to do in the whole world. "Leave it to me."

"There we are. All settled," Maxamillion said proudly. He set a friendly hand on Rune's shoulder. "You go ahead and take a three-day weekend. We'll have a meeting early Monday morning and talk about the future. Oh, and remember, you don't answer to St. Rachel or anyone else around here. You only answer to me, officially. And as far as I'm concerned, especially within the Praetorium, you are equal to a Saint."

Rune cocked her head to the side again, unable to repress her smirk. "Does that mean I get the same budget that they do?" she asked impishly.

His chuckle came out as an unattractive snort. "God, you sound like St. Benedict. I'll give you the budget you need just like everybody else when you can show me what you need the resources *for*." He turned then to head back toward his office. "Have a good weekend, Rune."

"Good night, Maxamillion," she replied, daring to use his name.

As soon as she was back in the elevator, she let a huge sigh of relief. "Okay. I don't think any of them suspect a thing." And now she had some time off to do with as she pleased, answerable to no one.

That couldn't have worked out better if she had tried to coordinate it. Maybe she was getting used to this "corporate spy" thing.

CHAPTER 5

St. Benedict waited in the dark hallway, his back against the unpainted concrete, his arms folded in front of his chest, his head tipped forward so the fedora covered his eyes. He had abandoned the suit jacket the minute he got back to the Praetorium, and even with his heating augmentations, his skin felt the cold biting. He couldn't make himself care, treating it like the punishment he rightly deserved, though it was inadequate to cover the least of his sins. He only realized how he must look when the elevator door in the wall opposite him binged open, throwing a strong beam of light that temporarily blinded him before his augs compensated.

The only sign that St. Rachel had been surprised by his appearance was the slight pause before exiting the elevator. Without further acknowledgement, she turned to proceed down the rough concrete hallway. Her movement triggered the lights to stutter on overhead, which had all gone out when he had stood still for too long.

St. Benedict fell into step behind her, keeping his head

tipped down so his whole world consisted of her sashaying ass in her dark burgundy business skirt. He couldn't admire the view; he only focused on counting her steps, measuring her gait, judging her thoughts based on her response to his presence.

"If you're here to—" was all she got out before he stepped up and kicked her square in that perfect round, peach of an ass. She toppled from her heels, snapping one of them as she flew forward, but if it had been anyone else, he would have been a cad for doing that to her. He knew he had just made her three times deadlier, but he didn't care.

Her inevitable tuck and roll came off masterful, and the fact the knife flew back at him before he could see it told him that she had partly expected an attack. Just not that specific one.

The knife buried itself into his shoulder, which meant she wasn't really trying to kill him.

Still hurt though.

"Asshole!" she shouted as she scurried back to retrieve her still-whole shoe to charge at him. She stopped her charge when she realized that he hadn't done anything to block or parry her knife.

"Why didn't you go for my heart?" he asked, cupping his now messed up arm against his chest, taking the pressure off of it but lifting the weight.

Her rage fell away, and she dropped the shoe to come to his aid. "Why didn't you dodge, you idiot?" she scolded, furrowing her brows at the mess.

She didn't sense the danger.

As soon as she was close enough, he let go of his cradled arm, snapping his hand around her throat. She froze, her eyes meeting his. He knew of three immediate counter moves she could do right that moment that would spill more of his blood and break a few bones.

Yet she was a Saint. She knew this wasn't just about doing harm to each other.

"Yes, St. Benedict," she said in an agreeing, condescending tone. "I *am* taking you very seriously right now."

"You are going to leave her alone," he said, his voice very soft and very deadly.

St. Rachel took a step back out of his grip, and he let her go, though he would have preferred she try and break his offending wrist. It was the least he deserved.

Instead, his counterpart fixed her hair. "I will use what *resources* I need when I need them to accomplish my missions."

"I'm never going to fuck you," he said flatly, cutting straight to the heart of the issue between them.

It didn't have the whip effect he hoped it would. "I never wanted you to," she replied coolly, which was a bald-faced lie. "Especially now. All lovesick puppy, moping around her all the time. You're disgusting. If we were still under the Cardinal's control, I'd recommend you for an emotional programming update. You're damn near useless."

"Maybe we should go together," St. Benedict said, grabbing her hand to pull, which she immediately resisted but could not entirely escape. "Let them climb into our heads again and tap dance around our synapses."

"Let go of me!" she barked.

His laugh was maniacal, like a broken thing. "Oh, come on, St. Rachel. Haven't had a good mind fuck in awhile..."

"Get off!" She pushed him away, and something in the panicked tone of her voice snapped him out of his manic madness.

Space opened up between them as they repelled away from each other to the opposite walls of the hallway. He went back to hugging his arms against his body, taking the weight off his impaled shoulder. They remained that way for a long, long moment.

"I'm sorry," he finally said, unable to look at her as he said it.

St. Rachel straightened her hair, which had become disheveled in their scuffle. "Apologizing is just another sign you're..." She didn't need to finish the thought.

"Becoming more human again? Maybe that's a *good* thing,

St. Rachel." His eyes challenged her and begged her to understand at the same time. All she had to give was resistance and her fear of what his changed behavior might mean. That he was slipping further and further away from something she understood and could count on.

St. Rachel moved to retrieve her fallen files from where they floated in mid-air, not that she actually needed to. They would have followed her wherever she went since they were just a digital representation of files. "Then you're useless to *our* mission, and you know it. We promised to end this forever and make *all* of them pay, whatever it takes. I know your goal was Masterson, but you damn well know your goals are not mine at all."

"I know," he conceded.

She took a step closer. "And we're getting closer. This is *my revenge* too." She shook her files at him for emphasis.

He met her eyes. "You need to leave her alone," he said softly, not a threat this time, more like a plea.

St. Rachel's perfect lips pursed together into a thin line. "I will use whatever tool I need. Like a Saint." She straightened with the bearing of a warrior goddess passing judgement. "Does she know you're down here, fighting her battles for her?"

He wasn't going to answer that question, and when he didn't, she sniffed once, then retrieved the broken shoe from the floor. Holding it with the other together in one hand, she accessed her interface menu with her eyes and began sliding through the branching lists with a glowing finger. In a few seconds, her shoes reset, whole and new. She tapped the menu again, and they appeared on the feet of her avatar.

"I really don't give a … care," she said, picking the word with careful control. He could imagine what she meant to say. "But if you're at all interested, she's up to something."

He narrowed his eyes at her. "What something?" St. Benedict asked, not even bothering to be coy.

His refusal to play the game made his counterpart more uncomfortable, not even having the safety of their banter to protect herself. She flipped her impossibly perfect hair to continue down the hallway, dismissing the question.

"What something?" he repeated, more forcefully.

St. Rachel turned, striking a pose that would have been the winning shot in a fashion magazine, smiling brightly. "Well, that's just the thing: she's being rather secretive about it, isn't she? And since her magic gets in the way of my normal means of acquiring information people don't want me to have, I can't really tell you, especially when I have you and Maxamillion blocking me at every turn. All I can tell you is if you don't find out what she's planning, I'll have to, and I don't exactly have time for this kind of juvenile playing-at-spy crap. Now, if we're done with the pissing match, I've got work to do, and so do you. Excuse me." With a nod, she proceeded down the hallway to her virtual office which she didn't open so much as walk straight through the closed door and disappear.

St. Benedict didn't even bother pulling the knife from his shoulder as he jacked out, letting his virtual body disintegrate, the knife included, before he blinked his actual eyes open. He gave a passing glance to St. Rachel, sitting in her own chair a few feet away, her eyes shut serenely as if she only slept.

That accomplished nothing, he thought, rubbing at the sore spot on his shoulder where his nerves were still convinced they had been hit with a knife. It would be a couple of hours before the ghost sensations wore off.

Completely jacking out changed the light over his head from a bright white to a cool blue. Beyond his pool of light, the dark churned with people working at their various terminals, oblivious to him as if he were another machine. In many ways, he was.

As soon as the switch happened, he sighed, then waited for the medical tech to remove the sticky pads from his chest and temples that watched his life signs in case something went wrong while his mind was connected to their network space. What did he think confronting St. Rachel would accomplish really? He knew hurting his relationship with St. Rachel could

mean his life in the right circumstances. He was pretty sure she wouldn't sabotage or go out of her way to have him killed, but it could mean the difference of a split-second reaction.

Once he was clear of the medical equipment, he spun his legs to sit up. Rolling his shoulder in its socket, he grunted at a fresh stabbing shock from the ghost knife wound.

"Do you want some painkillers?" the med tech asked.

He nodded silently and held out a hand to receive the pair of blue pills, swallowing them down dry. He stood then, speaking to no one as they went about cleaning up and resetting the jack-in rig.

Dinner had been delivered in the Praetorium kitchen with a decent line of techs and analysts lined up, moving in a neat, shuffling queue to help themselves from the silver serving trays. Initially, he decided to ignore eating until he spotted Malachi, his best friend according to the man himself, moving to intercept him. The thin tech looked less disheveled than usual. His hair was shorn on the sides instead of long and unkempt. Well, the top was still a little longer, but it looked on purpose instead of it-just-grew-that-way. Not only that, his goatee looked damn near professionally groomed. There was only one reason for the cleaned-up look, and internally, St. Benedict groaned. He could anticipate getting an earful about how things went with Zita's family gathering for their Naga holiday celebration honoring Manasa Devi, the Hindi goddess of snakes.

"So, impressing her parents went well, I see," St. Benedict said, cutting off whatever Malachi had been about to say before he could say it, effectively controlling the conversation.

"Huh," Malachi checked a step, "oh, yeah." Shyly, the tech ran his fingers through his nice haircut, grinning from ear to ear. "Her parents were pretty impressed, all things considered."

"Things like having two legs and *not* a proper spinal column?"

Malachi shrugged. "It's ... an issue, but there isn't a whole lot they can do about it. I got the impression, more than anything, her mother is content that I make as much money as her daughter."

"And her father?"

"Eh, let's not talk about her father. Needless to say, I didn't make a complete ass of myself, and Zita considers that a win."

"You are a brave, brave man," St. Benedict said as they moved with the line.

Malachi's committed relationship to Zita had been going on ever since St. Benedict first met the tech almost five years ago. Multi-race couples never had it easy, especially when anatomy came into play, but he also remembered the first time the self-proclaimed geek revolutionary had laid eyes on the beautiful and brilliant Naga doctor. Lovestruck understated it. There had been a betting pool for a few weeks on how soon Malachi would be found dead from being crushed or poisoned until St. Benedict tattled to Maxamillion, and the boss put a stop to it. St. Benedict never asked the details on how Malachi and Zita made it work. All he knew was that it did, and Malachi had never been happier in his life.

"How's Rune doing?" Malachi suddenly asked, interrupting St. Benedict's thoughts.

"I have no idea. Why do you ask?" St. Benedict lied, and it even sounded convincing.

"I just saw her a few minutes ago," Malachi reported.

"Well, then you would know better than me," St. Benedict pointed out as they finally reached the plates. He proceeded to grab one and look over what was on offer.

"She blew out her biometric lock to her apartment again. I replaced it, but I'm thinking I need to get her a magic-based one. I can't really tell why it keeps happening. I mean, is it just because her magical nature overwhelms the buffers, or is it connected to her emotions or something?"

"Well, she's not a typical Talent," St. Benedict reminded him. "It's probably got something to do with that."

"That whole Magi thing, right. I tried to find out if there was any research done about Magi and tech, but no such papers, which honestly, I find passing strange, you know what I mean?"

St. Benedict cocked an eyebrow. "Passing strange?"

Malachi grinned. "Zita and I are watching a lot of Jane Austen lately and stuff like Jane Austen. It's kind of creeping into my language, I guess. No one talks like that anymore."

"I like it. Keep it," St. Benedict said, selecting a pesto chicken to add to the plate. "Society could use some fancier words. And as for the paper thing, sounds like a great opportunity to be the first on the scene."

Malachi dramatically sighed and rolled his eyes. "Right, when am I going to find the time? Between you, St. Rachel, and Maxamillion, I'm about to go cross-eyed blind. They're going to have to carry me out of here in a straight-jacket and throw away the key."

St. Benedict shrugged. "Sorry, not sorry?"

"Your sympathy is deeply felt," Malachi said with a dryness that was undercut by the smile he couldn't suppress. "Anyway, if I'm going to get her a magical lock, I'm going to have to talk to Maxamillion about it first. See what he thinks. It would be a Magic Guild purchase, and things being what they are..." The tech rolled his wrist in a gesture meant to fill in the rest of the sentence.

Relationships between the Magic Guild and the rest of the tech corps of Chicago had always been bad, but since Rune's arrest had forced her House into probation, losing its voting rights and status within the guild, those relationships had become even more strained. Even with Corinthe Corp having brokered a deal that allowed them to take control of Rune's convict contract, for which they had paid the Magic Guild through the nose, it had by no means brought them closer. If anything, it seemed to have made things even more strained, for many saw them as another corporation chipping away at the autonomy of the magic community.

St. Benedict couldn't argue against that, but the whole situation had made him furious. Not only had Rune personally lost her freedom when the Magic Guild should have protected her; she had been put into an impossible situation that threatened her Wizard House. That challenge had exposed her as Anna Masterson and a former escaped convict. The Magic Guild had known Rune's secret by then and why she had been falsely held by the corporate prison system the whole time. They were supposed to be helping her. And yet, with everything that had been at stake, the Magic Guild had allowed the challenge for Head of her House. They should have never let things go that far.

The idea of reaching out to the Magic Guild for anything set his teeth on edge. "You should reach out to her cousin. He owns a magic shop. I bet he could hook you up." St. Benedict added a baked potato and sides of sour cream and chives. The next container added roasted Brussel sprouts and broccoli. It all looked prepared to perfection, yet the smell of it brought up an oily taste in the back of St. Benedict's throat.

"Who was her cousin again?" Malachi asked, taking two chickens, forgoing the greens and proceeding to drown his baked potato in every topping the food service had provided.

"Elias Leveau. I'll send you his contact info," St. Benedict said, already doing it through his augmentations as he moved to set the loaded plate on a tray. Only using a series of blinks and eye movements, St. Benedict pulled a list of contacts from the edge of his augmented vision, finding the number of Elias's shop, before shooting it off to Malachi to find at his computer when he got back. Through his hologram, he passed an eye over the desserts, looking for a piece of chocolate cake.

"Thanks, man," Malachi said, oblivious to the multi-tasking the Saint was doing. The other man was too intent on grabbing up three desserts to fill the remaining space on his tray. How the heck he ate so much and remained so skinny was one of the great mysteries of the age.

"No problem," St. Benedict replied. Finally satisfied with the tray, he moved to leave.

"Hey, where you are going?" Malachi called. "I thought you and I would go eat with Zita."

The elevator binged immediately, to the Saint's relief.

"Sorry, Bud. I haven't slept in thirty-five hours. I'm going straight to bed," St. Benedict lied.

"Well, okay. I'll talk to you later. Have a good sleep."

St. Benedict gave the obligatory acknowledgement just as the doors slid closed, but his mind had already left the conversation.

Poor Malachi. He didn't deserve such a crap friend as him.

Soon enough, the door binged open in the residential hallway. It was thankfully empty. Stopping in front of *her* door, he waited, listening for any sound of her on the other side.

His heart pounded rapidly in his chest.

Setting his hand against the door, he willed to know what was happening on the other side, but no augmentation in the world could give him that answer. Already he could feel the magical field that her apartments generated because of her presence in them buzzing on the edge of his perception. Coming near her apartments came with a price in the form of a constant low-grade migraine. Not that he cared.

Tech and magic didn't mix too well, and since his whole body had significant amounts of tech within it, being around magical sources had the chance of spazzing them out, even with the considerably sophisticated and expensive buffers installed to insulate against magic interference. They helped, but his prolonged exposure to magic over the last year made him wonder if he was reaching the limits of what tech could do. It seemed like he was driving a car with the brakes on all the time, burning the buffers down faster as he went.

It didn't stop him from coming to her room, from longing to be near her. The more he tried to deny himself her presence, the more he longed for it. He was already a psychopath; he didn't need her to know how badly.

Sighing, he forced himself to acknowledge that no amount of willpower was going to suddenly grant him the ability to see beyond the wood barrier. Sure, he could hack into cameras, but no camera had survived in any of Rune's personal spaces to date. It was frankly a marvel that the biometric lock worked three times out of five.

Setting his own hand over the handle, he waited the three seconds for the scan, then heard a sharp mechanical clack as the door unlocked. He was one of only five people who had access to her lock other than her: himself, St. Rachel, Malachi, Maxamillion, and Carmine who ran the cleaning service. Kicking himself, he realized he forgot to knock, which was what a civilized person should do.

Acknowledging that it was too late, he still tapped on the door. "Rune? Are you in?" he called, trying to sound casual and friendly, as if the tension that lived between them didn't exist. Inside, it was dark though, a clear sign she wasn't home, or she was asleep. But he had sworn he had felt her magical aura?

Shifting the tray in his hand, he pushed his way in. After all, was he a spy or not?

As he came in, the lights came up, starting from a low fade and rising to half-light according to Rune's preset preferences. The sun had set an hour ago, though the days were getting longer. So she could still be working?

He cursed himself for an idiot again. He should have checked her office or at least the biometric map that kept track of the location of every employee in the building. Though even that tech had trouble when it came to Rune, even with her company issued phone as the anchor point instead of the usual bio-chip that most employees got to enter and exit the buildings and departments.

Setting the tray on the granite counter of her kitchenette, he went to the door of her bedroom. He had ensured she got the best apartment the company had, which had meant unceremoniously relocating the former occupant to a lesser space one floor down. St. Benedict had lost no sleep over it, even if it ruffled a few feathers.

This was the least he could do for her, and he knew it wasn't enough. It was after all still a prison, one he had dragged her into.

His dress-shoed feet moved silently over the fine, soft

carpet made of microfibers that changed color with the touch on a screen fixed to a wall. Rune had selected a forest green, making the place feel like it had been floored with soft, wild grass. It went well with the slate gray walls she'd chosen for the changeable wall paint. These features of the apartments were part of what made this space extra special as well as the extra bedroom that he had set up as a magic office, even bringing over the few things he could from her old office to decorate it with, including her Tiffany glass lamp and all her books on magical study. Yet he knew she barely went in there, like she was deliberately avoiding it. Still, he checked there first. While he was sure she must have been in her bedroom, it felt wrong to surprise her there. So when the office proved empty, it left it as the only other option.

"Rune?" he asked softly into the dark of her bedroom. Like in the main room, the lights of the bedroom brightened, which they wouldn't have in sleep mode. Her bed waited, neatly made, covered in a dark claret-colored comforter. At its sight, the bed beckoned him to fall into it himself, wrapping himself in her scent. Ignoring its blatant seduction, St. Benedict turned back into the main room, heaving a sigh. He went into the kitchen and found a tray cover in one of the cupboards to cover the dinner he had brought her, leaving it on the counter for her to find.

Just as he decided to stop being a stalker and get out, he laid eyes on Rune's phone lying on the seat of the couch. Ever since he betrayed her and brought her to the Praetorium, she had been very good about keeping it with her.

Where is she?

"St. Rachel's getting into your head," he said out loud, and while that was true...

He triple-blinked his eyes, bringing up the default digital overlay. Immediately, his head began to ache. The last time he felt this much magical feedback was months ago in Rune's bar.

The one that burned down.

He brought up his holodesk, which appeared around him

in a circle of light, a keyboard forming under his glowing fingertips. The act intensified his migraine into a pair of burning ice picks behind his eyes. He winced, and for a second, closed his eyes against it, forcing his breath through his nostrils as he waited for it to abate as the buffers caught up to the overflow. When he was master of himself again, he set about his task. Reaching to the side of the holodesk, he pulled up out of the surface of light a representation of a file box. With his glowing fingers, he flipped through the labelled files, stopping on the program he sought.

"File 342id89 open," he ordered. Instantly, the file unpacked itself, forming a screen in the air before him. Lines of code initiated at the top part of the screen, filling in his program code as it linked itself back into the Corinthe network through him. As that worked, a text box appeared at the bottom, and St. Benedict typed in Rune's employee code, initiating the companywide search. "Come on. Give me location data," he muttered. "Where are you, Rune?"

After an eternity, he got back two reports. One said she was located in the very apartment he stood in, but the second box had a long error code, followed by text that read, "Subject Not Found."

St. Benedict stared at the second message for a long time. "Magical interference..." he muttered to himself, as if he needed to hear the words out loud to believe what he was thinking. "The perfect smoke screen ... to hide an escape..."

He shook his head, then shut everything down, leaving himself still standing alone in Rune's empty apartment. His headache immediately lessened. That's when he heard a soft shushing sound coming from somewhere far away. He leaned his head to focus on the sound.

Water. "The shower," he said softly to himself. She was taking a shower.

"God, I'm an idiot," he muttered to himself, rubbing his forehead where the headache still lingered.

"Dammit, St. Benedict, you're being paranoid," he scolded

himself. But he couldn't move. All his instincts were screaming at him. Something was wrong.

He crossed back to Rune's bedroom.

"Rune?" he called out once more but opened the door less cautiously this time. The steam billowed out, caressing his face. "Sorry to bother you, but... we're having a computer malfunction, and I wanted to check that you were alright?"

Lame, lame, lame, he thought at himself.

She didn't respond.

"Look, Rune, I'm sorry I'm invading your privacy like this, but can you just verbally confirm for me that you are here, and then I will get the hell out of your hair?" he said.

Still nothing.

Now his heartbeat sped up, all his instincts screaming that something was deeply, truly wrong. He crossed the bathroom space in two steps and ripped the curtain back.

If he had been only a few seconds later, he would have missed catching the magic lines of a door as they disappeared into the tiled wall on the other side of the shower stream.

Rune was nowhere to be found.

"Dammit!"

CHAPTER 6

R une sighed as she shut the door. Leaning back, she listened to the noises of the house. It was an unassuming house, a two-story standard of Chicago's 1920s real estate boom. Several incarnations later, it had updated electricals and plumbing as well as the original molding. Standing in the foyer with its flowery carpet and various kitschy knick-knacks on the wall, she thought it was plebeian compared to the luxury apartment she had just escaped, and she wouldn't trade it for anything in the world.

Unfortunately, it also didn't really exist.

Or at least, this version of it didn't.

What she sat in was a projection, forged out of the pure magic of ECAM, the Eternal Consciousness of All Magic. At least that was what she liked to call it. Her way of going home without going home.

"Oh, you're back early," the friendly voice of her uncle called out.

Smiling, Rune pushed away from the illusory wood and

glass door to cross into the dining room to her left. Sitting at an oblong table big enough to seat six rested a middle-aged-to-pushing-older man, who would have once been thought Hollywood beautiful in his youth, but now wore the signs of age proudly in the white at his temples and the wrinkles around his eyes. He sat in an athletic tank and casual brown pants complete with suspenders hanging from his shoulders. He would have looked more at home at the end of a bar, especially with the second low-ball glass sitting next to him and the still full, unmarked bottle.

"Hi, Uncle Lucas," Rune greeted the original inspiration for the lucky devil, winding her way around a chair to come to her uncle's side.

Pushing back the old-fashioned Hamburg hat from his forehead, he leaned forward to receive his kiss on the forehead, then gestured toward the kitchen with his low-ball glass. "Elias and Margaret came by, left you dinner if you want it."

As an astral projection of herself, she ignored why the offer for her to eat was a ridiculous thing to say and wandered into the kitchen obediently. "Did you eat any?" Rune asked, looking inside the take-out box with a fancy logo on the side from one of Elias's preferred restaurants. It contained an equally fancily prepared chicken, complete with collard greens. Someone had even sliced a strawberry into a tiny fan shape. The food was obviously untouched.

"It looks good. I think you should have some," she said, focusing all of her will on picking up the takeout box and bringing it to the opposite counter where the cupboard for the plates were. It took a lot of power to actually interact with the objects in the real world through the created projection in the ECAM, but Rune desperately wanted to feel like she was actually home.

"I got all I need," Uncle Lucas said, shaking his low-ball glass of mostly ice before sipping up the dregs.

"You promised Maddie you'd keep living, and a liquid diet is not the way to do that," Rune said, using more effort to get the plate to the table.

"Oh! Hey, I got that," Uncle Lucas said, jumping up at the sight of the floating plate.

"I'm almost there," Rune objected, but he scooped it out of the air and safely deposited it. Instead of objecting, she pulled out a chair and sat, or seemed to sit, beside him. "Okay, now eat that all up."

"Yes, my lady," he said dryly, his pursed lips directed at the plate clearly conveying his true opinion. Still, he took the fork she held out to him and started picking at the food.

Then the seat dropped out from beneath Rune, landing her on butt. "Oh dammit," she cursed.

A low-ball glass appeared in front of her nose. "Drink this, kid. You'll re-corporealize."

"I need to do it myself, and I can't if I don't practice," Rune said and crawled out of the chair. "What I can't understand is there isn't actually any gravity in the ECAM, so why don't I just float in place?"

"You believe in gravity, which why would you not, it's always been there, so the ECAM is trying to fulfill your belief by creating a semblance of gravity," Uncle Lucas explained.

"Lucky me," Rune grumbled as she stood up. Taking a deep breath, she focused on her feet. "I believe the floor is real without much effort. The chair should be the same?"

Uncle Lucas shrugged. "I don't know what to tell you. The mind likes to play games with itself."

"And look—I can pull it out easily enough," Rune said, doing just that. The chair complied. She stepped over to sit down. "And now just." But in that split second before she gave over her weight to the chair, she felt a shot of panic that she would go right through. So, she went right through.

"Okay, nevermind. I can just stand," Rune said, getting back up and folding her arms.

Uncle Lucas chuckled, bringing his glass up to his mouth. Before he could drink, Rune cupped her hand over it. *That* felt real enough. "Nope, three bites of chicken first."

He narrowed his eyes at her. "You know, if you really were here, I'd have you up over my shoulder and tossed out into the snowbank," he said. But he obeyed just the same, taking three bites of chicken followed by a healthy gulp of his drink.

After a moment, Rune reached into the pouch on her belt that held the recorder crystal, bringing it out to show her uncle.

"Oh, by the way," she started, sliding him a sly look sideways, "I got it."

"You got ... it?" Uncle Lucas arched an eyebrow at her.

Rune held her prize up for him to see, the softly glowing crystal pulsing dully, unaffected by the energies in the ECAM within her protective illusion. He held his hand out for it, but she closed her hand around it.

"It's not really there with you, remember?"

He closed his fingers and grunted. "Alright, then show me."

Holding the crystal gently in a tripod of two fingers and thumb, she blew gently on the crystal to activate it. Wisps of smoke emerged as if the recorder was living coal being blown back into life. "I was in a Kodiak subsidiary today. I managed to access one of their computers to get this."

Out of the smoke, a disc of light burst above the crystal face, then morphed to form the glowing words of the recorded address in the same type as it had appeared on the computer screen. Above the Goldcoast address, a neighborhood in Chicago that had once been posh but now had become the realm of middle management, floated the name of the woman: Jasmeen Clarmont. Rune motioned her fingers through the smoke, and the address faded to show the picture of Jasmeen from the file, smiling that professionally detached smile.

"And you're sure you didn't get caught?" Uncle Lucas stressed, his voice deadly serious with worry.

"As sure as I can be. My magic has been consistent with interfering with recording devices. And I was real slick about it. I had the secretary let me use their computer to write up an on-the-spot report, so it justified my being in the room. These companies treat Corporate Talents like a curiosity that then everyone ignores. I think we rank below the janitorial staff."

"Never piss off the guy who cleans your toilet or makes your food." Uncle Lucas bobbed his eyebrows twice at his truism before taking another swallow of his drink. "Not much has changed in centuries."

"Except magic practitioners used to be respected," Rune declared.

Uncle Lucas shrugged a shoulder. "You'd be surprised."

"As far as I can tell, no one has noticed anything. So, I would say my first foray into corporate spying was a success." She tossed the crystal in the air and caught it with a satisfied snap of her wrist.

But Uncle Lucas continued to frown. "I thought you had friends in your company. I mean, not just St. Benedict, but members of his crew?"

"I... Well... Not really..." Rune half-lied. "When I first arrived there, well, everyone pretty much left me alone. Let me recover. Frankly, I haven't really wanted to make friends. I mean, there's Malachi and Zita, but they are all so busy and on different schedules, and honestly ... I don't *want* to belong there. That's not my... my *place,* and it never will be."

Uncle Lucas nodded as he listened, and Rune hoped her word salad of a statement made sense. She felt the urge to keep explaining, but honestly, she just didn't want to talk about it at all.

"And St. Benedict?" Uncle Lucas said. There was a weight to those words that Rune didn't understand, as if he expected an answer to something, but she had no idea what his question was.

Rune smiled with fake serenity. "St. Benedict is not my friend," she said airily as if she didn't care. She was just stating the facts. "He doesn't care about me. I'm an asset to him and always have been. Someone to be acquired and..." She sighed. "If I'm honest with myself, I knew that. I've known it since the beginning of my relationship with him. And I know the whole time we were partners was a means to an end. He simply

played the game the whole corporate world revolves around and won. It's no different than—" she stopped, not wanting to say his name.

Uncle Lucas's eyes were deeply sympathetic as he clearly knew what and who she was thinking about. It made her angry, and she set her jaw, forcing the words out to prove they had no power over her. "It's no different than what Justin did to me."

"Justin was your husband," Uncle Lucas said.

"Yes, I know that," Rune snapped. Why was he stating the obvious? "I mean, everyone knows that, right? I pick men who are hellbent on using me with charming smiles and clever lies. I'm an idiot. I know."

Uncle Lucas reached out and laid his hand over hers. She stopped, surprised how real it felt to her.

The once-devil-turned-man held her gaze with his own, his eyes gleaming with a hint of that fire that burned inside him. "You are not an idiot," he stressed.

"Yeah, I know," Rune dismissed, but he didn't let go and held her impossibly in place. She looked down at his restraining hand. "How are you doing that? You don't have any magic anymore. You're just a man now."

"Yes, I am a man. As a man, and one who was once a very bad one, you did nothing wrong loving him. It was *his* fault. He was the one who failed to live up to and be worthy of your love."

Rune shifted her shoulders uncomfortably. "I didn't love St. Benedict," she deflected. "Let's just not talk about this anymore."

After a heartbeat, Uncle Lucas let go, and Rune sighed, shifting gears.

"And anyway, it doesn't matter. I *was* screwed. This *was* the best way out, and it *was* only a matter of time before they came for me. I'm very aware of how close I came to ending up back into Kodiak's prison system. So, you know, I got lucky." Now if only she could get herself to feel that it was true.

Rune met Uncle Lucas's unwavering, comfortable gaze. "Okay?"

"Yeah, okay." He cleared his throat. "So what's the next move?"

Rune sighed and regarded Jasmeen's image. "Well, if I couldn't save myself, I can try to save her. Honestly, I'm probably in a better position now to do something to help her. So, the next step is you telling me how to escape."

"Right now?" Uncle Lucas asked in surprise.

"Yes, I have the next three days off. If I'm going to do this, it is now or never," Rune said confidently.

"Well, alright then." He held his hand out to her.

She regarded it with a wrinkled nose. "Uh..."

"Take my hand, kid," he urged.

Focusing with all her might, she did. Then he shook it. As in really shook it. "You don't need to try that hard. Just relax and..."

There was a strange pop sound and feeling. While the room had colors before, they were brighter and sharper. Everything around her seemed more real.

Uncle Lucas let go of her hand, and this time put the second lowball glass into her hands. "Now drink up."

The glass felt cold and a bit slick from the condensation. She stared at it, realizing that it was real. "What... What happened?" she asked.

"I pulled you through with our retainer bond," Uncle Lucas said, this time willingly eating a bite of chicken. "You've done it before."

"Yeah, but that took me doing a formal 'retainer I summon you,' and using my own magic and... and there had to be at least three of you..." She looked around herself at the carpet, the chair, her feet on the ground. Then she got brave and bounced in her chair.

Nope. No going through that. She really was there in the real world, not just as a projection.

Another thought occurred to her. "You mean I could have crossed over out of the ECAM at any time?" she demanded.

"Yeah," Uncle Lucas said. "As long as it was me."

"Why you? And why didn't you tell me?"

"That I could break you out of prison at any time, even though doing so would be committing another crime, this time by both of us, which would only bring you more trouble?" He lifted his hat and scratched at his hairline. "As for why me... I may be a simple human now, but I am also a being that is in two places at once. You can call it my own special and incredibly specific 'Talent.'"

Rune furrowed her eyebrows. "Then ... why are you doing it now?"

"My mistress asked me to," he said simply. "And now I believe you need a ride, right?"

She nibbled her lower lip. "No, but can I borrow your phone to call a taxi?"

CHAPTER 7

Rune took a deep breath as she stood outside Jasmeen Clarmont's apartment door. At least, she hoped this was the right door. There could have been a chance the information was out of date, or Rune got it wrong. She couldn't know for sure with a number instead of a name on the front. Up and down the halls of the corporate apartment building, most other tenants had taken more ownership of their doors. Rune had passed several decorated with family name signs and various recognized spring holidays, mostly Easter, but a few others as well. The lack of homey touches on this taupe-colored door made Rune unsure as she screwed up her courage to knock.

For a long, tense moment, there were no other sounds in the hallway. Then the small light of the digital peephole came on. "Wh-who is it?" came the timid voice of a woman filtered through the speaker.

"Ms. Clarmont? My name is Rune Leveau. I'd like to talk to you," Rune said to the light.

"I-I-I don't know who you are. Just leave me alone," the

obviously frightened woman called through the door. The light went off.

"I can't do that, Ms. Clarmont," Rune said, doing the old-fashioned tactic of calling through the door. "Please. Let me in. I'm here to help you."

The peephole light flipped back on again.

"Please go away. I have neighbors," Jasmeen said. "I'll call the police."

Rune knew it was a bluff. She had been through this sort of situation before when she had apprenticed with Maddie. But it didn't matter. Rune didn't have the skills or desire to force her way through the door. She continued to stare-down the light, fiercely thinking. As long as she had the light, Jasmeen listened. The fact that Rune stood there for so long saying nothing and the light was still on told Rune the woman did very much need help. She was just waiting for Rune to say the right thing to give herself permission to open the door.

"You can always find help at the Lucky Devil," Rune said with the strongest conviction she had ever felt in her life. She needed to help as much as Jasmeen needed it.

Another long tense moment, then there was a low mechanical grind, followed by a click, and the door popped open.

The woman standing at the door was a mere shadow of the picture Rune had seen earlier, and it took all her practice in such situations to keep her face from reacting. Standing before her was a testament of depression. The Terrycloth bathrobe belted around the woman's body had food stains on it. Her hair was tied up in an oversized, multi-colored kerchief, making the top of her head look like a Mardi Gras beehive. The circles under her eyes were deep impressions around each eye, and her skin had a sallow yellow tinge to it. There was also a smell.

As she stood there, Jasmeen clutched the top of her robe at her throat, like it was a magical cloak that would protect her from harm, appraising her intruder with a long eye.

Rune waited patiently for the woman to speak first, to

judge whether to actually invite her in or not. She then leaned out to look up and down the hallway, but no neighbor peeked out.

"You'd better come in," Jasmeen said, stepping back to open the door the rest of the way.

"Thank you." Rune nodded in acknowledgment, relieved.

After shutting her door and waiting for the automatic lock to flip, Jasmeen adjusted her bathrobe belt, then fiddled with a fine gold bracelet clasped over her wrist.

"Do you drink coffee?" she asked, turning into the kitchen of her company apartment, an aisle design with faux-granite countertops.

"Uh, sure," Rune lied.

Jasmeen poured her a cup from a stained carafe, and Rune had to resist the urge to offer to do her dishes for her. She was handed her cup before her host filled up one for herself, grabbed the sugar bowl, then exited the kitchen to go sit at the dining room table.

"My cleaning service hasn't been in in a while," her host muttered as she slid some old dishes among the papers that took up the other side of the table. Rune could believe it but only smiled politely.

"My table doesn't look much better. Don't worry about it," Rune said, unbuttoning her coat before sitting. She set her cold hands around the coffee cup, which was still warm enough for the task. Taking a deep breath, she steeled herself. Here it was, the moment she'd rehearsed constantly for the last couple of months. "I'm really sorry, first off."

Jasmeen paused as she dropped too much sugar into her own cup. "Sorry for what?"

"For not being at the bar when you came looking for help," Rune confessed.

The other woman's darker fingers tightened around her pink coffee cup, her gaze staring into the foamy depths as if she could see all the mistakes of her life laid out. "It was my last shot. When ... my friend from work ... gave me the coin

and told me what to do... that I would find someone to help me there... it seemed... I guess it was too good to be true."

"It shouldn't have been. You should have found me there, and instead ... you met one of my associates, who in his own twisted way, thought he was doing me a favor."

"Is that what you do: trick people desperate enough to come to you? 'Deal with the devil,'" Jasmeen snorted. "I suppose it makes sense. The whole devil theme is a big clue. It was a very clever trap."

That stung Rune's heart. "It was never meant to be."

"And now my company has found out that I tried to break my contract and run. That's what *I* get for making a deal with the devil." Jasmeen didn't seem like she was really talking to Rune anymore. Her gaze went far away as she mechanically sipped her coffee.

She was a woman who had already given up. Rune recognized the look, and the fact that her own face had moved beyond that expression meant that Jasmeen could recover too.

Rune sat up a little more in her chair, physically and mentally shifting. "Have they fired you?" she asked.

Jasmeen sighed, letting her walls down as if it took too much energy to pull them back up. "Technically, no. They can't exactly fire me for looking for another job, and I can't exactly leave without a different one, but I've also been blacklisted, so I'm not likely to get another offer, and they can make my life a living hell for as long as they want." Jasmeen untied her hair and ran her fingers through the bundled up braids in their enormous bun. "I would give anything for a way out of this situation. Work has been... it's been terrible. No one will talk to me unless it's business related. I can't access my cafeteria anymore, and my grocery per diem has been cut back. I can't even buy a chocolate cake to drown my sorrows." She gestured to her television set. "That's been offline since it happened, and the repair person said it would be three days to come fix it, and that was five days ago. I expect they'd cut my utilities if they didn't need me to have access to the internet and still show up for work."

"They control your utilities too?" Rune asked, cocking an eyebrow.

Jasmeen shot her a harsh look. "Where have you been? Of course. The company bequeaths you everything you have as part of your compensation. I just didn't realize they could take it away from you too. Technically, they aren't supposed to, but I guess technically doesn't mean a whole lot."

Rune looked around, nodding as she recognized the modus operandi. "Like I said, I'm really sorry about this," she repeated, wishing she could come up with something else to say.

"So what you going to do about it then, if you're so sorry?" Jasmeen snapped, slapping the cup down hard enough to splash a little coffee onto the table. Her host didn't notice or even move to clean it up, glaring instead at Rune.

The Finder couldn't meet the glare but grabbed a couple of napkins from a half-buried basket of them and began patting up the spilled coffee.

"I... I don't know yet," she admitted.

Understandably, that did not impress her mishandled client. "Well, that's just great. So you... what? You came over here to assuage your guilt?"

This was the most fire Rune had seen from the woman yet; unfortunately, it was directed at her. She set the browned-up napkins to the side and folded her hands in front of her to hide the shaking. "No, I came to find out why you turned down my friend's deal if it is your only option."

Now it was Jasmeen's hands shaking really hard, and she went back to the quieter, more beaten slump. "Because if I hate how they're treating me now, I don't want to find out what my company will do to me if they knew what your *friend* wanted me to do. Now I'm all out of options. So what do you think you can do to help me?"

In that moment, Rune realized the major flaw in her plan. Everything she had plotted had been to get to that point: to be able to talk to Jasmeen and see what she could do to help.

It had stopped short of what she would be *able* to do next.

"What do you want to see happen? Ideally?" Rune asked, using one of Maddie's go-to questions. There was often a big difference between what people said they wanted and what they really wanted. Jasmeen was no exception.

"I want out! I want to get out from underneath Gary's thumb," Jasmeen screeched. "I *did* what you're supposed to do. I *went* to HR. *They* didn't care."

Rune reached into one of the pouches of her belt, pulling out the slip of paper Jasmeen had sent her months ago, careful of the well-worn edges. She held it out to Jasmeen.

"Can you tell me about the deal St. Benedict tried to make with you?" Rune prompted.

Jasmeen glanced over her note, then immediately crumpled it into a tiny ball, to Rune's personal horror. "Look, lady, I don't know you. I don't know anything about you. What are you, some sort of mage or something?"

Rune wrinkled her nose. Mage? That was a new one. She had heard the term before, but most people called her a wizard, or wizardress, sometimes witch. There were countless other styles for Talents, depending on the culture, history, and/or education, but none of them really felt like they fit Rune. "Yeah, something like that. I Find stuff," she said as if that made any sense.

Jasmeen wrinkled her nose. "You *Find* stuff? You're the Finding Mage? What, like lost keys or something?"

Rune chuckled. "Yeah, too often, but I can do other magic as well. It's the one I'm best with."

Her client chuckled along with her. "So, what... You're going to *Find* me a way out of my predicament?"

That made Rune laugh harder. "That is the idea, if you'll let me."

"Why?"

Rune blinked, the laughter dying in her throat, wondering if she'd missed a joke or something. "Why?"

There was no mirth left in Jasmeen's face, as if that burst

had been the last of it. "Yes, that is the question. Why do you want to help me? And don't tell me it's out of some sort of exaggerated sense of guilt because I'm not buying that. I've been in business too long to believe bullshit like that."

"Except that really is the reason," Rune argued.

Just then, a knock came from the front door.

Jasmeen froze, staring wide-eyed at the too thin metal door, clutching the front of her bathrobe again.

Rune stood up, all her senses on alert as well. "You want me to answer it?" she asked softly.

Her client shook her head, panting hard, eyes wide with fear. "They know! They must know. They got this place bugged, I'm sure. They know I'm talking to you. I'm stupid. I was so stupid!" she whispered, working herself up to hyperventilating.

The person at the door knocked a couple more times.

Rune grasped Jasmeen's shoulders and squeezed firmly. Instantly, the other woman, barely a few years older than Rune herself, snapped her attention from the door to her.

Rune gave her what she hoped was a reassuring smile. "It's alright. It's going to be alright. I'm just going to answer the door."

"No! Don't!" Jasmeen hissed, bursting forward to seize Rune's sleeve, then her arm, pulling her up short.

Rune nodded, taking a step back to let off the tension on her poor coat. "Okay, okay," she said with light ease. "But we should still take a peek. You have a peephole, right? Maybe it's just the repair guy?"

Jasmeen gave a tiny moan of fear. It was going to take a little more than that.

The Finder touched the back of the frightened woman's hands, still clinging to her sleeve. Reaching within herself, she Found the source of warmth in her core and thought of peace. Her warming trick raised the temperature of her hand and passed gently into Jasmeen. It wasn't enough to really be an empath spell, but Jasmeen's shoulders lowered a fraction. She took a deep breath, reasserting her professional mask, the one in her ID picture. "Okay, okay."

Her client pushed herself to her feet and bravely went to her front door.

"I'm right behind you. Don't worry. I can protect you," Rune assured. While they crossed the short distance, Rune wished her second sight allowed her to see through walls.

The person on the other side of the door continued to knock with the air of someone who could do this all day. Jasmeen stopped just inside her kitchen, stretching out a finger to lightly press the view button on her peephole. Immediately, the digital projector displayed the image.

"Oh crap," Rune cursed under her breath.

"That's him!" Jasmeen hissed. "That's the man who's trying to force me to..." She let the statement trail off.

Rune moved past Jasmeen to open the door, only to find that it didn't yield.

"No, don't!" Jasmeen hissed.

At least Rune's Talent was good for Finding the button to unlock the door. It buzzed and snapped open. She yanked the door open and leaned an arm against the doorjamb.

"What?" she barked irritably at the grinning man on the other side.

"Whatcha doing here, Rune?" St. Benedict asked, cocking his head to the side, smiling with an intimidatingly manic smile.

"I'm here to help *my* client. Whatcha you doing here, St. Ben?" she shot back, not in the least bit intimidated.

"I'm just looking to keep my errant charge out of trouble. You wanna get your ass out here?"

"I like my ass where it is. Thanks for checking." She promptly shut the door in his face. Automatically, the lock locked.

"What are you doing?" Jasmeen hissed.

The Finder crossed her arms. "He'll have it open in a minute. Listen, do you have a business card or something you can pass me? Quickly," she whispered urgently at Jasmeen.

"What?" Her client blinked uncomprehendingly. As predicted, they heard the sound of the lock winding, like it was trying to figure out how to open and had temporarily forgotten.

"Crap, that's fast. Pass me something of yours, anything, hurry! A thing you are personally, deeply connected to! Now!" Rune demanded, opening her hand.

Without thinking, Jasmeen yanked off her bracelet and dropped it into Rune's waiting hand. "This was my grandmother's," she said.

"Perfect," Rune said and immediately stuffed it into a back pouch on her belt. "I will give it back to you when I see you again. I promise."

Just as she got it tucked away, the door swung open, the Saint letting himself in. Rune caught a glance of the hologram hovering over his palm before he collapsed it back into his palm with a closed fist.

He glanced between the two women before offering a more polite smile to Jasmeen. Gentleman-like, he doffed his fedora, holding it against his chest as he bowed slightly at the waist. Rune wondered that he didn't add the heel click for added villainy.

"I'm extremely sorry for our intrusion on your privacy, Ms. Clarmont. We're going to get out of your hair. Now," he said, directing the last with a tone of warning at Rune.

"I don't answer to you, St. Benedict, and Ms. Clarmont is *my* client. So, I think you are the one who needs to leave."

St. Benedict's eyes flared at her defiance.

"I... I'm not your client," Jasmeen said, confused and alarmed, her eyes darting to St. Benedict. "I'm not with her, I swear. I didn't..." She covered her wrist guiltily where the bracelet used to hang and glared at Rune, who didn't respond or move to hand the bracelet back. She was pretty sure the woman wouldn't take it now if it incriminated her in the Saint's eyes. The fact that she was so afraid of him infuriated Rune.

What else had he done or said to her that she didn't know about?

"It was really nice to speak to you, Ms. Clarmont. We'll talk again," Rune assured, infusing as much encouragement

as she could in her voice. But it was clear that she had already lost her. Which was emphasized as St. Benedict set a hand on Rune's shoulder.

At the sight of the gesture, Jasmeen's large eyes went even wider. "You're with him?" she stated, shocked.

Rune tried to yank her shoulder from his hand, but the damage was already done.

St. Benedict instead took a step in toward Jasmeen, his height over her enough to intimidate the already frightened woman. "Ms. Leveau has currently entered our employ over at Corinthe Corporation. She is our newest corporate Talent. *Did* you engage her services? I understand she can read your fortune, chase away pesky sentient magic vermin, or even clear your aura." His voice dripped with sarcasm. Rune's palm itched to smash across his face.

The betrayed woman looked to Rune. "You tricked me!" she spat, the same ire Rune had for St. Benedict directed from Jasmeen to her.

"Jasmeen, I swear to you—" But it didn't matter what Rune swore. Her word meant very little now.

"Change your mind about working for us?" St. Benedict cut in, taking another step in. He didn't do anything else; in fact, he even had his hands in his pockets, but the menace was so clear that even Rune could feel it. "Believe me, our offer is far more generous than what you are currently receiving," he passed a gaze over the disheveled apartment, "or not receiving."

"Thank you," Jasmeen said coldly, her fear shifting into a spine of iron, even if tears budded from her eyes. "I want you to leave my home. Now."

Recognizing her defeat, Rune nodded and turned to leave, St. Benedict right on her heels.

CHAPTER 8

"So, I guess you think you're very clever?" St. Benedict asked, once the elevator doors closed on Jasmeen's hallway.

"Yes," Rune answered simply. She didn't look at him as she said it, making it difficult for him to read her expression.

He wanted to shake her. He wanted to seize her shoulders and ... hug her against him and keep her safe and tell her ... not to put herself in danger, to just stay safe... He wanted to beg her forgiveness... He wanted her...

He shoved the images of everything he wanted back in the box in his mind, forcing himself to flip back to where he belonged.

In control.

He glanced over at the interface display in his vision. The interference field he generated was still operational, keeping their appearances on recorded devices blurry and anything they said a mess of words, but they needed to get out of the building stat. If they hadn't been on the fifteenth floor, he

would have made them use the stairs. Maybe they should have anyway.

"Are you working for someone?" he demanded.

Rune was completely oblivious to the danger they were in.

"Yes, I'm working for Corinthe Corp. Just like you," she answered, again with that simple detached tone. He knew she was putting it on, and it was damn childish. Though having her ranting and raging at him for interfering in whatever she was doing would have been worse at that moment.

"No, I mean..." He took a step in, trying to not feel like a spy thriller cliché. "Are you working for somebody else?" he hissed quietly.

"Like who?" she hissed back, mockingly imitating him exactly.

"Like the Magic Guild or..." He actually had no idea who else, but anybody could have seen her as a weak link and gotten to her. Promised her freedom or protection or... He had no idea what else Rune could want enough to risk her well-being over, but that unknown scared him.

"I have not been in contact with anybody at the Magic Guild," she said tartly. "I'm here for my own reasons."

The elevator doors opened with a friendly bing. Rune exited, letting St. Benedict trail behind her. Outside, late winter/early spring ice-rain streaked the tall windows. Gray light coated the Goldcoast street in a depressing mush of weather. While Ms. Clarmont's apartment was situated in one of the nicer Chicago neighborhoods, St. Benedict still didn't envy her situation one bit. She'd be losing this place soon if she didn't make up her mind to take his offer.

Especially now with Rune's interference, his pressure campaign against Ms. Clarmont was in serious jeopardy.

"You have no business being here," he said.

"I have been assured by our mutual boss that I have independent autonomy from you *Saints*. I'm free to decide where I come and go. Right now, this is my day off. I'm not 'running away' or trying to 'escape.' I'm not trying to jump ship," she said in relaxed conversational tones, flipping up the hood on her coat when they approached the glass exit doors.

"How did you get here?" he asked as the rainstorm kicked it up a notch and thundered dramatically.

She leaned against the glass to look up at the sky as if by that she could judge what it intended. "I used my new company OmniSin to order a cab, which is how I assume you found me since that card is traceable, right? So, why are you asking me stupid questions?" She glanced up and down the streets, but there were no other cabs waiting or even driving by at that moment.

She was right; that was how he had tracked her. He had been relieved when her Omnisin had pinged the network. He removed the transaction, not that anyone would have seen it, but he took no chances. He needed to cover her trail.

When he didn't answer right away, she eyed him. "Am I wrong?"

"Wrong?" he asked, his mind having already moved on to the next series of problems he'd have to solve to get her back into the building without tripping any of the other security features.

She scoffed with disgust. "You found me with the OmniSin. That was my mistake, right?"

He growled in his throat. "Do you understand the awful risk you took? What if St. Rachel had discovered you first?"

She shrugged. "Whatever. It's fine. I need to talk to you anyway. Where's your car?"

"I parked it in the building garage. This way." He jerked a thumb toward the door leading to the underground parking lot.

"Perfect," she said as if they had just agreed on something and headed toward the labeled door.

Again, he followed. What was going on? He should have been the one dragging her out of there, but instead, he was following her lead. The thought of shoving her in the trunk to teach her lesson passed through his mind, but he dismissed it. It was actually dangerous to transport people in trunks,

so it would have defeated his entire purpose in coming to rescue her.

She spotted his car right away, and they walked toward it side-by-side, like they used to.

He continued his scan of the space. The place was half empty; it was the middle of the day in the middle of the week after all. But his display highlighted quite a few potential spots for ambushes to hide if they were so inclined.

The car beeped in welcome as it sensed his approach, unlocking the doors on both sides in attentive response. Without being told, Rune went to the passenger door and climbed in, bringing her hood down while she did so. The car ignited itself and the pre-set seat warmers engaged as indicated by the LED lights blinking up and down the edges of the seat themselves.

He felt considerably better once the doors were shut, the bullet-proof glass and re-enforced doors guaranteeing that their mutual foes couldn't take them both out now by conventionally bullet-driven means.

He opened his rogue hacking program and pulled out all the cameras he had been dealing with in the building and the garage. The program had intuitively fixed the cameras as he had walked through the building, looping most of the surveillance to show empty hallways and unopened doors. Now that he was in the car, he interacted to pull the program to the forefront and skimmed through all the "corrections" it had made to be sure they hadn't missed one.

Then he checked his secondary scrub program. Using his quick fingers, he replaced all of the bits of footage of Rune's arrival with scenes of nobody and nothing. It wasn't perfect. Anyone knowing what they were looking for, namely a Saint like him, would be able to see the "bent corners," but these cameras purged every seventy-two hours. He was tempted to shorten the purge time, but that change could be noticed. Better to let the system run its natural course.

Rune didn't say anything as she watched his ballet of light

work. As a final measure, Benedict reset his link to his car, which had connected automatically, but he wanted a clean connection and switched IPs just for extra, extra precaution.

"Is it safe to talk now?" she asked.

"We have no reason to believe that Kodiak's subsidiary is keeping a particular eye on this little errant corporate employee. But I fully expect..." He let that thought die on his lips.

Rune cocked her head to the side. "I can't even guess at what you were about to say, so if you could just fill it in for me, I would appreciate it."

"It's not safe to tempt Fate," he finally said.

Rune nodded. "I knew there was a risk in coming here. I banked on my magical interference to help me out."

St. Benedict shook his head. "Not with these cameras. They've got plenty of buffer."

She leaned back in her seat, thinking. "I should have borrowed one of those interference things from Malachi or something," she said as if that had been her biggest mistake in all this. "Good to know."

Instead of saying anything more, he roughly shifted the car into gear and pulled jerkily out of the parking spot to head for the exit. As he pulled out into the street, the rain decided it really did want to be water instead of ice and pounded down on the roof of the car, thick as a car wash. Lightning flashed and thunder rumbled.

"Lovely," Rune mumbled.

St. Benedict turned onto the street. In his vision, his augmentation projected a "threat" overlay as he scanned the street. Figures walking on the street appeared as outlines in green. Cameras spawned circles with data lists in entirely too small to read type, but if he focused, the list would open larger for clearer reading. He ignored all of them now, focusing instead on the car in front of him, which decided at that moment to hit the brakes.

"Oh come on!" he shouted uselessly at the car, slamming on the horn then immediately regretting it. "Stupid, stupid,

stupid," he muttered under his breath.

"I thought we didn't want to attract attention?" Rune asked in that same damnable neutral tone that made it so difficult to figure out if she was making fun of him or not. When had she learned that? He glared murder at her, and she didn't blink or look away.

"What I need is for you to tell me what you are doing here," he stated.

"That's fine. I'll tell you. Because I need your help," Rune said flippantly, using his own tricks to take control of the conversation from him.

It was infuriating.

She settled back in her seat, then waved a hand forward. "The cars are moving."

St. Benedict stuttered and focused on driving again.

Once they were in motion, Rune cleared her throat. "Jasmeen told me about what you want her to do in order to get your help with her situation," she said, breaking the tension between them.

"What did she tell you?"

"That you want her to do something dangerous. Something that she's afraid of doing and only then will you help her move to another job and a new life," she said.

"That is correct," St. Benedict answered. He could feel tension press against his chest, threatening to cut to his heart. "Did she tell you what exactly?"

"Isn't that cruel?" Rune asked instead of answering.

He sighed. "It's what I need to do to be able to grant her the resources. Rune... Our resistance... the Praetorium... It doesn't run on charity. It can't. What we're trying to do there, it's important, but half the time we're working on an elaborate web of shoestrings."

"So, how much do you need to help her?"

"It's not about the money. It's about information, okay? Information is the only real currency, and right now what we need from Ms. Clarmont, nobody else can get us."

"Because of her position within Kodiak?"

"Yes." He nodded. "If our need for what she can get us wasn't so high..." But it didn't matter. It was, and Maxamillion had been adamant. "There's a risk in moving her too, for us. Taking an employee away from a company like that? There's a chance it could come back to us, or it could expose the Praetorium, or even Corinthe itself for interfering. That risk has to be worth it."

They navigated through the slush-clogged streets into downtown Chicago, moving down Michigan Avenue, past the Art Institute and Millennium Park, before turning toward I-290 headed west. Most people on the streets were rushing through the rain to wherever shelter was for them. Tourists were thin on the ground. The cars around him were driving like all Chicagoans, as if the rain wasn't happening, hydroplaning be damned, which created a strange bumper car-like atmosphere on the streets.

"Couldn't ... *I* find that information for you? It's literally what I do," Rune asked, slowly parsing her question out.

"Of course not," he dismissed, stopping for the hundredth red light. Dammit, he wished they were already back at the Praetorium.

Abruptly, Rune sat up a little more in her seat. "Did you feel that?" she asked.

"Feel what?" he asked, checking the car's perimeter again. In his vision, he thought he saw a flash coming from the rear of the car, but when he replayed the last three seconds from his recorded brain, the little video playing on the corner of his ocular display, he saw nothing in the pouring rain. He couldn't tell if it had been a digital noise or an actual reflection off a car or a magical something.

"What did you feel?" he repeated.

"Not sure. I just had a feeling. It's gone now," Rune said, leaning back in her warmed seat, snuggling against the back.

"If it happens again, let me know," he said. If he had been on edge before, now he was doubly so.

"Anyway, what's 'of course not' about it? You want information, right? I can get that."

"How?" he demanded just as he passed through the last set of lights before getting onto the entrance of I-290 that crossed up and over I-90, the interstate that went North/South from the Loop. He had to check himself from taking the exit onto I-90, which would have led him to Rune's old place and her old life.

That habit was gone for both of them now. His fault, he knew, but the pang hit all the same.

Rune didn't seem to notice the entrance or his almost taking it. "We use the same trick I used to get Jasmeen's address." Rune said, thinking out loud. "We plant a magical source, a magic 'cherry bomb' or something. It messes the computers up. I come in to clean it up. While in, I get access to a computer to 'write up my report,' you give me some do-hickey to hack their system, and we get the info you need. Wham bam!"

Before he could consider the merits of her plan, the car went haywire.

Rune wasn't sure what happened, but all the lights on the car's console went on at once, including the radio, blasting whatever station it was on at full volume. The Saint jerked the wheel in response before righting back into their correct lane, getting an annoyed horn whizzing by them on the left. Frantically, Rune managed to get the volume down by pressing the manual button.

"What the hell?" she cried once she could hear herself again.

"Yeah, that was odd," St. Benedict commented.

"Is the car alright?"

He began gesturing in the air in front of himself. "I'm running a diagnostic. Just hold on."

"Shouldn't we pull over?" Rune cried in alarm.

"No need. The car's fine. I've got this under control," he

dismissed.

"Will you just ... put it in auto-drive or something if you're going to do that!"

He huffed, but then the car did a musical beep sequence, and a disembodied female voice said, "Initiating auto-drive mode: highway."

Rune sat back, that feeling she had been wrestling with since they got into St. Benedict's car persisting. Using her peripheral, she watched the stick between them shift itself from third gear to fourth as the car sped up to match the speed of those around them. He possessed one of the most high-tech, sophisticated AI cars the current world could offer yet had insisted on a stick shift. Still, that wasn't what was bothering her.

Taking a deep breath, Rune closed her eyes, then released the breath slowly. To St. Benedict, it would look like she was resting her eyes, but instead, she opened her secondary sight. No longer needing her actual eyes to be open to "See," Rune scanned the world around her. Everything in the vicinity of the car was a burst of a thousand beams moving forward and backward through time.

Normally, it was utter chaos, but Rune took another breath in and dismissed the future and the past from her perception. Highways were notorious places for movement, and it was difficult enough to see the present. Not only was there the cacophony of moving cars carrying individual, tiny worlds inside them, there was the rain pounding on the pavement and metal. It still created a barely discernible mess of motion and sound.

So she narrowed her focus to this car and its occupants. At last, it became easier to See. The car in the present was still a mass of energy moving through space, its little world sparking along as it passed and was passed by other vehicles on the road going in both directions. All worlds sparked when they touched, full of potential energy. In those places where sparks lived, spontaneous magic could most easily occur, if one was careful when messing with them.

Rune certainly wasn't interested in drawing on the torrent of possible power; she simply wanted to See. She watched, feeling the car around her moving. She realized that their car sparked far more than the rest of the other cars.

"You okay?" St. Benedict asked, his voice coming through as an echo of itself. Whispers of his thoughts danced around the words, *What's wrong? Are you hurt? Don't hate me. Am I annoying you? Can I make you feel better?*

Rune inhaled deeply and huffed, pushing the extra noise away. "I'm fine."

The sparks were becoming more persistent. There were dozens of them, all centered around a tiny ball of nothing. Or rather something that had coated itself in the intention of not being seen.

I want to Find what is in that blank space, Rune said to herself.

Following her bidding, the magic snaked out of her as a golden thread, weaving about as it attempted to obey her. Realizing the directive was simply not strong or specific enough, Rune shifted her heart hand to touch the whorls of her belt. Instantly, the connection strengthened. It straightened into a cord that Rune could physically touch, even though everyone around her would not see or feel it unless the magic was directed at them.

Her cord of magic connected to the closest nothing ball surrounded by sparks, and there was a chirpy feedback. Rune seized her cord with her right hand and snapped it. There was another mechanical shriek, and she pulled, yanking it toward her.

"Oh crap," she muttered as she opened her actual eyes, adding the real world overlay to her magical one.

"What's wrong?" St. Benedict asked, glancing sideways at her.

Rune tugged a few more times on her magic, maintaining her connection, but the thing on the other side was physical and couldn't simply pass through the also physical door.

"Rune, *are* you okay?" St. Benedict insisted, stressing each word.

"Yeah, okay," Rune said absentmindedly as she pulled up on the cord. The object she caught slid up with it. "St. Ben, can you roll this window down for me? I'm out of hands."

"Uh, sure," he answered and hit the button on his door. Immediately, rain splashed Rune's face as the glass lowered. Tugging her magic cord like a fishing line, she pulled in the object out of the wet. As soon as she cleared it, the window went back up.

"What the hell is this?" Rune exclaimed as she stared at the struggling metallic spider-thing her line had caught.

To Rune, it looked like it was fighting the line, but to anyone else, it would look like she was making the thing float in mid-air. Its little leg-pincer-things kept thrashing and passing uselessly through her magic. She wiggled her cord to make it spin so she could get a better look at it.

It was approximately the size of her hand if the body was her palm and the legs her fingers. Other than that, it was made entirely of some chrome-like metal with small multi-colored lights all over its body. The lights fired and darkened in a myriad of sequences that if it had been a living thing would have telegraphed to Rune as panic. It also made a digital-edged screeching sound that pulsed in a discordant rhythm.

"Where did that come from?!" St. Benedict cried, taking back control of the car from auto drive. The sudden transition forced them to skid into a stuttering hydroplane before St. Benedict corrected, and the special tires shifted to grip the road in some technological miracle Rune did not understand.

"This is what I was sensing," Rune declared, holding her prize catch out for him to see clearer.

"Don't bring that closer to me!" he said, shouldering at it as if it gave him the heebie-jeebies. "It's an Infiltrator!"

"That sounds bad," Rune stated, now holding the thing out farther from both of them.

"Yes, it does, doesn't it?" St. Benedict waved his hand over the dashboard. While Rune had been seeing the world through her magicked eyes, she hadn't noticed that St. Benedict had fixed whatever had been wrong with his dash. Now, he re-ignited it with various pink, green, and blue lights, all following controlled sequences and patterns over the surface of a digital representation of the car.

"Where did you buy this car? Raves-R-Us?" Rune commented on the light show, mostly to distract herself into staying calm as the spider-tech thing had given up on the magic line and was trying to make swipes at her face with its little metallic arms.

"Just don't let it touch anything," St. Benedict said, then verbally commanded his digital interface, "Run status check!"

The light show became more focused now, moving back and forth over the representation of the car. Smaller red lights popped up everywhere.

"Oh no," St. Benedict cryptically said. He let go of the wheel. A split keyboard appeared under his fingers, and he started typing furiously.

"What are you doing?" Rune cried. "You're driving!"

Suddenly, they swerved around the car ahead of them, sliding up on the shoulder and then proceeded to cross three lanes of traffic.

"Not anymore!" St. Benedict shouted, abandoning his keyboard to try to grab the wheel back and force it to respond to him.

It did not. Instead, it was more like a toy car where he would turn the wheel one direction, but the car had decided to go the opposite.

"Auto-drive ini—Auto drive initia— Auto drive, auto drive, auto dri-dri-dri-dri..." the disembodied voice repeated.

St. Benedict gave up and plunged both hands into his hologram, his fingers glowing bright as he interacted with the car's computer interface directly. "The speed control has been co-opted! And for extra fun, the brakes are *not* working!"

He paused a half beat. "Good news is the collision avoidance system is still working!"

"Yeah!" Rune said with dry sarcasm.

They skidded around a curve. Rune had to let go of her connection to her belt to grab the "oh-shit" bar to keep from slamming sideways. Immediately, her magical cord weakened. Sensing its chance, the infiltrator spider began wiggling even more frantically, whipping around on what was left of the cord and coming too close to Rune. "Okay! Okay, dying was not on my agenda today!"

"Don't let it touch you!"

"And I have had enough of you," Rune decided, grabbing one of the thing's metal legs. Using unfocused magical energy, she zapped the machine. It sparked a tiny death cry then went limp.

"No!" St. Benedict cried. "We needed to analyze that!"

"You still can. It's still here," Rune said, holding it out to him.

"You burnt out the circuit board!"

"You said don't let it touch me! It's one or the other." Just then the car bucked and shuddered alarmingly.

"Infiltrators work in groups, and they are going to get us killed." The hologram of the car between them began to shudder and blink until it went out completely. "And now I can't detect them!"

Actual sparks flew as something under the car broke away and skipped backward down the highway. The car following swerved to avoid the shrapnel, then laid on the horn as if that would help the situation for anyone.

"Okay, then what do you want me to do?" Rune asked, dropping the bot thing she'd fried into the backseat.

"Nothing! You can do nothing. It's a tech thing. Just sit there," St. Benedict said while he tapped rapidly at the digital keyboard that was also blinking in and out of existence.

That's when a tire blew.

The car went sideways and scraped along the cement barrier on Rune's side.

Rune screamed.

"Emergency tire pressure!" St. Benedict shouted, and the car pulled away from the barrier, levering itself back up into position.

There was an inflation sound, and the disembodied voice said, "Tire emergency patch engaged for temporary use only. Slow car to 30 miles per hour and see next available maintenance garage immediately."

The car automatically began to slow, and the back corner was noticeably lower than the rest of the car.

"Okay, more good news," St. Benedict said, flashing Rune a smile from where he leaned against his driver's side door. "The voice command is still working."

"Great," Rune growled. "Make the car stop!"

"Car: emergency stop!" he shouted.

"It is not safe to stop in the current lane. Attempting to pull over to the nearest shoulder or exit in order to safely come to a stop. Please secure your seatbelts."

"They are secure!" Rune argued.

Then the car sped up again, passing another honking car too closely.

"Okay, you want the bad news or the worse news?" St. Benedict asked.

"Shut up! I am not going to die in a bad dad-joke, comedy routine," Rune shouted as she sat up to scan. "Why are we not pulling over to the side?"

"The voice command just lost control of the speed gauge. Which means I might have to try a direct interface?" he said, unsure as if he expected her to be able to concur on that idea.

"St. Benedict! Just do something!"

Real sparks burst from behind as something fell from the roof of the car to land and bounce on the pavement behind them. A groove appeared in the car ceiling.

"I'm trying! They're tearing the car apart!" he shouted. He hit the button on the door to roll the window down, tearing his fedora off to toss into the backseat. He unbuckled and leaned out to look over the car roof. Rain spat across the space straight into Rune's face.

He ducked back in and pulled on the storage compartment between the seats where he usually kept his weaponry. "I'm going to have to shoot blind. I can't detect them!"

"*I* can detect them!" Rune shouted at him.

"What?" he called over the roaring highway wind. Another gouge appeared in the ceiling as he yanked out his gun.

"I can see them in my secondary sight! How do you think I saw that one?" She stabbed her finger at the spider corpse in the backseat.

He wiped a hand over his face and through his damp hair. "Why didn't you say so!?"

"Oh my gods! I hate you!" Rune unbuckled and turned around in her seat, then pointed throughout the car and the roof. "There. There. There. There and there! Also two underneath."

Two of the spark bundles were crawling from the damaged tire to the other side across the top of the car.

"They're going for the other rear tire." Rune pointed. She heard a kerchunk sound to her left and turned in time to see St. Benedict pull up his no-messing-around handgun, the control bracelet blinking red around his wrist. He took a deep breath, then ducked his fedora-less head out of the window.

"What the hell!!?" Rune squealed just as a semi-truck hit its horn hard as it passed on his side. "St. Benedict!!"

She dove for his legs, trying to haul him in.

"Hold me steady!" he ordered instead, his opposing hand curling in to grab his "oh shit" bar.

Bang went his gun. A metallic screech followed a burst of sparks as one of the spider-things went flying off and into the cement wall. St. Benedict's body twitched with the recoil, making Rune clamp down even harder.

"I hate this, I hate this, I hate this," she repeated.

Glancing around with her secondary sight, Rune could see St. Benedict's maniacal smile as he aimed at the other one.

He shot but missed. In response, it crawled away out of his line of sight.

Letting go of one of his legs, Rune flung her power hand out toward the thing. Obediently, her magic cord snapped out, seizing the sparked ball and forcing it back.

"Ha!" St. Benedict crowed, and he nailed the thing with another shot, bursting it into further sparks.

Rune turned her magic onto her ridiculously stupid partner, flinging several lines of magic into his chest and pulling his stupid ass back into the car. She had to fling herself against the passenger side door, using her own weight to counter balance.

"Whoa!" he cried, banging his forehead against the doorframe. "Son of a—" was all he got out as he clutched it in both his hands, even with the one still holding the gun.

"Shut up. At least you're still alive," Rune snapped. Slapping her hands together, she flattened them on the dashboard. Her magic went straight to the nothing hole of sparks inside the car.

"Please don't blow up the car," she prayed, then jolted magical energy through the whole frame. The sparks popped and imploded, dissipating into nothing.

There was a change in the sound of the car's engine. Everything on the dashboard spazzed for a second, then reset to normal.

"Auto car: pull over onto the shoulder!" Rune shouted.

The car immediately obeyed her, changing lanes smoothly between two cars and then onto the shoulder, finally slowing down.

Then it revved again as several spark bundles converged inside the engine. The radio blasted, and all the lights went on. She had missed the one that had interfaced into the car's computer itself. Using every bit of ready magic she had within her, Rune flooded the whole car this time. Every electrical bit spasmed into life—every light, every signal—in one glorious bright flash, then they all snapped like a light switch being flipped off.

St. Benedict screamed, clutching his head as his own aug-mentation took the full feedback from her magic. He had been connected to the car.

The next second, the car went completely dark.

Mercifully, they had entered a fairly straight section of I-290. Instead of flattening themselves against the concrete wall, the car did the normal thing and coasted. When she felt safe enough to, Rune pulled on the manual emergency brake handle. It took forever to come to a complete stop, drifting the last few feet to drag along the wall, which helped.

Once the car was still, Rune turned to St. Benedict to gloat or chide him—she wasn't sure which—except, to her horror, he was unconscious. His head just lolled from side to side, his back against the door, slumped over in the cramped space of the driver's seat.

"Oh gods, I fried him!" Rune cried as she reached for him. "St. Ben! St. Benedict, are you okay? Are you... please be okay?" She lifted his head up a little and felt around his neck for his pulse.

To her immense relief, she found it. Next, she went for his eyes, tilting his head up to peel them open. Where she expected to see dilated irises, she found his augmentations had caused the blue light that opaqued his real eyes. The light was blinking.

"What the heck does blinking mean?"

He didn't answer. Blood trailed from her partner's hairline. Rune jumped as the warm liquid hit her fingers.

"Oh crap. Crap. Crap," Rune said, then went for her belt to pull a pre-package of gauze from one of her many pouches of many things. "Come on. Don't die on me, please," she pleaded as she brought the gauze to his forehead, only to stop as she realized that his eyes were open again, the blue light now steady as he looked directly at her.

"St. Ben?" she asked, her voice coming out fearful.

At last, he blinked his actual eyelids twice, and on the third blink, the blue of his augmentation dissipated back to his human, green-blue color.

His blank expression crumpled into a painful one. "That hurt," he croaked out.

He hissed as she laid the gauze once more against his forehead, but she didn't remove her hand.

"We've stopped," she informed him.

"Oh, good. I was *not* in control of that situation." He tried to shift to a more comfortable position, then immediately gave up. "Okay, I think I need another minute."

"I saved us," Rune said, more because she needed to hear it herself than to brag.

"I know," he said, placing his own hand over hers. "Thank you."

She cleared her throat. "So, what do we do now?"

"Well," he paused a moment just as a semi buzzed past them, not even slowing down, "don't get out of the car. We'll be roadkill," he said dryly before he shifted himself to sit up more. Rune backed away. The move earned him a painful rap on the kneecap that he spent a few minutes hissing over. "Don't suppose you managed to not fry your phone with that little trick of yours?"

Rune fished the rectangle back up from the floor where it had fallen during her tangle with the spider. She tapped the power button, but it remained a black, now useless parallelogram. "Nope, fried it crispy."

"Okay, and I can't call for help either," St. Benedict reported. He moved his hand in the air. "My magical dampeners really took a strain. It doesn't look like that did any permanent damage, but Malachi will be running me through the battery of tests when we get back."

"And that leaves us with using more magic to call for help," Rune concluded.

St. Benedict leaned his head forward on the stirring wheel. "Yup, looks like."

"Will it hurt you if I do?" Rune asked.

He shook his head back and forth against the wheel. "I

don't think it should. And if it does, I'll suck it up."

St. Benedict sat back and flipped down the visor, sliding over a cover to reveal a lighted mirror. Or it would have been lighted if the car had any power. There was enough ambient daylight for him to examine his cut forehead despite the dark and gloomy weather. She opened hers as well and took a look, though she had a pretty good idea what she would see.

Sure enough, her hair was lightly feathered with grey-white streaks, making her normally golden-brown hair look dirty. Deep crow's feet framed her eyes and mouth and the indent between her eyebrows. The rest of her would have aged as well; she didn't need to check.

"You used too much of your magic," St. Benedict said.

Rune slid the mirror closed with a sharp snap. "No, I didn't. I'm not even over fifty at the moment. I'll be fine." It wasn't that he didn't have a point, but a night of sleep would fix the issue. "I am pretty sure not using magic would have mattered more if we had crashed into tiny pieces."

"Fair point," the Saint conceded.

"Yup, least of our problems."

"Oh, crap," St. Benedict suddenly said, leaning his head back against the backrest. "You know what the bigger problem is now? What are we going to tell Maxamillion about what happened?"

CHAPTER 9

"Whhhaaaat? St. Rachel screwed up!" Malachi said the minute Rune and St. Benedict got back to the Praetorium. The excited tech couldn't have been laughing harder as he approached, grabbing both Rune and St. Benedict's arms as if he meant to gather them into a conspiratorial huddle. "Thank God you guys are okay."

"Yeah, we're fine," St. Benedict said, cocking an eyebrow at Malachi's merry reaction. "Though it's not exactly a ball of laughs."

"Sorry. Sorry, I know it's not funny, but since you guys are alive and fine, it's hilarious." He launched into another round a manic chuckles.

"Darling, this is unseemly of you," Zita, Malachi's life partner, said as she slithered up. The Naga wore her white doctor's coat, which was St. Benedict's least favorite outfit on her. It meant a lot of wasted time for him.

At her admonishment, Malachi got it together better, and she wound the end of her tail around one of his ankles, slipping it under to stroke his leg in a small sign of affection even as she turned to Rune.

"I'm going to start with you," she said professionally as she gently took Rune's arm in a friendly but insistent manner, "though you don't look too worse for wear. St. Benedict, you are with Malachi. He's to run the full bio-diagnostic BEFORE you jump into ANYTHING. Is that clear?" She pinned both men with her piercing gaze.

Malachi crumpled immediately under it, as if his snake-like partner had turned into a Medusa all of a sudden. St. Benedict didn't react, only did his signature slide of his hands into his pockets. Zita's eyes narrowed the tiniest bit at him, and he conceded a slight nod of his own. Satisfied, she and Rune walked off as if they were girlfriends toward Zita's exam room off the main area of the Praetorium.

St. Benedict didn't take his eyes off Rune until she went through the door, then turned to find Malachi grinning at him with a knowing look that the Saint did not like.

"What?" he demanded, readjusting his fedora, which had been partly crushed in the car.

"I'm just so glad you two worked things out," Malachi answered before turning away to lead St. Benedict to the Praetorium's tech-build workshop on the opposite side of the main room.

"What do you mean by 'worked things out'?" he asked, coming up beside Malachi.

"Nothing like a death-defying, action-adventure, car chase to get things back on track," Malachi said. St. Benedict casually skimmed over the clusters of terminals filled by the various techs and analysts not so much working at all of them as ... twittering ... like a bunch of hens at a cocktail party. More than half were shooting him surreptitious looks.

"It wasn't a car chase," St. Benedict said as he shoved Malachi through the open door of the workroom before stepping in and shutting it firmly behind him. "And what the hell are you telling everybody?"

"What? Nothing!" Malachi said a bit too defensively.

Changing tactics, St. Benedict crossed his arms and leaned on the door. "Let's start with what are people saying out there?"

Malachi went to his work bench, picking up a handheld electroscope, which he fiddled with. "Nothing. Not much."

St. Benedict didn't move or shift or say anything more, just let Malachi's natural nervous jitters do the work for him.

"Look, we've all just been... Okay, come on, man. Ever since you brought her here, people have been unsure of what's going on exactly. You guys were partners one minute, but she was independent, which you know, made sense because she's magic and stuff. Then the next, she's working here, and you're acting as if you couldn't care less about her. Which, you know, doesn't surprise anyone, but we all sort of hoped... And I get *why* she's here, the whole thing with her House and Kodiak trying to arrest her and everything. But everybody is..."

"Is afraid of me," St. Benedict interjected.

"Not everybody," Malachi assured, "but yeah, more than you'd want on a volleyball team, and considering how St. Rachel's treating her, she's the number one pariah around here. Rumors are flying."

"What has everybody been saying?" St. Benedict asked, deflating a little.

"They are all afraid to cross you by associating with her."

That floored St. Benedict. And really, it shouldn't have. He leaned back against the door and covered his eyes with one hand. "Shit."

Malachi stood awkwardly in that long silence for as long as he could stand it, then he lightly tapped the Saint's shoulder. "Anyway, let's get started."

"Yeah," St. Benedict said, and he pushed away from the door to go to the jack-in chair next to Malachi's workbench.

The workroom was exactly that, the place where computers got built and maintained, which meant the walls here were covered in shelves, and the shelves were covered in the guts of electronica. It made St. Benedict feel like he too was only another machine, another tool to be used and maintained.

Normally, that suited him just fine. Thinking about himself that way gave a clarity of focus and kept him aligned with *his* mission. St. Benedict the machine with a pleasant, enigmatic smile that became whatever the people around him wanted him to be. He was skilled in making people feel what he wanted them to feel and manipulating that into what he wanted them to do, all the while feeling nothing himself.

Except he wasn't a machine anymore.

At the end of the day, when he lay in his bed in the dark, willing sleep to come, he had to grapple with the truth that he couldn't just flip off that switch anymore. His thoughts would flit to her. His body would ache and his guilt would tear at him. If he sat in Malachi's chair and begged the tech to remove his humanity, he wouldn't be able to do it. Would he ask him to do it anyway? Didn't he deserve this suffering?

Malachi pulled up his stool beside the Saint as he attempted to untangle the cords with their bio-pad ends. "Man, you shouldn't let what they think out there get to..."

"They are saying..." St. Benedict began as he flipped his hat up onto the worktable and began undressing for his examination, "that it was all a game. That I never had feelings for her, which was one of the previous rumors, that Ms. Leveau had finally warmed my cold, dead heart, and in typical Saint fashion, I manipulated her into position until I could claim her for the Praetorium."

Malachi sighed. "I suppose, yes, that is more or less what they all think. But hey, those are just rumors, right? *I* know it was more complicated than that. She was in real trouble, and she needed a safe place to go..."

"I still betrayed her," St. Benedict said, dropping his ruined suit jacket onto the floor, followed by the vest underneath.

"Yeah, but come on. There were all these extenuating circumstances," Malachi continued, pulling out the medical pads to attach to the diagnostic nodes.

"And why do you think I betrayed her?" St. Benedict asked,

surprised at himself and what he was about to do.

"Well, it's because she's your friend and your partner," Malachi said, struggling for the right answer. "Yeah. She's your friend. You like her, in your Saint-like way... You know what I mean—"

"I'm in love with her," St. Benedict confessed, saying the words before he could stop himself.

The statement was so clear, straightforward, and honest that Malachi didn't even seem to register it at first. "What—what?" he said as he froze, his eyes wide, perfect circles.

St. Benedict didn't repeat himself, just focused on unbuttoning his shirt while toeing off his shoes.

"Holy shit," Malachi breathed and literally fell off his rolling stool, having to catch himself on the edge of his desk, dropping the nodes. "Holy shit, St. Ben— Did you just say ... out loud..."

Pulling the buttons free, St. Benedict threw the shirt down and seized the metal box hanging from the double linked chain around his neck, his Saint Box.

Pushing through his instinct to hide this secret, he held it out to Malachi. "Right before we become Saints, each candidate is forced to select something that means the most to them, more than anything else in the world. The Archdeacons who study and train the candidates analyze everything about them in order to learn what that person or thing is. Then a connected symbol of that precious thing is chosen and placed inside the box with magic."

St. Benedict's hands were shaking as he spun the chain around his neck, bringing the re-enforced clasp around to the front so he could unlock it, and it took a full minute to get it to open. Once the clasp was free, he thrust the cursed thing out to the only other person in the whole world he finally decided he trusted.

Malachi didn't move at first as he stared at the box. The tech had seen it before, but every member of the Praetorium knew never, never, never ask the Saints about them. St.

Benedict never cared if it was a rule that Maxamillion had imposed or not. He had told himself it didn't matter to him, but his hand shook as he held it out.

"Take it!" St. Benedict finally insisted, which stuttered Malachi to life, raising his own hand to receive it quickly. Still unsure, the tech glanced up at the Saint, then refocused on the box. "You..." he swallowed, "you say this is magic?"

"Yes." St. Benedict's eyes didn't waver from the silver etched box, his fingers already itching to snatch it back.

"Why would they do this?" Malachi dared to ask. "The ones that ... made you?"

"To control us. Whoever holds that box as the 'master' has only to order us to do something, and we are compelled to obey. Even die."

"Wait, you mean..." Malachi's eyes shifted back and forth as he thought furiously. "You mean, that if they tell you to... I don't know... stop breathing."

St. Benedict sucked in a breath, and Malachi startled. He held his hand out desperately. "No, don't! Keep breathing! Keep breathing, man. I didn't mean..." He almost dropped the chain, but St. Benedict set a hand on the tech's shoulders.

"Yes, if the *master* told me to stop breathing, I simply would. If they told my heart to stop beating, it would. But you are not my master, Mal."

Relieved, Malachi's shoulders slumped. "Who is?"

"Maxamillion, of course. The box has to have a master, or it kills me anyway."

"God, that is horrible!" Malachi declared, and he wasn't wrong.

"And when they do this, you have to willingly make the vow for the spell to work. Of course, they try to control what you vow, but there is nothing they can do when you actually make it."

Malachi's eyes asked what his voice could not.

"I vowed to always remain faithful to my wife. If I ever break that vow, this curse would revert to her, and it would

kill her instead. Only then would I be free."

The tech stared down once again at the box. "That's how they compel your obedience. If you're willing to give up the thing you love most in the world..."

"I can be free, yes. Hence why they really want it to be something you truly care about more than anything." St. Benedict shifted back and sat down on the edge of the jack-in chair, folding his arms across his open-shirted chest. "It was also my way of saying 'fuck you' to them. If they had forced me to have sex with anybody who wasn't my wife, I'm pretty sure the spell would break then too."

Malachi's eyebrows furrowed. "Then ... why didn't you..."

"Because I have no idea what that might have done to... to her," St. Benedict admitted. They both sat in a long silence, lost deep in dark thoughts.

Then, Malachi leaned forward, putting his elbow on his knee to rub furiously at his forehead with his hand. "Why are you telling me this now?"

"Because ... I'm in love with Rune."

"Oh, fuck."

CHAPTER 10

Zita growled as she slapped her way through the various medical drawers, searching for some tool that just wouldn't come to hand. Rune waited patiently on the exam table, her coat off and draped over a chair, her boots tucked beside. She definitely wanted a shower, just from the copious amounts of sweat she had burned out of herself in all of the excitement.

At last, the banging became too much for her. "Is there something I can help you find?" Rune asked.

"No, no," Zita said just as she slid open a bottom drawer and seized on the box of latex gloves from the bottom, tearing open the top. "The techs have been in my stuff again. They keep stealing the small sized gloves so they can tear them up for finger cots and whatever else, instead of just requisitioning their own." The glove Zita was attempting to pull out, flung another onto the ground before the Naga could catch it, eliciting another internal scream from her. "No, really I'm fine."

"I don't..." Rune started, unsure if this might result in her getting her head taken off. Rune liked Zita, but she hated snakes, which meant she always had a low level of apprehension around Zita that she just couldn't shake or entirely ignore as much as she wanted to. "...believe you?"

"Good, I would have questions about your mental state if you did," Zita said, abandoning the fallen glove to shove her dainty hands into the pair she pulled. "Do you feel any sharp pains, any dizziness, anything of note?"

Rune shook her head. "Honestly, I'm just shook-up. Anything that actually hurt has healed itself by now. We don't need to do this."

Zita yanked up a clipboard, shaking it at Rune. "But I need to fill this out because it's company policy, so sit there and let me do this!"

Rune raised her hands in surrender. "Alright, alright. No worries."

The Naga sighed, her little explosion already cooling off as she dropped the clipboard onto her table and slithered over. "I'm sorry. I apologize. This is not about..."

Keying in to the signs, Rune nodded her head. "Did you get your results back from the review board?" she asked, remembering the Naga's plight, being a certified doctor in India but unable to get that same certification here in the states.

"No, it's worse than that," Zita admitted. "They are requiring further documentation, but now they're asking for things I don't even know where to find. It's just one more damn red-tape hoop to jump, and I don't even have legs!"

Rune didn't really know what more to say to that, and any joke she could make would sound wrong no matter how clever she tried for, so she nodded and stated the universal truism of, "That sucks."

"Can't one of the Saints just do their thing and push it through?" Rune asked.

"They may have to. I just thought, with Corinthe's corporate backing, that this time..." Zita plucked up her otoscope, bringing it up to flash the light into Rune's eyes as she spoke.

"That this time, I would actually make some damned headway. I wanted to get it because I deserved it, not because someone tricked them into it." She flashed her light in Rune's second eye. "I mean, it's getting so bad, it's actually starting to feel like one of Malachi's crazy conspiracy theories."

"Speaking of Malachi," Rune started, hoping it didn't sound like too rough a topic change, "he was dancing gleefully about St. Rachel messing something up. Do you know what that was about?"

"We've had an incident concerning her current project," Maxamillion declared, coming into the space without knocking. He wasn't running, but there was an energy in his movements that conveyed urgency and concern. "How are you, Rune? Are you okay?"

Surprised by his concern, Rune nodded opened-mouthed like an idiot instead of saying something.

"Yes, she'll be fine," Zita assured him. "I'm running some quick checks, but she walked in here under own power and has been cognitively talking with me, so I'm not at all worried that you're hurt any more than those few scratches."

Maxamillion caught Rune's hand, running the pad of his thumb gently over one of the aforementioned scratches. It hadn't bled much, looking more like a red marker line than an actual breach of her skin. "I'm glad it wasn't worse. I saw the pictures from the car, and I *feared* the worst."

Rune knew what he meant. Once their rescue had come to pick them up, she had gotten a good look at the outside. The body of the car had been shredded, like some sort of titanium tiger had been using the sides and hood as a scratching post.

"I am more concerned about St. Benedict," she said, and Maxamillion let go of her hand. Rune had the distinct feeling she had said something wrong but wasn't sure what that could be.

Their fearless leader slipped his hands back into his pockets and took a step back toward the door. "We will be having a meeting soon to discuss the developments. I would

like you there, Rune, to offer up your unique perspective."

"Of course," Rune agreed, though she had never been included on any meetings in the Praetorium so far. Once he had gone, she turned to Zita. "Something magical must have happened."

Zita nodded in agreement. "That would be something that St. Rachel wouldn't necessarily plan for."

Rune sighed. "Well, I suppose this is what I signed up for." She pushed herself back up to standing. "Thank you for the check-over."

"If I find anything in your blood results, I will let you know, but I do not expect to," Zita acknowledged.

Rune smiled and left to go back out to the main room of the Praetorium.

"No way, dude. Your relationship is already doomed," Malachi stated, slashing the air with his hand as if that would cut it off.

"What are you talking about?" St. Benedict asked, narrowing his eyebrows at his friend.

"You're not healthy for her at all," Malachi stated with continuing conviction, crossing his arms as he wheeled his stool around to face down the Saint.

"If you don't start elaborating, I'm going to punch you and do unspeakable things to the rest of the holes in your head," St. Benedict said, half meaning it.

Malachi pointed straight at the Saint's nose. "That right there. That is why you cannot, under any circumstances, pursue Rune, and it has nothing to do with whatever is going on with your Saint Box. You are so toxic in the way you handle other people when you do not get your way. And I haven't figured out yet if it's your fault or not. I mean, the Saint Program and their brainwashing... but it doesn't matter, does it? You bully and threaten and then make a joke about it, and that's not how you need to be a good partner—"

"I don't—"

"You do! You so do. And it's great. Don't get me wrong. You're a really effective coercer, but that makes you literally the worst person for... well anyone, but especially Rune. And right now, I think the only way you might be able to get around the curse on your Saint's Box would be for you to marry someone else. I mean, make Rune your wife... well unless, you used your wife's name in the curse."

"I did."

"Okay, so maybe that won't work either, but that is beside the point. I like Rune too much to let you—"

"I haven't done anything!" St. Benedict nearly shouted.

"You took away her agency! She's only *here* at the Praetorium because of you. I mean it was a fucked-up situation, and I don't really know what you could have done differently, but you took away her ability to choose. She's not going to forgive you after that, nor should she!" Malachi defended.

"What the hell is this? You taking a women's studies class?!" St. Benedict growled.

The shorter man didn't back down. "How many times have you called her stupid? To her face, in moments of stress?"

St. Benedict's mouth opened to get even more defensive, but instead, some stumbling syllables fell out without the cohesion of a sentence.

"And that's my point," Malachi said, this time quieter and more sober. "If you're not someone who builds her up, then you're not someone ... worthy of her..."

St. Benedict felt like his skin was going to crack and split open, the emotions roiling inside him bursting out. If only his "friend" had shot him in the head, it would have been quicker. The emotions needed to go somewhere, and putting his fist through Malachi's face kept seeming like a better and better option.

There was a glint of defiance in Malachi's eyes as his crossed arms and stiffened jaw challenged the Saint to do anything about what he had just said.

"And what do you think I should do instead?" St. Benedict asked with deadly quiet.

Uncertainty crossed Malachi's eyes, and St. Benedict felt a pang of regret. He needed to turn his anger down a notch.

"You should just leave her alone," Malachi finally said.

"I'm trying to keep her safe!"

"Yes, of course you are, by controlling her. And fine. Do that. Just don't freaking lie to me about loving her then. Because guess what? You can't do both. And yes, Zita and I have been going to couple's counseling, but you know what? I like that it's making me a better partner for her, so stick it up your ass!" Malachi stood up abruptly then, knocking his chair back so that it flopped over before marching over to the door.

"Where are you going?!" St. Benedict shouted.

"Oh, are you going to *make* me stay?" Malachi challenged.

"No, I don't care. Go wherever the fuck you want, you pathetic excuse for a stenographer."

"That doesn't even make sense!"

"I know!"

"Fine!"

"Fine!"

Malachi stopped with his hand on the handle of the door. They were both panting hard as they stared the other down, more worn out than if they had actually exchanged punches.

After a moment, St. Benedict gestured to the door. "You going or not?"

"Eat a dick," Malachi said and slammed the door as he left.

St. Benedict would have laughed at the playground-level response, but he was too angry.

CHAPTER 11

The Praetorium buzzed with chatter as techs rushed around. It seemed like whatever had happened with St. Rachel's screw-up had affected not just Rune and St. Benedict's trip back from the city, but every super-secret, need-to-know project that the Corinthe Corp ran.

Across the space, she spotted St. Benedict coming back from being checked out by Malachi. He gave her his sexy half-smile, and she had to resist the urge to rudely turn away and walk off. But frankly, she was getting so tired of this.

"Everything okay?" he had the audacity to ask.

"Yes, I am fine. I have been called to a meeting," she said.

"Oh, lucky for us. I am pretty sure I am at the same meeting. Shall we walk?"

"Don't you need to see Zita next?" Rune asked.

He shrugged. "No, not really. If I go now, she'll start to think I'm easy, and I like being chased." He looked at Rune as if waiting and expecting her to react to his joke. For a split second, she thought about giving him the reaction he sought,

even if she didn't feel it.

No. Not this time, she thought.

He didn't flash uncertainty or discomfort like she expected to her non-reaction. Instead, he looked away, chuckling at his own joke. "Yeah. That's funny," he mused to himself under his breath in a way that felt more like he meant the opposite. "Okay, well I'm walking to the meeting, and if you go in the same direction, then ... that is your choice." He waited another moment, then moved to walk along the wall of the underground facility toward the conference area near the jack-in machines.

There really *wasn't* another route to go to get there, and Rune couldn't think of another more important reason to not go to this meeting, so she had to follow. Besides, she hoped to get more information about what was going on and what it all meant. For both her and her client.

The meeting "room" was more like a table with glass partitions all around, set up in the middle of the Praetorium. It was open at the top, but for some reason, when Rune passed through the gaps in the glass, the noise from the main room disappeared. She would have said it was magic, even though she knew that wasn't possible. The table in the middle was a long oblong of fancy wood with cushioned chairs tucked under it all around. A prep cart with fresh drinks and snacks was being set up at one end by a very anxious-looking service worker. Rune picked up on the distressing tension as she entered the space and sat down at the farthest spot from the only currently seated occupant at the table: St. Rachel.

The beautiful woman was leaning her head on her hands, her fingers buried into her golden hair as everyone assembled around her. Maxamillion stood beside her, his arms folded as he observed everyone assembling. St. Benedict faced the active monitor the size of a small movie theater screen lighting up one of the glass walls, reading the listing of code and the various charts that meant gibberish to Rune. None of them were speaking to each other. Even with all the movement from everyone claiming a seat, those three only waited in an oddly still tableau, like they were waiting for a photograph to be taken or something.

As chairs filled up, a nice-looking analyst in a button-up shirt with his sleeves rolled up to his elbows pulled out the seat next to Rune. He slapped down a stack of papers on the table and gave her an acknowledging smile. She returned it, but before either of them could say any more polite greetings, St. Benedict came up behind him.

"That's my seat," the Saint stated.

The nice young man opened his mouth as if to protest or apologize, but no sound came out as if his brain hadn't decided which one. He finally glanced an apology at Rune and shut it entirely before reclaiming his stack of papers to skitter away.

St. Benedict didn't say anything more either as he cleared his throat, unbuttoned his jacket, and sat down as natural as he pleased.

Rune glared at him, but he never looked at her, so she poignantly stood up and went around the table herself. There was only one chair available on that side, and it was right next to Maxamillion, so she claimed it. Her boss gave her a warm acknowledging smile, completely oblivious to where she had just come from, and instead stood up to start the meeting.

"Alright, people, grab your drinks and snacks now because this will probably be a long discussion, and it won't be nearly as long as we need, so you better have gone to the bathroom already." There was a circle of grumbling around the table, and more than one person leaned in to help themselves from the black coffee carafe that was set in the middle with a tray of cups. Rune decided to follow suit and plucked a cup herself to fill with hot water from the white carafe that the food tech handed to her. She started to scan for the tea box when it appeared under her nose.

"There's the cranberry-orange ones you like," Maxamillion said as she took the box from him. He had already selected some Turkish blend that he had previously insisted was an

abomination against true Turkish teas, but he drank it anyway. Noting the torn wrapper made her smirk.

A couple people down her line seemed to notice the little exchange and met Rune's eyes a second before doing the gossipy shift away.

Well that's just great, she thought as she focused on her own teamaking and ignored the rest.

Eventually the meeting got settled, but all through that time, St. Rachel had not lifted her head up once. It fell to Maxamillion to start, taking to his feet once more.

"As many of you have undoubtedly heard, we have been attacked," he said plainly. The lack of reaction from the table confirmed his statement. Taking a fob out of his pocket, Maxamillion clicked it at the active glass wall. The screen changed from the various running programs to a written bullet list. It was almost laughable, showing a PowerPoint presentation for something as deadly serious as a cyber attack, but no one in the room even cleared a throat.

"This morning, around 2:30am, St. Rachel ran an operation following AR protocol against Synthtech. At the time, there did not seem to be any issue. Everything was as expected." Maxamillion flipped to the next slide. "We do not know for certain what went wrong or what tipped them off, but Synthtech's defenses kicked in at 3:42am."

Malachi raised his hand, and Maxamillion gestured to him to speak. "While defenses were tripped, there was not an immediate response until later this morning. We can confirm that now. It is highly likely that Synthtech did a full diagnostic and assessment before taking action against us."

"And it is at 3:42 that our attack was shut down," Maxamillion finished, with mutual nods between himself and Malachi. He picked up a piece of paper from the table. "Ross, who several of you know as RB, was the first to report this to us before he went silent."

"Is he...?" someone asked.

Maxamillion pursed his lips together. It was all he needed

to say. Around the table, heads bowed. Though Rune didn't know Ross personally, she felt his loss all the same from the reaction of those around her.

"This is all a bit too big of a counterattack for them to have not been planning this as a legit first attack against us in advance," St. Benedict piped in. "It's very likely that Synthtech was in the middle of setting up their own offensive and, once they caught us, saw no reason to delay any further."

"Our priority is not to assess the damage yet," Maxamillion stated. "This is about saving what we can. Our network is under assault, and we have to turtle-up. Pull in what resources we have and can protect. Retrenchment protocol is now in effect, people. Update your teams. Direct any questions or problems you can't handle to the Saints. It's what they are here for."

There were other exchanges and questions as the table more or less broke up, but they weren't relevant to what Rune was focused on. She needed to ask Maxamillion her own question, one she didn't need to announce to the whole room. So she waited and thought and pointedly did not look at St. Benedict, even though she couldn't ignore his presence in her periphery. Her best chance to speak to their leader would be when most everyone else had been addressed. The panicked tension in the room was near palpable, and she didn't blame them. The one thing everyone had said about her "incarceration" was that Corinthe Corp could keep her safe. Apparently, everyone else in the Praetorium had believed that too, and their faith was shaken.

"Rune," Maxamillion's voice finally cut through, addressing her out of her thoughts. Most of the room had moved on, and they stood almost alone.

"Sorry," Rune said, covering her inattention. "I guess I'm a bit in shock after all of this."

Maxamillion sighed, unbuttoned his jacket, and sat back down in one of the chairs, tapping a button which opaqued the glass around the table. "You're not kidding. I thought that would take more time, that it would be a longer meeting, but…

I guess not," he said, dropping his formal speech for something more real and human. He knocked back the dregs of his tea.

Rune did the same before speaking. "I want to talk to you about Jasmeen Clarmont."

Maxamillion lowered his teacup back to its plate with a calculated slowness. "I know the name but remind me."

"She came to me for help at the Lucky Devil. St. Benedict..." She knew how she was going to phrase this diplomatically when she started the conversation, but the right words shot right out of her head as soon as she needed them.

Fortunately, Maxamillion nodded as he remembered. "Yes, yes. Then St. Benedict stole her right out from underneath you."

"Yeah, more or less," Rune agreed, glad she wouldn't have to be more tactful than that. "Since joining your company, I've been keeping tabs on her."

Maxamillion rubbed at his temples again. "I am sorry. With everything going on, I haven't been able to keep up on all the moving parts."

"I want to bring her in," Rune said, cutting to the chase. It may have been a mistake, being too direct, because Maxamillion went still at her request. "She's a victim in all this, and she had no protection, and that wouldn't be the case if it wasn't for me."

"If I recall, she wanted to leave her company and had taken steps to do so?" Maxamillion said.

Rune pursed her lips, wanting to lie or spin it, but instinctively knowing it was a bad move. "Yes, she was desperate to get away from the corporate elites harassing her."

"Yes, but it also means her exposure is not our fault."

"You're withholding your help because she won't 'play ball.'" Rune lifted her fingers to make the air quotes sign.

He sighed. "That makes her not our problem. She made her choice—"

"Which is no choice at all," she finished, nailing him with a sharp look.

Maxamillion leaned forward to rest his elbows on the table. "Yeah, it is a raw deal, and I'll admit I haven't really been paying attention to this situation. With the work we do, we can't simply save everybody. We have limited resources—"

"It's mercenary!"

"It's practical. You can't have a community without everybody paying in, and that is what this is." He gestured at the Praetorium beyond the whited-out walls. "This is about our own, and we are under attack. I know it's not convenient, but if she chooses to, she can come to it."

Rune's eyebrows shot up at the declaration. "You mean, if I can get her here, you'll protect her?"

"If she comes under her own power, she can have asylum, but I cannot expend any more resources to go get her. That includes you." He held up a hand to keep her from standing up. "Don't forget why you're here. I'm doing everything I can to keep *you* safe too, but don't think for one moment the other corporations wouldn't give a lot to have you under their control."

"I am cognizant of the dangers," Rune agreed. She stood. "I'll get out of your way then."

Maxamillion stood too, strangely awkward for the usually suave corporate lord and master. "Thank you for coming by."

"Well, it was an order from the boss," Rune said, stiffly. "Though I don't think I contributed very much to the discussion."

"I know. I'm sorry about that. I just wanted to see that you were alright."

Something in that declaration made Rune raise an eyebrow. "I'm fine," she said, forcing a fake smile.

"Good. That's alright then." Maxamillion tapped the top of the table with his fingertips, like a piano player in a panic about the next tune. "If there is anything else you need, just let me know."

Rune nodded. "Thank you. I will. And you be safe too."

Just then, someone came to the glass door and rapped on

it before cracking it open. "Sir, there are several calls waiting for you, and St. Rachel would like a word."

Maxamillion sighed and gave Rune a tired look. "Alright," he declared, re-cinching his tie as he prepared for battle. "Time to get back on the court."

Once back to her rooms, Rune wasted no time. She charged straight in and locked the door behind her. It didn't mean it was truly locked. The electronic key system would open to anyone with clearance, such as the Saints or Maxamillion or security. So it was more symbolic than anything. Jasmeen needed her help, and she was going to be damned if she let anything stand in her way. It didn't solve all of Jasmeen's problems, but it certainly was a start. Rune could only imagine what would have happened if the Infiltrators had found them at the hominal woman's apartment instead of on the road.

The first thing she did was use her replacement mobile phone. Normally, she wouldn't have done this, but since Maxamillion himself had given her the official 'okay,' this was an official call. At least, that was the excuse she was going to use later since she was interpreting his words for him.

Having acquired the phone number along with the address, Rune had it already stored in her phone.

But it just rang. And rang.

"Come on, come on, come on. Pickup, pickup, pickup," Rune whispered out loud.

When the phone went to voicemail, the voice recording confirming she had Jasmeen's number, she hung up and called again. Endless rings and no answer.

Before she could leave a message this time, there was a knock at the door. With a pang of panic, she hung up instantly.

She could feel the silence drag out too long since the knock, so she pocketed the phone and went to open the door.

St. Benedict stood there.

She didn't say anything, simply waited. He had probably tapped her phone and was here to ask her about it. Of course he would be watching, the one who was charged with keeping her in line and under control.

They continued to stare at each other, both seemingly waiting for the other to make the first move. She remembered him telling her it was one of his psychological tricks, to try to make the person he was interrogating speak first. He'd use the uncomfortable tension in the silence to see if he could get them to start admitting things they didn't intend to even say, just to fill the silence. Well, she had no intention of falling for that trick. She could be just as comfortable in the silence as he...

"Rune, I don't know what to do," he suddenly said, breaking eye contact with her to look down at the ground.

She furrowed her eyebrows at him. *Is this a new tactic?*

"Can... Can I come in?" he asked.

Lacking a better answer, she stepped back, pulling the door with her so he could enter. He did, fiddling with his hands. First, he slipped them into his pockets, taking them out again before finally lifting his fedora off his head to run his fingers though his hair before settling it back.

"What's going on?" Rune asked, still wary of a trap or a trick.

"I know," he said. "I know what you're going to do."

Rune shut the door and leaned her back against it as she crossed her arms. "Okay."

"I want to help you," he said too quickly. His haunted eyes were almost crazed with anxiety. *What the hell is going on?* "But I get it. Why would you take help from me after ... everything." He turned then and started pacing. "Also, I *am* torn because I should stop you, right? It'll keep you safe if you stay here, but I can't do that, can I?"

She snorted disgustedly. "You can do anything you want."

"It's like I said: I don't know what to do. So I thought... I *thought* alright, just come here. And... And ask you?"

"Ask me what?" Rune cocked her eyebrow.

"What I should do?"

Frustration burned through her chest. She pushed off the door and went to open it again. "I promise I'm not going anywhere, so you don't have to worry—"

"I'm in love with you, Rune."

That stopped everything, from Rune's tracks to her heartbeat. Her mouth went dry, and her grip on the doorknob seemed to be the only thing keeping her standing. "What?"

St. Benedict slapped his hands against his thighs as he started pacing again. "I'm in love with you, okay?!"

She furrowed her brows as he stormed around while shouting. "You're not making it seem like that is a good thing."

"Because it's not! It's a very bad, dangerous thing," he said, cupping his hands as if he could hold that dangerous thing between them. "I can love you, or I can keep you safe. I can't do both. And I know keeping you safe should be more important, but I can't... I want you so badly that I stop being smart and start doing stupid things."

"Making decisions for me is a smart thing?" Rune snapped.

St. Benedict flinched. "No, no, it isn't... I mean... Ahhh! This is why I'm here. My brain doesn't ... work anymore."

"Then go talk to Malachi about it. What do you want from me?"

"I want... It's because..." He stopped, his words failing to come out in the right order. At last, he slumped like a defeated, washed-out man. "Holy Hell, I sound like an idiot."

She couldn't help it. She snorted into a laugh with all the dignity of Miss Piggy. The tension in the room drained away, and St. Benedict tossed up his hands and dropped into one of the armchairs in the "living room" section of the space. As he flopped, his fedora popped off his head. He caught in his hands before tossing it onto the table. It landed right side up and slid a few inches across the glassy surface.

Rune moved away from the door to come up behind the other armchair sitting perpendicular to him. She leaned against the top. "Say you're sorry," she stated.

He cocked his head at her. "I already said I was sorry for

how I treated you at the—"

"I wasn't ready to receive it then. Say it now."

"I'm ... sorry."

"For what?" she pushed.

"I'm sorry for..." He eyed her for answers, but she gave him nothing. "Everything?"

Rune had hoped it would matter, that his apologies would resonate, and she'd feel different. Yet all she felt was her sadness and disappointment when she looked at him. He had walked into that room declaring that he loved her, and it had surprised her, but not thrilled her like in her fantasies. It simply wasn't enough. Apologies had never made a difference with her ex-husband's behavior, and she certainly knew that words were simply that with St. Benedict. He was a self-admitted liar. He would say anything she wanted to hear, and it wouldn't mean a thing to him.

Maybe he was telling the truth, maybe he wasn't, but the fact that she even questioned it poisoned any feelings she may have about it.

"Thank you," she said stiffly, accepting the apology as much as she realistically could and went into her bedroom.

"Rune, wait," he called, but she didn't.

St. Benedict watched her walk away and resisted every urge he had to grab her by the shoulder and make her stop. He knew what she was going to do, though he had no idea how she was going to do it. "Rune?"

She didn't answer, only went into her bathroom. This silence was torture, and he was starting to resent her for it because he was pretty sure she knew what it was doing to him. When she went into the bathroom, he hesitated outside it, though she hadn't completely shut the door. Sighing, he braced himself to wait for her to do exactly what he knew she was doing.

CHAPTER 11

Pain lanced through his skull. A familiar pain that only one thing invoked.

"Dammit! Rune!" He burst forward, slapping the door open. It rebounded against the wall.

The room was empty again.

CHAPTER 12

Rune pounded on the door of Jasmeen's apartment, conveying all her anxious urgency with each knock.

Still, her client didn't answer.

Rune had rung the bell several times but received the same result. Despite Rune's furious pounding, the hallway remained quiet and undisturbed. If she held her breath, she could hear very distant sounds of someone's TV playing, but otherwise the soundproofing in the place seemed to be insulating her racket. That was what a mid-level corporate job got you.

Lacking other options, Rune searched around the door, looking for some hidden key. Even though the lock on the door was a thumbprint reader, there was often a physical backup of some kind in case the reader shorted out. Unfortunately, neither the top edge of the door frame nor the underside of the standard brown doormat yielded a key of any sort.

Rune now wished she were an Opener, a Talent whose magic abilities leaned toward being able to open most anything with a lock. Lacking that straightforward Talent and cursing herself for not thinking to study it, Rune gripped the knob to simply extend her own power. Sure enough, a thin thread of yellow emerged from the knob.

Find me a way to open you, she thought, focusing her intention into her magic.

The emergence of the thread, however, made the dimly lit screen of the digital lock flicker rapidly. Rune released the knob immediately for fear that she was about to fry the lock, making it that much harder to get it open. Obviously, Jasmeen's lock didn't have a lot of magical insulation.

Yet the gold thread remained, reaching out from the knob to shoot toward a door down a few feet and across the hall.

A neighbor must have a spare key, Rune thought as she turned to go ring that person's doorbell. After a few breathless moments, the door opened to an older woman half Rune's height. She looked Rune up and down, as unimpressed by the mage's coat and boots as Rune was with the neighbor's gray and pink sweater and hair full of curlers.

"Can I help you?" the neighbor asked stiffly.

Rune forced on a smile. "Hi, I'm a friend of Jasmeen's next door."

The woman looked over her glasses. "So?"

Rune faltered a moment. That wasn't the response she had been expecting but decided her planned out speech would still work. "It's ... just... I haven't heard from her in a couple days, and I know she's going through a hard time, so I'm worried. Would it be alright if I borrow the spare key and just check on her quick?"

"How did you know I had a spare key?" the neighbor asked, narrowing her right eye.

"I... uh... Sorry, it's just... Jasmeen told me that if I never needed... I mean ever needed to get into her apartment that you had the spare I could use?"

The neighbor pursed her lips very disapprovingly, then sighed and turned back into her apartment. "Come in," she said in the most unwelcoming way possible before shuffling off into what seemed to Rune an apartment kitchen similar to the one Jasmeen had. The neighbor went over to a rack that held several bunches of keys from what had to be various decades. She pawed through them a moment, reading tiny tags connected to each one. "Everyone leaves me their spares over the years," the woman grumbled, glancing at Rune's surprised face.

While she pawed, a noise caught Rune's attention, and she glanced out the front door.

St. Benedict, wearing his long trench coat, looking like something out of a noir movie, stood panting in front of Jasmeen's door, trying to turn the knob. It didn't open for him either, so he raised up his other hand, firing up his augmentation. Rune's heart leapt into her throat, and she ducked back into the neighbor's doorway before he turned to see her spying.

Crap, that was faster than I expected, she thought.

The neighbor returned with a slow shuffle back over to Rune, holding out the desired key which glowed yellow to Rune's perception. "Tell her she can just bring it back whenever she wants, and if she gets mad about me letting you in, you can tell her to trust it someone else then. I got more things to do with my day than babysit other people's keys."

Considering the stacks of keys on that rack, Rune highly doubted that but wasn't going to say such a snarky thing aloud when she was almost home free. Instead, she smiled pleasantly. "Thank you very much. I—" was all she got out before the older woman seized her upper arm in a painful pinch and rushed Rune out the door. It shut rudely without another word.

Facing the music, Rune turned to what she expected would be St. Benedict staring at her but discovered the hall empty again. For a second, she wondered if she had just imagined him, only to notice that Jasmeen's door stood slightly ajar. It seemed safe to assume he had used his augmentations to hack his way through the lock. Pocketing the key, Rune debated what the best next course of action would be.

St. Benedict debated what he should do next. Despite his hurry, Rune had obviously gotten there first and left with Jasmeen as he found no evidence of either woman in the apartment and no sign of forced entry.

"Dammit," he muttered under his breath. It had taken him too much time to sneak away from the Praetorium without anyone noticing, and now he had lost them.

The undignified yip that escaped him when he turned around to see Rune leaning in the doorway of the apartment only added to his discombobulation.

"So she's gone?" Rune asked, completely cool and nonplussed as St. Rachel had ever been.

"Uh, yeah, apparently," he replied, looking left and right like an idiot.

She pushed off the door frame and flashed a key at him as she strolled in. "I was just over at the neighbors getting the key."

He wanted to demand that they return to that same safe haven immediately. Instead he said, "I'm here. What do you need?"

Rune flashed him a glance, her eyebrows halfway up in surprise before diving back into a furrow. He could practically feel her gaze scour him to figure out his motives.

"Well, I think ... *I* should actually confirm that she is gone and not... you know, dead in her bed or something."

He nodded, taking that information in and its implications. "Well, uh, I don't sense anything, both with my natural and augmented senses. As far as I can tell, she simply isn't here."

Rune walked the rest of the way into the apartment and leaned in to scan the bedroom. The bed itself was made, but piles of clothes and things were stacked haphazardly on it, allowing for a large space in the middle. "So she packed up and left," Rune concluded.

"From the looks of things, she struggles more with depression and anxiety than masked corporate thugs in the night," he agreed.

The Finder sighed, a degree of tension melting out of her shoulders. "I actually feared what I'd find would be much worse."

She turned back to go to the dining room table, still not meeting his gaze. The table was still a mess, much as it had been earlier when he had last found her there. Rune ran her hand over the top of the table, landing on a small haphazard pile of business cards. She plucked one up and turned it around between her fingers. It clearly had their target's name printed on it with the Kodiak logo in one corner. "She must have cleaned out her purse too," she said.

He had to agree. Bits of old tissue, random cough drops, and receipts along with the stack of cards implied such a thing.

"I'm sorry," he said, and now she finally turned to him to meet his gaze. "We should have taken her when we were last here. If we had, she would be safe at the Praetorium right now, even if it would have been an exciting car ride to get there."

Rune's own eyes hooded at that statement. It had been the wrong thing to say, though it was the truth. He felt all his logical arguments bubble up in the back of his throat, readying to defend his position.

Then Rune's eyes went opaque with a sheen of softly glowing light, magic obscuring her irises, killing anything he had been about to say. She held the card out before herself, facing the door. His skin began to tingle and a small pressure-pain, like a mild ice cream headache, formed between his eyes as she used her Finding magic with the card as a catalyst. He had seen her do this several times, using the intention in the card of being found to Find someone. After a moment, the feeling abated, and Rune sighed as her magic dropped away.

"Wherever she is, she's too far away for me to Find." She slipped the card into the pocket of her coat before pulling out the chair to sit. "Dammit. All that tells me is she isn't in the building anymore. Otherwise, there would *be* something."

"Maybe... if we go back... If we get to somewhere where I can get deep-web access... I could..."

"No, wait. I have an idea," Rune said softly. She closed her eyes and straightened her posture, opening her palms forward. He had seen her do this before. When she opened her eyes again, they were once more filled with pure white light. Even without her irises, he could feel those lighted eyes roving all over his body, like she could stare into his soul. He let her look, saying nothing. She had already seen him spiritually naked before. He knew it looked ugly, even if he had never seen the sight himself.

Then her eyes drifted away, examining the apartment with her own version of augmented sight. "She was—is—will be here," Rune said, her voice echoing in that uncanny way. Without voice modulators or anything implanted, he had no idea how she did that. The sound sent shivers down his spine it was so eerie. Especially when she spoke the action verb, as he heard her say the past, present, and future tenses all at the same time, which shouldn't have been possible either.

"No, Rune," she said to herself, her voice's thrum retreating as she spoke, "focus only on the past."

In her unblinking trance, Rune turned and went into the bedroom. She picked up the bathrobe that lay on the corner of the bed, slipping it on as if it were her own. It was the same one Jasmeen had worn only hours before.

He dismissed the question of how long it had it been since that robe had been washed and kept his focus on Rune. She had told him Finding was an imprecise art, combining a person's connection to their things and their intentions.

Once she belted the robe around her waist, Rune's expression shifted to distress.

"She was afraid." Her arms slipped around herself, as if against a freezing storm.

St. Benedict resisted pulling her into his own. His need to comfort her would only interfere with her work, and she would not thank him for it.

Then, Rune's eyes closed. "She was desperate. There was nowhere to run."

More power wafted off of Rune as she concentrated harder, pulsing which flared a headache behind his eyes, disappearing as fast as it appeared. She reached out a hand, and it drifted to lightly caress the tabletop. "She typed at her computer," she said as her own fingers moved like typing. Now he could do something. His ocular implant recorded the finger strokes and superimposed it onto a keyboard.

"Can you see what she is doing?" St. Benedict dared to ask.

Rune squinted and leaned forward to stare at nothing at the table. "I can't read it. It's just a bunch of code and... and it keeps wavering. It's really hard to read." Rune paused and turned once more to the empty chair in front of the spot.

But St. Benedict recognized it once his program finished translating the keystrokes. "She used a deep-web shield. It would be a big risk to reach out to anyone using her open network connection," St. Benedict said.

Rune sat down in Jasmeen's chair. Another wave of magic pulsed off her. That's when he noticed Rune's belt. She had worn it everywhere she went when she worked on behalf of Corinthe Corp. What caught his eye this time was that it glowed. Or rather the runes worked into the tooled leather of the belt itself and the attached pockets were alive and active, funneling beautiful strings of light through their grooves.

"That's new," he muttered.

"What is?" Rune asked.

"Your belt." He reached out two of his fingers to touch one of the channels. "I've never seen it—"

A warm rush of energy flowed up his fingers, cutting off his words. It was like he had just touched the end of a live wire, but Rune caught his hand. There was another shift, like a second live wire, but this one seemed to ... equalize. The intense, weird feeling bloomed into pain, so intense that it pulled a grunt that morphed into a cry.

"Turn off your augmentations!" he heard Rune cry through the pain. For an eternal second, he managed to wonder why she just didn't let him go.

Then he triple-blinked, bringing up his interface. "Emergency shutdown!" he said, gesturing with his other augmented hand in a series of gestures that looked like a one-sided handshake. The relief was immediate as everything other than the essential augmentations powered off.

Then he blinked his own eyes, unsure of what he saw. It was everything. And too much of everything. Rune, haloed in light. She was gorgeous, like a real Saint. Color had returned to her eyes, and they glowed with intense green and brown of grass and fresh earth at the edge of a river.

His free hand moved of its own volition, and he cupped her sweetheart face, drinking in the music that was her eyes.

They were in a telephone booth. He had the impression that this was the past, in a world that did not exist. Leaning forward, the energy raced between them. He wanted to kiss her, and he was going to, and he did.

Except he wasn't, he was just holding her face, stuck in a moment while living the past in the present. *I kissed you, and then...* His voice echoed, but he wasn't saying it; he heard it. *I shouldn't have done that.* He said *that* all those months ago after he had kissed her the first time. In the strange vision he was having, he saw that moment reverberating all around them.

This is Rune, he realized. He realized this was what Rune was thinking about when he was so close to her. He could see her now, could see how much she had wanted him to kiss her then and how hurt she had been when he had tried to take it back.

He'd never be attracted to a woman like me, he heard her think.

That's not true, he thought. Why couldn't he say it?

"You should let go now," Rune, the now-Rune, said sharply.

The weird vision blinked away, snapping him hard back into the actual present.

He wasn't holding her face at all, though their noses were dangerously close together. Instead, his fingers were gripped around her belt. Rune's eyebrows rose as her breath caught, or was that his breath?

Then she took a half step back. "Next time, don't grab onto my belt when I'm using it like that."

"What happened?" he asked, doing as she said and releasing his hold on the stiff leather. Her own hand had been clutching the top of his, and he realized she had been trying to get him to let go.

"When you grabbed on... I'm not sure, but you got locked into what I was doing, trying to see the past. I'm going to have to do some research on why, but you have to remember, I carry the entire power of my House within my belt. Touching a conduit of a wizard's house is like—"

"Grabbing onto a live wire," he finished for her, nodding. "Sorry. That was stupid." He withdrew himself and stood up straight.

"Yeah, it was," she agreed, standing up to remove the unwashed bathrobe before laying it over the back of the chair. "Or lucky. Did you see something we could use?"

"Ah, yes. Before I ... grabbed you." He flourished his hand open with a magician's pizzazz, and a holographic image of a globe floated above the palm. Then he spread the light open, forming a holodesk around himself in a semi-circle. Windows of light appeared before him as well as a keyboard. He immediately began typing the keystrokes he saw.

"How can you remember all that?" Rune asked, her voice filled with disbelief.

"It's the only thing I can't shut down, the augmentation that supports my short-term memory. It essentially makes me eidetic," he said, his fingers flying across the keys that were only there to him.

The screen in front of him filled up quickly. An icon of a digital mouse appeared on the edge of the desk, looking up at what he typed, cocking its little head curiously as it reared up on its back feet. Rune reached out a finger and attempted to poke

the little light mouse in its belly, only to have her finger pass through it. It still reacted to her touch, however, batting away at her with its free paws.

"There. That's everything," St. Benedict said, then he tapped the mouse icon on its little head. It swiveled its attention back to the screen and crawled up the invisible wall to dive into the window. As soon as it disappeared, little highlights appeared over different words, starting from the top to the bottom. "It's searching for keywords, but I think what is most relevant to us is right here," St. Benedict said while his program ran. Using two glowing fingers, he highlighted the sections of text he wanted and physically removed them from the doc, creating a copy that he then pasted into another window before slashing across it with three fingers to make the window spin around so Rune could read it the correct way.

"What is this?" Rune asked, leaning in.

"A messenger exchange on what I assume is a secured VPN server. Our Ms. Clarmont is not too unsavvy after all."

Rune's eyes scanned the exchange. "A secrets broker?"

"A real classy job title, huh?"

"Well, it does what it's supposed to, I suppose, because I have no idea what that is."

"That's because you're a good girl, at least up until recently. You've had no need for a secrets broker, but for people like Jasmeen who have run afoul of the corporate law and order, it can be a place of last resort," he answered smugly.

Rune narrowed her eyes at him. "Funny, I thought coming to the Lucky Devil for help had been her place of last resort."

He checked himself at that, tamping his smugness back into the corner where it belonged. "Yes. I suppose it was for her since she wasn't involved in the magical world much, but I could also argue that it was one of her last 'safe' options," he said, throwing up the air quotes around the word "safe." "This could get her just as killed as doing nothing and waiting for her company to seize everything and throw her out on the street. Or worse, haul her off to jail."

Rune's eyebrows pursed together hard. She knew just as well as he did what corporate jails really were and the horrors that happened there. "That makes no sense. She hasn't committed any crimes."

"She's broken her contract. Those things are entirely enforceable and in the eyes of her company, more-or-less criminal. It's one thing to try to jump ship, but what she's done here—running out on her contract? They can and will hunt her down if only to make an example of her. If she works with the wrong secrets broker, they'll help her and then sell that information to the company's bounty hunters for double the profit."

"Do all secrets brokers do this?" Rune asked.

He took a deep breath in, only debating for half a second not to tell her. "Yeah, they do. She's as good as dead."

"Unless we find her first," Rune said resolutely, meeting his gaze and daring him to argue with her.

CHAPTER 13

Rune lifted an eyebrow at St. Benedict's mobile phone. "Dead World?" she read out loud.

"Yup, Dead World," the Saint agreed, smirking.

Rune brimmed with derision. "We're going to find the entrance to a secret enclave of underground hackers using a mobile game?"

"How would you do it?" he asked, staring down at his screen, flicking through his alerts. "I haven't played in a while. This all got backlogged. Missed several new quests too." He glanced up at Rune, smiling his foxy grin at her. "What?"

"I guess I'm having a hard time reconciling with you playing video games," Rune said.

"You make me sound like I have no personality whatsoever," he said, mockingly wounded.

"You'd have to have a soul first," she shot back.

His eyebrows shot up. "Ow. Seriously, ow. Okay. Well, okay then. Just ow." He chuckled as he looked back down at the screen.

Rune couldn't help but chuckle back, realizing she may have zinged a little too hard but glad he was treating it as a joke. For a second there, it felt like how it used to before ... she lost her freedom. "So the plan is for you to play your game for a while until you find out where the location is for this place?"

"More or less." He continued scrolling through his notifications. It kept pinging every few moments.

"Thank you. That cleared things up nicely." Rune folded her arms and looked up and down the street. They were downtown in the Loop on S. Federal Avenue, a short street between Jackson and Wells that only existed in this two-block section. It had the least amount of traffic as most of the corporate drones were flooding down the main arteries of the Loop toward the various CTA buses or trains with a healthy flood heading down to the iconic Union Station to catch Metra trains out to the suburbs. Being on a side street didn't mean they were completely alone however, and she stepped out of the path of a pair of long coated suits as they blew past her like she didn't exist, too engrossed in their conversation to notice anything outside of themselves. Following their progress with her eyes brought Rune back to St. Benedict, who had stopped looking at his mobile phone, his gaze resting on her. Or at least she thought it rested on her. It was hard to tell since his eyes were opaque with the blue light that indicated he was using his augmented sight.

Then his eyelids fluttered into a triple blink, and the light dissipated to reveal his blue-green irises were indeed focused on her. "You wanna play too?" he asked, typing something quickly into his phone.

She re-cocked her eyebrow at that. "How?"

He glanced up and down the street. "Come with me."

They walked a few doors down until St. Benedict ducked into a shop with some pretty sophisticated tech displayed in the window. To Rune's surprise, no one alive seemed to be monitoring the place. Instead, there were several long display cases holding equipment within, all behind shatter-resistant

glass. None of this bothered St. Benedict as he walked up to one of the counters and waved his glowing tipped hand over the surface.

Obediently, a holographic display opened up above the counter. A huge list of all the products available popped up in square boxes with rounded corners, the images dancing inside as friendly elevator music played. With his two fingers, St. Benedict flicked right, dismissing the list for another, then skimmed down that list to stop over what looked to Rune to be a pair of sunglasses. There were three available ones, and he selected the last one, double tapping it. The other icons disappeared as the one he selected grew larger. Stats appeared beside the image, which rotated now in a slow circle, looking so real Rune wanted to reach out and touch them just to be sure they weren't. St. Benedict seemed to ignore the image as he scrolled down the stats. He read past the layman's English focusing on the specs list, which were just a whole bunch of numbers and letters that meant nothing to Rune.

"Yup, this is perfect," he said and double tapped a big friendly "Buy!" button. The display erupted into confetti, and an OmniSin reader rose out of the display case. Instead of a card, like the one Rune used, St. Benedict passed his hand over it, and the light turned from orange to blue. Rune was never quite sure if that meant that he was actually using his OmniSin or if he just hacked the thing to make it believe it had accepted a payment. Either way, it was enough to satisfy the reader, which sank back into the display case.

Then nothing.

"Um, what are we waiting for?" Rune asked after a long moment.

"For the product to come up from the back. It can take a few minutes," St. Benedict said. He checked his mobile game. "We should have time to get in on the next wave."

"The next wave of what?" Rune asked, not liking that he was making her play Twenty freaking Questions again, especially since she wasn't entirely sold that finding this underground hacker ring would lead them to finding Jasmeen.

St. Benedict leaned in to show her the map displayed on his mobile phone, just as a section of wall behind the counter slid to the side to reveal a... well a robot, rolling out.

It looked like a drink cart covered in the store's logos with treads instead of wheels and a small blinking light in one corner. On the top of the robot sat a box with the glasses pictured on the front. It stopped in front of its customers and lifted up its top, turning it into a tray that extended on two little hydraulic arms. The product slid onto the display case before the robot replaced its tray and retreated back the way it came.

St. Benedict immediately began to tear into the box, pocketing the power cord as he activated the glasses. Lights danced back and forth along the temples, the bar that went over the ears, flashing from red to orange down the rainbow spectrum to a dark purple, then back to red. Holding up his phone, St. Benedict seemed to be syncing the glasses to it. Then he handed them to Rune.

"Go ahead and put them on. You're all set," he said proudly.

Rune accepted the glasses but didn't put them on immediately. "How much did these cost?" she asked, examining them. They looked like a normal if pricey pair of sunglasses.

"Don't worry about it," St. Benedict dismissed.

"Oh crap, that expensive huh?" Rune correctly interpreted as she slid them on. Then she blinked and turned her head, gazing through the barely shadowy glass and not seeing anything different. Barely effective as a pair of actual sunglasses. "Okay, I don't get what the big deal is—"

A zombie leapt out at her from the doorway. She screeched and startled away, banging into St. Benedict. He caught her and raised one of his hands just in time, the tips glowing, launching something that looked like a disc of pure light straight at the creature. The light sliced through the zombie's neck, and the creature froze up, then collapsed to the ground before disappearing altogether in a burst of pixels.

"What the fuck was that?!" Rune shouted, tearing the glasses off her face to see what wasn't there.

"It's alright. It's just an augmented reality game. You're fine," St. Benedict said, sounding like he had really enjoyed her reaction.

She unabashedly smacked his arm. "You scared the hell out of me!"

He continued chuckling and held out two rings of soft rubbery plastic that had a pair of lights fixed in the middle, glowing much like his augmented fingers. "Here. Put this on. It'll be able to track your hand gestures and then you'll be able to slay zombies too."

She let him slip them on her fingers, pursing her lips at the whole set up. "I don't think I like this."

"It's a lot of fun. Don't worry. I'll show you," St. Benedict assured her.

This time when Rune slipped on the glasses, a menu appeared to her one side. Also in her hands, she could see what looked like a large machete. When she opened her hand, it dropped, then disappeared. "Where did it go?"

"Double-blink at the word menu at the bottom of your sight," St. Benedict instructed.

She did as told, and the block word "WEAPONS" flashed and was immediately replaced by a wheel of items. As she looked at them left and right, they scrolled by. Most of the slots were empty, but then the machete reappeared. She held up her hand, instinctively reaching to grab it. Her hand showed she had, but she still felt nothing... because of course she *was* grabbing nothing but air.

"Oh, this feels weird," she said as she flicked her arm back and forth, seeing but not feeling the machete move. "Like playing pretend."

"There is an accessory that gives you something to actually hold so you can feel it, one second," St. Benedict said, reopening the store menu to scroll for it. This product appeared a lot faster than the first one. It was just a black, rubber grip, but once St. Benedict put it in her hand, she could feel it grow heavy, giving her the sensation of holding a blade handle. "It'll change weights and shift itself, depending on what weapon you have selected within five pounds."

"Cool," she said and meant it.

A red indicator exclamation point flashed at the top of Rune's vision.

"Fresh horde is incoming," St. Benedict said, stepping up beside her, the lighted discs appearing in his hand. Outside the store, Rune saw what he meant. A horde of decaying bodies were shuffling along the sidewalk. They were equally grotesque and cartoony. Many were unrealistic colors: blue, green, purple, etc. A couple in the center were even shiny silver. "Don't worry about them. I'll take care of this bunch..."

"What?" was all Rune got out before he leapt forward and flung his discs of light at the first line passing through the door. The disc of light, to Rune's be-glassed perception, cut into two or three necks, dropping the zombies to the ground to disappear into be-pixeled nothingness. In place of the bodies, other stylized objects appeared, but St. Benedict ignored them. Rune couldn't get a clear look as they were obscured by more rotted legs passing through.

"And playing this game is going to help us find Jasmeen?" she asked dryly.

"Yup. A tip though: try to save the silver zombies for the end of a horde because they can double your experience earned." He stepped to the side to avoid a swipe. "Okay, I'm getting my butt kicked this way. You can switch to 'active mode' at any time. Using your phone screen is called 'public mode.' Do you see the flying eye to the left?"

"Yeah?" she said, turning her head, which just traced the icon to the left. "I see it. Now what?"

"Poke it with your glowing fingers when you want to switch modes; if it's open it's active mode. Closed is public mode. Okay, I need to get serious about this." Then he moved.

Now he fought with his whole body, the light discs

appearing in his hand as he ducked and wove through the mostly empty store. Instead of getting two or three hits, the discs would bounce four to five times. Not every hit dropped a zombie but within seconds, the whole horde had succumbed and disappeared save the two shiny silver ones. The discs of light bounced off of them, and St. Benedict switched weapons, this time holding an impossibly enormous hand-cannon, lifting it up with one hand as if it were made of air.

Which it was.

He cocked it like a real gun, grinned and fired. A purple-blue explosion erupted from the muzzle in a glittery ring as six shots blasted out to fly on their own trajectories, tearing through the silver zombies. One dropped to the ground and erupted into floating items, but the other continued its shamble. It reached out a hand toward St. Benedict's unflinching face, then Rune flung her machete at the zombie. The angle of the throw actually landed the overlong knife in the head of the silver game character, and it flopped to the side to explode like its companion did.

Surprised, St. Benedict looked toward Rune, his eyebrows disappearing beneath the brim of his fedora. She grinned and shrugged. "I think I get the idea."

Rune felt the thumping through the concrete long before she actually heard it. Through her new glasses, she could see bouncing lighted lines overlaying the grubby cement walls. "I'm getting the feeling that these glasses are really just for entertainment," she said dryly.

"You would not be wrong about that," St. Benedict agreed as he dismissed another floating window that tried to run parallel to them on the wall. It looked like some sort of pop-up advertisement. "But there is gold in them hills."

"So then what are we looking for?" Rune asked, following as she dismissed her own floating screen. There were also these little notifications that kept appearing at the top of her vision only to disappear just as fast. They looked like phone calls and messages, but since they were both linked to St. Benedict's phone, she ignored them as not her problem.

"I'll know it when I see it," he assured, flinging a silver disk at a singular straggler zombie coming around a corner.

They had been killing zombies for what felt like an hour, following some sort of trail that only St. Benedict could really decipher, and she was honestly starting to resent it. Periodically, she tried to reach out with her Finding for any small hint of Jasmeen, but the threads never brightened and only made her glasses stutter. Luckily, only she could see that, so she kept trying.

The second she got a glint of Jasmeen, she was ditching her unwelcome escort again.

"Ah, here we go. This way," St. Benedict said, taking a sudden turn down a refuse-bedecked alley. The short bit of dirty pavement framed by fire escapes and dumpsters screamed danger to her. St. Benedict strolled down it like he was walking in a park on a sunny day.

The unthinking confidence of men, she grumbled internally.

She flicked at the eye icon in the corner of her view, switching over to public mode, not wanting to be distracted by zombies in case real dangers jumped out at her.

They walked down about halfway, St. Benedict's blue glowing eyes scanning everything until he stopped to turn left.

"This is supposed to be an underground, secret ... thing?" she asked as St. Benedict led her down a flight of concrete stairs lined with pipes and darkness.

"Don't be worried. We'll be fine," he assured, turning back to offer her his hand, which she did not take.

"Look, don't get me wrong." She glanced forward into what appeared to be a tunnel into the building with no door on the front. The thumping dance music echoed out of it dully. "The atmosphere doesn't bother me at all. I've walked creepier, smellier, sinist-ier underground walkways before. It's just

incongruous, that's all."

"Incongruous?"

"I mean, how can they call themselves secret if they're also violating a noise ordinance or two?" She side-stepped a standing puddle of water at the bottom of the steps that looked like it was already in the process of supporting a tiny ecosystem.

St. Benedict chuckled as he waited for her to come up beside him. The hallway seemed to compensate for its low ceiling by being double wide.

"The thrill and excitement is part of the advertising. Come on, my lady." He offered her his crooked elbow, and she took it with a sigh.

"What is it?" he asked, picking up on her reaction.

"You're doing it again," she muttered.

He paused. "Doing what?"

"Controlling the situation by controlling the information," Rune stated, pulling her arm away from his grasp. "You won't tell me what we're looking for. You're just making me dependent on you for the information, so I won't ditch you again."

He stopped then, his blank blue eyes staring at her face. Then he triple-blinked, making them disappear so she could see his real eyes, now clearly pinched, the space between them puckering. "I…" But he didn't finish. Instead, he licked his lips, then snorted a breath of air.

"Okay, then," and he brandished his hands before himself and gestured. Immediately, a holodesk appeared in a tight circle around himself. The move reignited his eyes. He took a half step forward, then paused. "Do I have your permission to come close? You need to be inside the circle for me to show you."

Surprised, but curious, Rune nodded. He came up behind her then, though maintained a breath of space between their bodies. His holodesk resettled so that it was in front of her. With a few quick gestures, he brought up a snapshot of the zombie game. In the picture was one of the floating icons, a circle with a briefcase shape floating within. "Alright, you know how we've been spinning these icons to get items?"

"Yeah," Rune acknowledged, leaning in to look at the picture closer. St. Benedict spun two fingers in front of the image clockwise once, and the image began playing like a video. His hand in the played-back memory appeared to spin the icon. Actual St. Benedict then tapped the playback once to make it stop.

"Did you see it?" he asked.

Rune narrowed her eyes. "Play it again."

He repeated his gesture, starting the video from the beginning. She leaned in closer, and that time she saw the superimposed image popping out of the lines the animation made as it spun. It was another icon next to a very clear pointing arrow. "What is it?"

"A scarab. And an arrow giving directions," St. Benedict said, gesturing wide with both hands to make the holodesk disappear from around them.

"So that's what you've been following?" Rune asked, putting it together. She readjusted her glasses, which still showed her the glowing lines and icons of the game but casting none of that light on the dim walls of the underground hallway.

"It's not in the same place, but yeah, someone distributed the clues all throughout the game. Just keep looking for that scarab and something that indicates direction, and we can find the hacker group."

"Why couldn't you just tell me that before?" she challenged, noticing an in-game icon at the end of the hall floating in a slow, lazy circle. She switched back to active mode so she could go over to it to smack instead of waiting for an answer.

She was surprised when she got one. "You were right. I was holding it back so you wouldn't ditch me," he confessed.

A couple of items floated out of the icon in little animated bubbles, but she didn't bother attempting to pop them. They would pop on their own and populate in her game's inventory either way. Rather, she focused on the spinning icon. Sure

enough, once it was in motion, she could see the scarab sitting atop the long body of an arrow. She turned back to him, still standing with his arms at his side, eyes looking like they were waiting for her judgement.

She licked her lips. "I won't ditch you as long as you help me find Jasmeen," she said. "But if you try to stop me—"

"It's your call," he said, interrupting whatever she was about to threaten. It didn't matter. She didn't really know if she had a credible threat, but whatever it had been was gone from her brain under the gaze of his emotionally naked face.

"I'm not leaving her out here to get taken by Kodiak," Rune stated to make sure they were clear.

St. Benedict nodded. "Like I said, it's your call. I'll follow your lead."

She took in a big breath of cold, fetid air and sighed. "Alright then." She spun the icon again, this time extending a finger into the animation to see... just to see...

"What are you doing?" St. Benedict asked with genuine curiosity.

"I'm wondering if this is like the business cards. Someone left this here with the intention that they be found, so..."

"Maybe you can use your magic on it to Find a more direct route to them," he finished when she didn't.

But try as she might, her finger just didn't interact with the actual icon. "No good," she muttered, disappointed. "All I feel is air. I suppose it technically is on another plane of existence. The digital realm." She spoke that last bit with a spooky flair. St. Benedict's grin reached his eyes.

"Scavenger hunt it is then," and he offered her the crook of his arm to take just as a zombie alarm rang out.

Rune threw her digital machete in what was becoming her signature move at a slobbering creature just past St. Benedict's shoulder. She moved past to face the onslaught spawning at the end of the hall.

"First things first."

CHAPTER 14

Getting into the improvised club turned out to be fairly easy. The bouncer at the door passed a reader over Rune's OmniSin and St. Benedict's augmented hand and let them into the writhing chaos beyond when it blinked blue. Rune didn't want to know how much he'd just paid to get past the door.

"Holy crap," Rune said, though she couldn't even hear it herself.

Bodies of all types were writhing in a mass of lights that painted them every color of the rainbow and several in between. The space itself must have been a warehouse at one time, but now it was home for the dancing crowd, the DJ's nest on a stage at one end and the overworked bar on the other.

When they entered the pop-up club, Rune slipped the glasses up to the top of her head, so she wasn't distracted as they tried to enter, and doing that made the game pause automatically. Now that they were through, she pulled them back down to her nose.

"You shouldn't do that in here. It might be a little much!" St. Benedict tried to say, his voice getting swallowed by the music, but Rune waved him off.

"It's no different than trying to use my Seeing sight!" she dismissed, shouting.

And it was. Overlaying the chaos of the room were the additional icons from the game, floating and totally unaffected by the actual colored lights passing over them. A reality on top of a reality. "At least we're not moving forward and backward through time!"

"We're going to need drinks to do that!" he quipped, then seized her hand in his own. "Come on!"

They wove through the crush of bodies, only staying together by their resolute determination to hang on. To Rune's surprise, there seemed to be other people playing the game even here. The game itself highlighted those people with a floating white light above them that had different avatar icons to represent the players below for ease of co-op gaming.

"What do you want to drink?" Rune thought she heard St. Benedict say, though it was based more off her interpretation of his gestures toward the bar.

"I don't," she shouted back. The last thing she wanted right then was to have her senses dulled.

St. Benedict motioned to insist but gave up when Rune waved him down, so he shrugged and attempted to flag down one of the two bartenders. They were rushing around trying to make drinks fast enough to keep the crush of people from overwhelming their bar. It was all chaos and noise, so Rune turned back to cast an eye over the back wall of the bar. She didn't expect to spot a scarab, printed on one of the labels on a liquor bottle against the back wall.

She chuckled. It was something Maddie would do.

Wapping at St. Benedict's arm, she pointed it out.

He narrowed his eyes in the dimness before popping them open wide in understanding. By that time, the bartender had come to them, and St. Benedict gestured at the bottle. The bartender nodded but didn't turn around to retrieve it. Instead, he reached under the bar itself and pulled out two smaller versions of the bottle, which he uncapped in a smooth motion from the bottle opener concealed in his hand, along with a key with a chunk of wood bolted to it. He set both on the bar and gestured for St. Benedict's OmniSin, which he scanned, then moved on. St. Benedict handed Rune one of the bottles and grabbed the other with the key. They moved away from the bar to a spot along the wall that actually had some space, beneath one of the red lights. There he held up the block of wood. Someone had written two words across it: "Family Bathroom."

St. Benedict looked up to scan around, but Rune touched the oversized token. Instantly, her head whipped to just down the wall. She touched St. Benedict's shoulder and indicated. He nodded and took a swig from his bottle. Surprised, Rune did as well and found a heavy dark lager within. It was surprisingly good.

They drifted to the door through some gyrating bodies. At one point, someone made a grab for Rune, a strong hand around her waist to pull her in to a dance. She tried to escape, but the guy wrapped his other hand around her and wouldn't let go, grinding against her hip. His face moved wetly closer to hers.

Then St. Benedict was there, basically shoulder checking the guy as he got his own hands on Rune. Her non-consenting dance partner seemed surprised and confused at the intrusion. The guy gave an ineffectual "Hey!" that no one could hear over the music, but by that time, St. Benedict had stepped in closer and kept backing them both up and away.

Rune didn't mind. With the crush of bodies around them, she would rather be pressing into one she knew. She tried to walk backward to escape the crowd, but the pressure of St. Benedict's hand against her back stopped her. Looking up, she met his eyes—and caught her breath.

He was doing it again, that intense feeling that made her think he maybe wanted her but could also be a manipulation.

She just wanted to pull away and hide, but then his lips formed the words, "Dance with me?"

Shyness made her drop her head, but she started gyrating her hips tentatively to the all-encompassing beat of the music. His own body met hers, matching her rhythm, her pace. The song warped into something slower and grindier. Rune slid her hands up St. Benedict's chest, just under his coat, to wrap around the back of his neck. She could feel how much he was sweating underneath, but she didn't mind that so much. He pressed his face into her hair and bent lower, gyrating deeper, and she smiled in spite of herself.

This is so silly, she thought but retreated from that idea. His own eyes were closed, and he seemed to be enjoying the dance. Enjoying touching her, being close to *her*. She had to admit, it was so good to feel his strong, lean body pressing against hers.

Eventually, she stopped when her back bumped into the wall. St. Benedict cupped her body with his own. It caught her breath, and she tilted her head up, believing he was about to kiss her. She was shocked to find she wanted him to. She had wanted it for so long.

Then another hand slapped the wall beside her, not connected to either of them. St. Benedict shifted again, blocking another, wilder dancer who made up with enthusiasm what he lacked in skill.

"Are you alright?" St. Benedict asked, his lips close to her ear so she could hear him. She nodded, recapturing the tug of her magic. Then she grabbed his head to turn his ear toward her own lips. "It's just over there a few feet to my left," she said. He nodded, but before she released him, she stuck her tongue in his ear.

His whole body flinched and spasmed. An involuntary, indiscreet moan escaped him and the guy dancing too close startled at it, then moved away.

"Okay, the way is clear," she said, releasing him.

The look he gave her was equal measures intense and chiding as he realized what she had done.

She just returned a very smug smile back at him. "I've learned a lot from you Saints," she shouted at his ear as she turned to move along the wall to get to the door.

It didn't look like much of a normal door, being double wide, basically one large slab of metal. There was an industrial-sized doorknob with a slot for a key which turned easily once inserted.

A pair of drunks wavered by, one holding up a hand to St. Benedict to high five. The other howled for them to "have fun in the 'family bathroom.'" Both idiots fell over each other laughing.

"Oh great," Rune muttered, then thought, *Now I have that image in my head,* ignoring the fact that it had already taken up residence. They entered the quieter bathroom, and St. Benedict slammed the door shut to lean against it.

Inside the bathroom... well it wasn't exactly a bathroom. The walls were half-tiled like it had been one in a previous life, but instead of the usual toilet or sink, there was a simple shelf underneath a mirror flanked by two florescent lights. On the mirror, someone had written with what looked like red lipstick, "Deposit Key Here" and an equally red arrow pointed down to the shelf. A dozen other blocks of wood-laden keys already sat there. Beside the shelf was an opening that someone had sledgehammered into the wall and fixed a set of metal stairs leading down. Electric lights illuminated the bottom at least a floor down. It was enough to see by.

"This way?" Rune asked.

"Yup," St. Benedict confirmed and took point.

"This seems a little much," she commented.

"A little much?" her escort inquired, following behind her as she went down the stairs.

"All this elaborate subterfuge. It's very..."

"What?"

"Spy movie?"

St. Benedict chuckled. "Everyone wants to be sexy and mysterious. Even underground hackers."

"You'd think 'underground hackers' would be enough."

"The most effective hacking is some of the most boring, undramatic work imaginable. Not exactly something Hollywood can easily make a movie about. At least, not one anyone wants to actually see." He said the last as they reached the bottom of the stairs.

Rune stopped and stared at the room they entered. It was much like the Praetorium, in that there were consoles everywhere in the open warehouse space, with different little clusters of computers. Various, mismatched carpets had been laid out, overlapping each other and overlapping various, vinelike cords to cut down on tripping.

"So this is a hub room," Rune muttered.

Like its twin above, this bar was another cobbled-together rectangle. Dance lights beamed straight up at various intervals and neon signs twisted behind, illuminating the various bottles. Unlike above, the place had a solemn quiet over it like a library with only the faintest thump-thump-thump of the party still raging on the floor above them.

She reached into her pocket, grasping the business card left by Jasmeen. Extending her Finding magic, she focused on Jasmeen's intention within the paper. Sure enough, a gold thread snapped into being, but it hovered with no clear direction to go.

Which was odd.

In response to the magic, though, a wave washed over the room, making monitors blink for a second. Immediately, Rune killed it, and the wave stopped. People reacted, grumbling and muttering, but everyone also took it in stride and returned to what they were working on.

"Can't do that," she decided.

"They're probably used to it. They're hijacking power from elsewhere and using the party upstairs to disguise it," St. Benedict said softly.

"Are they playing Dead World?" Rune asked, pointing over to an area nearby where figures seemed to be moving among the metal building supports, slashing and dancing about each other, all wearing glasses like hers. The carpets didn't reach that far, leaving that area with open and cracked concrete.

"Probably, but there are a few other games that are popular right now," St. Benedict said. "These hubs are usually run by one specific person, usually an information broker of some sort or another. We may not find anything, but we can start a search."

"Doing it the tech way," Rune muttered. "But that is the way Jasmeen probably would have gone if she wanted to try to change her name and disappear?"

"Really dangerous, but she may have been desperate enough," St. Benedict agreed.

"Sitting in her apartment and doing nothing would have been dangerous too right now," Rune stated, moving toward the makeshift bar since they couldn't just keep standing in the doorway forever. "Maybe she got a heads-up somehow about the attack."

"Nothing about her situation is ideal," he agreed again as he shadowed her.

"Not even the people trying to save her," Rune muttered.

No one looked up as they crossed. She supposed that since they had entered in properly, everyone present just assumed they had every right to be there. The place was so calm that the bartender had already positioned herself to intercept them as they approached. To Rune's surprise, the bartender turned out to be an Ogress with LED caps on the ends of her tusks and strands of LED lights woven into the braids of her hair.

"I see you already have drinks from above, but can I get you anything else?" the Ogress asked politely, setting a pair of menus before the newcomers. "The kitchen is open all-night too if you'd like to order food."

St. Benedict immediately slid the food menu over to himself, and Rune's own stomach growled at the realization that it had been a long time since she last ate. She glanced over her shoulder and noticed that there was a distinct lack of prices on anything.

"How much for the crab cakes?" she muttered, skimming through the descriptive text, trying to pick out numbers among the words.

"All food is complementary," the Ogress recited.

St. Benedict leaned over and whispered to Rune, "This place charges a fortune by the hour for the terminals, and they include food. Within reason." He turned back to meet the bartender's steady gaze.

She nodded tiredly. "Yes, within reason," she confirmed.

"Fine, I'll have the crab cakes," Rune said.

"Okay, good," St. Benedict agreed. "And I ... need a few more minutes." He continued studying the menu like it was a map to great treasure.

Rune sighed. "While he's looking, can I ask if you've seen someone come through here?"

The bartender leaned a hand against the bar, propping the other on her hip. "Are you corp cops? Or the sheriff's department?" the Ogress asked, though there was no hostility in the question, only fact gathering.

"Neither, ma'am," St. Benedict stated, equally as matter of fact.

The Ogress snapped some bubble gum that she had apparently been holding in her mouth as she measured them for truthfulness.

Rune continued to meet her eye for eye. "There's someone we're trying to find, so we can help her."

"Well, I don't know her," the Ogress said, swiping the bar with her rag.

"But I didn't even tell you who I'm looking for," Rune noted.

"I'm aware," the Ogress challenged.

"Look, you need to understand, I am ... the Heir of the Magdalene. I'm just trying to help her." But that didn't invoke the reaction Rune had hoped for.

Instead, the bartender crossed her arms. "Just because I am an Ogre doesn't mean I have anything to do with the magical community," she stated in cold, clipped tones.

"Oh," was all Rune could say to that as she stared perplexed with her mouth literally gaping open and closed as she struggled to come up with some coherent thought.

"Do you prefer the Irish nachos or the Tex-Mex nachos? This version seems to have the real queso instead of that artificial cheese stuff," St. Benedict piped in, pointing out the two selections from the menu.

Rune paused to glance over at the menu. "Uh, Tex-Mex…"

"Sour cream?" he asked.

"Sure."

"Okay. Can *I* ask you a favor?" the Saint asked, turning the question to the bartender, who now had her own look of uncertainty deflating her bristle.

"Yeah?" she replied.

"Can we get extra sour cream on the side? And a couple more of this divine beer?" He took a swig from the bottle to make his point.

The Ogress pulled out a number tab and stabbed it into a standing twist of metal made for that purpose, leaving it to twang on the bar. "I'll be right back," she snarled, slapping the towel off her shoulder, smacking it on the edge of the bar. She disappeared into the back, and the other bartender at the opposite end gave a worried glance the way his partner went, then went back to ignoring the offending customers.

Rune leaned on the bar. "Alright," she said, sighing. "I am open for suggestions."

"It was worth a try," St. Benedict said. "Person to person information gathering, while it can be less reliable, is also harder."

"I don't need a pat on the head. I need actionable information. Can you provide me that?" she snapped.

His spine stiffened. "Yes, yes I can." He killed his bottle, picked up the number stand, and scanned the room before gesturing at an open terminal. "There."

While most of the terminals were clusters of four, this one

happened to be a cluster of three. The open terminal had its back facing the wall. "Just the way you like it," Rune noted as St. Benedict dropped into the worn and cracked black leather of the obviously purloined office chair. It squeaked noisily as he settled in and flipped on the monitor mounted in front of him. The monitor itself seemed to be suspended on an adjustable arm. With ease, the augmented man did his magician's trick and ignited his hand to pass over an OmniSin reader fixed to the desk. It beeped blue, and the whole apparatus came to life.

"Not the comforts of home, but it will do," he noted, then snagged a spare office chair to pull it closer. The person in the terminal facing east from their north eyed them both for stealing his extra commodity.

St. Benedict flashed him a smile. "You're not using this, right?" he asked with too many teeth.

The neighbor beside them opened his mouth to object, eyed St. Benedict's hat and glowing blue eyes, which had come on when he had paid their fee, then thought better of it. Instead, he turned back to his screen without answering.

Satisfied, the Saint pulled the seat up closer and patted it for Rune to sit down next to him. He then stuck the number stand on top of his monitor, which turned out to have a suction cup on the bottom for exactly that purpose and proceeded to type with that unnerving level of speed that always flummoxed Rune.

Not knowing what else to do, Rune leaned back in her acquired chair and crossed her arms. She didn't have to wait long.

"Alright," the Saint said, pausing in his work, still speaking in their library-level tones. "I've put out an inquiry for any information about our target, and we'll see what we get back."

"So what do we do now?"

"We wait, get something to eat, maybe play some more Dead World?"

CHAPTER 15

After disintegrating the last zombie from the sixth horde she had encountered, Rune logged out of the game to go finish her crab cakes at St. Benedict's station. She had actually been having some fun, and honestly, it had been a while since she had done anything truly for fun. Her existence since getting arrested and handed over to Corinthe had consisted of work and magical studies.

No getting out socially and very little activity that wasn't work. She hadn't admitted it to herself, but she had gotten weary.

But I'm technically a prisoner, so it only made sense, right? I'm not supposed to have fun. I'm lucky enough to still see the light of day and have the gilded cage I do at the Praetorium. The weight of those thoughts encroached as she took her seat next to the Saint, who in a lot of ways shared the same fate as herself. No wonder he showed up at her bar so often before.

St. Benedict continued to stare at the screen, filing through lines of code in a sort of language that Rune herself didn't understand at all. He had come and played with her for a couple rounds after they had been initially served their food before getting a series of calls from the Praetorium with urgent questions. Apparently, he had been getting the calls the entire time he had been with her and had to catch back up with anyone who had wanted his attention.

"Can I ask you a question?" She popped a delicious piece of the crab cake she had ordered into her mouth.

He held up one finger to ask for a moment, then typed something really quickly and exaggeratedly hit enter as he sat back to regard her with his opaque blue eyes.

"I swear the Praetorium would erupt into flames without me," he muttered, then laced his fingers over his stomach and smiled. "Okay, go ahead."

"Are you free to leave the Praetorium? I mean, you're not really a prisoner there, right?"

At the question, he fingered the Saint Box Rune knew he wore under his shirt at all times. Or most times, since there had been an incident or two where he gave it to her as a way to Find him again. She gestured at it. "I mean, I know that keeps you bound to Maxamillion more or less, but you're not like me, right? You're not an inmate. You can just leave whenever you want."

"Technically, so can you," he noted.

Rune cocked her head to the side and narrowed her eyes. "No, not really. I only get to leave the Praetorium when I'm hired out on a gig."

"Or when you're using magic to escape to go save a ... previous client."

They both exchanged sickly smiles.

St. Benedict broke first, readjusting himself in his seat. "You're not an inmate, Rune. Maybe Maxamillion didn't say it, but we're not 'holding' you. I did what I did to save you—"

"I'm aware of that, thank you," she said tersely. "I understand the logic of all of this, how I came to be in this position, and what the alternatives could have been, okay? But you're also still wrong. I'm still a prisoner."

St. Benedict's smile didn't disappear, but it was as wooden as a puppet's. "Only on paper. But you know, don't take my word for it. Talk to Maxamillion when you next get the chance. See what he says."

Thankfully, an alert sounded on the computer screen, ending what turned out to be a tense exchange.

"Is that what we've been waiting for?" Rune asked, leaning in to peer at it.

The Saint scooted closer, tapping at his keyboard to bring up the alert. "Oh yes, indeed. We got ourselves a fishy." His voice drifted off as he read the screen. A text box appeared, and he typed a few exchanges back and forth.

"What's happening?" Rune finally asked when she could take it no more.

"Negotiating," he muttered. "This guy thinks he's a big shot."

"Negotiating what?" Rune pressed, leaning in closer to read the screen.

"There's an information broker who apparently ... sold our target a new identity, and he is willing to share with us the same information for a prince's ransom."

"You've got to be kidding?" Rune asked, disgusted.

"I know. Who does he think we're looking for? The Next American Pop Star?"

Rune closed her eyes. "You're negotiating with him, aren't you?"

"Don't worry. I'll take care of this," he said and kept typing. "We've got all kinds of wiggle room."

"Sure," she replied dryly, "it's not like there is a woman's life on the line, and we've been hanging out here too long, playing video games."

Her partner didn't respond as he focused on his negotiations. Stressed, Rune sat back in her seat and stuck her hands in her pockets. She had let him do this to her again, made it so that he controlled the flow of information she needed to complete *her* mission. As her fingers quested for something to

fiddle with, they encountered Jasmeen's card. She could feel the intention burning within it, begging for a slip of power to enable her to Find whomever it was that helped the office worker attempt to escape—an attempt that proved useless since the one who helped her was immediately betraying her to the highest bidder. Jasmeen was in so much danger.

As Rune fingered the card, she remembered that her power had worked when she had tried to invoke it earlier. She had been seeking out where Jasmeen was now, but they were in a place that Jasmeen probably had been, hence why the magic hadn't had anywhere to go. But it had detected something of Jasmeen. It could mean the person they sought was somewhere in that very room. Rune's heart began to pound, and she let her gaze slide around the space.

"I'm going to go get another drink," she said to St. Benedict, who nodded but didn't look up as he typed.

Standing, Rune kept her hand in her pocket and walked toward the bar. She didn't need much, just a specific direction. With the tiniest fraction of power, she invoked the Finding. There was a pull, an invisible pull that indicated a direction. The computers around her didn't seem to notice her magical intrusion into their world, and she changed her own steps to follow her new lead. As she passed the first cluster of terminals, she did her trick again. The pull continued forward, and so did she. The screens blipped the tiniest flicker, but nothing that the people focusing on them even noticed. Same happened when she passed a second cluster of terminals, this set tucked in the opposing corner from where St. Benedict had set up station.

A few more pulses from the paper steered Rune to a lone figure sitting in the opposing corner. He was round of face and round of body with a mess of hair that seemed like it wanted to be a beard but hadn't fully committed yet. Thick glasses perched on a splayed nose that also had a small slit in one of the nostrils, like he had a nose ring at one time which had been torn out.

Luckily, there was an empty chair a few feet from him, strangely abandoned with no station needing its chair quota filled. Rune spun it to face her quarry and slid it over. He didn't even notice her until she plopped down into it with a casual confidence she actually felt.

"Who the hell..." He startled, looking her up and down as his face fought to figure out which emotion it wanted to go with at her sudden appearance.

"Hello there. The Devil has come to collect her due."

The hacker stared at Rune with a pale blankness as if his brain had shut down completely. The long silence between started to become awkward.

"You can't be here," he finally said. Actually, he nearly shouted it, which drew some annoyed glances from the two others working nearby.

Rune raised her eyebrows at that declarative statement but didn't uncross her arms or move to leave. "You provided an alternate identity to a desperate woman named Jasmeen Clarmont."

A couple of wide-eyed blinks were her answer, so she just kept going. "After providing that alternate identity, you let her go on her merry way. You maybe never even met her in person, but you took her money, didn't you? Money she probably couldn't afford, but that wasn't enough. Now you are selling her secret to the highest bidder in order to increase the amount you earned off of this woman's desperation."

"You..." the hacker finally squeaked out. Apparently, his brain was almost complete with its reboot. Though, Rune wondered if her metaphor might not be a metaphor. She knew St. Benedict had a computer in his brain, but how widespread or available was that sort of augmentation?

Whichever it was or not, the human part of the hacker started to shake, lifting an accusing finger. "You can't be here. No one is supposed to—"

"Do I look like I care about supposed to?" she snapped, her anger at the whole situation bleeding through. "Believe me, the worst has already happened to me so I don't fear a whole awful lot right now."

"How did you find me!?" the hacker growled. "You shouldn't have been able to trace me—"

Before he could finish completing his first sentence, Rune opaqued her eyes, making them glow pure white. "Do I look like someone who needs a trace to find you?"

The hacker shifted away, and the others at his terminal finally noticed, their monitors going frizzy as Rune's power aura rose.

"Goddamn Talents," the guy with headphones cursed, getting up with his laptop and moving away from the disturbance. The other two went slower but did the same, packing up their gear to vacate what was obviously becoming an altercation. "You still think you have all the power."

Feeling whatever safety the other hackers provided abandoning him, the one in Rune's sights panicked and stood up, though whether to run or ask for help was uncertain.

"Sit down," Rune barked, still not having stood up from her chair. The only real change she had invoked was her voice now thrummed with a weight of power, the strange slight echo that translated and intimidated the little hacker in front of her. At least, it seemed like it did because he obeyed, sitting back into his chair.

"You... You can't ... do this," he said softly, almost like he was pleading now.

Rune toned back the power infusion, letting her eyes return to normal. "Jasmeen Clarmont. You are going to tell me where she went, and you are not going to give me trouble about it."

At that, the hacker's upper lip twisted into a snarl. "I don't have to do a damn thing."

Rune sensed St. Benedict before he arrived, moving up to the opposite side of the hacker just as the same man made to stand again. He landed a heavy hand on the man's shoulder, pressing him back down into his chair. The caught quarry obeyed, his eyes bugging out even wider.

"Compadre the hacker," St. Benedict purred. "Imagine seeing you again. And here I was trying to run a trace right across the room."

"S-s-st. Benedict," the hacker stuttered. Unconsciously, he plucked at the tear in his nose with thick fingers, and Rune could imagine that the scar had been created by the Saint.

"Of course, you already know him," she sighed, keeping her seat while she let her partner do the intimidating.

The hacker looked between the two of them. "Oh god, you work for him?" He jutted his thumb back at St. Benedict.

"Actually, I work for her, and I believe she gave you an order," St. Benedict answered first, squeezing on the guy's shoulder.

"Okay, okay. But not here, please. You're already damaging my rep," Compadre pleaded. "We got private rooms. Please, we can go there. I'll tell you anything you want to know."

"Your call," St. Benedict said, directing the last to Rune, who arched an eyebrow. He didn't answer her silent question, only waited patiently.

"Alright, fine. Private room it is."

"Okay, okay," Compadre said, reaching for his keyboard. "Just let me log out first."

"Nope," Rune said, and St. Benedict seized his hands before he could touch it. "St. Benedict, log him out."

The Saint obeyed her order, and the hacker continued to alternate between pouting and growling. The rest of the room was entirely disinterested in what was going on, everyone keeping their eyes on their own screens and in their own business. Only the bartenders noted anything, and they made no move to intercede.

"All done here," St. Benedict said once the monitor went black, and he had reached down to unplug the whole unit just to be sure. "Lead the way, Compadre."

"Shut up. That's not my handle anymore. Not after you and Max X burned it." The hacker got up sullenly without further prompting from St. Benedict, though "leveraged" might have been the better word for it.

The hacker formerly known as Compadre's bulk was far more apparent once it distributed itself on his frame. "This way," he said, snatching a Maestro Bigger Gulp cup from a cup holder sticking out of the monitor station that Rune hadn't noticed before. He lumbered and they followed, making their way down the wall to an innocuous metal door with a reinforced glass window in it. He stopped with his hand on the handle and then looked at St. Benedict, waiting.

"Hey, this is your shakedown," the hacker said. "I'm not paying for it."

At that, St. Benedict passed his hand over the small black box beside the door. Its light blinked-on blue, and the door unlocked as the room's light turned on automatically. A computer rig sat inside with its own overly cushioned captain's chair. As far as Rune could see, it was the same as the set-ups out in the main hall. It was just in its own private room.

"The whole place is soundproof," the hacker formerly known as Compadre said, then noticed Rune still in the entryway, "when the door is closed."

She came the rest of the way in and shut it. Sure enough, the ambient noises from the next room were gone, along with the sounds of the rave party above that she had grown ear-deaf to. The hacker sniffed, satisfied. As he pulled up to the terminal, however, he found himself shoved and rolled back hard against the wall by St. Benedict who took control of the set-up.

"Nope. You tell me where to go."

More swearing in Spanish, but the Saint ignored it as he brought the rig to life.

Rune crossed her arms again and leaned against the door. "We know Jasmeen reached out to you for help. What exactly did she ask for?"

"Better answer her, Compadre," St. Benedict warned. "Password key?"

"It's not Compadre anymore, I told you. It's the Jade Scarab."

"Your new handle or the password?" St. Benedict asked.

"Both," Jade Scarab said.

That earned him a derisive look from the Saint.

"What?" Jade Scarab took a long sip from his Gulp cup. "We can't all have cool, pre-packaged code names just handed to us. Jade Scarab has a decent reputation now because I didn't sell out like some assholes we know."

"What's he talking about?" Rune asked, directing the question at St. Benedict.

"He used to be part of Maxamillion's original crew when he was still an underground punk revolutionary."

Jade Scarab spat. "Before he turned corporate sellout."

"Before he got smart," St. Benedict said softly as his focus became absorbed by the windows that auto opened on the screen.

"Smart, my ass." Jade Scarab started playing with the straw, making it hum an annoying squeak as he tugged it up and down.

"At least he didn't give up on the cause." St. Benedict took a step back from where he was hunched. "My god, Compadre, how many different deals you got going on here? Blackmail, contraband, illegal downloads?"

"I am an information broker," the hacker said with an edge of pride. "I find things that people want and get them to those that can pay the most. It's an honest living."

"It's anything but," St. Benedict sneered. "You're a parasite living off this city's infection."

"That's right because that's all there is! This society is a rotting corpse, and all that's left is—"

"Yes, yes, you're both very poetic," Rune cut in, having had enough of the pontificating. "Give us everything you did for Jasmeen and a list of everyone you've sold that information to. Or rather give him..." She gestured at St. Benedict, then said to her Saint, "Better you make a copy, right? We don't want to linger here longer than we have to."

St. Benedict nodded and saluted. "Exactly."

Jade Scarab panicked, pressing forward to lay a hand over

the screen as if that would stop what was happening. "You can't! That's my entire work! You can't just take it!"

Now St. Benedict's eyebrow shot up. "A whole trove of secrets, is it?" He crossed his arms, smiling wickedly as he leaned against the rig desk, pushing the monitor out of Jade Scarab's hand since it was only suspended by the armature. Jade Scarab whimpered as it went, clearly understanding how screwed he was. Rune supposed his entire ability to operate with so much dangerous and costly information was because no one would normally be able to find him. His protection had been in his anonymity. Rune might have felt compassion toward him, but Jasmeen's terrified face slipped through her thoughts.

"Take it all," she said coldly.

"What! No!" Jade Scarab cried, but St. Benedict didn't even hesitate. He turned his back to the portly hacker and triple-blinked his visual augmentation to opaque his eyes blue. Immediately, he seemed to be downloading, screens opening and closing in flashes on the monitor screen, as St. Benedict's long piano-man fingers flew over the keyboard.

Too fearful to attack St. Benedict from behind, the Jade Scarab turned in his chair to Rune, pleading. "Please, you can't do this to me."

She cocked her head at him. "What do you say to people who say the same thing to you?" she asked.

He furrowed his brows into an ugly rage. "I *help* people! I help people when no one else can or will. If they didn't have me, they'd have nobody!"

"You feed off of people. It's far from the same thing," Rune spat. Then she remembered. "Who else have you sold Jasmine's information to?"

His eyes flexed wide, then flitted between her, the door, the clock over the door, and back to her.

He's waiting for something, Rune intuitively thought. *Those hunting for Jasmeen?*

"Did she tell you that we were trying to help her?" Rune

asked the hacker. His eyes went wider.

In that moment, she realized the trap.

"Saint B—" was all she got out.

Then there was a fantastic boom outside the room followed by shouts and screams.

Her Saint went for the door, looking out the small window. "It's a raid."

"A police raid?" Rune asked.

"Doesn't matter. Big soldiers with big guns, and we need to go."

He opened the door, and Rune came up just inside his guard as they both exited the small room, leaving Jade Scarab behind. Rune knew they needed a way out. Even as people scattered throughout the large room, there were only a couple of official exits out of the place, and they were filling up with armed bodies. They needed an unofficial way out.

Rune called up her sight and threw out her magic, focusing on one intention: escape.

A scatter of gold threads slashed out into the room, many very small, but three solid gold ones as thick as twine popped into existence. She grabbed one that took them along the warehouse wall and seemed the closest. "This way," she said, and without questioning, St. Benedict followed.

His eyes remained opaqued, scanning around them, assessing for the nearest dangers.

She would let him focus on that while she focused on escape.

They skimmed along the wall, following her thread as shouting echoed. To her surprise, the thread bent around a corner. It didn't normally do that. Most of the time when she tried to Find something, the threads just went directly to the person or thing, and she was left to figure out how to get from A to B. This was something new, and there was no time to study it.

Following her strange thread, she went around the corner into a square area that looked like it had once been intended as a loading dock for large shipping trailers. Slanted ramps led down to two enormous doors, large enough for a pair of semis to fit through parallel and not encounter each other. Both the Finder and the Saint eyed the enormous doors and could instantly tell that they weren't going to open in the time frame they needed, even if they could locate the controls to do it.

Instead, Rune headed for a human-sized door next to the enormous ones. She hadn't seen it at first because it had been painted the same beige as the walls. But her lighted thread went straight through it, the more normal thing for her magic to do. Feeling more on solid ground now, she ran up to it. A darkened, hatched-glass window reflected back a ghostly visage of Rune and her glowing white eyes as she grabbed the doorknob. It didn't even shift.

"It's locked!" she cried as she put all her strength to it with no avail. Yet she could see her gold twine moving straight through the door. "This makes no sense. My magic leads us straight here!"

"Here, let me try," St. Benedict said, reaching for the handle only to stop as he peered through the hatched window. Beyond was a short hallway, and they could both see a second door on the other end. Through the far hatched window of the other door, more armored people seemed to be trying to get through it.

"Crap!" Rune cried as they both leapt back from the door, lining up against the wall on either side.

"But my magic... this was the best way to escape!" she cried, swiping the game glasses off her head to slip into one of the inner pockets of her coat. The magic woven into the coat would keep them from getting crushed.

"We'll have to find another way out," St. Benedict concurred with no judgement, just looking back the way they came with business-like calm. Yet beyond them, the shouting had only gotten worse in the main room. From Rune's perspective, all the other possible exit threads dissipated into tiny bursts of sparks. All but this last one, glowing thick as a rope.

"There is no other way out," Rune said, thrusting her thumb at the hatched door. "This is the only one left."

"You still see this as a way out?" St. Benedict asked, meeting her gaze with his own opaqued blue.

She felt the urge to doubt herself, given the circumstances, but her gold rope had actually gotten thicker in the few heartbeats since she last looked at it. "Yes," she said sounding like she had complete confidence. *If I don't trust in myself, I'll never be free.*

The shouts were getting closer. "Hey, you two! Out here now!" someone shouted, but Rune couldn't see them as they were hiding around the corner.

St. Benedict opened his coat and pinched at the lining. Like she had seen him do before, he pulled something from his coat, tearing it free. Cyberspies and their tricks.

"St. Ben, what are you do—" was all she got out before he broke what was in his hand, snapping something that looked like a pen in half.

"Don't look," he said belatedly as one end ignited into straight, white-blue fire. He stuck the impromptu torch into the lock, melting it into slag. Within seconds, he had cut through. "Go!" he urged as he seized the handle on the door and pulled it free from the liquid metal.

"But the soldiers..." She tried to say, but he grabbed her shoulder and pushed her through. Rune flinched as small droplets of melted metal landed on her exposed hands, but she didn't let it stop her as she bolted through.

He came in right behind her, pulling the door closed when a rifle butt stopped it at the last second. A masked man shouted incoherently as he tried to pry the door open. More gloved fingers appeared around the edge as others tried to overcome the Saint's not inconsiderable strength. Rune pressed in herself to help hold it, but they were losing their battle.

Then St. Benedict shoved her, knocking her back onto her butt. The move seemed to give him a push off to surge forward, and he swung the door out, slamming the door into a set of helmeted faces as it suddenly gave way to their efforts.

Time seemed to slow down without any aid of Rune's altered sight. She saw St. Benedict exit into the brighter room. He whirled, his coat flaring out around him as he gripped the door. There was a pause as their eyes met, but it could only have been for a second because his spin never slowed. He gave her his grin, then the door slammed shut. The metal at the door joint glowed once more molten hot. A heartbeat later, there was a bang as St. Benedict's body was slammed against it, his face pressing against the small square of industrial glass in profile.

By then, Rune had found her feet and had rushed back to him. His one eye looked at her, though how she knew with them opaqued, she couldn't say. The eye winked, then he was gone.

The door thumped and rattled as the view in the window was replaced by one of the tactical-masked faces. More shouts, demanding that she open the door, but Rune only backed away. She felt torn, like she needed to do something to save St. Benedict, but he had made sure she couldn't, and she had no other plan.

I need to run, was her only tangible thought, disconnected from her emotions. "He'll…" She closed her eyes. "I… I believe in you, St. Benedict." She knew he could survive. "He'll get himself out. I need to run so he can do it."

She spun around, clinging to the hope burning in her chest. He had done this so she could escape. She needed to escape.

"Find Escape. Safety." Before her magic flared, the intention of escape renewed, leading her away down the very short hall.

This door banged rhythmically, and she could just make out the soldiers on the other side swinging a battering ram. Lumps punched into the door on her side. All she could do was stand there and watch helplessly. There was nowhere else to go, and her Finding rope still showed this as the way out.

This is insane! she told herself, trembling as she struggled to have faith in her magic.

The battering ram bent the door, and one more slam knocked it off completely.

"Grab her!" a voice barked as she stood her ground. To retreat was useless as they would be on her in seconds.

An explosion rocked the ground.

Smoke and dust kicked up, and she instinctively turned away from it, covering her face with her coat sleeve. Debris flew on either side of Rune's head. Even with the protection of her coat, she coughed and coughed, trying to get a clean breath in. It was like the air itself was attacking her.

Someone grabbed her. She tried to fight them off, but it was all she could do to keep coughing and trying to breath. Something... a bag? a mask? was shoved roughly over her head. She faintly heard two clicks on either side of her face, then cool air blew. Within seconds, Rune's coughing stopped as she focused on taking in lungfuls of clean air. Her cloudy head cleared, and she realized she gripped a mask covering her face.

"Keep breathing!" a familiar voice ordered. As her vision cleared, Rune looked through the mask's visor into another masked face and a pair of angry eyes glaring through it.

"St. Rachel!" Rune croaked.

CHAPTER 16

"**W**here's St. Benedict?" St. Rachel demanded, giving Rune an urgent shake.

"He's still inside!" Rune managed to say, stumbling out of the building at last.

St. Rachel "helped" by seizing the front of Rune's coat and hauling her toward the alley beyond.

Rune tried to dig in her heels. "No, wait! We have to go back for him!"

"No, we're leaving now!" St. Rachel countermanded. "Knowing him, he'll probably beat us to the rendezvous point."

She didn't let go of the front of Rune's coat as she moved through the slowly dissipating smoke, clearly some kind of knockout gas. Rune stumbled once on something squishy on the ground.

"Step over them. Watch your feet!" the Saint snapped.

Staring down in shock, Rune saw the darker form of a body. All about them were soldiers lying on the pavement where they fell.

"Are they dead!?" Rune asked, panic rising as her brain was not prepared to cope with that idea. Her foot kicked a small canister still spitting a small trail of smoke.

"No, unconscious, unless someone here's got a heart condition," St. Rachel replied with matter-of-fact coldness, not slowing as she picked her way over the bodies. "Last thing we need is a real body count. Keep moving."

"Why didn't their helmets..." But the question died as she realized the soldier's helmets didn't protect them from the smoke because they were just wearing plastic face shields with no air filtration system. They hadn't expected to need one.

On the chest of one were the white letters CPD; his armband read Paladin Police Force. Kodiak's policing force.

A pair of vans appeared out of the smoke, black painted with the doors open, but St. Rachel threaded past them as well. At last, they came to the warehouse on the other side.

"Does he know where that is? How did *you* find us?" Rune asked, shoving off St. Rachel's hand at last to walk on her own. The Saint let her go but kept moving, approaching a slightly ajar door.

St. Rachel didn't answer immediately, instead lining up beside the door and checking inside it, her handgun at the ready.

Satisfied, St. Rachel swung back and pinned Rune with her stare. "On the other side is an unmarked gray car. That is our escape." She opened a pocket and pulled out a set of keys. "If we get separated, I assume you can 'Find' your way to it with these?" Her tone was snide when she said "Find," but Rune didn't let it stop her from taking the keys, clutching them tightly in her hand.

Instantly, she sent her magic into it. Predictably, her thread fired through and out, the key soaking up her magic like it was water, directing her through the warehouse. Smaller threads branched off to connect to another set of keys in St. Rachel's own tactical vest.

"If you should get there first—" A shout cut off her words,

and both women ducked lower.

"If we get separated, then I wait for you and St. Benedict," Rune whispered what she assumed were the rest of the instructions.

"No, if we get separated, and you get there first, you drive away—"

"No!" Rune reacted before the Saint could finish, shaking her head. "Not going to happen."

"Those are the orders. You drive away. Do you hear me?"

"Why? Why are those the orders?" Rune demanded.

"We don't have time for debate. We need to go now."

As if on cue, the shouts intensified at the end of the alley.

"Come! Now!" St. Rachel hissed, and she moved into the warehouse, her gun locked in line with her shoulder. Rune had little choice but to follow. Besides, her magic indicated this was the way to go. Trusting it had gotten her this far.

The inside of this warehouse was much like the other, only it was an open space that went up two stories without the various support pillars throughout. It made the room seem very vulnerable and open. A handful of crates on either side did not help that perception. High above, a series of catwalks covered the ceiling with dramatically long ladders leading up to them in the corners. The only light in the place streamed from windows high above on either end, leaving the space semi- to nearly dark.

"Masks off," St. Rachel ordered and pulled hers free. Her usually beautiful self was gone, replaced with a grim-faced woman, her hair pulled in a tight blonde bun and no make-up. Rune actually found her more striking. A warrior queen. Her eyes were opaqued green, and Rune realized in that moment that she had never seen St. Rachel use her augmentations.

Once Rune had cleared the door, tugging her mask off as ordered, the Saint pulled the door shut behind them. "Hold this."

She thrust her gun out to Rune. The Finder took it, even though she abhorred the thing and everything it stood for.

The grip was sweaty-warm and the small light on St. Rachel's bracelet went from blue to red, meaning it would no longer fire until the person who was registered to it reacquired it. If Rune had it too long, it would initiate a self-destruct, though she had no idea what that meant it would do exactly. It made holding it even more uncomfortable.

St. Rachel didn't even notice as she pulled out a pen-length stick, exactly like the one that St. Benedict had used. She snapped it, and one side ignited into the mini torch. She jammed it into the seam where the door met the jamb, immediately melting it all into slag. When the torch died, she flipped around the small stick in her gloved hand and pressed a button in the top. Whatever she was blasting at the other side instantly seemed to cool the slag, hardening it.

The Saint tossed the two ends of the device and reclaimed her gun. "Let's go," she said as she moved into the space, weapon at the ready.

Rune moved to follow but then her magical thread wavered and recoiled. Stopping, Rune stared at the keys in her hand. The thread of her magic had wound itself around the key, spinning like a hive of disconsolate bees, trying to find a place to land.

That's wrong? she asked it silently to herself. She tried to focus on Finding the car. *So I can escape,* she thought.

The magic still wavered and buzzed. Her magic had never done that before. It was acting so strangely.

She took a deep breath and tried to clear her mind as best she could under the circumstances, even as her feet did the work crossing the warehouse space along the wall. The magic got thinner and thinner as they went.

"St. Rachel, stop!" Rune said, quickly grabbing the Saint's shoulder.

"What are you doing?" St. Rachel hissed, but Rune didn't answer her, her eyes going wide.

The second she had laid a hand on St. Rachel's shoulder, the second thread, the one to escape, dimmed to almost nothing. Snapping her hand off, it reignited brightly.

If she went with St. Rachel... she wouldn't make it to the car. She wouldn't escape.

Rune focused her intention on the second thread. "I need to find a way to escape," Rune said to it, using the words to clarify her purpose in her mind.

Obediently, the thread shifted, no longer going forward, but going behind her, to the nearest ladder up to the catwalk.

"We need to go up and over," Rune said to St. Rachel, indicating the ladder as she touched the other woman's arm again.

Once more, the thread faded. Rune's heart skipped a beat as she realized what that could mean.

There was an escape route but only for her.

And it was clear St. Rachel believed she had lost her mind. "Absolutely not!" the Saint hissed.

Still, Rune wasn't going to leave her behind. "Trust me, St. Rachel. I—"

Yet she refused to listen. The dangerous woman stalked toward a far door Rune could barely make out across the dark, open space.

"St. Rachel!" Rune hissed as loud as she dared. "Not that way. *Please.* You have to trust me."

"You either come with, or I will haul you out by any means necessary," St. Rachel hissed in return, pausing with her gun trained forward.

Instead of arguing, Rune hurried back toward the fire escape. If she couldn't convince her, she could possibly lead her.

"Get back here!" St. Rachel shouted imprudently, doing as Rune hoped.

The Finder got to the ladder first and was well up it by the time St. Rachel got to the bottom. "You bitch!" the Saint cursed at her, but Rune didn't stop.

"Come on. This way! Please!" Rune urged.

St. Rachel redirected her gun to point at the Finder. "Get down here right now, or I will shoot you, I swear!" she threatened. That did make Rune stop, her gaze jumping from the gun to St. Rachel's very serious face.

"You said the mission was to get me out alive," Rune argued.

"He didn't say anything about your kneecaps."

They continued to stare in stalemate. In this situation, Rune thought she'd have felt more fear, more concern, but all she felt was angry.

"You're an idiot," Rune spat at the woman, and St. Rachel actually reacted to that by lifting an eyebrow, her only indication of surprise.

Then the door that they had come from, which was now only maybe ten feet away, blew off its hinges. There had been no warning, just a massive boom as the door flew back to skip across the floor before coming to a flopping landing.

It took everything Rune had to not let go of the ladder. At the moment of the boom, she hit her head against the metal rungs, but she managed to keep her hold, her arm shoving through the space to wrap around the whole thing. St. Rachel also stumbled but turned as she caught herself on the bottom of the ladder. She retained the grip on her gun and pointed it directly at the new opening, now larger than the door had been.

A figure marched in through the dust of the rubble and the new plume of smoke from whatever had erupted the wall. The man was someone Rune had never seen before, and in the dim light, it was hard to make out his features. Yet St. Rachel cursed, her opaque eyes widening to perfect circles.

Then she fired.

The figure moved, and to Rune's perception, seemed to blur as he crossed to the semi-prone woman. St. Rachel's first two shots missed, but as he got closer, her third seemed to stagger him. Rune didn't wait any longer but pulled herself the rest of the way up the ladder to relative safety.

As the intruder stumbled back, St. Rachel shifted more onto her feet, her gun stance locked as she stepped closer. She seemed to be putting herself between Rune's ladder and him. And from what Rune could see, the figure was definitely a him.

He stood tall, probably six foot plus, but his body seemed

off. Like his arms and legs were slightly too long for his frame. Across the body armor he wore were the words emblazoned in white, purporting his affiliation to the FBI.

St. Rachel kept her gun trained on him. "St. Dominic," she shouted.

Oh great. And he was a Saint too.

The newly named figure lifted his head and straightened, running a hand through his dirty blond hair. Rune couldn't tell if he was wounded or not. His black clothing disguised any signs of trauma, and he didn't seem to be favoring any particular body part. Instead, he grinned, which turned his face from automaton menace to the good-old boy FBI agent that TV shows were always casting.

"St. Rachel," he said cordially as if it were a fortuitous meeting of old high school classmates. He spread his arms wide, showing his empty hands. "Imagine meeting you here. You're not the Saint I was expecting to find."

Rune's heart skipped a beat. She had an idea who the new Saint had been expecting, and she doubted St. Benedict was the only one they were looking for.

"I love to be full of surprises," St. Rachel said.

Staying in a crouch, Rune slowly started the long turtle walk along the catwalk, very aware that too much motion would probably attract the enemy Saint's attention.

As if cognizant of Rune's actions, St. Rachel also stepped sideways, moving toward the open area of the warehouse. Her eyes and her gun remained focused on the danger in front of her.

"Where are you going, St. Rachel?" St. Dominic asked, a warning tone in his voice. He turned with her, keeping his focus on her as he smiled. "It's a bit far to run. Or are you just trying to stall me so someone more *important* can get away?"

St. Rachel only glared, her jaw and her gaze locked, giving nothing away. Rune was grateful as much as she was terrified by what the Saint was doing. They may have been enemies, but they were on the same side, and Rune didn't hate her enough to want to watch her die, or anyone to die, for her sake.

"So where is *he*, hmm?" St. Dominic asked, switching tactics while triple blinking. His eyes flashed as they too went blue with augmented sight. "We know he was here. Him and Anna Masterson."

Rune's heart leapt into her throat upon hearing her original name.

"I have no idea who that is," St. Rachel lied, still moving away toward her original exit, but it was simply too far away to be practical escape.

Rune knew it was.

Yet it did keep St. Dominic's attention away from Rune's position.

Crouched, Rune couldn't see down below as well as she had on the ladder. But she could see the hidden world up above. Other things were stored on the catwalks that hadn't been visible from below. Forgotten boxes and equipment in different places, creating a strange sort of up-in-the-air maze. There were even abandoned tools lying about; it was almost desolate and dystopian. Like the equipment told a tale about workers past that Rune could not even begin to decipher or understand. In the farthest corner from her position, however, Rune saw a half-lighted sign that said "EXIT," and her gold thread zigzagged for it. She could only speculate that it was a fire escape.

Rune moved as quickly as she dared, catching glimpses of the two facing off Saints below.

St. Dominic approached St. Rachel, matching her step for step with his empty hands outstretched. He had the same cocky confidence St. Benedict would display in the same situation, but there was something more menacing about it. St. Rachel, for one, did not let down her guard one iota. "There's only two ways this goes, St. Dominic: we both walk away, or we both die. The only choice is which do you want?"

"You're that sure it'll be a fight of attrition, do you?" Then St. Dominic moved, faster than Rune could even follow. St.

Rachel fired in the same instant. It was unclear if she hit her target because he dodged away, rolling at the last second to appear at her side. She swirled just as fast, keeping her gun on him.

"Okay, you can still hit me," he agreed, rubbing at his chest. She had in fact hit her target. "That is going bruise in the morning. But the real question is, can I dodge more times than you have bullets?"

"That wasn't a miss," she countered.

"You didn't hit my head; you hit the Kevlar. I would call that a miss," he replied. And then he moved again.

They did the song and dance twice more in quick succession. Him moving toward her. Her firing, deflecting him away. Then on the third pass, he went left instead of right. It was a stupid mistake. An obvious mistake, and yet St. Rachel fell for it. Her shot not only missed. Her arm pointed straight up to the ceiling, just as Rune passed over.

The bullet missed her. Instead, a bulb shattered from the shot, raining down glass. But what it did do was make Rune yelp involuntarily.

St. Dominic and St. Rachel stood in that strange pose, their faces inches apart, like dancers before the first chord was played.

"Oh you clever woman, of course," St. Dominic purred, his voice carrying in the empty space. Then he lifted his wrist to his mouth. "The target is on the catwalk. All agents converge now—"

St. Rachel wrested her gun arm away and brought it down at a slant across his face. This time blood sprayed. He went down to the ground. It made no difference. The door slammed open in the direction St. Rachel had wanted to go and black-clad agents poured in from both directions.

"The catwalk!" St. Dominic shouted, catching St. Rachel's foot just before it crashed into his face.

The soldiers headed to the ladders, clamoring up them a hundred times faster than Rune could. She didn't even try to be subtle now but stood and ran across the catwalks. She couldn't afford to look below, but she could hear St. Rachel still fighting, both Saints exchanging blows as fast as a tap dancer on caffeine and each sounded awful. Rune focused on her own feet, jumping and leaping over the boxes and detritus in her way. The thread she followed seemed to compensate for the change of circumstances, leading her left, then forward and right, which seemed to take her on a counter-intuitive path that the agents weren't compensating for.

I wish I had my shield crystal! Rune thought desperately, as too many bodies were still moving in her direction, narrowing her ways to go without falling to certain doom.

A large block of a soldier leapt toward her.

She raised a hand. "Shield!"

For one brief moment, a concave circle of yellow stuttered into and then out of existence.

The agent she meant to block, however, reacted as if something other than light had blasted at them, and they ducked away. Rune hurried past, skipping over a rolled-up tarp like a deer.

"Stop or we will open fire!" they kept shouting at her, but the Finder didn't believe them for one moment. Instead, her gold thread burned brighter, spooling back into herself as she moved along it, filling her with confidence that the direction she was heading was freedom.

She got ahead of them and ran full tilt for the exit door. Slamming her hands on the bar, she pushed with everything she had.

The door didn't open, but she passed through it anyway.

CHAPTER 17

Rune found herself in a dark stairwell instead of the open-air fire escape she had expected. The ground beneath her was dirt, or rather, metal stairs so buried in dirt it would take an excavation team a week to dig it all up. In fact, all around her was dirt from the walls to the ceiling, and there was no light at all except what came through the emergency exit door still standing open. Even that was meager.

Whirling, she seized the door to slam it shut, but the bottom edge got caught on the dirt.

The armored soldiers came straight for her. She tried to scramble back on the uneven ground, grasping at the dirt coated walls.

As they passed over the threshold, however, they disappeared. She could distantly hear the clank-clank-clank of feet hitting metal and voices shouting urgently, but she couldn't see where they had gone.

Rune forced herself to take a deeper breath, clearing her head. They couldn't chase her. She had gone through into an in-between place, one of the countless areas of the city where two worlds met, trapping a forgotten space, locked forever in its own universe. Such in-between ways were hard to find and harder to access or even navigate. Without her own magic, Rune would have never known it was here, and the fact that she managed to cross into it without deliberately trying had probably only been possible by the thread's guidance.

At that thought, she looked down at the spooling magic thread as it spun around the key in her palm. Refocusing on her two desires, to find the car and escape, the thread burst out once more, zipping down the stairs. It was meager light but gave her enough to navigate. While everything in the stairwell was coated in dirt, a banister stuck out from the wall. It was enough for her to balance herself as she made her way down the unevenly coated stairs. It felt like an eternity to reach the bottom, but once she got there, she found herself in a four-way split of earthen tunnels, wiggling away like enormous snakes had plowed through. There wasn't a sound in the space; even her footfalls were barely registering.

A longing for St. Benedict flitted through her, along with fear for his safety. She pictured him dead or taken, but she pushed those images to the side. She had to have faith if they were going to escape. *I wish I could still be angry at you right now,* she thought at him. *It would have made things easier.*

Holding out the key, she saw her twined threads took her left. Determined, she kept going. The thread whispered ahead of her, taking her along the wavering corridor as she prayed she didn't run into anything hungry or, even, at all. After several minutes with only her heartbeat for company, she found a ladder bisecting the tunnel. Her light danced up the rungs, and even if it hadn't, Rune would have taken it just to get out of the claustrophobic tunnel.

At the top, there was no manhole cover or anything. She just found herself standing on the street. It was so disconcerting that she stumbled as she tried to step on a rung that wasn't actually there anymore. Her hands grasped at nothing

in the air before her feet found the flat of the ground. Spinning around, she backed up against the side of a brick building, looking up and down the street she had appeared on.

She could hear distant sirens, but otherwise the street was empty of people. She saw no easily read signs, street or otherwise, that could give her a better idea where she had been spat out by the tunnel or even if she was still in the same city. In-betweens were strange places where space and sometimes even time could shift.

Yet Rune still had her magic thread. It zipped merrily down the street ten feet along a row of parked cars before stopping around a nondescript grey sedan.

Sighting it, Rune hurried to the car. Before she could come around to the driver's side and use the key, the car activated itself, turning on its interior lights and unlocking the doors. She wasted no time marveling at the trick but ducked inside. Once the door shut, the car automatically locked itself, leaving Rune with the sound of her own breath as she gripped the steering wheel.

"Well, I guess that verifies that I'm still in Chicago," Rune said to it. It also meant she wasn't far from where St. Rachel and St. Benedict were.

Releasing shuddering breaths, Rune slid her hands up the sides of the steering wheel, feeling the bumps of the grips on the underside. She knew that St. Rachel had ordered her to leave.

Like hell she was going to do that.

Setting a hand against her chest, Rune focused on St. Benedict in her mind. Another deep breath in and she meditated on every detail of him: his smell, the pressure of his shoulder against her cheek when he held her, the pain she felt when she thought of his betrayal, the longing she tried to ignore, the... the love she felt for him that she tried to deny.

Her magic sparked instantly, the cord in her heart tied to his popping into reality as if it was always there, even though she just didn't see it.

He is alive!

She could feel it along the tie that bound them together.

He is alive!

She tried to follow it, to see down that cord, like she sometimes could with people she cared about, but the images were jumbled and chaotic. He was fighting. Slashes of pain, color, and blood filled her vision, then snapped her back inside the car.

Panting, Rune looked around the vehicle for a tool or weapon, anything that might help him. Then she remembered that the Praetorium cars had a lock box in the middle arm rest where most people kept change or tissues. She lined up the sensor pad with her thumb, wondering if it would open for her and was genuinely surprised when it popped and unfolded itself. A tiny gun rack lifted automatically inside, extending a gun handle even higher to be taken. The second rack was already empty, and Rune thought of the gun that St. Rachel had been carrying.

"St. Rachel?" a voice called, and Rune startled a yelp. "St. Rachel, did you get Rune?"

"Malachi! It *is* Rune," she corrected. Before her on the car's panel, a hologram manifested with a little box of dancing lines that moved only when the tech on the other end spoke.

"Rune! Thank whatever theoretically existent deity is out there listening. Are you alright?" the tech squeaked, then continued without waiting for an answer. "Where are you? Wait, you're in the car. Obviously. Where is St. Rachel or St. Ben?"

"They're both still inside," Rune said, staring at the still waiting gun. "I'm the only one who made it out so far."

"Damn it," Malachi cursed. "Okay, okay. We're going to have to work with that. You are ordered to drive back to the Praetorium as fast as you can, the most direct route that you can. Don't worry about being seen. I'll be covering you the whole way here. You just need to focus on driving safely."

Somehow that order decided things for Rune, and she seized the grip on the gun. There was a musical beep as the weapon released into her hand, and Rune belatedly grabbed

the syncing bracelet, which she snapped onto her own wrist. "Unregistered user," a disembodied female voice reported. "Please enter authorization code for this weapon's use."

"Rune? What are you doing?"

"I'm going to go back and help," Rune said resolutely. "Give me the authorization code for this weapon."

There was a dead silence as the normally jumpy line in the sound box went completely straight. "Oh my god. You are as bad as he is. No wonder he loves you."

Rune's heart beat a rapid tattoo at that inadvertent declaration, even as Malachi tried to choke it back in one drawn out, run-on sentence. "Um, anyway, that is... uh, crap... irrelevant... to this situation, but you aren't even trained on that weapon, and you need to get back because this is getting really bad, and we've lost too many resources to this whole thing, and Rune you gotta go now, Maxamillion's orders."

"I don't care about what Maxamillion ordered," Rune said, her brain gripping on to the last thing said.

Just then a scream tore through the air from somewhere too far away. Rune froze, knowing without knowing that it was St. Rachel.

"Rune, you need to get out of there right now!"

"Look!" Rune snapped. "I'm going back—either with a gun or without one."

A pregnant pause ticked away the seconds she didn't have.

"Bracelet unlocked for use," the disembodied voice reported, the light on it going from red to green.

"No one ever freaking listens to me," Malachi grumbled.

Rune didn't respond to that; instead, she opened the door and exited. Upon exiting, she almost immediately dropped the weapon, the weight unfamiliar and nothing like the toy gun feel she imagined it would be like. Renewing her grip in both hands, she pointed the end toward the ground. Looking back and forth, she was relieved to find the street remained empty despite the echoes of sirens and shouting. Everything sounded strangely louder and quieter at night, and that night was no exception.

"St. Rachel," Rune breathed, barely closing her eyes before her magic shifted to obey her will. Maybe it was her clarity of purpose, but the thread didn't even hesitate as it shot away, giving her a clear path back the way she had come. She hurried along it, her coat bellowing out behind her in a conspicuous flash of red and white.

The thread didn't take her the same direction she had come from. It slashed along the night-covered bricks of whatever industrial building she hurried along and whipped around the corner. She didn't whip with it, but instead did what she had seen the Saints do countless times: she aligned herself with the edge at her back. Panting a couple of breaths, she flipped her head around the corner for a quick look.

"Dammit," she huffed. "I didn't see a damn thing." She tried the trick a couple of more times, but in the seconds-long glances, she just got impressions of brick and darkness.

"Dammit, dammit. What are you doing? Rune, you're not a Saint." She paused as she realized the truth of that statement. Of course she wasn't, and she was guaranteed to fail if she tried to be. Closing her eyes, she immediately snapped them open, activating her secondary sight. The world illuminated in a flash of color, light and dark, as she saw the literal fabric of existence, both time and space and several other dimensions she couldn't put words to.

Then she focused, narrowing down all those dimensions to the here and now. Taking a grip onto her magic thread that connected her to St. Rachel, she used her new perspective to look down the thread, her mind moving along it, seeing ahead of herself, and this time seeing everything that was immediately around the corner and no further. People were moving, figures and the bubbles of their worlds moving between and within buildings. Searching for her. She could see both herself and them and measure her relationship to them. It was a form of omniscience as she focused on the idea that she wanted to Find: the pathway through them with the least amount of

violence only.

The thread snapped at that thought, becoming strong and clear. Confidently, Rune moved.

As she went, she could hear them, the people looking for her. Their feet thumped on the ground even as she skimmed silently between the warehouse's tiny paved alleys. Interestingly, her thread seemed to be communicating ideas back to her as it led. She got a distinct urge to stop in the middle of the space and crouch. Rune followed the urge just as a beam of light blipped over her head and passed on.

She didn't move as the beams of light turned and twisted at the end of the alley, like they were mounted to heads that were looking back and forth.

Searching.

Rune held still in the darkness of the alley, feeling terribly exposed. There were boxes blocking the way she had been going, more apparent now that the lights were giving them an edge. They created a long shadow exactly around where she crouched.

All she could do was focus on her breath. She forced herself to take slow, quiet breaths. Her heartbeat tattooed hard against her ribs.

Then there was a distant sharp yelp of pain, echoing from down to the left. It caught the attention of the people searching at the end of her alley. All lights turned straight for it. Then they moved, disappearing from her view.

Her thread gave her an impression that it was safe to stand up, but she hesitated. Through her own enhanced vision, she saw another person coming along the wall, the opposite way from where the others with the lights had gone.

Rune pointed the gun toward the end of the alley. If they ran past with the others, then fine. But if they came down the alley...

She didn't know if she could actually do it. Her resolve wavered along with the gun point. Whoever it was, they were a life. A sentient life that she would snuff out with the pull of the trigger. But she had no doubt that the ones that were searching for her would not be so merciful.

The figure slowed as it neared the edge of the alley, lining its body along the edge. They had no weapon that she could sense, but Rune allowed her sight to incorporate the immediate future of the person before her. Unfortunately, she didn't have the control she needed for such a thing. Her senses flooded with all the possible futures that could happen and then locked onto one. She will fire the gun. She will drop the gun, and she will scream as the body of the man will fall to the ground. St. Benedict will die before her.

And then the future aligned with the present. She hadn't fired. In fact, the gun was to the side unfired but still deflected as St. Benedict pulled her against his chest with the other arm.

"It's alright. It's me. It's me!" he panted, out of breath.

Rune felt her legs go jelly as she realized what she saw hadn't happened. She would have fallen if he hadn't been holding her up.

"What happened? Rune, are you alright?"

"Yeah, yeah. I'm fine. I just..." She pressed the heel of her hand against the dull ache behind her eyes. "I was trying to see the future, and I think I got sucked down one possible path. I'm just glad that..."

He didn't let her finish that thought but pulled her closer, hugging her hard. "I knew you would find your way out," he said into her hair. At some point, he had lost his coat. His shirt was soaked through with sweat.

"Are you hurt?" he asked, and she almost laughed if she could get a breath in herself.

"Are you?" she asked instead of answering.

"I'm fine." He took her hand, now empty of the gun, because he had it now.

She wasn't attached to it anyway.

"Okay, let's get out of here," he said and tugged her after him.

"No," Rune said, grabbing onto his arm to stop him. "St. Rachel."

St. Benedict's body went still. "What about her?"

Rune pulled on him to get him moving. "She's in trouble. This way. She's fighting another Saint. We have to help her."

His eyes went wide as he followed. "Which Saint?"

"St. Dominic."

A stiffness entered St. Benedict's shoulders with an expression Rune had never seen before. "Which way?" St. Benedict asked as he marched past her.

Her Finding thread shot out before her. Without hesitation, she followed it with him running parallel beside her. Rune felt no fear, only a cold understanding of their mission now.

At the end of the alley, they paused, and St. Benedict checked around the corner. Through Rune's Sight, she saw three figures standing in front of the warehouse.

"The thread goes through there," she whispered to her partner.

He nodded and went around the corner, Rune right on his heels. As he marched with purpose toward the three figures, he raised the gun, his blue opaqued eyes blazing. Rune immediately ducked inside a doorway's alcove. He fired two shots in quick succession, and the streetlight halfway between burst into shards of sparks. It was followed by the light over the warehouse door a split second later. The three soldiers spun and shouted, but neither Rune nor St. Benedict were as blind as they suddenly were.

She waited while the sounds of struggle filled the new dark. She could make out the figures as they left their impressions on reality. The closest didn't even get a chance to react before St. Benedict put a near point blank shot straight to their kevlar chest protector. From what she had been taught in her brief introduction to such things, as per Corinthe Corps corporate requirements, she knew such a shot could still kill, but it had a greater chance of rendering the target stunned. Sure enough, the first agent dropped to the ground, curling around himself like a bug.

By this time, the other two pivoted in, lifting their weapons.

St. Benedict stepped in and slammed his elbow into the second soldier's chin. The helmet did nothing to protect from the attack. They stumbled away, dropping their weapon. The third came up to St. Benedict's other side. Without slowing his motion, St. Benedict sidestepped to the side just in time to be missed by the soldier's muted shot. Then, St. Benedict brought down the grip of his gun slamming into the soldier's wrists. They bellowed, which St. Benedict cut short by wrapping an arm around the guy's throat. The Saint discharged a shock from his hands. The soldier went limp, and also succumbed to gravity's pull.

The second soldier had recovered.

"St. Benedict!" Rune warned.

Her shout startled the second soldier. They looked her way, so they didn't see the second shock coming from St. Benedict until the air filled with a distinct tang of burnt hair and urine. This time, the soldier stayed down.

St. Benedict wavered on his feet. Rune rushed over and grabbed his shoulder to steady him.

"Can't do that again. Two discharges at that level was pushing it," he said as he steadied.

Another cry of pain that could only be St. Rachel rang out.

It spurred St. Benedict to the door. He wrenched it open and swung in, his gun pointed and ready, this time to shoot to kill if possible. Concentrating on St. Rachel, Rune's thread fluttered in, wavering as it didn't seem to be able to find a clear and safe path for Rune to get to her goal.

"Oh, and there he is. St. Benedict himself," the new Saint crowed.

St. Benedict answered the greeting with a continuous series of gun blasts. That's when Rune sensed it, a way to get past. Then she peeked around the door.

The two male Saints were charging at each other across the empty space of the warehouse. On the ground, ten feet away from the door, the light of her Finding highlighted St. Rachel, lying on the ground.

Blood covered her face, and much of her hair had come out of her ponytail. A portion of it fanned her head like a broken halo. The Finder would have thought her dead except her Finding magic wouldn't be highlighting her. Once a person left their body, they became a thing, and that was a different Finding all together.

Trusting herself, Rune ran out at a crouch to where St. Rachel lay. She went to seize the woman's arm and hesitated when she realized the woman's forearm had been snapped. White bone was sticking out gruesomely through the skin. Instead, Rune seized her other, more intact arm to pull her up to sitting.

St. Rachel moaned.

"Come on. We have to go," Rune whispered as loudly as she dared, ducking under the arm and getting a grip around St. Rachel's waist. Rune did all of the work to get her standing, but once on her feet, St. Rachel stumbled forward. They had ten feet to cross to the exit. It might as well have been ten miles. Rune could hear the two men fighting behind her, but she ignored them. Focusing entirely on her task, she kept talking to St. Rachel.

"Stay with me. We're just putting one foot in front of the other. There you go. Just keep walking. We're going to get you help."

Once they passed the threshold back to the outside, Rune sent out a Finding to lead them safely to the car. This time the thread led them straight. All they had to do was keep walking. St. Rachel's head lolled dangerously, and she slumped against Rune. The broken arm dangled eerily, and Rune knew that couldn't be good for it, but the Saint didn't seem to be feeling any pain. She wasn't conscious enough for it.

"St. Rachel, stay awake. Come on. We're going to get you help, but you got to keep walking," Rune ordered. The Saint didn't even argue, and that scared Rune most of all. She kept moving, however, one foot in front of the other, even if Rune had to support her all the way to the car.

There was a huge sense of relief as soon as they passed through to the narrow alley between the buildings and then back on to the street. Their escape car chirped open as Rune approached with St. Rachel. The Saint collapsed into the backseat and lay there unconscious and unmoving. It took Rune going around to the other side to drag her the rest of the way into the back. Blood oozed everywhere, and that was when Rune noticed the blood trail they had left behind when they walked. She felt quickly for the Saint's pulse and held her breath almost too long before she found it, faint, but there. But St. Rachel's skin felt cold to the touch.

"We need to call an ambulance," Rune said, her mind slipping into panic as she realized that St. Rachel could very well die before they got her help.

"No time," St. Benedict said, startling her as he came up behind her.

CHAPTER 18

"Your ear is bleeding," Rune said, staring at the rivulet of red coating the side of his face.

"It's just nicked. My eardrums are fine," he stated matter-of-factly as he moved to the driver's side. "Is she still breathing?"

"Yes," Rune said, though she wasn't a hundred percent confident about that. She clambered into the backseat, scooping St. Rachel's head into her lap.

St. Benedict passed her a first aid kit from the front, and Rune rummaged through it while he tore the car out of the parking spot. He gestured over the console, silently summoning up a holographic display. "Nearest emergency room," he snapped.

Off in the distance, Rune could hear sirens echoing raucously, but she ignored them as she focused on her patient. She found one of the large gauze pads near the top of the case and tore into the packet with her teeth. The thick pad spilled out, and she applied it to the worst cut on St. Rachel's head, which had turned her blonde hair into a sticky clump.

The Saint moaned, her eyes fluttering as she tried to will them to open.

"St. Rachel, can you hear me?" Rune asked.

"St. Rachel!" St. Benedict barked immediately after.

"St. Bene-dict," St. Rachel croaked. Her eyes marginally opened, and she turned her head toward the front. "Alive?"

"Yeah. Yeah, girl, I'm alive," he said, then spun the wheel, making the tires scream and forcing Rune to both brace and cushion St. Rachel from crushing against the door. "Now you gotta stay alive. You hear me? We're getting you help soon."

"You gotta drive in such a way that *gets* her there alive!" Rune shouted.

St. Rachel groaned and pawed at her side. Rune noted it and pulled back the Saint's hand. It was covered in blood.

"Dammit," Rune muttered and dug out another pad to press against her side. St. Rachel cried out in pain.

"What is it?!" St. Benedict demanded, panicking.

"I got it. Keep driving!" Rune snapped back. The pad filled up with blood, and Rune could not take her eyes off the broken arm with its glaring bone sticking out. She dug back into the box. "Dammit. How can this thing not have a healing crystal or something I can use!"

St. Benedict didn't answer. Outside the car, other cars were screaming horn-blasts at them.

Then she remembered her own belt. She had two in a pouch, but she couldn't get to them with St. Rachel dying all over her lap!

An eternal few seconds later, the car screeched to a stop. St. Benedict was out of the car as it bucked from being forced into park too fast.

"Help! We need help now! Help!" he shouted, his voice echoing hollowly off the overhang of the hospital emergency room.

It seemed like forever before a gurney pulled up with three people in scrubs. A fourth in a white coat came up, yanking out a stethoscope to shove into their ears.

"Rune! You have to get out of the way!" St. Benedict screamed at her, even as she tried to figure how to get out of the car without dropping St. Rachel's head while all these other bodies were pressing in to get to her.

"We got her," the one male nurse assured as he slipped a neck brace around St. Rachel expertly.

Rune completely let go, dropping one foot to the ground, still unsure how to escape without falling out of the car. Then a vise-like grip seized her upper arm to haul her the rest of the way out. St. Benedict backpedaled them clear as St. Rachel was transferred from the car to the gurney by the professionals.

"What happened?" the doctor asked as they followed into the hospital.

Rune didn't know what to say, since "she was in a fight" would involve police, but not telling the doctor how she had been injured came with its own problems.

It didn't matter though because something sparked along St. Rachel's face, making everyone jump a moment. "Cybernetics. We need a medical cybertech in here now," the doctor ordered as they went back to wheeling her into a small room to the side of the horseshoe-shaped emergency room.

"What kind of tech does she have?" the doctor asked, blocking Rune and St. Benedict from entering the small room. They were a slight person with short hair and delicate features, with eyes that had seen too much and were too hard for such a young face.

"Extensive," St. Benedict said tersely. "Proprietary."

The doctor glared. "Fucking corporate elites," they muttered, then turned to the room, diving in among the swarm of people around her. "Treat what you can see. Let's get a sleeve on that arm and get the bleeding under control. Let's hope she isn't bugged to blow."

There were a few dry chuckles, so Rune thought the statement was meant as gallows humor. They hooked St. Rachel up to monitors and bags of fluids. The patient groaned and tried to move.

The doctor flashed light into her eyes. "What's her name?"

"St. Rachel," Rune said before St. Benedict could speak or stop her.

"Rachel, can you hear me? Do you know where you are?" the doctor asked.

St. Rachel didn't say anything, but she lifted her good hand and flourished the fingers. A hologram burst from her palm. It flashed red with a small representation of a woman. A stat list appeared beside the figure that flashed red in certain body parts, leaving the presumably unharmed parts of her a dull blue.

The doctor's eyes went wide at the sight, but then they refocused to read the stat lines.

"Okay, we need blood here. We have an internal puncture," the doctor said and proceeded to rattle off a dozen more medical terms at lightning speed that Rune could barely understand. She got broken ribs, fractured arm, and internal bleeding, and that was about it. While St. Rachel's head wound bled terribly, it was deemed superficial with no signs of trauma to the skull itself. Even understanding that much, Rune just gripped the metal doorframe of the alcove, feeling completely helpless.

"We need to get her stable and up to surgery prep," the doctor said. "Where's the blood bag? Chris, I swear to god, I am going to have you fired!"

A nurse pushed past them, carrying a bag of blood, and she hurried to set it up next to the fluid bags. As she set up the bag on the drip stand, St. Benedict grabbed the nurse's arm.

"You can't use that," he said.

"Let go of me," she demanded, flinching away. "It's universal—"

"Doesn't matter!" he barked, reaching up to pull it down.

"St. Benedict, let them work," Rune tried to intervene, seizing his arm. He shook her off but also let go of the woman and the bag.

"You want to tell me what her blood type is then, or is that proprietary as well?" the doctor sneered.

"It is," St. Benedict said through gritted teeth.

"St. Ben, tell them what they need to know," Rune urged.

He met her eyes with a complicated, shattered look. "I... I can't."

"Give her the blood—" the doctor decided.

"Use mine!" St. Benedict barked instead. "We have the same composition of blood."

That made the doctor pause. "What? What's in..." but their eyes moved back and forth in the distance, as if the doctor were reading something in their head. "You have some special enzyme in the composition of your blood?"

"Yes," St. Benedict confirmed.

"Fine, fine. Take him for testing and get it back to me, high priority," they said to the male nurse who helped pull St. Rachel from the car.

"Are either of you hurt?" another different nurse asked, looking from the mess that was St. Benedict to Rune.

"We're fine as far as I know," she said, glancing at him and more poignantly, at his blood-encrusted ear. "I guess I don't really know about him." She gestured at St. Benedict, who stared past as the nurses and doctors worked on St. Rachel.

It was like watching his mask shatter. The normally cool and collected Saint who hid everything behind a smile and a wink was gone. His gaze was long and haunted, staring at St. Rachel's face, now swallowed by a breathing mask. The look was raw.

"We can't take her to surgery until we know we have a supply of blood that will keep her stable. Focus on stabilization," Rune heard the doctor say, snapping her out of her own zeroed-in moment. Sounds came back louder, and she had a passive thought that maybe she too was in shock, but she dismissed it because she had no idea what it would be like if she was.

"Why aren't you taking my blood?" St. Benedict demanded, jerking when the male nurse tried to push him gently toward another bed.

"We need to check you out first and then we need to test your blood," the nurse explained patiently.

"Just hook me up to her," St. Benedict said, tearing at the sleeve of his shirt.

"No! No, we can't do that, sir. Sir!" the nurse said, holding up his hands to stop St. Benedict to no avail. The Saint tried to push past toward St. Rachel, but the nurse continued to block him. "You need to sit down now. We cannot do anything that endangers your life to save another. Please!"

"Get out of my way. Hook me up to her," St. Benedict demanded, shoving the nurse back.

The nurse was prepared however and braced to hold him. "If you don't calm down, we will have to call security!" he grunted.

"St. Ben, stop!" Rune said.

"We are not going to directly hook you up. That's insane," the doctor shouted, returning to the commotion, standing between the bed and the nurse as another barrier.

"I've done it before!" St. Benedict argued.

"Look!" the doctor shouted. "I don't know what circumstances you were in that *that* was necessary, and I don't think I want to know, but this is not a battlefield situation. She is stable. She will *remain* stable. Whatever technology you have in your bodies is your business, but it seems to be helping to keep her alive. Now comply with our request, or I will have you taken into custody and then she will not get the help she needs. Do you understand!"

St. Benedict's eyes went blue with murderous light.

"Back down!" Rune shouted, stepping between the doctor and him. He kept pushing in, however, moving to what she could only assume was throttle the doctor. She and the male nurse pushed back.

"Security!" the doctor shouted, though the uniformed people were already moving in.

"Is there somewhere we can go?" Rune asked the doctor. "A side room. I'll calm him down. We were just fighting for our

lives, okay? That's his partner there."

The doctor met her gaze, and an instant understanding passed between them. Rune understood completely that the doctor was genuinely trying to help them, and she could see the doctor understood St. Benedict's reaction. They waved the guards to stop.

"In there." The doctor gestured to another room exactly like the one they stood in next door, only that one was empty and had a sliding door.

Rune nodded and shoved hard. This time St. Benedict yielded, allowing her to herd him into that room.

Once he was past the threshold, she slid the door closed and slapped the light panel. The lights didn't go completely off, but the half-light turned out to be perfect. St. Benedict panted, leaning against the empty bed, his fists gripping the sheets, and Rune held his shoulders as she pressed him to sit down.

The second his butt hit the sheets, he tried to pop back up again. Rune grabbed St. Benedict's head and forced him to look at her. "St. Benedict!"

He stopped all his other aggressive fidgeting. His nostrils flared as he breathed. Blood had encrusted the side of his face, and his struggling had opened a fresh break in the scabbing, wetting Rune's hands as she held him. It was only then that she realized he had lost his fedora. Such an inane detail, but at that moment, it made him look even more damaged.

"She's going to be alright," Rune said. "You got her to help."

His breathing became more labored, honking painfully, before his face crashed into tears. "God, what the hell!" he tried to say. He pressed his hands against his forehead, desperate to hide his face.

Rune braced her hands on his shoulders. "You're in shock. You've done this before, remember? You know what's happening. This is a normal reaction."

His arms wrapped around her, and she didn't resist them. His head pressed painfully into her shoulder as he held on hard. She cupped the back of his head, petting her fingers through his hair gently. It didn't take long. The distant sounds of the emergency room were ever present, but for that moment, Rune felt disconnected from it all. There was only him, and her, and holding on to each other. She had a passing thought that crying would be good for her too, but the tears didn't come. She felt unbelievably calm. They didn't say anything to each other. They didn't have to.

Soon enough, St. Benedict took a shuddering breath in as he forced himself back under control, and the male nurse pulled the sliding door open to peek inside.

Rune gestured for him to come in. The nurse brought in a rolling cart and slid the door shut again.

Getting out of his way, Rune stepped to the side and sat down next to St. Benedict on the bed. She slipped her hand into his, and they interlaced their fingers, holding on just as tight as they had moments ago. St. Benedict didn't lift his head at all as the nurse started wordlessly setting up to draw the blood sample.

Rune finally got a good look at the man's name tag. It said "Joey" with a smiling merman next to it. Also in this light, she realized what she took as black hair was in fact a dark blue. There was webbing between his fingers.

A Lake Michigan Naiad.

Though, she knew native Naiads didn't call themselves that since it was a Greek term for the water nymphs hailing from that part of the world. Early settlers had unfortunately named them that when they first arrived, but Rune couldn't for the life of her remember what their official water tribe term was. To be fair, it had been a stressful night. She highly doubted Joey was his real name, just the easier anglicized version of his name.

Abruptly, the nurse cleared his throat, and Rune realized she had been staring. "She's doing alright," Nurse Joey said, referring to the only "she" that mattered at that moment.

He must have thought her staring was her pleading for him to tell them some news. She couldn't blame his assumption. It was an ER and probably the most prevalent question they heard.

"Thank you," Rune said, nodding acknowledgement.

"I have to check you over, and then we can take your blood for testing," he continued to explain, gesturing to the cart.

"Okay, that's fine," Rune said on behalf of herself and St. Benedict, who sat there deflated. "St. Ben, sit back."

She bent down and pulled off his shoes, setting them to the side. The nurse automatically went to a cabinet nearby and pulled out a gown that opened to the back. "I'll step out unless you need help." He spoke to Rune though it was clear his words were meant for St. Benedict. "Get changed. The doctor will be right in to—"

"I don't need that," St. Benedict said tersely, gesturing at the gown. "I have various cuts and bruises; this is the only one that might need stitches." He pointed to the one near his ear.

"I'll take care of it," Rune interceded before the nurse could object. "Just give me a couple of minutes."

Nurse Joey nodded and left.

Rune didn't say anything more to St. Benedict, only shrugged out of her coat, went to a sink near the door, and turned on the tap. The water was already warm, and she splashed some onto her own face. Brown and rust went down the drain, and she would need a real shower later, but just that little bit did a lot to help her feel more grounded. She found a towel stacked in the same cabinet with the sheets and hospital gowns. She snagged two, one to dry herself with and one to get wet. She took the wet one to St. Benedict, who continued to sit there, staring at his hands.

"I'm sorry, Rune. I'm sorry for all of it." He lifted his gaze to her face as she began to wipe gently at the blood on his face. He didn't seem to feel it. "Are you alright?"

"I'm fine," she said matter-of-factly. "You need to let them do what they need to do to help her. We need to do what we can. We aren't safe yet, right?"

St. Benedict sniffed in deeply, and Rune watched as he

put the pieces of himself back together. "We need to contact Maxamillion," he agreed. "We'll have to guard St. Rachel, make sure she stays here."

Rune furrowed her eyebrows. "You think they would kidnap her?"

"Something is out to get us, Rune. By all rights, we should have stayed in lockdown in the Praetorium." He didn't finish his implication.

She didn't need him to. Instead, Rune went to the door and gently slid it back open, letting in the sounds. They were less frantic, but she peeked around the corner and saw St. Rachel bundled up in wires and tubes. The nurse still waited outside and stepped forward when he saw her.

"She's stable for now. They are about to move her up to surgery, so we need to get the blood donation now," he said.

She nodded. "He isn't going to get undressed, but he has the same holographic interface she does with his bio stats. Will that suffice for checking him out?"

The nurse's eyes pursed into a question. "I'll ask."

They exchanged nods, and he disappeared to presumably go find the doctor. Rune went back in to attend to her partner. St. Benedict had taken over wiping away the dirt and blood from his face and hands. He ran a finger along the scar hidden under his hair.

"We can't leave her alone," he said.

"Will you behave yourself if I go stay with her?"

He nodded. "I'm calm now."

Rune decided to take him at his word. She turned to go, but he captured her arm.

"Thank you," he said, his voice heavy, like he had to drag it out of an abyss to say anything.

She laid her hand over his. "I wasn't going to leave her."

"You should have."

"Yeah, everyone kept saying that. But that isn't who I am," she said resolutely. "I don't know. Maybe I'm wrong."

"No, it isn't, is it?" He lifted his gaze to her then. "Rune... I am so sorry."

"It's fine," she said, taking her hand away. "We all got away. We're going to get help and you tried. I know, I get it. You tried to help me find Jasmeen, even after you told me it was too dangerous, and it turned out you were right, so—"

"I'm sorry for betraying you," he said.

She flinched. He hung his head again. "I know, I get it. It's not enough to simply say sorry, but I am. I was such an idiot and got us both stuck in a situation that undermined you and trapped you in this cage. I tore everything away from you: your bar, your family, your life."

"St. Benedict, stop it. I'm tired of the burden of your pity party," Rune said, staring down at the hand wrapped around her wrist. He released her with a jolt, like he didn't realize what he was doing. "I... I understand, okay?"

She expected him to respond to that, but when he didn't, she found she needed to.

"I'm not an idiot. I know what the circumstances were. I was trapped either way, and there was nothing that could be done to stop that, and if it wasn't for your intervention, I would be in Kodiak's prison, whatever they're calling it now, and not in this semi- quasi- facsimile of freedom."

"I promised to protect you," he said.

"So fucking what?" Rune snapped, the emotions she was trying to keep down rising to the surface anyway. "It's not like what I wanted mattered. You don't owe me anything."

"I owe you—"

"Look, I get it. Okay? I'm not upset with you." A sob escaped from Rune's throat unexpectedly. She pressed the back of her hand against her mouth even as her eyes blurred. "Dammit."

Maybe it was everything that had happened over the last hour, but she felt that if she took her hands away from holding herself, she would fall to pieces.

"I lost everything, okay? I don't blame you for it, but I still... I watched my bar burn down. Liam died! I lost my freedom, and I'm grieving it!" Her voice broke on the last truth. "I'm grieving it, and I'm not going to be okay, okay? I lost everything that makes me *me*. Again!" She wiped her sleeve against her nose, which was leaking now, copiously. "Jasmeen. Helping her was the last little bit of myself that I *didn't* lose, and it was *my* choice. Ever since I've met you, you've been trying to take *my* choices away to keep *me* safe, and I just want you to *stop!*"

"I know. I'm sorry," he said as much as with his haunted eyes as with his words.

She didn't know what to do with that. He wasn't fighting her about it. She had so many ready responses to the different arguments he could make, point after point, but the one response she hadn't prepared for was for him to agree with her. Her feelings had nowhere to go.

"What do you mean, 'you know'?" It came out as an uncharitable sneer.

He stood up. "How many times have I betrayed you? From the moment we met? I keep doing the same things over and over again, and I know I'm doing it, okay? I know. I'm just..." He turned and kicked the wall past the head of the bed. It made a dull thump, and for a heartbeat, Rune thought he had punched a hole. "I don't have the right to ask for your forgiveness. I don't deserve that... And I can't *make* it right, either. I can't give you your freedom or your life back."

"Just stop—!" Rune said.

"Is everything okay?" Nurse Joey asked from the doorway.

"Yes!" Rune shouted, then collected her feelings to stuff them hurriedly back into their box inside herself. "Sorry, sorry. Yes, we're just ... working some stuff out."

"Okay. The doctor is going to be in soon to check your holographic thing," he said, obviously struggling with the term for it, and Rune was no help. She didn't know it either. "They're moving your friend up to prep for surgery in a couple of minutes."

St. Benedict bolted to the door. "She can't be alone."

"St. Benedict, sit down!" Rune ordered and he did. She walked over and took his wrist in her hands. "Do the thing

that brings up the hologram platform with your bio-data on it." He yielded, flourishing his hands so the surface of his palm ignited. With a few gestures, his own little holo facsimile appeared, along with a list of his injuries.

"Here is his bio-data, nénado'wet," Rune said, recalling up the word for "healer" in Potawatomi. She had no idea where her brain had spit that word out from, but Nurse Joey double-blinked in surprise. His jaw relaxed an inch, and he nodded. "I'll let the doctor know, Lady," he returned. Now it was Rune's turn to blink, realizing that he had also recognized her as the Head of one of the Houses of the Magic Guild, status notwithstanding.

"Thank you," she nodded.

Then a klaxon went off in the emergency room.

CHAPTER 19

St. Benedict rushed out of the room with the nurse, Rune right behind him. Everywhere white lights were flashing from units near the ceiling. The horrible sounds seemed to be coming from those units. It was so sharp and grating, Rune had to slap her hands over her ears.

"What's going on?" she tried to shout, but she could barely hear her own voice.

"I don't know," St. Benedict seemed to say, though she was mostly guessing from the shape of his lips. He said something more she couldn't figure out and then turned to go into St. Rachel's room. The staff were still inside, slowed but not stopping their work to assist the unconscious patient.

St. Benedict went to the doctor and leaned in to speak in their ear as loudly as he could. Whatever he asked, the doctor shook their head no. The doctor tried to say something more. Rune moved to intervene, afraid St. Benedict would lose control again and attack the doctor, but instead her partner met her gaze.

Fear.

Then he came to her. He leaned into her ear. "We need to get out of here," he said.

"What's happening?" Rune asked, their cheeks meeting so she could speak and be heard back.

"They're coming for us," he said. "We need to escape, try to get to a safe house."

"But St. Rachel…" But she already knew. If they tried to move her, she died.

She looked at the woman lying on the bed, her personal enemy, helpless and on the verge of dying.

"We're not leaving," Rune said.

"I know," St. Benedict agreed. "Can you make a shield, like you have before?"

"Without my crystal, I can only try," Rune said.

"Try," he agreed.

Rune scanned the emergency room. There were several people in the space being escorted out by nurses and security personnel, all in various stages of treatment. The medical staff looked discombobulated.

Three separate security guards moved about the room with flashlights, flashing the light into passing faces like it was a cruel teenage prank.

It was clear they were looking for someone. One spoke into the radio at his shoulder while another, who was a Catwoman, moved toward the entrance of the room. Just as they approached, three more figures in black pushed their way in, brazenly shoving a nurse to the side. The Catwoman held up her hands, calling "Hey," at the figures, but the foremost one immediately rushed them while the other two bolted past.

Then the Saint from the warehouse appeared. He looked rough. His lower lip was split, and his opposing eye was on its way to swelling shut, but even more importantly, he looked pissed.

"St. Benedict!" he shouted, his eyes snapping from across the room.

Rune felt St. Benedict's hand on her arm squeeze tighter. She nodded and went deeper into St. Rachel's alcove, taking a position next to her side.

She grabbed the vulnerable Saint's limp hand, the one that was not broken, and gave it a squeeze. "It's going to be alright, St. Rachel. We're going to keep you safe," Rune said, even if no one, not even herself, could hear her. Outside the door, St. Benedict moved forward along with a pair of very brave nursing staff.

"You cannot be back here!" Nurse Joey attempted to intervene, bravely blocking the way. He was immediately bullrushed by another one of the agents. St. Benedict rushed up and grabbed that agent's arm, freeing the nurse, who shoved at the same time. The two males threw the agent back.

The agent should have fallen onto the enemy Saint, but he jumped up and over the man's body like he wasn't there and came down with a cross punch into St. Benedict's face. Blood sprayed across the central nursing station. The nurse sitting there screeched in shock as she backed away from the violence, the landline receiver still in her hand forgotten.

The enemy Saint grabbed St. Benedict by the back of his shirt and hauled him back, throwing him onto the floor. St. Benedict landed hard. He grimaced as he curled around himself. Rune was sure he hit his head on the floor. He had already taken so many hits from their first attempt to escape, she had no idea how much more he could take.

As he squirmed on the floor, trying to get back up, his attacker stepped over him to kneel on him. The other Saint moved sluggishly himself, betraying his own fatigue and injury.

St. Benedict kicked out with both feet. It was awkward but effective, scoring a hit on the enemy Saint's knee. St. Dominic collapsed, bellowing in pain, and St. Benedict rolled to crawl away, freeing his legs from underneath the man.

Rune moved to grip the door frame of St. Rachel's alcove, wanting to go to him to help and knowing she was the only thing left between the oncoming confrontation and everyone

behind her. She glanced behind herself at the fearful medical workers, their eyes wide, their vows to do no harm so close to being tested.

"You should all go!" she told them, gesturing for the other side of the nurse's station, hoping that the agents attempting to move in would let the bystanders pass in favor of their real target. It was a grim hope, but all the situation could allow.

"Everyone out!" the doctor ordered. "Leave everything. Go now."

Most were reluctant, but everyone obeyed, moving past Rune and exiting to the other side of the nursing station quickly. Only the doctor remained.

"You should go too!" Rune shouted over the still-blaring sirens at the doctor.

The doctor glanced at her as they continued working on St. Rachel. "I don't leave my patients to die," they said so matter-of-factly it could only be true.

Rune realized she had no choice but to accept that. A glimmer sparked in the doctor's eyes, and for the first time, Rune got a good look at the silver name tag on their coat.

"Thank you, Doctor Khan," Rune said.

Then she closed her eyes and went into her center. If there was ever a time for all the practice and meditation to pay off, now was it. She felt her magic uncurl within her.

Snapping her eyes open, she turned and left the alcove just as St. Benedict made his mad scramble back toward her. Like their foe, she stepped over him, placing herself between. In her mind, she pictured the shield of light globing before her.

"Leave me! Get him!" St. Dominic screeched, waving away the agents who were trying to help him while the third attempted to go around the long way, finding himself blocked in by the retreating staff.

Extending both her hands out, Rune was relieved to see her shield before her, glowing golden bright. "Stay back!" she shouted as one of the agents approached the shield, hesitating at the sight of it.

"What do you think that is going to do for you, Talent?" St. Dominic sneered, regaining his feet with the help of the last agent. His leg was bent wrong, but then with a hefty grunt, he forced it straight with a painful, bone-crunching snap-snap. The most that crossed the Saint's face while he did it was a pang of discomfort. Then he gave the leg his weight with a few sauntering steps.

"You come any closer, and I'll short-out your entire cybernetic everything. Then I'd like to see you fix that knee," Rune declared, holding her ground. The shield only glowed brighter.

"She means it, St. Dom," St. Benedict said, pulling himself back up to standing, his own augmented eyes glowing bright blue.

St. Dominic stopped his saunter a mere few inches from her shield, making the surface snap and crackle. Smirking, he flicked it with his finger.

All the power in her shield flashed, and St. Dominic's hand went rebounding back, taking him with for a couple of wobbly steps as the shield blinked out of existence.

"Dammit!" Rune cursed.

"It's okay. Keep trying," St. Benedict said, pushing past her to throw himself back into the fight just as the agent who went around approached.

St. Dominic continued to wobble, needing to grab the nursing station to take weight off his bad leg. His easy repair had been a bluff apparently. By then, two brave security guards came between, protecting the people still trapped in their alcoves on the right side.

"No, don't!" St. Benedict tried to say, but it was too late. The other Saint grabbed both guards, and their bodies violently seized. There was a snapping sound, and the enemy Saint's eyes were completely opaqued and flashing.

The second he let go, the guards dropped to the ground, unconscious and smoking. A terrible ozone smell filled the limited space.

St. Dominic's fingers glowed, electricity still snapping in

his hands. Then he staggered back, the light from his hands and eyes dropping as he staggered back into the third agent behind him.

"That was a mistake, St. Dominic!" St. Benedict crowed, laughing as maniacally as a Viking in the heat of battle, wiping blood from his mouth. Then he vaulted over the nurse's station, finding his own second wind.

St. Dominic rolled up to intercept him.

St. Benedict threw a punch. It was parried. The Saints exchanged a series of swings and punches that Rune could barely follow.

One of the agents recovered enough and came at St. Benedict from the side.

Her Saint was too slow and went down with a tackle.

"St. Ben!" Rune shouted. She rushed forward, shoving the agent off him as the two men scrabbled undignified on the ground.

St. Dominic towered over them, swinging down with a pair of gripped fists, his eyes blazing opaque blue lightning.

Rune gripped the air in front of her breastbone where the old shield crystal would have sat. Pretending that she still held that precious gift, she focused again on calling up the shield. Her fingers spread as magic tore down them. The light flickered into a shield.

But the magic wouldn't hold.

St. Dominic arrested his attack just before he would have hit the shield, but the shield flickered out on its own.

The horrible blond man glared down on her with pure contempt, his mouth drawn back in an ugly sneer.

Then his face froze.

His whole body seized.

The sneer turned to a grimace of pain.

He buckled forward, bending in half as blood dripped from his nose onto the tile of the emergency room. She thought St. Dominic was going to fall on them.

Rune lost her balance and slid back onto her butt. She

tried to push herself clear on the slick tile, but St. Benedict's body was in the way. He was trying to struggle back up to fighting. The agent she had knocked over made it to his knees and attempted to punch the back of Rune's head, but St. Benedict blocked it from the ground as he wound both of his legs around the agent's neck.

Rune kept her eyes on what was happening to St. Dominic. A strange glimmer of light flashed over his opaqued blue eyes, something unearthly white.

Then he stopped and straightened. His eyes were still completely opaqued as he stared forward, his hands hanging limply at his sides like a marionette on a final string. Above him, a light fixture burst, throwing sparks. The people still in the emergency room screamed while others continued to evacuate them. The other lights flickered, making an eerie sight behind the insensate Saint, unreactive to anything that was happening around him. His eyes kept glowing, growing brighter. They were intensely white, burning so brightly, making it harder and harder to look at him.

Then a hologram erupted around the Saint's body, seemingly projecting from every pore. The hologram overlaid his form, creating a ghostly blue surface, obscuring the Saint's actual features. The hologram was of a man, tall and lean, with dark rockstar hair and looks. He wore a simple black, v-necked shirt and skinny pants that hugged his frame. The figure leaned his hips to one side, blinking as if he were trying to orient himself in the space, then ran both his hands through his overly long hair.

"Well, look at that," he said, lifting up the hands of St. Dominic now covered in the holographic skin. "It worked. Now for fuck's sake, what is going on?" He turned to survey the scene with a detached disinterest.

"This is a mess, St. Dominic. Now we're going to have to take care of all these people," he said, rubbing his forehead in exasperation.

Rune stood up in absolute shock. She couldn't believe

what she was seeing. As she rose, the figure turned to her, his eyes at first passing over her as if she were nothing of importance, only to double back in the next breath. His own eyes went wide in mutual recognition.

"Justin?" Rune could barely make a sound as she spoke his name.

"Oh hell," the hologram of Justin responded, "it's... it's you. You're alive." He extended his hand as if to cup her cheek. She wanted to pull away, but she was too stunned to remember how to. A warm hand that tingled touched her. In her mind, she knew it was actually St. Dominic's hand covered in a projection, but she still couldn't pull away.

"Justin," she said again, as if saying his name would make him more real.

The other hand came up and held her face. "Anna. I just... Anna!" Arms came around her and pulled her into a tight hug. Automatically, she hugged back, her body going on autopilot as her mind tried to re-engage. The hug didn't last long as the image of Justin released her, laughing.

"Where are you? Where is this place?" he asked, sweeping her hands into his own, his joyful eyes looking from her to the space and back to her. "It's a hospital. You're in a hospital. Anna, are you hurt?"

"No, no. Justin," she sputtered, pulling her hands away from him, keeping them up to ward him off. "Just... Just give me a moment. I don't... I don't..." She stepped back, trying to take him in. "You can't be here. I saw you die. The tape... the video... there was a video. I saw you die."

His smile fell a little as he studied her expression. Then it switched again to a smile. "It's alright. This is going to be alright. I will take care of all of this. I just—"

"Rune, get away from *it*," St. Benedict said. He had staggered to his feet behind her, the other agent unconscious, she hoped, on the floor.

"Shut up, St. Ben," Rune said instead, stepping closer so that she edged out in front of him, addressing the apparition in front of her. "Justin, I... I have a million questions to ask you but right now—"

The hologram grinned that famous rockstar grin that haunted her dreams. "Yes, we need to get you out of here. If you're not hurt, you are free to leave, yes? I'll have a car summoned. I can take you away from all this."

Rune's heart thunked hard. They were nearly the exact words he had said to her all those years ago when he proposed, promising to take her away from the pressure and expectations of her parents.

"No, Justin. I can't go with you." She glanced back at St. Rachel's room, the vulnerable Saint still lying there. A couple of nurses had rejoined the doctor and were now standing with them in front of the bed, making a sort of human wall.

Justin glanced up at them as well. "I can have this all taken care of. It's no problem. I don't know what you've gotten yourself into, but there is nothing I can't solve." He tried to cup her face again, but she pulled away.

"Call your people off," she demanded.

His jaw went stiff in that one-eighty way he had when she did not go along with his plans. He seized her arm, forcefully gripping. "Are you with them? Anna, what have you done?"

St. Benedict seized Justin's thumb, pulling it back hard until it made a painful crack. Justin didn't seem to feel it, but he lost his grip on Rune's arm, and she pulled away. She backpedaled several steps to get clear. St. Benedict shoved, making her former husband stumble.

At last, Justin looked at St. Ben. If his face had gone dark before, it was full of hatred and death now.

"You!" he spat.

"Yeah, I hate you too," St. Benedict said and lunged to throw a cross punch. Justin grabbed the hand, stopping it in mid-swing with inhuman strength. A sick grin split Justin's otherwise handsome face. St. Benedict didn't slow but instead set his foot against Justin's chest and pulled free, kicking himself back and knocking them both to the ground.

Justin recovered first, scrambling across the tile floor like an animal to climb on top of St. Benedict. He seized the Saint around the throat.

St. Benedict struggled to hold him back, already so weakened by the fighting.

"I'll make sure you never hurt her again!" Justin roared. He lifted one hand, keeping the other pinning St. Benedict down by the throat. It snapped and crackled with electricity. He brought the hand down toward St. Benedict's sweaty face. The Saint struggled, but he couldn't dislodge him. Instead, he got one of his own hands free and seized Justin by the elbow. Despite this, the hand continued to lower inch by inch.

"Justin! Stop it!" Rune cried. She rushed forward.

"Stay back!" St. Benedict bellowed. "His hand—" It was all he could get out as he struggled.

Rune didn't care. She seized one of the guns that had been dropped in the initial fight and pointed it right at Justin's head.

"Let him go, or I swear I'll blow your head off!"

Justin stopped at that threat, tipping his eyes up to see the end of the barrel. Rune felt unbelievably calm holding the weapon, the end steadily pointing. She meant every word.

"I don't believe you," Justin said quietly.

Rune shot the gun.

A piece of tile leapt out of the floor beside both men. The remaining people in the room screamed, and Rune redirected the gun calmly back at Justin's head. "I'm deadly serious," she said without missing a beat. "Let. Him. Go."

They held gazes for an endless time. Justin didn't move, and St. Benedict panted beneath him, still struggling to push the sparking hand away.

Rune saw he would move a second before he did it.

She realized in that same second that she wasn't going to pull the trigger. St. Benedict was going to die.

The world rolled in slow motion, as if her alternate sight was activated.

She shouted.

The hand crackled.

Then there was a pulse.

Rune couldn't see it, but she felt it. It ripped instantly through the room. The lights and all the machines blinked out at once. The damn klaxon finally died. Then emergency lights came on at once, casting a strange pall throughout the room.

The hologram of Justin disappeared, revealing St. Dominic underneath. Without his strings, the puppet dropped hard to his knees before falling unconscious to the floor beside his would-be victim. St. Benedict gasped for air, his eyes closed.

And behind Rune, Maxamillion held a strange pomegranate-sized orb. More people were filing in behind the Prince of the Resistance, taking charge of the room. Rune recognized them as agents from the Praetorium. Calmly, Maxamillion lowered the orb, dropping it into the pocket of his trench coat. He stepped up to Rune and extended his hand for her gun, giving her a gentle smile.

"Stand down," he said calmly. "The cavalry's here."

CHAPTER 20

E verything after that went by in a hurried flash.

Rune recalled Zita appearing and taking charge of St. Rachel's care. The wounded Saint had been stabilized enough to move, and after some conferring with the ER doctor, Zita was able to convince them that the specialized care St. Rachel needed could only be provided by the Corinthe corp. Doctor Khan didn't seem to like it, but they didn't have a whole lot of choice, especially after St. Rachel received an infusion of specialized blood.

After that, St. Benedict stayed by St. Rachel's side as she was wheeled out to a waiting, unmarked ambulance. It was Maxamillion who led Rune into a waiting SUV complete with a living driver. A privacy shield had been installed inside, separating the driver from his passengers, and Rune appreciated it. She knew Maxamillion wanted to have words with her, and the idea that someone she didn't know would be listening in on what was said made her stomach sick. She knew she was in trouble, and while she was pretty sure she couldn't be "fired," she knew she was most likely going to lose a whole slew of privileges.

Dawn crept through the cracks of the city, and she felt utterly exhausted. Maxamillion didn't speak to her once he got in beside her and shut the door. Instead, he immediately got on the phone, talking a mile a minute. She couldn't think clearly enough to follow what being said, and frankly, she just didn't care. Her mind was filled to bursting with a thousand shocks and realizations.

The foremost: Justin lived.

As she grappled with *that*, the car jerked into motion. She looked to the coming dawn and saw instead rainclouds, swallowing it up. Streaks of water slashed against the window as the rain dumped onto the city.

It was so fucking metaphorical.

"Are you alright?" Maxamillion asked.

She didn't even realize at first that he had gotten off his phone call until he handed her a bottle of water. She stared at it like it was a foreign object whose use eluded her.

"Rune? Are you alright?" he repeated.

"I…" She wanted to lie or say some acceptable platitude, but she just couldn't. Not right at that moment. "No. No, I am not okay. I don't think I've been okay for a long time."

"I am so sorry," Maxamillion said.

"Okay," Rune replied after a hiccupped moment, unsure what to make of that declaration. "Not what I expected you to say."

He arched his perfectly shaped eyebrow at her. "You just saw the walking, talking ghost of your first husband. I don't think there *is* a right thing to say for that."

"I suppose not," Rune agreed. "So you knew?"

She studied Maxamillion's expression as he thought about his answer. "I'm not sure," he finally said. "There were unverified rumors for sure and strange circumstances surrounding those rumors. But there are always rumors and conspiracy theories. Most of them contradict each other."

"I suppose you are under no obligation to tell me any of those rumors," she stated dryly without judgement. She was just stating the truth. "I suppose St. Benedict knew of these rumors, too."

"They have been a central tenet of his mission to find the Masterson Files," Maxamillion agreed.

Rune took a deep breath in and let it out. "I suppose they were like the rumors of *my* continued existence as well."

"Those proved to be true," he agreed.

"So did Justin's."

He shrugged one shoulder at that. "I'm not ready to make that conclusion," he said, then amended. "I saw what you did, but it was a projection, correct? Overlaying another body. There have been several projects working on advancing holographic projection technologies. I hadn't seen a working one in action before."

"You knew how to diffuse it," Rune noted. "You came prepared with the exact thing."

"I knew how to incapacitate the Saint without harming him further. Unfortunately, it took out the emergency wing as well and that will come with its own problems. St. Rachel was already unconscious, and St. Benedict wasn't out for more than a minute."

"Oh, I..." Rune swallowed. "I didn't realize St. Benedict was knocked out."

"And don't tell him I told you. He'll be fine, or at least he won't be harmed from that." Then Maxamillion's phone binged five times in quick succession. He sighed and pressed two fingers against the bridge of his nose. "It never fails. I solve one problem and make a dozen more."

"I'm sorry," Rune said, though she didn't really feel it.

"It's not your fault," he said. "I should have warned you about the rumors. You are right. I had thought many times to have a meeting with you to show you everything that we suspected to date, but I thought it would be better to let you have time after losing everything. I'm actually shocked you've recovered and wanted to work so quickly."

"I didn't think I had a choice," she said. "I am your inmate, after all. I owe you work. I'm just grateful you're not torturing me."

"Rune, you are not my 'inmate.' The only reason I gave you anything to do in the company at all was Zita suggested it might help you with your recovery from it all. We were all worried about you."

That information surprised and touched Rune. "I thought everyone was just avoiding me... but what you're saying is you were all just trying to give me space?"

The princely man settled back in his seat, now looking out his own window. "I couldn't do anything about the cage our society placed you in, but I had hoped that if you had your choice of cages, I could make one for you that would be barely noticed. Much like mine."

"Are you saying, 'we're all in cages'?" she said, wryness creeping into her voice, much to her own surprise. Maybe she wasn't as numb as she thought she was.

"Well, yes. Everyone in Corinthe Corp is. We're all people that the corporate authority deemed problematic to their interests. My underground resistance barely made a dent in their lives, but as a corporate entity ourselves..." He sighed again. "But this just shows me what I didn't want to admit to myself. We're losing sight of our own mission. It took your act of defiance for me to see it."

"You abandoned Jasmeen, the exact kind of person you said you were designed to help. You leveraged her," Rune stated. Again, these were the facts.

Maxamillion slammed his fist into his thigh. "Yes!" Then he remembered himself, adjusting his dress coat before passing a hand wearily over his eyes. "Apologies," he said. "I... Believe me. It's been a very trying twenty-four hours. We've lost half a dozen of our people, and they're not even dead. They are simply gone. And yes, Jasmeen is one of them."

A silence dragged out between them. "I'm not going to

apologize," Rune finally said. "I don't mean any disrespect to the situation, but I don't think what I did was wrong."

"No, it wasn't wrong. What was wrong was the whole situation in the first place. You are calling me out correctly. I am becoming the very monster I've been fighting, and this was something I have been afraid of. I let St. Benedict make the call regarding Ms. Clarmont. I was measuring resources and cost/benefit analysis and..." He fell silent.

"And forgot about the person factor," Rune supplied when he couldn't.

He looked at her with an intensity she found unnerving. "You always see me, don't you? Ever since we first met, you just look right through all of this to a man's very soul."

The pronouncement surprised her. "I guess. I don't realize that's what I'm doing if I am."

"You know, I trusted St. Benedict then too, in regard to your safety. This is not an excuse, but I take responsibility for my part in what happened. I ordered him to make that deal with your enemies in order to rescue... it's more like *take* you out of the situation."

"I *understand* the circumstances that landed me with you," Rune said impatiently, getting really freaking tired of explaining this over and over again. "What I don't understand is why everyone else doesn't see that I KNOW. I'm not stupid. I *know* what was happening, and I know what was at stake!"

"And that is why you're trying to do the same for Jasmeen Clarmont?"

That brought Rune up short.

She wanted to say no, but what had been her plan?

To get Jasmeen into the Praetorium... just like me. Why? Because it was what I thought would be best for her, she thought.

"We're all in cages," Maxamillion repeated, reading her face.

Rune shook her head, more at herself than anything. "And now I don't know how we're going to find her, if she's disappeared into the Kodiak's system... and now Justin knows I am alive, and I know he's alive. If he's working with Kodiak as well, it just got even more dire for me, hasn't it?"

"There is a lot we don't know," Maxamillion agreed.

"What baffles me is how could Justin have not known *I* was alive?"

"Simple." He opened his palm to her as the example. "How did I not know that you had a way to escape the Praetorium with my best agent and were gone for half a day before we realized it? There is a power struggle going on inside Kodiak. For all their flaunted influence and their grappling for more, they have turmoil within that we have been exploiting. Yes, someone at Kodiak knows you're alive and someone else now. It benefitted that someone within Kodiak to keep that information from … your ex but now he knows. Their internal balance is shifting again. And what that means for our current situation, we will need to see."

"Do you think it could stop what is happening?"

"God, I hope so." Maxamillion reached for one of the tiny bottles of water in a back pocket of the SUV and cracked it hard, downing the whole thing in one go. "The next question now, is what do you want to do?"

"Pardon?" Rune asked, her thoughts having dwelled on the memory of seeing her ex-husband's face again in the length of the pause.

"Do you wish to keep hunting for Jasmeen? In this regard, it is your call on how you want to proceed."

She cocked her head at that. "Is it even possible now, if Kodiak has taken her?"

"Malachi has also been searching for her on the down low, right under my nose," Maxamillion said with dry humor. "Apparently there is mutiny on all sides. He will want to show you what he's discovered and compare notes with you as soon as we get back. Whatever other resources you want are yours."

She furrowed her brow at that. "What do you mean 'other resources'?"

"My original plan had been to make you the head of your own department, the magic division of the Corinthe Corp,"

Maxamillion said. "That comes with a discretionary budget and your choice of personnel. I want you to work with the people you feel most comfortable with and can support you. You choose your missions; you execute them. You help people like you did before."

Rune sat stunned at what she was hearing, but she took a moment to roll the implications around. "I want Malachi," she said.

"Done," Maxamillion agreed.

"I'll think about everyone else," she said.

"Of course." He nodded.

"Would that mean you're still my boss? I only answer to you?" she asked, the first question to pop into her brain.

"No, that's not the arrangement. I am the CEO of Corinthe Corp. What I'm proposing here is more like its own company with its own CEO head, you, both companies under the same banner, but we would be more like equals."

"Why?" Rune asked. "Why would you want to give up control like that?"

"Because I've been alone on the top too long, and I'm losing perspective. I think the last couple of days have proved that very clearly. I need more checks and balances, and I think you're the kind of person who can help create that." Then he looked away, his dark skin flushing to his ears. "And because I really want to ask you to dinner, and I can't do that if I am your boss."

That was a punch in an already tender metaphorical stomach. He glanced back uncertainly at her, like a teenager who had just asked a girl to prom.

She double blinked. "I didn't realize..."

He squirmed in his seat, which just made it funnier and cuter. "I understand that this is not a good time for this discussion. Like I said, you were recovering... and there are other considerations. I was just hoping when things settled ... into a routine, that you would maybe consider..."

"What exactly?" she prompted.

"Going to dinner with me," he said.

"I would love to," she answered honestly. Now it was his turn for his eyes to go wide.

"Oh," he said, stunned. "Are you sure? You just learned your husband was alive."

"Ex-husband, yes. There are some things I need to sort out, but you said that we could wait until we've gotten things back under control right?" She chewed on her lower lip. "Would you still be up for going out with me, knowing that part of the reason I said yes is to prove to myself that he doesn't own me anymore?"

"I'm okay with that," he agreed. "It's just dinner, after all. I enjoy your company, Rune. I would like to spend more time in it."

"Good. Then I think I would too. When things settle down. Thank you, Maxami—"

"Max."

"Thank you, Max," she amended.

Now he grinned in such a boyish way that the smooth businessman was gone, and he looked like a teenager wearing his dad's suit. "I must be blushing like a fool," he said.

"About as badly as I am."

CHAPTER 21

"**A**re you hurt?"

"Not as badly as she is." St. Benedict stared at St. Rachel's face, lost underneath her wounds and the breathing apparatus they kept over her face. Zita squatted on the other side of the locked gurney, writing something on a chart. No one had said anything to him since getting into the ambulance.

"This was my fault," he murmured, the metal taste in his mouth heavy.

"Yes, it probably is," Zita said stiffly. The tip of her snake tail twitched rapidly, conveying her anger in a way that the coldness of her tone did not.

He buried his face in his hands.

Rune knew.

She knew, and it wasn't because he had told her the truth. No, instead this was a million times worse. Now the truth had been all stirred up and made complicated. He knew she didn't really understand what she saw and what it could mean. There was no way she could understand. Hell, he barely understood what he saw.

Justin Masterson.

St. Benedict needed to do something.

Patting around his clothes, he went through his pockets. "Where's my phone? I've lost my phone, dammit."

"You don't need it," Zita said. "We are on technology lock-down, remember?"

"I need to—"

"Sit your ass down. It's a damn miracle that you weren't fried when the mini EMP pulse fired. If Maxamillion hadn't directly hit the other Saint... In fact, it's a miracle we didn't take out the whole damn hospital, just the ER with the ambient pulse! No big deal! Or for that matter killed St. Rachel in the process."

St. Benedict stared at St. Rachel again. "She saved her," he muttered.

"What?" Zita snapped.

"St. Rachel saved Rune," he repeated, then he snorted. "Then Rune saved St. Rachel. This wasn't supposed to happen."

"Don't say that," Zita snapped, pointing a finger at him. "I hate it when people who have screwed up say things like that. As if that would make any bit of difference now! Tell me, does that make a bit of difference to St. Rachel?"

"This is my fault," St. Benedict confessed again, bowing his head, staring at the texture of the metal floor beneath. This was what he wanted from Zita, to tell him what he was already screaming in his head.

Always contrary, Zita did not comply with that wish. "That wasn't your fault. Not directly," Zita conceded, her tone and her tail softening. "We're under attack. You are responsible for not staying where you and Rune would be safe, but *being* attacked, that is only on them."

"Kodiak Corp." It was both a question and a statement.

Zita's lips were a thin line. "Yes. This looks like retaliation for destroying their lab and Dr. Klauson. It was just slower in coming than we thought. Malachi thinks that was part of the plan, to outwait us until we got complacent."

St. Benedict's spine stiffened as he stuffed all his guilt and self-loathing back in the well-worn box in his mind. He had waited too long, but now he needed to tell her. "I need to talk to Rune," he said.

"She is in the other car with Maxamillion. He's briefing her now," Zita stated, refocusing on her clipboard before reaching over and using a digital wand to activate St. Rachel's bioscan hologram in her hand.

St. Benedict half stood and attempted to move toward the front of ambulance. "Give me the com," he said to the driver and the other paramedic/guard up front, who sat there with a weapon across his lap.

"No!" Zita barked. "Sit back down. Total communication silence until we get back to the Praetorium."

The guard in the passenger seat slapped the back of St. Benedict's hand as he tried to reach for the com anyway, chasing him back.

Zita held out a syringe threateningly, and St. Benedict put up both his hands and backed down onto the bench. "I will drug you into next Tuesday if you push me! You'll be fully briefed when we get there. We're in a complete network blackout for our safety. Maxamillion has called out a small army to retrieve you, and I almost argued against it! Now shut up and sit until we arrive. I am going to have to go into surgery with St. Rachel the second we get there, and I need to review all of her charts and her last bioscan, so stop making everything about you!"

Lacking any other recourse, St. Benedict did just that. While they drove, he watched over St. Rachel, willing her to consciousness. As if she heard him, her eyes flickered open. Zita noticed and leaned forward so the other Saint could see her.

"St. Rachel? You're safe, you're in a Praetorium ambulance, and we're getting you home," her doctor reported.

St. Rachel blinked twice in acknowledgment. This wasn't their first rodeo, but then she flicked her eyes to St. Benedict with a question. He held out his hand over hers, and light snapped between them, linking them together.

<The Finder?> she asked through the digital equivalent of telepathy.

<She's with Maxamillion in the other car. She's secure,> he reported.

St. Rachel closed her eyes in relief. *<So she wasn't hurt?>*

<Not badly. She got away and found me on her way coming back for you.>

<She came back for me?> St. Rachel reopened her eyes, pursing her eyebrows together to express with her thoughts. *<The idiot!>*

<If she hadn't, you would be dead right now,> he stated.

St. Rachel didn't comment on that, though he could sense her thoughts swirling underneath the surface. It wouldn't take much for him to dive into those depths, but he refrained. She hadn't invited him that deeply in, even as he got ambient impressions of what she was thinking. He reached out and laid his hand over her unbroken one, squeezing it gently.

"We got him," he said out loud.

Her eyes darted to him, and he nodded.

"St. Dominic. We've got him in custody."

She snorted, squeezed his hand back, and tried to give a little nod.

<When I'm able, I'm going to...> She didn't finish transmitting the thought. Images of what she wanted to do to him explained herself plenty.

"St. Rachel," St. Benedict said, dragging his voice through the words he knew he needed to say. "I'm sorry."

He knew it wasn't what she expected to hear. If she started shouting at him, either out loud or in her mind, he wouldn't have blamed her. He would take all of it. Instead, he heard the tragic truth that he always knew but never wanted to acknowledge in the ambient whisperings of her thoughts.

<I love you, I love you, I love you. Please love me back...> She closed her eyes as if that would hide those feelings like it normally did. Yet she was too weak and broken to mask her

thoughts like that.

"I love you, too," he said gently. It was the truth. Maybe not the truth she wanted, but it was the truth she needed. A truth he himself needed to acknowledge. He prayed too, that she wouldn't ask him to clarify, that she wouldn't ask him to define his declaration. Because he could never give her what she wanted, but to pretend that he didn't love this woman who had been with him every step of the way since they had escaped, that her loss would mean nothing to him, was a sheer lie he couldn't endure anymore.

St. Rachel's eyes bore into his own, and he let her see. If she could have scoured his soul for evidence to prove or contradict him, she would have. Tears brimmed from her eyes, spilling down her cheeks. He gently thumbed them away. "Sleep, St. Rachel. You're safe. I won't let anything happen to you," he promised. "I'll be right here."

She nodded again, and after a few breaths, she was deeply asleep. He still heard her thoughts through their connection, but they were the peaceful delta waves of sleep. He mentally backed out but didn't fully close the connection, just in case she wanted him there.

He met Zita's gaze.

"I love you too, Zita," he said.

She snorted as if it were a joke, but when he remained dead serious, she nodded. "Maybe there's hope for you yet."

CHAPTER 22

The Praetorium was an amazing mess by the time they returned. Even with the ambulance running its lights, clearing their way on the highway, it seemed like an eternity had passed before they pulled into the building.

St. Rachel was unloaded first and carted off somewhere with Zita and St. Benedict right behind. Rune didn't even try to get her Saint's attention. She didn't even know what she wanted to say to him.

Instead, Malachi greeted her the second she walked through the door with Maxamillion.

"There you are! Thank the non-existent deity you're safe," he cried, grabbing her shoulder with the camaraderie she had been missing since coming to stay.

"Wait, what about St. Rachel?" Rune said, hesitating. It felt wrong to simply move on when her state was so undecided.

"She's safe now. She's going to get the care she needs, and she is going to recover," Maxamillion said with unwavering certainty. He set a hand on Rune's shoulder. "In order to

continue for that to be true, we each need to do what we can to secure the Praetorium. And there are still people out there who need our help to get to safety."

Rune knew that, but she needed to hear it, as if it gave her permission to let go and refocus. She nodded, and Maxamillion squeezed her shoulder.

"I will leave you to it," Maxamillion said, bowing gallantly to her before turning to get swallowed by the crowd of people gathering to talk to him.

Malachi tugged on her shoulder to lead her to his alcove. "Come on. I've got a ton to show you."

She followed him obediently and then he spun in place suddenly, his newly cut hair already growing wildly and flopping into his eyes.

"Oh, did he talk to you?" Malachi asked, jabbing a finger in Maxamillion's direction. "About the job thing?"

Rune blinked in surprise, though she realized she shouldn't have been. She nodded. "Uh, yeah. I said I wanted you on my team—"

"Great, perfect. Weird-ass way to get a promotion, right?"

"He didn't really frame it as a promotion—"

"No, yeah, I know." Malachi spun back again and went the rest of the way to his alcove, but he only stopped for a moment to gather up a plastic bin filled with his personal items from his alcove. "I got things more-or-less set up. When things are not so scary death-death, we'll want to take over another facility. Corinthe's got a couple of them, and we don't need a whole ton of people, but for now, what we got will be fine."

"Where are we going?" Rune asked.

"Oh, this way," he said as if that were enough explanation. He led the way to another cluster of monitors at the farthest corner of the room. It was completely empty of anyone else, except for one terminal where the rest of Malachi's stuff waited to be unpacked. To her surprise, the blank concrete wall beside them opened to reveal a freight elevator. Two figures moved out, unloading a whole stack of mattresses, piled one on top of the other. Malachi paused at the door and watched with her as they were unloaded. Another cart emerged, pushing folded metal frames that would unsnap to form the beds.

"What's going on?" Rune asked, eyeing the beds as the large industrial doors of the elevator closed and disappeared behind the concrete wall.

"We've pulled in anyone and everyone connected with the Praetorium that we think may have been compromised. This place can convert into a refuge facility, and that's what we're doing. We've also found the mole," Malachi said tersely.

"*The* mole!" Rune said. The surprises kept coming.

"Maxamillion's personal assistant," Malachi said angrily, dropping his stuff haphazardly on top of his other stuff. "The one person I was confident wasn't the mole until she confessed of her own free will."

Rune had no real idea who this woman was. She had been on the outside of the corporate society and hadn't made a point of getting to know anyone new. She could understand that having someone so close to Maxamillion betray them like that would be devastating. "So she knew everything?"

"She knew enough, though she just thought this was normal corporate espionage: pocket an extra paycheck and move on with life. We need to move locations ASAP. We're going to be setting up in the secondary Praetorium location away from the main corporate building. It'll be safer there." Malachi plopped down into his chair and tapped some keys to wake up the small bank of monitors before him.

"We're leaving the Praetorium?" Rune asked, surprised.

"No, we're not. Not yet anyway. It's going to take us twelve hours at the minimum to lock things down and get them transferred over, and that's with them cutting every corner imaginable." He shook his head. "We got too big, and this is too dangerous. Thank the non-existent deities our mole cracked when she did. We have time to do this with minimal issues."

"What changed her mind?"

"St. Rachel getting hurt. Same old story. Someone falls for

a Saint, and then they do stupid things. Stupid for her, the personal assistant, I mean, this time, because we would have caught her otherwise."

Rune furrowed her brows at that. "What have you done to her?"

"She's fine," Malachi dismissed, typing away at his keyboard. "She's being held. She's aware of her situation, and she's cooperating. We've frozen her assets since she's a corporate employee, and we'll be investigating her officially. It's all standard corporate authority stuff, but for right now, our underground needs to go deeper underground. Separate from Corinthe for a while."

Rune slipped off her coat. "But that is not what we're doing?"

"No, I am to help you in finishing your mission and getting this Jasmeen Clement to safety. There are at least five other teams doing the same thing; it's part of what is slowing us all down. Lucky for us, I found our target already," Malachi said, focusing on his screens.

From her angle, Rune could just make them out. "You found her!" She exclaimed as she jetted forward, grabbing the back of his chair.

"Yes. Or rather, I know where she currently is," Malachi said, typing away at his keyboard. Windows opened and expanded on one of the three screens facing them. "And it doesn't look like they've moved her since I last checked."

"Where is she?" Rune peered at the screen, trying to decipher what Malachi was doing, her gaze jumping from one screen to another.

"One second, I'll show you," Malachi said. A few more tense seconds and he had his screens sorted out. He pointed to the one on the left. It held an image of a rough looking man with short horns coming out of his balding head.

"This is the guy who is running the team that is holding her: Priapus. He has been previously identified by Praetorium as one of those 'special agent squads' that live on the Kodiak payroll," Malachi said, making the air quotes with his fingers before going back to typing. "St. Benedict has tangoed with him at least once and St. Rachel twice. Not a Saint, just a very talented satyr. I'm pretty sure he picked his own code name, so that tells you everything you need to know about him really. He does have limited augmentations. Mostly in his right hand, which holds a mini rocket launcher of all things."

Malachi brought up a stat line along with a 3D rendering of Priapus.

"Priapus, huh?" Rune said.

"You know him?" Malachi asked.

"Well, no, it's just his name," she noted.

"Yeah, Greek satyr god of lust or something. The guy's got a poetic side," Malachi noted.

Rune shook her head. "It's not just that. I'm just surprised that he calls himself Priapus of all things."

"Why?"

Furrowing her eyebrows, Rune huffed uncomfortably. "Well, it's a slur name for a satyr."

"Is it?" Malachi cocked his head. "Like how bad?"

"How bad is any racial slur?" Rune countered. "It's a word in order to treat a person as an other and de-sensitize them."

"You mean, dehumanize them, right?" Malachi pressed.

"Sure if you think 'human' is the central definition of 'normal,' excluding the hundreds of other sentient species out there," Rune said dryly. She could see Malachi still not understanding when it occurred to her something that he would understand. "It's as bad as calling Zita a 'snake.'"

That Malachi understood, and his face went dark at memories of that very slur being used against his Naga life partner. "Well, Priapus chose his name, so that's his problem," Malachi said tersely. He brought up another window. It showed Priapus getting out of a black SUV like the others that had appeared at the rave.

"I got pinged during a search for an advertisement offering to sell information on someone that matched Jasmeen's description. This big lug responded using one of his avatars

that he doesn't know we know is his in the deep web. Shortly after that, he shows up here and a few minutes later..."

Malachi plays another video, and Priapus with two of his men are leading a familiar woman out of the warehouse, through the very door that Rune had escaped only hours before. They loaded her into the back of their SUV even as she struggled to keep from going in. The camera never got a shot of her face.

"She was there the entire time?" Rune asked, horrified that her Finding magic hadn't detected her.

"No, this was the day before. She was long gone by the time you and St. Benedict arrived," Malachi assured, though it was only mildly reassuring.

"How do you know for certain that is her?" Rune asked.

"Because a minute later, the worm we installed into Kodiak's subsidiary network system pinged back that her status had been changed, which can only be done with her OmniSin. Jasmeen's is installed subcutaneously as most Kodiak employees are now. It means they would have to scan her OmniSin from her hand in order to change the status, even if she were dead. Which she's not—her status there hasn't been changed to that, and the biometric data would report that."

"That sounds like something that could be very easily hacked and changed," Rune countered.

"Easily, oh heck no. But yes possible, but also not something they would want to do. This was for their internal system only. Since she's an employee, she is their responsibility, and so there are failsafes within the company network to prevent tampering even at the highest levels. This is the only way the social system works. Everyone within it has to believe in the security of the system or the system fails. Cracking it themselves and anybody finding out about it—that's how you get revolutions. No one in the corporate world wants that, so here we are. There's too much money tied up in all of this."

"I'm aware of the concept," Rune said tersely. "I had to survive it."

Malachi noted the change in her voice and looked up at her. She met his gaze.

"I was in the corporate system before, remember? When I was Anna Masterson. It's why they forced me to divorce Justin, so they could officially change my status in their system, and I was no longer their responsibility legally."

"I'm sorry, Rune. I did forget," Malachi said somberly.

Rune waved her hand, dismissing the apology. "It's fine. That's not what I'm getting at. My husband was declared dead in the system. So how is it I just saw him if someone didn't alter the system?"

"You did what?!?" Malachi stopped mid-type to stare at her.

Rune swallowed the lump in her throat. This was not the time to feel anything.

"At the hospital. Justin. He... I don't even know how to describe it. But he was there. He saw and recognized me." Rune gripped the back of Malachi's chair hard. It seemed to steady her. There would be time to have feelings later when Jasmeen was safe, and Rune had a whole bottle of whiskey and a stack of cookies. "The point is, they changed his status in their company registry, which is tied to his citizenship."

"Then they must have had his consent to do that. I'm not saying it's impossible to make someone disappear from the system. Just that they haven't done that to Jasmeen yet. She is still registered, and she would have to be dead to undo it. Even if she were dead, it all takes time and many hoops to jump through. Believe me, it's not easy to get people out of this system. It's designed to be that way, even from when you escaped it, things have gotten more and more complicated. Transferring within the system is easier than removing someone entirely."

"So can't you just transfer her to Corinthe's corporate structure or something?"

"We have the resources to do it. I just need permission to—"

"You have permission."

Malachi opened his mouth but paused as his brain caught

up to what she just said. "Yes, ma'am." He started typing again.

Rune nodded, satisfied. "How long will it take?"

"Let me see how far I can get with all the paperwork. It'll be a few hours even expedited to get everything to go through."

"As long as they don't kill her," Rune said.

"They won't. There is too much at stake," St. Benedict said.

CHAPTER 23

He appeared beside her, walking like a man with weights around his ankles.

Rune looked him up and down and dismissed a dozen things she wanted to say or ask, settling on, "How is St. Rachel?"

"Stable," St. Benedict replied, and he focused on Malachi's computer. "I came over to help you."

"Well, as you can see, we have this in hand," Rune said, retrieving her coat. "Malachi, are you fine if I go take a shower?"

"Yeah, boss. I got this," the tech said, eyeing St. Benedict and choosing to stay out of it. "I will contact you when I get things squared, and we need to make some decisions. This will be at minimum three hours, so if you want to get some sleep, now's the time."

"Thank you," Rune said, nodding and recognizing the wisdom of the advice, even if it seemed like sacrilege based on everything that was going on.

She said nothing more to either man and headed toward the door leading to the underground suites. And every step, she was aware that St. Benedict walked beside her. They said nothing to each other the majority of the way to their suites, just moving around each other as if previously choreographed. He opened the door for her, and she waited for him to come through.

"It wasn't Justin," St. Benedict said just before she got to her door. She turned to look at him. He shifted on his feet. "It can't be Justin. What we saw..."

He stopped, licking his lips as he struggled.

Rune sighed. "What do you think he was?" she asked.

That seemed to shift the Saint out of whatever loop he had stuck himself into. "A projection. Someone pretending to be Justin."

"For what purpose?" she asked. "Why would St. Dominic stop fighting when he was winning to project an image of my supposedly dead husband at that particular moment?"

When St. Benedict didn't answer her, Rune asked another question. "Why would Kodiak for that matter? If they wanted to trick me, why stop St. Dominic from taking you out and seizing me by force right then?"

Despair painted St. Benedict's face. He opened his mouth to speak.

"Please stop," Rune said, holding up a hand. "Whatever lie is about to come out of your mouth, just don't. I just do not care anymore."

He closed his mouth.

Sliding her fingers through her hair, Rune pulled on the roots in consternation. In that moment, she thought she might fly apart. "Did you know?" She dropped her hands. "Did you know that Justin might be alive?"

"Rune, what you saw wasn't Justin—"

She narrowed her eyes at him, the rage that had been buried under a surface of numbness flared up. "Did you *know*!? When we watched that video of him being killed, violently, did you know that he was in fact alive?"

St. Benedict straightened, his hands hanging heavy at his

sides. "Yes. I knew," he admitted.

"Why didn't you tell me?" Rune asked, her voice now deadly quiet.

"I tried... After... when we saved the Fairy Queen, I came over to tell you everything. You said..." He stopped, pain crossing his face.

"What?!" Rune demanded, shouting and not caring who heard, not that she thought there was anyone to hear.

"You said, 'Let him be dead'!" Now it was St. Benedict who shouted, his voice ringing off the walls of the hall.

The memory of her saying that ripped through Rune's mind. Her standing on the ladder, mixing the magic color-changing paint. Him showing up in his three-piece suit to talk. That put the anger to bed, buried deep without a cause. "I remember," she said dully and set her hand on the knob of her door.

"Rune, wait..."

"Please, St. Benedict," she grimaced, "I just want to take a shower. Please."

"Okay," he whispered so softly that she almost didn't hear it. She opened her door and went inside, feeling relief and emptiness when she shut it between them.

Just as she mustered the strength to push away, someone knocked on the door behind her. She opened it to find St. Benedict still standing there, bracing himself against the door.

"My life is yours," he said softly.

"What?"

"I meant it when I said it. And I want you to ask Maxamillion to give me to you."

Rune took in a deep breath. She was too tired for this. "Why can't you just leave me alone?"

He hesitated. "If ... that is what you want, then I'll go." He took a half step back, struggling with words he hadn't said yet. "I didn't ... intend ... to hurt you."

"I know that!" Rune snapped. "But you don't respect me, do you? What? I was just supposed to forgive you because you had a 'good enough reason'? That was what my husband expected too."

St. Benedict held up his hand. "I don't deserve to be forgiven. You're right. I violated your trust."

"You took it for granted!"

"Yes. I made a terrible mistake."

"And I'm just supposed to forgive you? Just get over it because it was for my own good," Rune spat, though she wasn't really talking to St. Benedict anymore. "Because I need to be saved. I need help. I can't do anything on my own."

"That's not true," St. Benedict said.

This time she looked at him. She imagined her gaze could incinerate him on the spot, but he didn't flinch away from it. Instead, he stood quietly, waiting with his hands behind his back.

"It's what you all keep telling me," she finally said in a low, even voice. "You know, I had allies before all this. I had retainers who genuinely cared about me, who chose me freely of their own will and wanted to help me. People I could *trust*!" She pointed. "*That* was what you took away from me."

"Do you want me to go?"

"No! I want you to understand what you've done. I want you to hear how this feels!" It was all coming out now, the pain she'd kept a tight grip on for so long.

She screamed and kicked one of the lower cabinet doors so hard, she punched a hole through it.

"Crap," she said, staring down at her damage. She pulled her foot out of the cabinet, the wood splintering more.

"Don't worry about it," St. Benedict said softly. "I've vanquished many cabinets here."

She stepped back slowly from it, staring at the hole. "I didn't mean to do that."

"It's okay. We're all under stress."

St. Benedict went to one of the cabinets and took out a glass. He then went to fill it with water from dispenser in the fridge door before offering it to her.

"It's not okay, is it? What you did to me. I've been saying it's okay and that I understand this whole time, but it simply ... isn't, is it?"

"Yes, it simply isn't. I knew that, and I did it anyway. You're not crazy," he agreed. "I do not know what the hell I'm doing."

"Neither do I most of the time," she agreed. "But it was bearable when we were in the mess together. And I mean, you've already apologized, so I don't know what it is I want from you. I don't know how to make it alright again."

"You don't have to make it alright for me," he said, waving a hand at her. "You don't owe me anything."

"But then how do we heal if we can't fix it? If I don't forgive you?"

He held out his hand to her. She gave it to him, which he covered with his other one. "I promise to never betray you again."

Her lower lip trembled. "I'm just afraid. I've been betrayed so many times in my life."

He went still, as if something had occurred to him. Before she could compose the question, he knelt before her.

Rune went still. "What are you doing?"

"I swear..." he said, then looked up at her face. It seemed to steady his purpose, and his face became more resolute. "I ... swear to honor and serve you as my Lady and Mistress."

She stood there confused. Then a rush hit her hard in the chest. Magic poured through her, and the walls of her apartment shifted and wavered. Instead of the refined opulence of the wood and stone, the room was replaced by the worn, beloved walls of her bar. It was complete in every way from the bar itself to the chairs and tables to the kitschy devils lining the walls. It continued to blink in and out of existence as thrums of power wound and bound the Saint to her.

Rune stumbled a step back against it all, and he cried out in pain, grabbing at his head.

"St. Benedict!" she cried, reaching for him.

"Rune?" The Finder stopped in her tracks at the

familiar voice.

Blinking into existence was her youngest retainer, Ally. The kid was off to college and looked it, standing there holding a book bag, wearing a Northwestern sweatshirt, her blonde hair in a tail behind her head. She wasn't the only one. The room stood filled with people now, all familiar faces, and a couple still new to her.

Alf. Elias. Margaret. Uncle Lucas. Franklin. Marcus. Ravinia. Her retainers. Her family.

They stood beside her, completing a circle around St. Benedict, still kneeling on the floor. His hand fell away as he too stared in awe, mouth dropped open at the figures who had joined them. As one, they all turned to look at him as well.

"You finally took your Knight," Alf harrumphed.

"Pay up," Uncle Lucas said, thrusting a hand toward Elias.

"Oh wow," Ally said.

But Rune's eyes never unlocked from St. Benedict's intense and resolute gaze. "What... What have you done?"

St. Benedict stood looking around the circle. Then he shrugged, his expression bewildered. "Go big or go home?" he offered.

And then the group and the bar began to blink-out again. As one, the retainers returned their gaze to Rune. Alf bowed his head. "We are glad to see you're alright, my lady," he said.

"Remember, kid, we are always with you," Uncle Lucas added, and then they were gone, leaving only Rune and her newest retainer alone.

CHAPTER 24

feel much better," Rune said two and a half hours later.

To St. Benedict, she looked better. Sitting at the counter of his suite, the same layout with different colors of stone and wood, she was a picture of renewed vigor. Her cheeks were pink from her too-hot shower, and her long hair hung still damp and messed up.

She was absolutely gorgeous.

He set a fresh glass of water in front of her. "Did you sleep?" St. Benedict asked as he as hacked whatever vegetables he could find to sauté into a pan for the ramen soup he was attempting to make.

"I did. I didn't think I would with everything that is going on," Rune admitted as she picked up a paddle hairbrush to try to pick through her volumes of hair. He got hypnotized watching her work, and the edge of the hot pan bit him, forcing him to snap his hand back.

"You okay?" she asked, pausing to look for the danger.

He waved his hand exaggeratedly. "Turns out hot things

remain hot when you put fire under them."

"Hmm, must be a law of thermodynamics or something?" she quipped like she used to, and his heart sang.

They seemed to be alright now, though he had no idea he was going to make that pledge until he had made it. But now he felt right. He had toyed with the idea once or twice, but actually doing it was nothing like he had imagined. For one thing, he had an ever-present ache now behind his eye. It didn't matter. They were together again. And he hadn't even had to tell her the whole truth. The relief added to his giddiness.

Now she separated her hair to braid it back, as comfortable with him as she had ever been. She knew she could trust him again. "I hope two hours is enough to do what we need to do. I feel strangely awake."

"I promise you a vacation when this is over," he swore, meaning it. "Do you want to see beaches or a forest of trees?"

"How about a quiet cave with a pool and a big fluffy bed next to a stack of books? And no one around except room service," she said.

"Vacation in Romania it is," he said.

"Wait, such a place exists?" she asked.

He flashed her a grin and set up his little pot to soft poach some eggs.

"St. Benedict, there is something I need to tell you," Rune said, growing serious.

"Go for it," he encouraged, knowing that whatever she said to him, he could take it now.

She took a fortifying breath in and sobered even more. *Apparently, it's serious.*

"Maxamillion asked me to dinner," she stated.

St. Benedict stood there stunned as she waited for his response. Then he got pissed. "He did what?"

Rune held up her hands. "It's not like that. I mean he asked. He's not pressuring me. But I want you to know that I also understand that nothing has really changed between us, right? I mean, I know you just swore to me as a retainer, and I get why you did that, but I'm not going to hold you to it, okay? When this thing with Jasmeen is over... or really it doesn't even need to be later, I can let you out of it right now—"

"Don't you dare," he said, cutting off that idea at the knees. "I want this."

She lowered her hands. "But what about your deal with Maxamillion? He owns your Saint Box, right? You can't exactly serve two masters."

"Then we'll get it from him. He said you could assemble whatever staff you want, right? We'll figure it out."

Rune nodded at that, accepting it. "But first Jasmeen."

He nodded.

"And I just wanted you to know that I am going to accept Maxamillion's invitation to dinner, okay? I mean, I have already accepted it, but I want things to be very clear between us, you know? Right?"

She looked up at him, anxious for understanding. What else could he do but give it to her?

"I mean, as long as it's what you want, then I have nothing to say about it," he lied, lightening his voice to reassure her. Or rather it was the truth. He *did* have no right to say a damn thing about it, but he wasn't okay with it. But that was his problem, not hers. He would just have to make sure that Maxamillion made her happy.

She sighed in relief. Then her eyes stared off into the middle distance, the familiar haunted look wrapping itself around her like a snake pretending to be a scarf.

He reached out and touched her hand. "It wasn't Justin," he said. "What we saw in the hospital. It wasn't him."

She double-blinked back to the here and now, regarding him, but no less haunted. "Then what was he?"

St. Benedict withdrew his hand. "I don't know, but it couldn't have been him."

Rune shook her head. "But it doesn't make sense? If it was a projection or something to trap me, then it was stupid and awkward."

"If it was a trap, it may have gone off before they really wanted it to, and it all went very wrong. Don't prescribe malice to something that can be explained by incompetence." St. Benedict pulled down two bowls in preparation for the soup. In quick sequence, he dropped in everything into an already boiling pot of miso stock and noodles.

"But wouldn't it also be stupid to dismiss the possibility that it really was Justin?"

St. Benedict sighed. "I suppose. How does it make you feel to have seen him again?"

"Honestly?"

"Only if you want to be," he said.

"I wanted to kill him. I know I was initially shocked, but then I just wanted to punch him in the face and not stop."

St. Benedict winced and cleared his throat. "There's a team working on St. Dominic, so there should be more answers soon."

"Yes, my job is to focus on Jasmeen," Rune confirmed.

They both fell into silence.

He had no idea what she was thinking, but he imagined various means to hurt Maxamillion in alphabetical order. "He was always one for the big romantic gestures." Her eyebrows perked up. "Maxamillion, I mean. Making you head of your own company like this."

"He's done this before?" Rune asked.

"He's the prince of grand gestures, though most of them have been centering around funding schools and dance programs and stuff. Girls and Boys clubs, get kids off the streets. But he's also funded a few small business start-ups." The Saint ladled soup into the waiting bowls, slipping the eggs in at the last minute. "I mean his own company is sort of fake, but actually real, but sort of fake; we talked about expanding this model to incorporate more corporate entities into a conglomeration, each with different mission statements and such."

"An extended underground resistance," Rune said, nodding.

"It was part of why he wanted an alliance with the Magic

Guild and the Faerie Court," St. Benedict said. "I'll admit, a little surprised that he decided to pull you in to the scheme."

"I *was* a small business owner," Rune pointed out.

Man, this woman knew how to make him smile. "Are you hiring?"

"That's the plan," she said, moving her brush aside as he placed the bowl in front of her. Her own smile and eagerness as she took up the spoon was worth the effort. He came around the counter to sit next to her on the stools as she continued laying out her plan. "The idea is Malachi will initiate the transfer for Jasmeen from Kodiak to my corporate entity. Maxamillion and I discussed it in the car when we were signing the forms to incorporate Digital Mage..."

St. Benedict choked on his first spoonful, forcing him to drop it and pound his own chest while he coughed and laughed. "The Digital Mage?"

"Do you like it?" she asked, passing him her glass of water.

"It's got style. That's for sure," he conceded before clearing his cough with a healthy sip.

"Anyway, we agreed that transferring Jasmeen to my company will have a more likely chance of slipping underneath the radar."

"That's only if the other side agrees to the transfer." St. Benedict blew on his soup, thinking.

"Which is where I come in," Rune said. She slipped her mobile phone out of her pocket and slid it over to him.

St. Benedict stared at himself in the mirror as he wiped away the last bits of shaving cream. He met his own eyes, studying the blue-green depths of them, the artificial coloring, a scar that no one recognized except him.

"You're a damn coward," he told himself, but he already knew.

"You ready to go?" Rune called, and he hurriedly tossed the towel over his sink and grabbed his fedora off the toilet. She

entered the bedroom fully dressed once more as her "mage" self. Her hair was half up in a pulled back braid with just a few errant wisps around her face that curled naturally. Her coat flashed, freshly whitened, its cuffs and lining a red vibrant. She had been drying it with a blow-dryer while he got changed and shaved. How she had snuck around a darkened alley in that flashy coat was its own mystery. He'd lay a lot of money down on it having something to do with magic but knew no one would take him up on that bet.

Rune leaned up against the door frame and appraised him with her warm, laughing eyes. God, he had missed them. To add to his performance, he took off his hat and turned on the spot, holding his arms out for her perusal. "What do you think? I clean up nice, right?"

"You definitely look the part," she conceded.

"So do you. All you're missing is the staff," he said. "Maybe a hat of your own."

"Yeah, that's wizard stuff and really only the staff. I'm a mage. Got a belt, lighter on my feet," she said, running in place a second with her knee-high boots, which had an excessive number of buckles at the top. But they were in style at the moment, and the combat design of the boot itself would serve her. They even matched her belt which seemed strange because he could have sworn the belt had been brown before, but now seemed darker. Again, he assumed magic tooled into the leather of the belt made it adjust its appearance to suit whatever outfit she wore.

"You look perfect," he said, smiling at her with his hat pressed against his chest.

The compliment seemed to hit its mark, judging from her pinking cheeks and shy smile. "Malachi should be here any—" Just then the suite door opened, and the tech of the hour entered unannounced. He stumbled over the threshold, loaded down with three computer bags and another square of tech equipment that St. Benedict knew Malachi would be plugging all those computers into as another buffer from cyber-attacks and detection. He had a couple of other smaller bags that were probably cords and was dressed in all black for onsite work. In his hands was a sealed black crate with everything else they may need.

"Did you remember the kitchen sink?" St. Benedict asked.

Malachi shot him an expected stink eye. "You could help me with this, you know."

St. Benedict only grinned but started when it was Rune who moved in to help, arriving in time to take a computer bag before she did.

"You could have just made two trips," Rune said.

"I desired the thrill of efficiency," Malachi retorted. He released the handle of the crate he carried to let St. Benedict unloop the computer bag from his arm, and then attempted to catch the crate again before it fell. He failed in both endeavors and ended up dropping everything. "Dammit, dammit, dammit," he muttered as he hurriedly opened the crate to check inside.

"What's that?" Rune asked, peering inside over Malachi's shoulder.

"A dummy VPN hub," St. Benedict answered before Malachi could. "We'll be able to log into the city network from anywhere without being noticed digitally."

"Yeah, if it still works," the tech grumbled as he pressed buttons and stared at it for signs of life. It beeped and flashed a few buttons, and Malachi let out a sigh of relief. "Okay, we should be fine." He tucked the device back into the crate and reorganized the rest of the bags.

Just then the suite door opened again, and Zita slithered in. "Oh, good, I caught you," she said, sliding up behind her partner to lay a hand on his shoulder.

"Zita, is everything okay?" Rune asked. St. Benedict could practically hear her thoughts go straight to St. Rachel's condition.

"Is St. Rachel okay?" St. Benedict asked.

"Yes, yes, everything is fine. She's awake already and

working from her bed, no matter what I say," Zita dismissed with a casualness that assured St. Benedict that St. Rachel was in fact out of any danger.

"We should strap her down to keep her in the bed," St. Benedict noted.

"Why? Do you want to end up in the bed next to her?" Zita shot back without missing a beat. "No, I want to say goodbye to my mate before he goes gallivanting off into the field, and I never see him again."

Malachi's face shifted to serious concern as he got back up to his feet. "I'm going to come back, babe. I'll be fine. I promise."

She laughed to cover her real fear. "Of course you will," she said, but St. Benedict could read the haunted look as easily as if her thoughts were printed on her forehead. Her smile didn't reach her eyes. The last time she and Malachi had gone into the field, he had been beaten to a pulp, and she had almost been killed. No amount of logic undid that sort of damage quickly. If ever.

Rune turned away politely as the couple embraced, flashing St. Benedict a worried smile. He knew she understood the dangers of the operation they were about to attempt; it was her idea after all, and she had planned everything. He had only added his expertise where needed and asked for. The whole thing was deceptively simple in actuality.

"Well, good luck to all of you. I'll see you at the other Praetorium," Zita declared, withdrawing and slipping her fingers into the pockets of her white coat. Her eyes were rimmed red, but she smiled encouragingly.

Malachi bent down again to reshoulder his bags. "Okay, let's go," he said stiffly and then marched through the door that joined St. Benedict and Rune's suites.

Rune exchanged nods with Zita before jetting forward to catch up, passing Malachi in her living room to take point toward the bathroom. St. Benedict tipped his hat to the good doctor, and she narrowed her eyes at him.

"You all come back alive, you hear?" she said as if everything that ever went wrong was singularly his fault.

"Yes, ma'am," he responded.

Once they had all assembled in Rune's bathroom, she shut the door.

"Well... this is intimate," Malachi said, turning to set the crate in his hands onto the sink to make space for the other two bodies.

"It won't be for long," Rune assured, and she stepped into the shower. "Montre sa ki kache," she said. His augmentation heard the language and spun in the corner of his vision, informing him a second later that she had spoken Haitian Creole. "Show what's hidden."

There was a shimmer of magic against the back wall of the shower stall, revealing the drawing of a door. It had changed from before. Rune had added a rough, passable drawing of the icon for the Lucky Devil bar, a stylized winking devil's head. Rune slid her fingers along the ornate stitches of her belt, pulling strings of silver magic from it as fine as filament. As if drawn by a magnet, the filaments were brought toward the edges of the door, locking in until all the edges were filled with light.

"Geez," Malachi breathed out in awe.

When the last light filament snapped into place, the door filled in with glow and then retreated to reveal a very real door on the other side. It was wood and pebbled glass with a much better stenciled drawing of the Lucky Devil winking at them from the glass. Strangely, the door was whole and appeared to cut right through the side of the tub.

Nodding with satisfaction, Rune opened the door and stepped through. Malachi hesitated, muttering all kinds of prayers that St. Benedict had never heard cross his lips before. It took a quick shove from the Saint to get the tech moving and through.

Yet when it was the Saint's turn to go through, he hesitated. He hated magic and yet loved the woman who wielded it. Stepping through the door would hurt, but Rune reached back her hand, her palm open to him. He took it, letting her pull him through. He felt a shiver of power, causing lancing pains behind his eyes, intensifying the ever present one, then it was over. It only lasted a moment, and on the other side was Rune's warm, smiling face.

"Well, that wasn't so bad," he said softly. They were close, and he suppressed an urge to lean in and kiss her. For a heartbeat, he thought she would cross that gap and then he would be done for. Instead, behind them the door shut on its own, and Rune turned away as if nothing had happened.

In fact, it hadn't.

They stood in the burnt-out shell of Rune's old bar, the Lucky Devil.

It hurt St. Benedict's heart to see it that way. They currently stood in the third of the three rooms to the bar, St. Benedict's favorite of them, the Lounge Bar. The once warm and welcoming neighborhood space was now ravaged and black. So much of the kitsch that remained on the walls, signs and pedestals that once held various devil statues, were damaged beyond repair. The tables and chairs were all gone, burned away with the remains cleared. Even the Lucky Devil's booth was gone, only bits of dried plastic on the floor where the Lucky Devil statue had melted.

The bar itself had survived the fire, protected by the same magic that kept the walls safe and ensured the integrity of the building. But everything else had been destroyed.

Rune floated amid this wreckage like a ghost near her grave. While this destruction wasn't his fault, St. Benedict felt no less responsible for it. Another debt that he owed her.

She laid her hand on a push broom someone had left behind next to a pile of refuse, mostly ash and bits of broken glass. "Looks like the other retainers were here to clean up," she said. She sounded steadier upon seeing her lost legacy than he would have thought she'd be.

"Hello?" a voice called out from the Main bar. All eyes shifted to the doorway that joined the two rooms and a thin faced woman appeared there. "Oh!" the new person said, holding a large dustpan in both her hands as if she expected to use it as a shield or something.

Upon seeing Rune, the woman jetted forward, then tried to kneel, rethought it and tried to morph into a bow, then failing that, dropped once more into a kneel. Her knees hitting the floor sounded painful to St. Benedict's ears.

"Ravinia?" Rune said, genuinely surprised as she held out her hand to help the young woman up.

"Yes, my lady. I mean, yes ma'am." Rune's newest retainer, or former newest until St. Benedict's vow, rose, still clutching the dustpan.

"What are you doing here?" Rune asked, glancing around, but no one else appeared.

"Alf said to come and tidy up a bit. That you would be needing the space soon," she said. "I wasn't sure which room you would want to be in, so I was just sweeping them all."

"Oh," Rune said, flabbergasted. "How did Alf know we were coming?" She glanced back at St. Benedict, but he shook his head. He hadn't called the steward of Rune's Wizard House, so he had no idea either.

"Oh that was me," Malachi said, shifting his crate in his hands. "Is there somewhere I can set this? My hands are starting to hurt."

"Oh! Yes, this way, sir," Ravinia said politely, then hesitated. "Unless you want to be in here instead?"

"Actually, I thought the back bar since the fire didn't get that far, right?" Rune suggested.

"Yeah, totally," Ravinia agreed and left her dustpan on the bar to come assist Malachi with his load. "Uh, can I help you... or rather maybe I should carry your..." She turned uncertainly toward Rune, who had one of Malachi's bags over her shoulder.

Rune waved at her. "No, no, you can help him. I'm fine."

Ravinia redirected and scurried up to Malachi, seizing the crate before he could stop her. "No, hey, I got that..." He trailed off when she turned and hurried off with it, her stick-thin

arms making it look like it weighed nothing. "Uh. Okay. I am still secure in my manhood. I am still secure in my manhood," he muttered as he followed her lead.

The retainer led them through the Main Bar to where the double doors to the Back Bar would have been. Unlike the Lounge and the majority of the Main bar, the back bar still looked whole as the fire had only gotten past the threshold. The remaining tables and chairs were pushed and stacked to the side, waiting for inspection and either destruction or restoration. On the bar in this room, a line of plastic sacks waited. Ravinia went straight for those, setting the crate next to them before digging into the sacks.

"Alf wasn't clear about what you would need, so I got one of every drink they had in the cooler and some basic snacks, but if there is anything else that you want, I can run out and get it." She looked to Rune eagerly, like a puppy.

Rune simply looked uncomfortable. St. Benedict understood her apprehension. It was Ravinia's brother who had burned the place and killed one of her employees and friend in his mad rage to steal her Wizard House from her. Ravinia had surprised them all when she sided with Rune, declaring her retainership to her. Granted, it was after her brother had been killed by the demons he had unleashed and only Rune could stop them, but it made her an unknown quantity in this whole situation. Technically, her loyalty should have lain with Rune, but did it really? Even though he had sworn himself, St. Benedict wasn't entirely sure what the rules were regarding this new position.

"This is more than I expected," Rune tried to assure her. "Thank you."

Ravinia nodded, accepting the acknowledgement, but she didn't seem satisfied because she immediately worried her hands.

"Is it alright if I set up on one of these tables?" Malachi asked, oblivious to the tension in the room. He tugged out one of them and tested it for sturdiness.

"Yeah, go ahead. You're the one who's going to be stuck here," Rune said, nodding at it. "Is there anything else we can do to help you?"

"Nope. I'll have this up and running by the time you get downtown, so just leave the bags here and get out of my way," Malachi said, completely focused on pulling equipment out of bags and setting it up to connect together with various cords.

"It's alright. He's got it from here," St. Benedict assured, setting a hand on Rune's shoulder.

She nodded, then glanced at the bags on the bar. Making a point of it, St. Benedict went over himself and selected a bottle of tea, then stuffed a protein bar into his inside pocket. Always a good choice when on an operation. Rune followed his lead, and the tension went out of Ravinia's shoulders.

"The van should be here soon," the retainer assured as she went behind the bar and picked up her own black backpack that matched her goth-like hair and clothes perfectly.

As if on cue, there was a knock at the back door that led directly out to the alley, then the door swung inward. "Actually, the van is here now," a familiar voice that St. Benedict didn't like said.

CHAPTER 25

"Marcus!" Rune cried with a lot more enthusiasm than she had mustered for Ravinia. The former demon hunter smiled, sliding the rest of the way into the room. Like Ravinia, he was new to Rune's service and attempted to bow respectfully to her, a sexy "my lady" slipping out of his mouth before she had him in a hug.

Laughing, the Viking-like warrior in jeans and leather returned it. "I'm glad to see you're alright, my lady."

"Oh enough with the 'my lady' stuff. I can't seem to get any of you to stop doing it," Rune declared.

"Absolutely not. It's funny enough watching you squirm," Marcus retorted, matter of factly.

"Well, I must say, you are far more jovial than when we first met," St. Benedict interjected, more to encourage the other man to get his hands off Rune as it was to point out his transformation.

The interjection worked enough because the demon hunter released Rune from his hug and stuck out his hand toward St. Benedict. "It's amazing what finding yourself can do for your disposition." He turned toward the door where his counterpart and alter ego, the Jersey Demon, sat waiting like a patient dog. The thing hadn't gotten any better looking with its squashed features and muscular, square body, but the red light in its eyes glowed warmly as it wagged its long prehensile tail on the ground.

"Oh, so therapy is working for you?" St. Benedict quipped, hiding the jab within.

"Actually, yes," Marcus replied without a hint of shame or embarrassment. "Learning to accept who and what I am has been a real load off."

"And what do you tell people your other half is?" St. Benedict asked, knowing that having a demon walking around was hella illegal.

"My gargoyle."

That set St. Benedict on the wrong foot because it wasn't the response he expected. Marcus lingered just a moment longer, the glint in his eye confirming that he knew exactly what he just did.

"Oh," St. Benedict said, cocking his head to the side. "Those are very legal."

"Yeah, I know," Marcus called back as he turned back toward the door to the alley. "Do you need anything loaded up?" he asked.

As he moved away, Rune gave St. Benedict a warning look to behave. The Saint couldn't argue with it. He had been a right jealous ass the last time he saw his brother retainer.

"We have everything we need," Rune assured him, grabbing one of the plastic bags of snacks, which Ravinia wordlessly took from her before she realized it and beelined out to the van.

"Alright, then then let's go," Marcus said and opened the driver's side door to let his demon clamber in first, again like a big old dog. He then slid into the driver's seat himself, shoving the Jersey Demon into the back of the nondescript van with

an affectionate, "Get back there."

Ravinia opened the back sliding door to reveal an empty space in the main body, then scurried around to the passenger side door.

"This way, my lady," she offered, and before Rune could protest, St. Benedict set a hand on the Finder's shoulder and gave her nudge to just take it.

"It'll be faster," he whispered, and Rune rolled her eyes but accepted. Ravinia joined him in the back, pulling out two upturned crates for them to sit on.

While she did all that, Marcus busied himself speaking into a crystal softly, and from what St. Benedict could hear augmentedly, it was to assure her other retainers that she was safe and with him. Then he shifted the van into drive, and that was when St. Benedict realized it was an electric van since it didn't sound like anything when it turned on.

As they threaded through the streets, Rune talked softly to Marcus up front, the Jersey Devil laying down on the van floor between them. She absently scratched behind the demon's ear, which made the thing purr softly.

Meanwhile, Ravinia sat twitchy beside St. Benedict, focused entirely on what was going on up front.

He found himself suddenly wondering what exactly Ravinia's Talent was. At the thought, the augmentation in his brain reacted, filling in the information that his memory hadn't retained. "Ravinia: Talent: Wind Manipulator" appeared in the corner of his vision. He rubbed at it, dismissing the extra info.

Okay, maybe she can hear. Wind carries sound waves, right? he thought. He could relate to how she was feeling.

He too wished he were up front with Rune, talking to her as they headed out on the mission, reassuring her, and tangentially himself, that everything was going according to plan. Not that she looked like she was *that* worried. Had it only been last year when she had been an anxious ball of nerves about every little thing? Now she looked as serene as a cat in the sun on the deck of a battleship.

He refused to eavesdrop. He had the tools to do it, yet he would not. Instead, he slipped his mobile phone out of his inner pocket. Turning it on, he noted the static sluggishness caused by being in the presence of so much magical force in the van, but it was no more annoying than going through an underground CTA tunnel.

With Malachi's custom VPN installed on his phone, he felt comfortable enough to pull up the social media he had funneling through a single platform and did a casual scan. He had set up programs to alert him about anything to do with the raid. He knew Malachi had already been running bots to check for anything that had his, Rachel's, or Rune's face in it, but that would run for hours if not days. Still, it was something to do, slipping through the feed and seeing where the narrative of what happened went.

Most posts were definitely focusing on the sensationalism of the anti-corporate hacking activities that had been happening on site. There was amateur footage next to professional footage of people with multi-colored clothes and strings of LED lights being hauled out forcefully by stoic officers in police riot gear or uniforms. Drugs were highlighted, of course. Nefarious dealings, seized stolen property on and off the net. As he thumbed through the feed, a single headline caught his eye. He stopped, letting his thumb hover over the bold face lines staring up at him.

"St. Benedict Church being tapped to intervene in search for missing wife," it read.

His heart double-timed as he stared at the headline. It started to skip up the screen, slowly being moved off as new headlines replaced the bottom. He tapped it before it disappeared completely. The article opened.

A picture of Rune stared up at him. She looked as surprised in the picture as he did seeing her. In the background, he could make out the blur and motion of a chaotic emergency room. This had been taken only hours before.

Beneath the picture read the caption: "Anna Masterson."

The article itself was all bull. Just some random details about a missing woman and "beloved" wife having gone missing and if anyone had seen her to please call the below number. It also took the extra step of saying no reward would be offered for information concerning her. He supposed that was one way to cut down on every person in the city of Chicago calling in every random tip for a lucky chance to make some money. But enough would call anyway, and one of them might have actually seen her.

St. Benedict stared at the phone number at the bottom of the article. This was obviously a message for him specifically. In his palm, he flourished his hand. A small hologram appeared there, and he turned his palm over. A small, one-handed digital keyboard appeared underneath it, and he typed in the number, sending it into his personal search algorithm.

He wasn't connected to any network personally. Connecting one's augmented brain to any external network without a jack-in chair was a dangerous thing to do on a normal day. But the internal drive in his head had an updated phone directory already installed, and he ran the number to see what would ping. He wasn't surprised when it came back with a private corporate number, starred blue to indicate special access required, used for privacy and exclusivity by the elites of society.

"Have to have everything special," St. Benedict muttered under his breath.

He continued to stare at the screen on his phone. As he waited, a text alert popped up. There was no name listed in the top of the alert window, but it had the same number. His fingers shook as he tapped it.

The text window opened, and three dots danced inside a thought bubble.

[Unknown: Ah, there you are]

Bile threatened at the back of St. Benedict's throat, but he swallowed it down.

[Unknown: Bet you're wondering how I was able to trace you through a news article? Well, I'm not telling]

The message continued filling up another bubble.

The thought of chucking his phone out the window passed through his mind and out the other side.

Instead, he typed slowly.

[St. Benedict: What do you want?]
[Unknown: For you to fall into a spiky pit, fill it with shit and snakes, and watch to see which will kill you off first.]

The Saint cocked an eyebrow.

[St. Benedict: Barring that?]
[Unknown: Anna, of course.]

He stared at it.

[Unknown: Look, I'm not going to play this game with you back and forth. I'm pissed off enough to discover you're still alive, and before you ask, yes, some heads have definitely rolled. But don't flatter yourself. Lying to me about you is bad enough, lying to me about *her*...]
[St. Benedict: You can't have her.]

The dots disappeared for a long three seconds. Then reappeared.

[Unknown: I can. That's a given now. It's really just a question of how. We both know what those other how's could be, but what would be best for her, for *my wife*, is for you to return her to me.]

[St. Benedict: She's not your wife.]
[Unknown: She's not yours either.]

St. Benedict almost broke the phone in his hands, he squeezed it so hard.

[Unknown: I can give her everything, everything I should have before. Wealth, luxuries, love...]
[St. Benedict: Choice.]
[Unknown: More choice than she's got now, that's for sure. I know what you did to her. How you imprisoned her. In the same cage as yourself. I can give her her life back. I can rebuild her bar; she can do whatever she wants.]

The bubble danced again.

[Unknown: She'll finally be safe.]

A knife thrust through his heart would have hurt less.

[St. Benedict: You've been doing your research.]
[Unknown: Now that I knew what I was looking for, it was incredibly easy. Especially since I'm not being sabotaged anymore.]

St. Benedict snorted soundlessly.

[St. Benedict: How can you say you will keep her safe, when you don't even know who's your enemy and who you can trust.]

The dots didn't reappear.

The Saint stared at the screen, willing it to respond. He had no idea with what, but as long as it communicated with him, he had time to make a plan.

Finally, they reappeared.

[Unknown: Your company will be destroyed, along with everyone you know or have ever associated with. I will take everything from you, including her. You're only choice is if you make it easier on her, or not.]

As threats went, it's vague, St. Benedict thought derisively.

[Unknown: I bet you haven't even told her the truth, have you? About who you really are. What you've done. What we did together. It's the only explanation I can think of why she would still even be with you, because she certainly wouldn't if she knew. Not even her heart is *that* forgiving.]
[St. Benedict: Damn you.]

He thought better of it two seconds too late. He could almost hear the mocking laughter through the next message.

[Unknown: Run the calculations. You know that I'm right.]

St. Benedict glanced up at Rune, still oblivious to what he was doing only feet away from her. Ravinia had become pre-occupied with staring out the window.

[St. Benedict: What do you propose?]

They pulled up a block down from the target building. When Rune hit the street, she turned back and smiled at Marcus still behind the wheel, a worried look on his face.

"It's going to be alright. I got this," Rune assured him.

"Call when you need us," he said, shifting the car out of park, but he waited for her to shut the door before he pulled away while Ravinia climbed back into the front seat.

Rune turned away and walked toward the building, St. Benedict falling in step with her. It felt like a lifetime since she had last seen the front of the Citadel building. As she approached the glass doors, she noticed the same three security guards standing behind the desk. Smoothly, St. Benedict pulled open the door for her, and for a brief moment she had a flash of wishing she did indeed have a staff. It wouldn't have meant anything to her, she didn't use staves to do magic, but it would have been something to hit these idiots over the head with.

As she approached the desk, the third guard who had given her so much trouble before recognized her with a narrowing of his eyes. "Lady Rune Leveau and St. Benedict to see Ms. Rosenwald," her partner said, coming up beside her to capture the security guard's attention.

It worked because it startled the third guard out of his glare, forcing him to look at the man beside her, dressed to the nines with all the money and style of one of the corporate elites. And he was acting as her assistant. Even more confused, he glanced between that and Rune's white and red coat, complete with the hood up, framing her face.

"OmniSins?" the guard requested, going back to the routine when faced with the unusual.

St. Benedict smirked and held out his hand, doing his magician's trick of flourishing his fingers, popping open a hologram to float there with his credentials. The third guard's eyes flared at the even greater indicator of wealth and prestige, at least as far as he knew, and scanned it with his reader, making his device turn blue. He didn't even hesitate to scan Rune's plebeian card.

"Elevator three will take you straight up," the guard said, pressing on a screen inlaid into his desk. Once he finished, he gave them a curt nod, and St. Benedict rested a hand on her shoulder. She didn't need the indicator, but realized only once they walked toward the entry gates to the elevators that he was making absolutely sure they did not give her any trouble for using the good elevators this time.

"It would be better if I could get this level of respect on my own," Rune muttered as they approached the third door. A small display next to it was counting down the floor numbers as it responded to the summons.

"Yes," St. Benedict agreed, "if only we had time to stage a protest."

She furrowed her eyebrows. "Don't make fun of me," she retorted.

He opened his mouth, then checked himself. "Sorry, that sort of thing makes me angry, and I'm being half serious, even if it doesn't sound like it." He reached to press the button to call the elevators only to stop and realize that there wasn't one, and then slid his hands in his pockets.

"Do you…" Rune looked at his gesture while he gazed over her head at the guard booth. "Is that why you do that? Put your hands in your pockets, so that you don't punch anybody?"

His eyebrows rose, and she knew she got it right. She laughed as the door dinged and parted open. "Oh damn. You've got a tell. I just figured out one of your tells."

St. Benedict sighed and entered after her. "I am the worst spy in the world," he muttered, shaking his head in faux defeat. He slipped his phone out of his pocket, glancing at the screen. Using two fingers, he pressed the "rapid shut down" command that would destroy the SIM card within as well.

"No escape now," Rune quipped as the door closed them both in.

The second it did, St. Benedict dropped his phone and moved. Rune yelped as he pushed her against the wall and shifted to press his face in the region of her neck.

$$\text{℩ ʃ}$$

"St. Ben—" she started to exclaim.

"We don't have time. Just react like I'm kissing you," he said quickly, giving her neck a nuzzle in order to make her squeal, which she did beautifully.

"What are you—?" She tried to ask before it warped into

a moan. He knew what kind of effect this would have on her. He felt her shiver under his touch. He had to resist the urge to do more.

"Something has happened, and I don't have time to tell you what," he continued to whisper, his lips dancing at the tiny hairs along the outer edge of her ear, "but you need to know, whatever happens, I have not betrayed you, and I never will again."

He pulled his face away and looked into her eyes to see if she understood. Her eyes glittered as he gazed down into them and like too many times before, he had no idea what it meant. He could read any face in the world, but never hers. Her eyes always demanded the truth from him, and he didn't dare give it to her.

She licked her lips with the tip of her tongue, looking absolutely wanton to whatever hidden camera that was absolutely watching them, no doubt about that.

"You should pick up your phone," she said, her voice husky and low, but there was a thread of anger underneath it. Or was he just hearing it there because it was what he feared most?

The door binged open before anything more could be said. In the split second between the bing and the opening, he moved back from her and straightened his jacket.

The receptionist, Petunia, stood there on the other side, smiling professionally as they arrived, her hands folded in front of her demurely.

"Mr. St. Benedict, it is so good to see you again," she said, extending her hand to him as he came off of the elevator, covering Rune as she peeled herself off the wall.

He doffed his hat to hold against his chest as he smiled back gentlemanly before taking her hand and kissing the knuckles. "Always wonderful to see you as well," he said suavely. The secretary honest-to-god giggled, then reclaimed her hand to give him an "oh you," pat with it. This woman was out of her time and would have thrived better in the 50's business world or at least a romantic version of that time.

Still blushing, she turned toward the glass hallway toward her boss's office. "Ms. Rosenwald is waiting for you if you'll walk this—"

"This is my partner, Lady Rune Leveau," St. Benedict interrupted and poignantly not following immediately. He gestured to Rune who stepped up beside him, letting the elevator close behind her.

The secretary turned back, blinking in surprise. It made her smile fall into more of a grimace. "Sorry, what?" she asked inelegantly, then looked to Rune. "Oh, yes, welcome Ms. Leveau," she recovered, replastering the professional smile, but St. Benedict doubted she remembered the Talent who had been there only a few days ago.

"If you care to wait in the reception area, I'll get you some water or tea, if you prefer, while you can wait," she started to say, indicating a collection of chairs in a circle on the other side of the glass wall.

Neither of them moved as they continued to stare with pleasant smiles at the secretary whose eyes darted between them. St. Benedict could practically hear the wheels churning in her head. "I'm sorry. I was given to understand the meeting was between just *you* and Ms. Rosenwald?" She indicated St. Benedict with a gesturing hand since a lady never pointed.

"*Lady* Leveau and I have an appointment with Ms. Rosenwald," St. Benedict said, giving the title a little bit of helpful emphasis to help the slow-witted woman out.

More panicked glances between them before a fluttering of her eyelids indicated that the Emily Post reference in her mind had finally gotten to the chapter about Magic Guild protocols. At least enough to know that any magic user with the title Lady or Lord before their names meant they were someone of some status on par with an executive. That was enough information to allow her to sweep her hand for them both to follow her. St. Benedict caught the glimpse of her true expression in the last half second before she finished spinning her face away. Definitely out of her comfort zone. Exactly

where he needed her to be.

He looked to Rune, offering her the crook of his arm. For a split second, Rune regarded it, then glanced to him with reading eyes. He knew he had done too little to earn her trust back, and this was too soon to test it, but there had been no safe way to tell her anything between whatever listening device preserved in his phone or whatever big brother set-up this company had installed.

Rune held out his phone for him to take before she turned and walked down the hall without taking his arm. It made him sick to his stomach, but the dice were cast, and there was nothing for it now.

CHAPTER 26

"**M**r. St. Benedict and Lady Leveau to see you, ma'am," the secretary reported to the intercom attached to the door outside the office Rune had stood before only a few days before. The full circle of it all smacked of destiny. *If this were a novel or a movie or something...* she thought.

No response came over the intercom, or from any divine hand for that matter, but Ms. Rosenwald's office door opened, and the woman herself exited her office with an excited light in her eye and both arms up in greeting.

"St. Benedict, my hero!" she declared, coming straight to him. The Saint had his own version of a professional smile on, though his never looked like it. He was far too good at being charming for that. Rune stood to the side and waited as Ms. Rosenwald performed an air kiss to each of his cheeks, European style. Then she looped her arm into his to lead him into her office.

"I have a bottle of work Chardonnay chilling," she said secretively.

"Well, before we crack into it, let me introduce you to my partner, Lady Rune Leveau," he said, pulling up on her arm to turn back toward Rune.

Ms. Rosenwald's eyes landed on Rune, and the Finder expected her to purse confusedly at her like the personal assistant had. Instead, they popped up with recognition. "Yes, I remember you." She glanced at St. Benedict, putting things together faster than her assistant had. "I apologize. I didn't realize you were a lady."

"I didn't feel comfortable using my title before," Rune said, giving her genuine smile since she didn't have a professional one. It was nice to be recognized this way. "I'm still new to this sort of work on the corporate level."

"We all have to begin somewhere," Ms. Rosenwald agreed, and Rune found herself liking the executive more when she wasn't under a mind-control love spell. This time she turned to the door and invited them both into her office, not reclaiming St. Benedict's arm this time. True to her word, a bottle of Chardonnay waited in a bucket on her sideboard with two glasses. Smooth as ice, she pulled down a third one and began filling the first glass before her assistant took over and poured out the remaining two.

Moving away from the sideboard, she offered the first flute out to Rune, much to her surprise. Rune wondered if it was because of her status as a Magic Guild Lady.

"I have to say I was surprised to get your message, St. Benedict, and now that I see who you've brought, I'm even more intrigued." She looked between them, calculating. "Is this a new business venture?" She held out her hand to accept the glass of Chardonnay presented to her by her assistant, who handed St. Benedict the last glass at the same time.

St. Benedict's smile widened, confirming Rosenwald's guess.

Ms. Executive folded her arms, still holding the Chardonnay in one had as she did so, her body language echoing an elegant, thoughtful pose that St. Rachel would use. It came off aristocratic. "Alright then, I'm game. What is your new business venture?"

"Magical services for a digital age," St. Benedict said before taking a calculated sip from his glass.

"The Digital Mage," Rune added, still smiling at her own pun. Rosenwald glanced at her, the wheels obviously turning in her head.

"And this is under Corinthe or completely independent?"

"Sister company with Corinthe, independent in everything except affiliation," St. Benedict agreed.

"So you're not here to see me to add to your war chest," the financial executive concluded, and she took another sip of wine, Rune recognizing the time-buying tactic to let her brain continue to think. "Ah, I see. You're here for some initial clientele."

Rune nodded and moved toward one of the two chairs that waited in front of her desk. The others followed the cue, Rosenwald taking her position behind her desk and St. Benedict to her right. "We'd like to extend to you our initial services as one of our premier clients," Rune said.

"You and your office," St. Benedict added.

"Well, I don't think we have enough issues with magic to require someone on retainer," Rosenwald stated.

"As the years have gone by, magic and the rest of the world have been integrating quickly," Rune said, taking point on the conversation. She stood up and went to the wall of items that she had seen the last time she had been in the office. "All such mergers have their unexpected issues and pitfalls. This would be no different."

Rune stopped in front of the one piece that had been whispering the most magic. "I didn't realize this before when I was here, but this piece is actually a missing magical artifact that was stolen from a Mage House a few years ago."

It was a round mask framed with feathers on each side and inlayed dark stones around the eyes. It could have come from a dozen ancient cultures, and magic wafted off of it in the corporate void. It would become a problem to Ms. Rosenwald's office eventually.

She poignantly glanced back at Ms. Rosenwald, whose own face had become as still as the mask. "That was a gift from a mentor," she said.

"I'm sure," Rune said with no hostility in her voice, only friendliness. "Still, possession of such an artifact comes with investigations and paperwork and possible fines. The Magic Guild takes things like this very seriously, especially any artifacts that have anything to do with dangerous magics."

"Dangerous magics?" Now an eyebrow popped up.

"Nothing active at this time. You would have to know how to activate this to do any real harm, but it wouldn't take much for a competitor to recognize this for what it is and ... bring someone in who wouldn't care about triggering it."

"Which is a major security weakness," St. Benedict added. Ms. Rosenwald turned back to him.

"Which I would imagine would be covered under our security contract with Corinthe?" she challenged.

St. Benedict quirked an eye, and Rune's heart skipped a beat for a second. That was a wrench in their argument.

"Would you call the fire department to take care of your pest problem?" he replied smoothly. "Or would you rather use an exterminator? They might know more about what they are doing, and your house might keep standing."

She narrowed her eyes in return. "Point taken." Her eyes slid to the artifact on her wall. "So you would like me to hire you to make this problem go away?"

"What we're offering you is this," Rune said, taking over. "I have contacts within the Magic Guild. I can make arrangements for this artifact to be anonymously returned. It will be at no cost to you—"

"No cost to me? Except the loss of a valuable piece that I paid good money for?" Ms. Rosenwald snapped, her true feelings escaping her control.

"I thought you said it was a gift from a mentor?" Rune asked pointedly.

The flex in her eyes confirmed that she had just been caught in her lie. Rune really hated playing this game, but she steeled herself. Jasmeen's life was on the line.

"Like I said," Rune continued, "I would return the artifact to the Magic Guild, at no cost to you, as the anonymous go between. There will be no control or connection to you with that object. My associate," she gestured to St. Benedict, "will do a review of your photos, social media, and those close to you to clear away, to the best of our abilities, any remaining evidence that could be used by another interest to hurt you with it."

"And what will *that* service cost me?" she asked evenly.

"At this time, nothing. I want to do this for you as a favor for a friend," he said, taking a sip from his glass. "I mean, good word of mouth about our endeavor, without giving too many details of course, would be most appreciated."

Some of the tension slipped from Ms. Rosenwald's shoulder. "I'm sorry, St. Ben. I just..." She readjusted herself in the chair, setting her chardonnay glass down on her desk to toy with the stem. "Ever since the thing with..." She swallowed, and the strong woman looked like she would shatter into a million painful pieces. "I've never been violated like that."

Rune brought the magicked piece over to the desk, setting it down on the surface while she pulled another small sack from one of the pockets of her belt. Unfolding it, she shook it out. "It sucks," she agreed.

The powerful executive looked up to meet her gaze. "I can't believe I let it happen to me. After everything I've done, everything I've worked for. I thought I was so smart."

"You shouldn't—" St. Benedict started to say, but Rune held up a hand at him to be quiet, all while not breaking eye contact with Ms. Rosenwald. He obeyed, settling back and taking another sip of his wine.

"Yeah. It sucks. It makes no goddam sense, and it isn't fair," Rune agreed.

"Why? Why did this happen to me?" the executive said in a small, girl-like voice. "I was so... so complicit in what

happened."

"We get trained, don't we?" Rune said bitterly. "We get told a story. Be a good girl. Let everyone give you kisses. Don't be a bitch. Don't be 'like that.' Don't disappoint everyone around you. Your wants and desires get turned against you and twisted, and before you know it, you 'wanted' it. You 'agreed' to it. So they didn't do anything wrong. Even if they roofied you, or got you drunk, or cursed you with a mind-influencing spell. You didn't fight it because you didn't want to be a bitch. And then you wake up, your entire being is screaming, but no one else can hear it."

Ms. Rosenwald didn't look away, her mask completely gone as the truth of Rune's words echoed within her. Rune shrugged. "I don't know. It does get better. With time and help, it does. And you'll slide backward, and you will move on, and you will find love and continue to live life, and you will be wiser, and you will wish it was wisdom you never needed to find out about. And you will hate him, and you will miss him, and you will be confused by it." Rune sighed. "I'm sorry. I don't know where I'm going with this... but maybe that's the point."

Ms. Rosenwald looked crestfallen as Rune lamely finished. It wasn't the answer she wanted to hear, but Rune had no idea what the right answer possibly could be. It certainly wasn't in the hundreds of platitudes that got bantered around when people didn't know what to say. There was no guarantee that it would ever get better, no guarantee that she would be able to move on from it. No guarantee it wouldn't happen again.

"There was another reason we came to see you today," Rune said, dropping the artifact into the bag forgotten in her hands. "We were going to use this to coerce you into helping us find someone."

St. Benedict choked on his wine, coughing hard.

Rune ignored it. "There is another woman I tried to help, one who has also had her whole life overturned, and now she is in real danger, and we need to get her out. We came here to soften you up with this issue, and it is a real issue by the way—we didn't make it up—but his plan was to get you to use your executive privilege to transfer this woman to our company before the corporate authority could do away with her. And since it is a big risk to you, we recognized that you would need to some persuading. Carrot and stick. But if we don't do this now, this woman could be lost forever. We need your help."

Ms. Rosenwald didn't blink once during her whole confession. Her gaze drifted down to the bag in Rune's hands, then to St. Benedict.

"Who are you people?" she asked, looking back to Rune.

"I am the Heir of the Magdalene, a Mage and protector of those who ask for my help," Rune said, the title flowing easily like the pledge of allegiance from elementary school, rarely said and never forgotten. "Will you help me save—"

"What do you need?" she responded before Rune could even finish.

St. Benedict pulled out a small thumb drive from his inner pocket, holding it out like magician with a playing card. "Plug this into your computer when you make the request. My guy will remote log in through it, untraceable, and will take care of the rest."

CHAPTER 27

"'m surprised that worked," Rune said when they got down to the street.

"You have good instincts. Maybe you should be the cyber-spy," St. Benedict quipped, but Rune didn't react to it, instead looking around.

"That's okay. Pass," she said. "Where is our ride?"

"Over this way," he said, tipping his head toward where he had been told the car would be. Despite his casual appearance, his heart pounded in his chest. He prayed the car wouldn't actually be there.

But it was.

Sitting parked in a special spot for the Citadel employees use only was a sleek black car that screamed of money while being just short of flashy, like a really cool undertaker. Even worse, it unlocked itself, and the interior light came on.

Rune stopped at the sight of it, even as he moved to the driver's side. "This wasn't part of the plan," she said. He pulled open the door and rested his wrist on the top. "What's wrong,

Leveau? I thought you said you trusted me again?"

She met his gaze with her own, and he tightened his buttocks together, forcing himself to not flinch or look away as the raging guilt inside tore him to shreds.

Stay calm, stay friendly. She can kill me later. She'd have every right to, he thought, and he meant it. The next betrayal, he would offer up his life to her and accept whatever she did to him. She just needed to be safe.

Despite her long perusal, she said nothing further. Instead, she came to the passenger side of the car and got in. He followed a half-beat later, hating himself. The car activated as soon as he shut the driver's side door. The onboard computer automatically engaged the engine and calibrated the seats to fit the passengers perfectly. Rune even giggled as it adjusted.

He wanted to tell her then, explain what was happening, and confess what he had done. Yet there was no way this car didn't have eyes and ears inside, just like the elevator. He had destroyed the SIM card of his phone, and even doing that had been a real risk of tipping the precarious position they found themselves in. He could only keep playing the game and hope for an opportunity.

Like his hands were full of lead, he reached for the steering wheel.

"Before we go, we should contact Marcus and Ravinia and let them know the change of plans," Rune said, setting a hand over his on the wheel to stop him. His skin tingled with the feel of hers, like she was fire, and he craved the warmth even as it burned. He could drive away with her right then and hide, find a secluded place where no one from any corporation could find them, and he could keep her safe from all of this. Keep himself safe from a heart that had learned to feel again because of her and was too vulnerable now for this world. He thought of his home, his true home, and wished he could take her there. It would be safe for the most part, but not from Maxamillion, who knew all his secrets. Yet losing her to Maxamillion would be better than...

"Yeah, go ahead and give them a call," he said, keeping his voice light, gripping the steering wheel with both hands like an anchor.

She nodded, but instead of reaching for her mobile phone, she closed her eyes only to open them filled with clear white light. "Retainers, come to me," she commanded in a voice that rang unnaturally with power. St. Benedict squealed painfully as he felt himself being yanked much like when he jacked into the digital world; his body remained, but his spirit was pulled into a... Well, he didn't know how to describe it. It was a place. He could discern that much, but it was full of everything and nothing churned into a liquid soup that moved nearly unfathomably fast. Except he *was* fathoming it. It made him feel sick, and a spike slipped through his head.

Then the world coalesced around him. The pain in his head eased, and he found himself sitting in a booth instead of a car. Rune sat beside him, completely at ease with what had just happened. Her eyes had returned to normal as she glanced sadly at the statue sitting across from them.

He recognized it himself, the statue of the namesake of her bar, sitting and smiling with an arm thrown over the back of the booth and an empty lowball glass in his other hand on the table. His mustard yellow hat sat tipped on his smiling head, allowing one small horn to poke out around the brim.

"I just can't imagine this place without him in it," Rune said as if he needed the explanation.

"I'm sorry, Rune," he said, the words slipping out.

She glanced at him. "It wasn't your fault that the bar burned."

Nothing more could be said to that as two more figures appeared, sitting across the table beside Lucky Devil.

"Rune? Is everything alright?" Marcus asked, glancing between the two of them, a million disaster scenarios running behind his eyes.

"There's been a change of plans," Rune stated. "Something's happened and we're being watched. St. Benedict." She turned to him then, surprising him. "You can tell me now. Whatever's got us bugged can't hear us here in the ECAM. I'm sure they're getting nothing but massive static right now from the magic I'm putting out."

He double-blinked at her, shocked. "What?" he asked, his brain not processing what she was saying.

She huffed irritably. "In the elevator, you said something had happened, but you didn't have time to tell me what." All eyes turned to him.

St. Benedict felt his panic bubble out. "Rune, first, I need you to know, I have not betrayed you. I just... I just didn't know what to do with them listening—"

Rune set another hand on his forearm. "St. Benedict. St. Ben, hey. It's okay. I trust you. I know. You told me as soon as you could. We're okay."

He looked from her hand up her arm to her beautiful face. He had never loved her so much in his life or felt more unworthy of her.

She huffed in annoyance. "St. Benedict, we don't have time to baby your feelings right now. Jasmeen's life is still in danger, and I'm guessing we are in no less danger, so come on, spit it out!"

Her sharp rebuke galvanized him, helping him flip the switch inside himself. "The thing calling itself Justin contacted me."

All eyes at the table narrowed at that. Marcus and Ravinia knew. "I'm assuming Rune told you?" he asked them.

"Yes, when she contacted us to come help, she told Alf who told us," Ravinia said, her shyness forgotten in the face of a problem to solve. "What did he want?"

"Vague threats of annihilation of Corinthe Corp if I don't turn Rune over to him for her own good."

"So, it's his car we're sitting in?" Rune said, jumping to the right conclusion.

"Yeah, I'm supposed to drive you to the preset coordinates in the car's GPS and trade you for Jasmeen. If I do this, he

offers to stop the attack against Corinthe, to force a ceasefire."

"And you agreed to this?" Marcus barked, his anger evident.

"I listened to what he proposed. I didn't agree to anything; he just assumed it."

"And now we're sitting in his car, so knowing him like I did, he'll assume that's a yes," Rune contemplated. "Okay, so how do we work this so that we can get Jasmeen back and not have to give me up?"

"If he'll give you in exchange for Jasmeen, was the meeting with Ms. Rosenwald pointless?" Ravinia asked.

St. Benedict shook his head. "No, the deal needed an excuse like an inter-company transfer to allow him to move Jasmeen out easily. It's convenient for him. It gives him cover, though I have no idea who he's trying to cover all this up from. He let us follow through on this part. I'm sure he's looking for the double-cross because he knows that I—" He stopped, then swallowed down his stupid hesitations, facing Rune. "He knows that I don't want to give you up for anything in the world, which is why he is leveraging your safety to coerce me. Everything else is just icing on the cake."

"And again, how do we work this so that we can get Jasmeen without giving me up?" Rune repeated.

Marcus snorted. "Even if your ex-husband were to take you this way, you're still a prisoner of the Corinthe Corp, and that will still take precedence. We could let them take you and then have Maxamillion file to get you back. Legally, he would *have* to give you back, and it's just changing one cage for another, at least for a short time."

"It's not the same," St. Benedict growled.

Marcus shot him a hot look. "Says the man who put her there."

"Says the man who falsely imprisoned me to begin with," Rune shot her retainer back, though he hadn't been her retainer at the time. Both men fell silent, chastised, and Rune looked to Ravinia. The slightly younger woman raised her eyebrows, clearly not sure what it was Rune might be asking her

with her eyes.

"I don't have a problem with it," Rune finally concluded.

St. Benedict choked on his objection, even as Marcus's expression turned grim even though it had been his idea. Rune looked at all three retainers at her table, waiting for objections that didn't come. "I need some answers anyway, and I'll be safe. I mean, if he wanted to kill me, I would have been dead a few times over, so there is some value to him, me being alive."

"Yes, my lady," Marcus and Ravinia both said dutifully, which didn't inspire confidence.

"St. Benedict, can you make sure that Maxamillion hires Marcus to retrieve me when things settle down? With an official warrant, I mean?"

He nodded and gave one of his fake smiles, not trusting the lump in his throat.

"Okay, we have a plan. Let's do it," Rune said with forced cheer that did not inspire the troops, but each vanished from sight, leaving the two in actual proximity sitting alone in a car.

Alone except for all the spy devices.

CHAPTER 28

The GPS led them to a warehouse near the Lake. Scanning the area, St. Benedict pulled into a vacant parking spot and shifted the car into park, leaving his foot on the brake.

"Winter boat storage," Rune said, reading one of the nearby signs.

"Good a place as any." He glanced at her, meeting her gaze.

"To hold a prisoner," Rune finished, her eyes reflecting his thoughts. "Well, I'm glad Ms. Rosenwald was able to arrange the car for us so we could go get Jasmeen directly. I can't imagine what she's been through already." Rune opened the door and exited. He followed suit, resisting the urge to take his gun with him.

"So what should we do now?" Rune asked, looking the building over, then all around. There was not a soul in sight.

"How about you check inside? I'll check the other side," he said, forcing his voice to be casual to hide the lie by omission. Again, she met his gaze with her knowing one, hearing the messages he didn't mean to send in the spaces between his words. There were eyes and ears everywhere, and if her plan was going to work ... he needed to trust her.

She turned away without saying anything more and went to the door. Like a ghost, she slipped through and was instantly gone. He had to hold the door frame of the car to keep himself from following her. All he could hear was the beating tattoo of his heart. It was so loud he didn't hear another door down the block open until it slammed.

Standing before it, as if in her own whirlwind of shock, stood Jasmeen Clarmont. Having a task at hand spurred St. Benedict to action. She didn't see him until he was less than five feet away. Then she startled, backpedaling away.

"No! Not—" She screeched, holding her hands up as if she expected an attack any minute. Her clothes were roughed up and torn in places, and both eyes looked swollen from crying.

St. Benedict stopped, holding up his hands for her to see that he meant her no harm. "Jasme—Ms. Clarmont, I'm here to help you," he said, keeping equal distance with her even as she backed away.

"You! It's because of you that—"

"I know. I'm sorry, but we have to go. I have to get you to safety. Now," he said, gesturing toward the street. The tiny whisper of a promise of safety did the trick, and Jasmeen's desperate mind focused on it.

"Why should I trust you?" she asked, begging for a reason to say yes.

The thought of simply grabbing her and forcing the issue passed through his mind. It would be easier. Also not what Rune would want.

He set his hands against his chest. "Please, I only want to help you. I made some mistakes, and I admit that, but now, I am only here to see you to safety. I can take you away from this, but we do not have time for me to prove it, please." He held out his hand, and she only stared at it. "I won't force you, but I can't help you if you don't help yourself."

She hesitated, slowly extending her own hand, her eyes

wary for any sign of betrayal. Just then, tires screamed near the end of the street. A familiar van revved through a stop sign. The noise and chaos startled Jasmeen away from him. He took a step forward, placing himself between Jasmeen and the street, his hands out in a waiting half-crouch. Again, he wished he had taken his gun but too late now for regrets.

The van pulled up, its tires squealing more as it hit its brakes too hard. Through the passenger window, St. Benedict saw the silhouette of a woman he thought was Ravinia, but he only got a glimpse before she disappeared from the driver's seat into the back of the van.

A heartbeat later, the back door slid open by the same frazzled young woman. "Get in!" she called. "Hurry." Then she bolted from the door back to the driver's seat.

"Jasmeen, come on!" St. Benedict said, but the rescuee already moved toward the side of the van. He had no idea why but accepted it and tried to lay a protective hand on her shoulder, but she shook him off. She was still not entirely trusting, but moving forward worked for him.

They clambered into the back of the van, and Ravinia pulled away before he had even gotten the door closed. He had to muscle it closed just as Jasmeen got thrown into him.

"Ravinia! Drive normally! They aren't firing on us!" he cried.

"Oh! Sorry!" the other retainer cried, no less panicked. She hit the brake too hard, and the only reason no one went through the windshield was St. Benedict grabbed the passenger side seat and used his body wedged sideways to block the space, making a meat wall for Jasmeen to bump against.

"Drive normally!" he shouted again.

Ravinia meeped, and there was a gust of wind, he presumed from her Talent, and then she hit the gas again. This time they moved at manageable speed, though *he* wouldn't call it normal, and she turned out of the area.

"Where is Marcus?" St. Benedict asked as Jasmeen moved off him like he had gotten cooties all over her. That was fine. She was in the van, and he disentangled himself enough to scramble into the front seat.

"He's following the plan," Ravinia reported, turning too fast on the wheel to make a turn toward the I-90 that led to the north side of the city. A homeless man begging at the side had a colorful opinion about almost getting side swiped, and St. Benedict couldn't blame him as he grabbed the panic bar himself and braced the other hand against the dash.

"The plan?"

Ravinia looked at him sidelong.

"What plan?" he demanded.

Rune entered the warehouse and let out a breath the second the door slammed shut behind her. No going back now.

Inside, several large boats covered in tarps sat in their cradles waiting for spring. Light filtered in through the above windows. It made the place seem almost haunted inside. Taking a deep breath, Rune fortified herself and took several steps inside.

"Hello?" she called out, deciding she'd rather face whatever was about to happen head on instead of waiting for it to jump out and scare her. Her call did exactly that for the youngish man who had been leaning against a car, reading off of his phone. He straightened like a startled deer, shoving the phone into his back pocket. He wore dark clothes but not a suit, something closer to business casual with a black pea coat. He looked her up and down and then nodded to himself as if she were exactly who he expected and went to the back passenger side door of the SUV to open it for her, waiting.

"I suppose you want me to get in?" she prompted.

"Yes, ma'am," he responded, standing up straight and formal.

She took a few steps closer. "Got to admit, you aren't what I was expecting?" she commented, hoping he would say something else.

"The seats have already been pre-warmed, ma'am. There

are both hot and cold drinks waiting, if you prefer," he listed. "The ride shouldn't be too long."

Shrugging a shoulder, Rune walked over and got in. Her ... chauffeur shut the door behind her, then went around the car to the driver's side. There was no sign of anyone with a gun or the muscle to force her to stay. No sign of threat anywhere.

Once the driver was in and had started the car, she leaned forward in the seat. "Don't suppose you could tell me where you are taking me?"

"Evanston, ma'am," he replied and shifted into gear.

"Oh. I didn't actually expect you to tell me." She settled back and pulled on her own seatbelt.

"I'm so glad you came."

Rune flinched at the sound of the familiar voice, murmuring so close to her ear. Even more startling, the sound came from the wrong side of her because there was no seat there, only the door and the traffic on the other side. Rune scanned the back compartment for some sign of another person but only saw the driver.

"Did you say something?" she asked him, realizing then she forgot to get his name.

"Oh, let me close that for you," the voice by her ear purred and a divider rose up from behind the front seats, shutting her in.

"Justin?" she asked, still scanning, this time for a screen or something to lay her eyes on.

"Yes, I'm here. In a matter of speaking," his voice digitized at the last word. "I'm calling into the car, so you can stop looking for me."

"You startled me," Rune said truthfully.

"You startled me when you appeared back from the grave at the hospital. Though I suppose on some level that location makes sense. That is what they do there, right?" He chuckled at his own amusement.

"You know, you didn't have to go to all this subterfuge and mystery. We could have just met at a coffee shop or something,"

Rune said.

"Well, once I understood your situation, I couldn't leave you there."

"My situation ... is none of your business anymore. You saw to that," Rune said tersely. When she thought she might run into her ex again, she never expected this sort of scenario.

There was a long, heavy pause. "You know I didn't want to do it, right? I didn't have a choice."

"You didn't even do it to my face," she responded, not trying to hide the bitterness.

"They wouldn't let me see you. It was part of the deal," he defended. Not whined like he would in the past. So maybe some things have changed. "I wasn't even sure that they didn't lie to me and simply killed you. I just didn't have any other moves left."

"I know. I saw the footage," she admitted.

Another weighted pause.

"I tried to protect you."

"You blamed the whole thing on me. Like I said, I saw the videos," she said.

"You don't know what you saw."

Rune's back stiffened. If she needed anything to convince her she spoke to her husband, the gaslighting was all too familiar.

"Look, I'm sorry, Anna. It was a bad time, and yes, you are right. It is all my fault. The whole thing. I was young and so stu—" Another pause. "I was so cocksure I could handle the situation. But you know, don't you? You were tortured too. You know what that does to a person."

"Yes, I know," she said softly.

"God, I'm so glad you are alive. And don't worry. I'm going to make up for all of it. Everything. You won't have to worry or be scared or look over your shoulder ever again. I can protect you now. You'll see."

"Why aren't you here? Why aren't you in the car with me?" Rune asked.

"Well, that is the other thing I need to tell you, but it would be easier to show you than explain, I think. Don't worry. Soon, you'll know everything, I promise."

Then the car jerked to a stop. If not for the seatbelt, Rune would have been flung out of her seat. "What—?"

There was no explanation forthcoming from the front because of the partition, so Rune scrambled around, looking for a switch to bring it down.

"What is it? Anna, what's going on?" Justin asked through the speaker, sounding panicked. Maybe everything hadn't gone according to his plan. She could hear muffled shouting outside the car, but she couldn't see much of anything from her side window other than the driver had opened his door and stood behind it. She did, however, find the switch to drop the partition next to the window controls.

Out front, crossing in front of the car was another SUV, more dark-blue in the late afternoon light than black. It blatantly blocked the street, and there were cars behind with drivers laying on their horns and more shouting. The driver's side door of the blocking SUV opened, and Marcus sauntered out, completely unbothered by the ruckus. Rune thought about getting out of the car but found her doors were locked, which she hadn't checked prior since she had no intention of dramatically escaping.

"Get the hell out of my way!" the young chauffeur barked, throwing his arm dismissively at Marcus. He looked like a scrappy little Terrier trying to scare away a larger Doberman all while hiding fearfully behind the door. If the larger man decided to punch him, the smaller man would go down. Marcus stopped on the other side, cool and confident as an iceberg. He reached into the inner pocket of his short jacket, and the chauffeur flinched back.

"Hey, I don't want trouble! I'm just driving her around!" the chauffeur squealed, ducking his head, uselessly preparing to get a face full of lead.

Instead, Marcus extended a stapled set of papers. "Under

the Corporate authority of the city of Chicago and on behalf of the Corinthe Corporation, you are ordered to turn over one Rune Leveau to my custody. She is a corporate convict who has violated the terms of her agreement."

The chauffeur hesitated, then cautiously took the documents. From her vantage point, Rune could just make out the city of Chicago crest at the top of the first page, and it seemed to have a seal stamp at the bottom. It looked very legit to her.

"But … I've been instructed…" The chauffeur huffed as he turned the page over.

"Anna, what is happening? Talk to me! Why have you stopped?"

Marcus shrugged. "If you prevent me from executing my duty, I will be forced to charge you with obstruction," he said, so matter-of-factly it could have been true. He seemed almost bored, like this was just another day for him.

The chauffeur futzed with the papers a little more, then groaned as he pressed a button in his door. The rest of the car doors unlocked, and he went to open the back for her.

"I'm sorry, ma'am. There's… There's nothing I can do," he apologized, holding the sheets out to her.

"Anna! What is going on!?" the speakers shouted, the sound degrading from the shouting from the speaker.

"I seem to be getting arrested. Again," Rune said, looking over the papers herself, mostly for show.

"Anna! Don't get out of the car. I can protect you," the speaker continued.

Marcus replaced the chauffeur, extending a hand to beckon her out, his other hand holding a pair of handcuffs. "Ma'am, I am going to have to ask you to exit the vehicle now. Otherwise, I am prepared to drag you out."

"Anna!"

"I don't think I have a choice," she said in a small, hopefully frightened-sounding voice. It felt strange to hear it again, but it would have been what Justin expected.

"Anna, don't be afraid. I will find you again, I promise," he said, obviously convinced by her performance.

"I know you will," she said, touching the speaker, assuming he could see her from some hidden camera because why wouldn't he have set one up? "I've waited for you this long."

She got out.

It did frighten her for a moment to feel the metal clamp around her wrists. Marcus handcuffed her from the front, and the chain between the two manacles was longer than she expected, her secret retainer keeping a grip with one hand. She didn't look at him or at the crowd of people gathering on the sidewalks or staring out of their cars as she was arrested. Even though this was what she wanted, it was hard to be the center of a spectacle. Marcus marched her over to his SUV and opened the back door, helping her in without making it look like he was helping her in. It was easier with the manacles in front of her than behind. Also, another hand from inside the back helped steady her inside.

"Maxamillion!" she said breathlessly.

The prince of a man grinned brightly and brandished keys that he immediately set to her handcuffs. "Let's get those off you," he said.

"Glad to see I'm not really arrested," Rune said, truly relieved to get the metal bracelets off. Though there were no marks, she rubbed her wrists with each hand to get the feeling off.

"On paper only, just to cover our tracks. We'll record some sort of punishment, though the statute may require more time on your sentence unless we think of a way around it."

"Being forcibly kidnaped by another company doesn't count?" She arched an eyebrow.

"Like I said, we'll see. I'm expecting your ex is going to try some other legal maneuvering, but so far everything we've done here is aboveboard and legit." Maxamillion offered her a small bottle of water, which she took. "Congratulations on your first successful Praetorium mission."

The driver's side car door finally opened, and Marcus

plopped in. They were off in seconds, and Rune picked up with her next question.

"So we got Jasmeen? St. Benedict and her got away fine?"

Maxamillion nodded, grinning again. "Malachi confirmed. They've picked him up at the offsite and are bringing everyone in. We should arrive at about the same time."

Tension in Rune's shoulders washed away. She leaned back her head. "Oh, thank the gods." She sighed in relief. "I was worried that my sacrifice was going to be for nothing."

"No, in fact, it helped us get the other situation under control," Maxamillion said, redirecting his focus ahead.

"You mean the attacks?" Rune swallowed a large mouthful, basically emptying the little bottle.

"SynthCorp. Confirmed. They weren't able to cover all our operations, and it looks like they split their resources too thin trying to follow you that they weren't able to stop our counteroffensive. Then with Mr. Masterson doing whatever he did on his end with Kodiak's influence, their activity is more-or-less exposed now. Corporate authorities are looking into it, and the news is only slightly behind the social media frenzy. Apparently, we weren't the only company they have gone after in the last month. We're just the latest ones to stop them. And since we didn't do anything directly to them that they can prove..." Maxamillion shrugged his shoulders. "Well, it's game over."

"I'll have to tune in later," Rune said, knowing she had no real intention of doing so. She simply couldn't care much about corporate politics.

Maxamillion cocked his head to the side. "You don't seem too happy about our success?"

"I guess I don't really know why it's game-over? I mean, corps break the rules all the time. Why is this any different?"

"Their stock is dropping. Public opinion of them is dropping. Other corps are pulling out their business interests with them or making overtures to do so soon. It's the same old story. No matter how human beings have organized themselves throughout history, we all want to pretend to each other that we're civilized and follow the agreed upon rules."

Rune took all that in, but she didn't really feel like she got it.

Maxamillion patted the tops of her hands. "You won, Ms. Leveau," he said warmly.

She looked at the man sitting next to her, so happy for her success. There was even pride in his face. Instead of standing in her way or trying to control her actions, he had done everything he could to support her.

She leaned closer to his smiling face and kissed him. Maxamillion jerked a little from surprise, but soon cupped her face and returned it. It felt like a good kiss. A satisfying one with trembles, tingles, and tastes of tongue. When it broke, excited jitters danced in Rune's chest. Her face hovered inches from his, smiling as he studied her for answers to questions he couldn't form.

"Now I feel like I won," she said, and they kissed again.

Somewhere, distantly, she heard Marcus clear his throat.

They broke away, but she could feel her cheeks burning. Maxamillion cleared his own throat and straightened his already loosened tie. "I'm just, uh, glad the plan worked," he said.

"Yeah, what plan was this?" Rune asked, looking from Maxamillion to the back of Marcus's head to the rearview mirror where his gaze reflected back.

"As soon as you left us, you know, after communicating with us, I called Maxamillion. I figured, why wait for you to be taken and who knows what else? He agreed and we managed to get this little sting operation together in time to stop you from going too far," Marcus explained.

Rune wrinkled her nose. "You had Maxamillion on speed dial?" she asked skeptically, though it obviously was true.

"I gave my personal cell number to Alf for any emergencies," Maxamillion explained. "He passed it to Marcus and Ravinia when you summoned them."

"Good thing too," Marcus said.

"I guess," Rune said, glancing out the window. They had

made it to the highway, and the gray road was only split in half by a few trees peeking over the edge of the gray concrete before merging into the matching gray sky above.

"You don't seem happy for the rescue," Maxamillion noted.

"I would have liked to have been consulted first," she said, not caring if it sounded petulant. "It was my operation after all. Though I suppose I don't see how you could have done that with the way things were timing out."

"I do apologize for crossing that line," Maxamillion said, but Rune waved it away.

"I would have also liked to have more of a chance to get answers. I wasn't too keen on being in anyone else's custody, but... I did *want* those answers. And I was starting to get them too."

"Was Justin in the car?" Marcus asked, still looking at her through the rearview mirror.

"No, but he called in. Making all kinds of promises, which honestly doesn't surprise me. Just..." She struggled to put words to the feelings inside. "It was just weird."

"Hopefully, we'll get more answers in time. I'm sure this isn't the last time we've heard from Justin Masterson," Maxamillion said.

"No, I suppose not."

CHAPTER 29

A s Maxamillion had predicted, they arrived at the secondary Praetorium more-or-less at the same time as St.
Benedict and Jasmeen. Ravinia looked shaken as she roughly
parked the van in front of a building that looked like an abandoned warehouse and got out of the driver's seat as fast as
possible. She squatted down next to the van and cupped her
head in her hands as Malachi pulled open the side door. He
almost stepped on her getting out but awkwardly managed to
get his body around her in a flail of limbs.

"Hey, you okay?" he asked the younger woman. She only
moaned and shook her head.

"Just give her space," St. Benedict said, pushing Malachi
back so he could clear the narrow exit for himself and then
Jasmeen. "She did a great job of driving despite how scary
it was," he added louder so that Ravinia would hear it. The
younger woman ran her hands through her hair, glancing up
as Rune approached.

Upon seeing her mistress, Ravinia bolted upright and

made obvious attempts to straighten herself out. "My lady! We did it," she reported, swallowing.

Rune laid a hand on her upper arm, smiling gratefully. "Yes, we did. Thank you so much for everything, Ravinia."

"It was my ... duty," she said, obviously not used to being thanked.

Not wanting to push the young woman further out of her comfort zone, Rune squeezed her shoulder, then turned to Jasmeen. The poor woman looked haggard and roughed up. There was bruising over her eyes, and the winter coat she wore had a few small tears in it. Despite how fast they had worked to find and save her, they had been too late to prevent all damage, and that kicked Rune in the stomach. "I am so sorry we didn't get to you sooner," she said.

Jasmeen's arms were wrapped around herself, but she lifted her head to meet Rune's gaze with her hollow one. Recognition washed over her features. "They said you traded yourself for me."

Rune nodded.

Tears beaded in the bottom of Jasmeen's eyes. "Thank you," she croaked, and Rune felt able to move, pulling the other woman in a hug.

"I'm just grateful we got to you in time," Rune added.

Once Jasmeen felt steadier, Rune escorted her into the building. A set of guards on duty directed them to a service elevator, and one of them helped pull the massive maw-like doors shut before passing a key card over a sensor and selecting an unmarked button. It only felt like they went down two floors before the maws were open again. Jasmeen gaped at the enormity of the enterprise beneath, and to Rune's surprise, the room turned to them and started cheering and clapping as they exited the elevator. Those still working at scattered stations among what looked like massive crates and equipment stood up and joined them. It was a cacophonous roar in the cave-like space. Rune had a passing thought that this may have been the Praetorium before the creation of Corinthe

Corp and its coffers. As the group disembarked from the elevator and approached, people came up and shook Rune's and her entourage's hands. The celebratory mood was infectious, and it was in that moment she finally felt like she had accomplished something.

Maxamillion saluted her as he was scurried off by a small group of techs and analysts to deal with whatever other urgent matters awaited his return. They were still in a crisis, after all. Zita also slid past, giving Malachi a quick kiss on the cheek when he wasn't looking without stopping her slither toward Rune and Jasmeen. The other woman had been gripping Rune's arm to keep herself together since they got into the elevator and pressed down even harder now as the Naga approached.

"Ms. Clarmont, I am Zita, the medical professional on staff. If you would come with me, we'll get you looked at," she said warmly with that perfect bedside manner that put anyone at ease.

Still, Jasmeen glanced at Rune, who nodded. "I'll be right behind you. You're safe now," Rune assured. Jasmeen relented, probably too tired to fight any more, and allowed herself to be led away.

Rune thought to turn to St. Benedict next, but he had already gone off to a conference table someone had set up across the space, propped up on a few crates. He headed directly to St. Rachel, sitting in a wheelchair and working no less hard. Rune could see from where she stood that St. Benedict quipped something in his sarcastic manner, which earned him a cool look from the other Saint, then she stood up with the help of a cane to reach across to pick up a load of papers that she threw at him. The papers flapped like an escaping bird, held together by a strong clip, and he managed to catch some of them while laughing.

This left Malachi and Ravinia, who stood behind her, waiting patiently.

"Thank you again for helping me," Rune said.

"We're glad to see that you are alright and thriving, my Lady," Ravinia said, cutting off whatever Marcus had been about to say.

They had an awkward exchange of glances as she realized what she had done, and he nodded silently that it was alright before turning their attention back to Rune. It made her wonder how much time her newest retainers had spent together ... and if something going on there.

"I can get you guys rooms and some food if you want to rest—" Rune started to say, but Marcus held up a hand.

"We want to report back to Alf and the rest, let them know how it all went," Marcus said. "We just need to know what is the best way out of here."

That surprised and saddened Rune a bit, though she knew it made no sense for them to stay. Still, a part of her had missed the camaraderie of her people. Even if she didn't know these two as well as the rest, their presence made her feel more connected to them all again.

Still, they were right. After all, she was still technically "being punished" for her crimes against society. It was a risk for them to continue to be around her, marking them as targets in the corporate game of 3D chess this world played. "Alright, if you're sure. It would probably be best to have you guys leave through my secret door."

"You have a secret door?" Marcus asked, following as she led them toward her suite.

Rune flashed him a smile. "I can make one," she said with a wink. "I'm sure there is an obliging wall here somewhere."

$$\zeta \quad \int$$

"Thank you, thank you, thank you," Jasmeen repeated over and over again as she hugged Rune fiercely. The Finder returned the hug just as fiercely.

"I'm so glad I was able to help you," she assured her, and they remained that way for probably a few minutes too long, but it had been a trying few days.

At last, they broke apart when an impatient voice cleared his throat.

"Don't worry, ma'am," Trent the security guard said. "I will make sure personally that she gets on the plane."

Rune nodded to him, grateful. "Thank you. I'm very relieved it's you taking them out to O'Hare."

Jasmeen picked up her bag of replaced belongings and turned to climb up into the large shuttle van along with several of the other people and families the Praetorium had rescued. While the worst of the attack seemed to be over, they were still being sent away to a safe tropical island for a lovely vacation, courtesy of the Corinthe Corp. After her vacation, Jasmeen would return to start her new life, free of her old company.

Rune took a step back as the van pulled away but didn't turn to go back into the building until the van turned out of the alley. Only then did she let herself feel relieved.

$$ \wr \; \int $$

"And there she is, the hero of the hour," Malachi declared as Rune came up to his workstation, picking her way around a forklift someone had long ago abandoned with the keys rusted in place.

She smiled as she pulled out one of the overly large computer chairs brought over from Praetorium and dropped down into its space-age-y softness. Malachi handed her an unopened can of fizzy water, which crack-hissed satisfyingly when she opened it.

"This place is a maze," she said.

"All a part of the cozy defenses here at ye olde Praetorium," Malachi stated. "They attack us here, and they will have to deal with all our nooks, crannies, and dead ends."

"So, this *is* the old Praetorium?" she asked.

He nodded. "Yup, you got it. This was the underground before we went commercial. So. How are you feeling?" he asked, grinning back at her.

"Honestly? Really, really, freaking good," she said, sucking down a foamy sip off the top. The fizzy water bit back with carbonation and the taste of freshly squeezed lime.

"Trent confirmed that your charge got on her plane, and the plane took off with no incidents," Malachi informed her.

Rune pursed her eyebrows together with worry. "They are safe, right? No, I don't know, assassin squads are going to show up and take her and everyone out?"

Malachi shook his head. "Absolutely not. We're monitoring, and if such a thing popped up, we can move everyone out of there without them even knowing something is wrong. The consequences if they did such a thing would not make it worth it. I mean, is there a risk? There is always a risk, but they are a lot safer there than here. We got plenty of Praetorium guards going with them. We're more likely to be hit than them, now."

Rune humm'd at that but didn't argue. Instead, she rubbed her eyes.

"You probably should go to bed yourself," Malachi noted.

"I'm too wired still. After I sit for a moment, I'll take some sleepy stuff myself, but I just ... need a moment, you know?" Rune said. "Now I need to figure out the whole Justin situation thing."

Malachi nodded, then his terminal beeped. "You just do that. I'll take care of this," he said distractedly.

"Don't worry about me," she assured.

Malachi had already gotten sucked into whatever problem on his screen.

Rune leaned back, letting the fashioned headrest hold her in a semi-recline. Looking across the Praetorium space, her eyes picked out St. Benedict. He stood next to the conference table working over projected a hologram surface with several others. St. Rachel appeared beside him, already standing. Rune supposed that was the virtue of being a Saint. While she spied on them, St. Rachel winced. St. Benedict set a hand on her shoulder, and she tersely waved him off. Still, he made her sit down and went to bring her something to drink from the kitchen nearby.

Rune felt a calm she hadn't in a while, watching the way he moved, his arms swinging up as he reached for a couple bottles of water. The way his fedora slid back on his head, a peak of hair straining to burst out and probably would before he reflexively reset it. The smile and wave he gave the person he passed. She thought about everything they had been through over the past year, marveling that it had been a whole year. So much had changed in her life in such a short time, but it was also true that these changes had taken years to bring about.

And she thought about what he had told her.

"I'm in love with you."

She hadn't wanted to dwell on that declaration, didn't want to take in what it meant. She had been too angry, too tired, too thrown by the curve balls of the last few days. But now that she was still and feeling honest, that thought kindled inside her, igniting a burning feeling in her chest that sent tingles out.

She loved him too.

Despite having seen the worst and the best of him, or maybe because. He was a screwup, his need to control things would always be an issue between them, but he had learned to yield, and if he could do that, she could see forgiving him. She wanted to forgive him.

Then her gaze landed on St. Rachel as he handed her one of the bottles of water. She took it, but he didn't let go, and she glanced up at him. He said something to her. She blushed but tugged the bottle away. From where Rune sat, she could see the Saint trying to put her mask back up, to hide the tender feelings Rune knew St. Rachel felt for him. He didn't let go, not until she looked up at him again, and then he used that hand to cup her cheek. He said something more, and she nodded, mesmerized.

A pang cut through Rune. *Or maybe that ship has sailed,* she thought. *I missed my chance.* She *had* told him, well, not no, but not yes. And she had told him about her plans with Maxamillion. There was also the kiss with Maxamillion.

No, it was clear to her that they had both made their choices, and besides, love was not something that needed to be defined as romantic to exist, right? She could and did love him, and they would remain good friends. *Maybe I can almost believe that,* she chided herself.

"Rune?" Malachi asked.

Rune started, so lost in her own thoughts she hadn't realized Malachi heard her.

"Sorry, what?"

Malachi cocked an eyebrow at her. "You alright?"

Rune shook her head, forcing a smile. "Don't worry about it."

But Malachi glanced over his shoulder and spotted what she saw. "They're working on the Synth Corp clean up. Though that's going to take days to parse out. We took them to the cleaners."

"What do you mean?" Rune asked. "If I dare ask."

"Well, no, I can't tell you, but," he said holding up a finger, as if only just then remembering something, "there is something I can tell you. You know that voice you've been hearing that's supposed to be your ex-husband?"

That drew Rune up short. "I'm guessing by the word 'supposed to' you mean—"

"Yeah, it's not real, or rather, the voice you are hearing is computer generated. An AI's voice." Malachi tapped some keys on the keyboard, and a small box appeared on the screen. "I was able to intercept this while you guys were in the field, through the access Ms. Rosenwald gave me. I didn't know what I was following when I did, it just seemed like a strange bit of code, but then..." He hit a key, and the box danced to life.

"You startled me when you appeared back from the grave at the hospital. Though I suppose on some level that location makes sense. That is what they do there, right?" the box said.

Rune furrowed her eyebrows. "How do you know

this is fake?"

"I can deconstruct it. Broke it down to the code and saw that it wasn't a recording, but synthetically generated. Here, hold on." He typed something into the box, and Justin's voice responded with. *"See, this is just a line someone can have me say as if I'm really talking to you."*

Rune's hearing went tinny for a moment as she tried to process this new information. "So they really are messing with me? Whoever created this? It wasn't Justin at all."

"Looks likely. That's what we've got to figure out now—why is Kodiak so hellbent on tricking you into their clutches? It just doesn't make sense."

"I guess so," Rune said as she glanced over at St. Benedict. "He was right then. He knew it wasn't Justin."

"Yeah, it's annoying, right? Those Saints always being right about everything," Malachi said dryly. "I mean, don't get me wrong, St. Benedict is my best friend, but that only goes as far as it goes with them."

Raising her own eyebrows, Rune leaned back. "Now what do you mean?"

Malachi leaned in conspiratorially. "Look Rune, I know. I know what St. Benedict thinks of me. I'm sure he's talked about how he doesn't care about anyone, that he doesn't actually have friends."

She nodded her head. She did know what he meant. "But it's not true."

Malachi grinned then shook his head. "It's not true. The only one he's fooling is himself. And lately he's been a lot better. Ever since meeting you. You are a very important person in his life. I hope you know that."

"I do," she agreed, meaning it.

"Good." Malachi nodded, settling back in his chair. "Besides, he's not really *that* good looking naturally." He folded his hands over his chest, a wicked gleam in his eye.

Rune laughed. "Okay, I'll bite. What do you mean?"

"I mean most of us here have had to have changes done."

He gestured to his own face.

"Oh, so you're saying you've had plastic surgery or something?" Rune said, affecting a scandalized haughtiness.

"Hey, do you want to see?" Malachi waggled his eyebrows at her.

"Sure," she said warily, a grin tugging on the corners of her mouth.

"I know, right? I actually chose to look this way," he joked as he called something up on his computer screen. Two clicks later, and Rune stared at a before picture of Malachi with the after looking back at her and leaning in so she could compare.

"Oh! It's your nose?" Rune said as her eyes darted from one to the other and back.

"Yeah, the cops busted it really bad. Had to be reconstructed." Malachi gestured. "I had a deviated septum before, so it became a two birds and one stone sort of thing. I also used to wear glasses, but they corrected my eyesight for me too. Glasses do a lot to change how a person looks."

"Just ask Clark Kent," she added.

He gave a half shrug and kept typing. "I know you've seen Maxamillion's before. Didn't change too much there, just a haircut and a shave... oooh, do you wanna look at St. Rachel's before?"

"Absolutely," Rune agreed, feeling like they were high schoolers hacking into the school's private records. She felt a bit disappointed when she saw St. Rachel. The before image was still pretty, but the woman in that image stared hollow-eyed at the camera. There were little things different with her face, like a mole or a slightly thicker edge to her jawline. Nothing damning, but Rune could more clearly see how St. Rachel's body and face had been altered to fit the more unrealistic ideal she embodied now. Her original face had been more real and the loss it represented more poignant for it.

"Oh gosh," Rune whispered. "Poor St. Rachel."

"Yeah," Malachi said, his own mirth having cooled as well. "Here let me show you Joey's. Joey's is a lot funnier."

They continued like that for a while. Joey's was indeed funnier since he had done that facial tattoo to himself and had no one or genetics to blame. Their goofiness had caught a few other people's attention, who then had to show their before pictures. Rune enjoyed the camaraderie and warmth, something she had lost and been missing for too long.

"Hey Malachi," Rune said, inspired, "can I see St. Benedict's?"

The group sobered a bit, looking at each other, unsure. Malachi took point, however. "We can, but I got to warn you, it's not a pretty sight."

"What do you mean?" Rune asked, concerned.

"The only before we got is from the Saint Program's own records..." one of the techs that had joined them explained.

"Yeah," Malachi agreed. "They did a lot of damage to him. My understanding is he almost died."

Rune didn't know what to say. Malachi searched her face, then shrugged. "Okay, just don't say I didn't warn you." He clicked and tapped at his screen, then an image filled the monitor.

It was as bad as Rune feared. His face was a bloody mess, both eyes swollen, and his jaw was obviously broken. A bandage wound around his head about where she knew his cranial scar was.

Rune stood up in shock staring at the screen. Her mouth dropped open. She couldn't breathe. Her ears rang.

"Aw, Rune," Malachi said, though his voice sounded so far away. "I'm sorry. I did warn you. It is pretty disturbing..."

He went to click away, but she seized his hand with a sharp grasp. He yelped in pain from her squeezing too hard, but she was heedless of all of it. She continued to stare.

It was him.

Justin.

Under the wounds and the bandages, it was him. She could see it so clearly now. She could *recognize* him. Something burned inside. An angry, mean burn with pressure behind it. Something was breaking. Something...

She turned her head as if drawn by a magnet. Her gaze sharply focused on the man across the room. He still leaned over the conference table, focused on his work below. As if feeling the weight of her gaze, he looked up and met her eyes. His face lit up a moment, a smile rising on his lips.

Then it fell.

His eyebrows pursed together in a questioning quirk, realizing something was wrong.

Then they widened fully.

She could hear his thoughts as clearly as if he were speaking it. *You know.*

She moved then. She ran.

"Rune!"

He shouted her name, but she didn't stop. She was down the hallway to the suites, the door banging hard against the wall. The Praetorium went silent, but she couldn't hear it. Her mind screamed.

Past the elevators.

Stairwell.

Up the steps. They flew under her feet. It should have been an effort, but it wasn't.

Down the hall.

"Rune! Wait!"

Through a door.

Against the back wall.

Her newly made hidden door glowed and opened before she reached it.

She swiped her hand and the door flung open.

She stepped through.

All was darkness.

She stood in that darkness for an eternity, but it couldn't have been more than a few seconds. Then the world around her formed from the ECAM, from the potential magic of the door, the spell, and the destination she had preset. Walls arranged themselves around her, familiar, safe walls. And then the color filled in, and she was home.

Rune stood in her own apartment above the burned bar, her back door leading out to her switchback porch behind her, her open kitchen to her left and her bedroom to her right. Someone had come in since she had been taken away and packed up things for her. Clothes and random objects covered various surfaces. She knew it wasn't a mess she had left, so one of her retainers must have done it.

It didn't matter. She was home.

Her legs gave out from underneath her, and a sob broke from her chest. And then another. And another. She cried and screamed, letting it all loose freely. She thought it would never end. But it did. It always did. And when she was exhausted and empty for the moment, she stood up and went to her bathroom.

She barely recognized her own face in the mirror. The cold water felt really good on her hot face. Leaving the bathroom, she cut through the second doorway directly into her bedroom. Her clothes were more or less thrown about too, as only a certain number of them arrived for her at the Praetorium after her incarceration. Her retainers had packed for her...

Her retainers. She should call one of them and tell them... Tell them what?

Rune sat down on the bed, and she sank deeper into the mattress than she did on her bed at the Praetorium. It was like sitting in the crypt of another life, being haunted by the ghosts still lingering there.

She felt so tired.

She stripped off the clothes she had been wearing for too many hours. A set of mismatched pajamas were laid out, forgotten, on top of her dresser, and she changed into them. She slipped into bed like it was her grave and fell impossibly asleep.

CHAPTER 30

Rune woke up instantly to the sound of someone pounding on her door. It had been banging awhile, but sleep wouldn't let her go, and if she was honest, she enjoyed the oblivion. It kept her from remembering...

Her eyes popped open.

She knew who was at the door.

The debate on whether to leave him there or not ended when the pounding stopped. She felt compelled to lift her head and look, but since she could see nothing from her bed except the door still filled with daylight, she pressed up and out. The floor felt cold under her feet, which woke her up further. She hovered at the doorframe to her bedroom. A shadow filled her back door window, obscured by the white vinyl blinds there. The doorknob rattled.

It took her a second to realize he was picking the lock.

"Oh, for gods' sake," she muttered and crossed the three steps to undo the lock and yank it open before he finished. Sure enough, St. Benedict's picking tools tore from his hands

with the knob, the bumper dropping to ping on the tile of her kitchen. She held the door and stared him straight in the eye.

St. Benedict opened his mouth to speak, but nothing came out. His eyes were full of pain, but that didn't affect Rune this time.

"I could kill you," she said, meaning every word. "I could kill you. I COULD KILL YOU!"

He moved as she started to scream, entering and shutting the door quickly behind him. Rune startled, backpedaling. "No, no!" She held up her hands to stop him. She saw him pull out his gun; the metal flashed in his hands.

He was going to kill her.

The gun slapped into her palm so hard it stung. His hands engulfed hers as they stumbled back together against her island counter. Dishes that were stacked there tumbled and crashed to the ground at her feet. He pressed against her. The barrel pressed against his chest.

"My life is yours," he said. His face was inches from hers, his breath brushing over her face. His hands were still cupping hers, keeping the gun there. "You can take it. You can take your revenge."

She stared at the weapon. Slowly, her head shook. "I can't..."

"You can if you want to. Nothing will happen to you. I promise." He held up his wrist where his safety bracelet hid under the sleeve of his trench coat. The light bead at the top blinked a soft green. "It's unlocked for general use. I came to attack you, to keep my secret quiet. We struggled for the gun. I died. That's all you have to say."

"St. Benedict..." Rune said, warning filling her voice.

"I can't—" He gasped, his eyes wet and angry but not at her. "I can't fix it. I can't make it up to you. I can't ask you for forgiveness. I don't deserve any. I won't put that on you. But I can give you this. I know you hate me. I know I lied. I know. Rune... Anna... I'm so... Aarrgghh!" He roared and pressed her hand with the gun harder against his chest. "Fucking do it!"

"NO!!" she screamed. She ripped her hand away and threw

the gun across the room. And then she swung. She hit and hit, her hand hurting, probably causing as much damage to herself as to him, but he didn't stop her. Her hits and shoves forced him back, and the whole time she screamed. She knocked his stupid fedora off his head.

"Damn you! Damn you! Damn you!! You fucking— Agggh!"

She had thought all her tears were dried up, but they burst forth again. She crumpled, and he caught her. They slid to the ground together, and she gripped his neck as hard as he gripped her back.

"I hate you!" she cried, giving one more burst of energy she didn't really have, slamming her fist into his chest one last time. A button from his trench coat popped off to tink across the tile.

"I know," he answered. His voice sounded thick, like hers. His red face streamed wet and ugly.

Things became quiet again, except for their labored breathing.

"Justin," Rune finally said. She sat back, rubbing at her face where it had pressed too hard into his chest. It was hard, but she looked him straight in the eye. She saw the damage she had done, his cheeks bright red from her slaps. Considering how hard she felt like she had been hitting him, she thought there would be more damage. "You have been Justin, my *husband*, this entire time."

He closed his eyes a moment and swallowed before opening them again to meet her eye. "Yes," he said with a voice of gravel.

"You lied to me," she could barely whisper.

"Yes." He couldn't hold her gaze now, looking down guiltily.

"I ... thought you were dead."

"I wanted to be," he said. "I pretended to be. Sometimes I even convinced myself."

She studied his features. This face that was familiar now seemed alien to her. She forced the bones to shift in her mind, to overlay the man she once knew as her husband with this man here. As his eyes widened under her scrutiny, she could see it plainly. She could see the younger man whose bones hadn't finished developing into the older man he was now.

"I couldn't see it before—"

"You did see it," he cut her off. He raised his head again. "You did see me. You were right. When you revealed yourself to me, you saw the truth of who *I* was." His eyes searched her face, like he was willing her to understand the extent of his sins. "And I made you doubt yourself. I questioned your perception and made you think..." His voice broke, and he pressed his hand into his mouth and bit down too hard.

Alarmed, Rune grabbed his hand and pulled it from his mouth. "Stop it!"

He ripped away, like her touch burned him and grasped his head between his hands, rocking like a mad man in an asylum. "I don't deserve to be forgiven."

"So you did it," Rune said, picking at the sharp pieces of her shattered mind for some semblance of logic. "You came back for me. You didn't abandon me."

The image of the damage he'd suffered and the words Malachi said echoed in her mind. "You should have died."

"I did die. The first time they jacked me in... I did die. And then they brought me back." He rubbed at the scar on his head.

She reached out and touched it. He went still under her hand. "Your brain damage."

"I lost a lot. I couldn't remember your face, only that you existed. It took me a long time to find enough pieces to put together what happened and why." He stabbed at his skull too hard with a finger. "I wouldn't remember your face now if not for the computer hard drive in my brain."

Rune couldn't take any more. She simply couldn't take any more. Standing up, she went to her bedroom and laid down under the covers. She just left him there, saying nothing more. She had a sense of him coming to her doorway, looking in on her, but she didn't care. She didn't care what he did now. She didn't want to talk; she didn't want to discuss it further. She wanted oblivion.

St. Benedict... Justin, hovered there for a long time. She couldn't *not* be aware of his presence, but he didn't come in or go out. It was the last thing she was aware of before she went to sleep again.

Rune didn't really awaken as much as bolt up in bed when the police crashed through her door. There were shouts and bodies as they piled in, pulling her out of her bed. Two of them took each of her arms, and she was lifted up and dragged into the living room before she could do much fighting back.

It was her repeating nightmare come true. People in dark clothes with shield-covered faces storming into her home, shouting and manhandling her as if she were nothing. In another life, she would have crumbled.

This time she screamed.

"GET YOUR HANDS OFF ME!!" Throwing up her own hands, she summoned a shield. Only again, it didn't work, not really. A flaring of yellow energy burst into being around her, kinetic forcing the hands off her arms, only to immediately blink out of existence. The intruders around her gave a startled shout, but when she tried to turn on her bare foot to run, she found herself blocked in.

"Where is he?" one of them shouted as the bulky, bear-like officer rushed her back against the wall of her kitchen. The shocking move ignited her magic-infused clock, causing it to burst smoke into the air which filled up with the time, date, and current outdoor temperature. A hand went around her throat, and she grabbed at the arm, trying to break it at the elbow to let her go. Two more officers came up and pinned her arms again, her back door rebounding against the right side guy's back.

"Where's the Saint?!" the first officer stated more clearly.

"I don't know," she answered truthfully because there was

no sign of St. Benedict anywhere. She didn't even remember how she got into bed, only the fight and the crying in his arms and the truth...

He is Justin Masterson.

The officer with his hand around her neck shook her, bringing her back to her current predicament. "Where is the Saint?" he repeated.

"I. Don't. Know!" Rune repeated, spitting the words in his face, her spittle hitting the surface of his shielded face with droplets.

"There is no sign of him, sir," one of the other black-clad monsters reported. The rest had swept through her apartment, searching the few rooms. She could hear them tearing things up in her bedroom, but she highly doubted he was under her bed or in her closet. It looked like the Saint had left her alone and unprotected.

Not that she needed his protection... even if that was an obvious lie at that moment.

"You will tell us where he is, or I am going to rip out your—"

"Let her go, officer," another voice said as a figure strode past them, obscured by her standing open back door. The rest of the officers backed away, giving the newcomer space as he turned and smiled at her.

Rune's heart dropped into her stomach.

"You ... were in Corinthe custody..." she started to say, but the one holding her throat squeezed again.

"I see you're a few hours behind current events," St. Dominic said, sniffing as if he smelled something gross. "I said to let her go, or do you want to go on a permanent vacation?" St. Dominic stated congenially as if he were asking a friend if he wanted to take his sister to the prom. It just sounded so wrong and threatening.

The pressure on her throat let up, but it only made Rune angrier. Some small part of her understood that she really should be afraid right then, and her usual response would have been to crumple into a million pieces followed by some begging. But it just wasn't in her anymore. It made her recklessly giddy.

St. Dominic studied her face, and she felt like he saw exactly what she felt. His expression didn't reflect anything, however; it held with a fixed smile, like his face was really a rubber mask from a 1950s Halloween horror movie. A few scratches and discolorations from his earlier fight marred the otherwise calm and collected persona. He stepped closer, his hands behind his back, wearing a new storm-gray trench coat that hung open and swirled around his body. A regular Bond villain.

"Where is he?" he asked Rune in a reasonable voice.

"I don't know. He was here when I fell asleep, and I haven't seen him since you guys rudely woke me up," Rune responded, no longer shouting herself, but no less angry.

St. Dominic leaned in an inch, studying her hard. Rune didn't look away but met his gaze head on.

"Then you are of no use to us," he said matter-of-factly. "Take her into custody."

The officers holding her arms pulled her forward to force them behind her back. "No! Wait!" she protested as she felt plastic zip ties going around her wrists. To her shock, a shudder of magical energy zipped through her, one she recognized as a nulling power that prevented Talents from accessing their magic. She had a similar set of such manacles in her basement, inherited, of course.

"You can't do this!" she continued, her mind racing for some compelling argument to stop what was happening. "When Justin hears of this—"

"He's not going to," St. Dominic stated, cutting her off with a slash of his hand.

Well, that answered one question. Apparently, it wasn't Justin who sent them. Or rather, the person pretending to be Justin. The faction who tried to trick her into believing it was Justin. Except that didn't make sense either because St. Dominic had just said...

She shook her head a little. This was all getting confusing.

"Get her out of here," the first officer ordered, interrupting her desperate thoughts to bodily drag her toward her back door. As she tried to brace herself against the floor, she kicked something a few feet across her tile. She only caught a glimpse of it, but it gave her the lightening idea she needed.

"I can find him!" she yelled.

"What?" St. Dominic asked, and the officers hauling her off stopped.

"Let me go... I can find him!" she repeated, trying to pull free and failing. "It's what I do, in case you didn't know. I'm a Finding Talent. I use magic to Find things and people. I can lead you right to him."

St. Dominic narrowed his eyes, then gestured for the officers to release her. It was a relief to stand on her own. "How?" he asked.

Rune nodded at the button on the floor, mere inches from an officer's boot-clad foot. "Can you pick that up? Please?" she belatedly added. The officer started in surprise, then did as she requested, bending down to pick up the button in one of their black gloved hands. Rune nodded.

"I can find him with that. It's from his coat. It'll work perfectly," she assured them.

St. Dominic's narrowed eyes kept up their study. "Why would you willingly do that, if that is in fact what you are going to do?"

"Because," she said, with all the honesty, anger, and conviction she had, "I have a few fucking questions for him myself."

CHAPTER 31

Rune hadn't actually needed the button to lead her to her ex-husband, ex-partner, ex-friend's whereabouts. The second they had taken the crystal-modified plastic cuffs off her, her Finding power had locked on to him strongly. It was strange because it was clear that he was several miles away, and her power never Found anything past a mile. But this time, she knew exactly where he was. Maybe it was his newer connection to her as her retainer that gave her Finding greater potency. She didn't know and didn't really care either.

It wasn't until they had almost approached the building that Rune realized where they were going.

The Secondary Praetorium.

Too late, she realized she made a terrible mistake. Of course, he would return to the Praetorium. The fact that St. Dominic had escaped and these yahoos had attacked her home, meant something there had to have gone terribly wrong.

He probably left me at my apartment because he thought I would be safe there if there was danger here, Rune thought, the car ride giving her more time to think things through. *How do I find my way out of this?*

It had been simply a thought, a quiet wish, but her magic responded. From her heart, light unfurled, golden and shining. It curled from her chest like a fast-growing vine, then darted forward straight, absorbing the Finding line to St. Benedict.

The only way out is through, she thought. Despite all the small, worried voices whispering in her mind, the thread remained strong and singular. This was the only way forward.

"That way," she said stiffly from her vantage point in the front seat of St. Dominic's car, pointing at the innocuous warehouse building where the secondary Praetorium had been set up. She could feel the weight of the three officers crammed in the backseat behind her, each armed and more than willing to put a bullet in the back of her head. They would have handcuffed her again if the cuffs they had brought wouldn't have interfered with her ability to navigate.

She closed her eyes, but all that was left inside was her fear for everyone else at the Praetorium and the burning anger inside. Every interaction she had ever had with St. Benedict, every word exchanged, every touch, every distant, sad look in his eye, was now under deep interrogation within her mind.

How could she have not known? Not realized the truth? Had she been under a spell? Why hadn't he just told her the truth?

"I love you."

The words stabbed through her innards. She pressed a hand against her chest.

"Feeling guilty?" St. Dominic said, intending it to be a jab, but she already hurt too much to truly feel it.

"Not in the least," she lied.

She gripped the gold thread, so straight and true and solid with no deviations or possible variations. She had never seen a thread like this before, and she knew what it meant. Her chance to take a different path had already passed. She was trapped now on a course she could not alter, only be carried along with the overpowering current.

There was almost no time to think further as St. Dominic led his army of cars to pull up and surround the building. Everyone piled out of the vehicles, including Rune, hauled out by an arm.

The gold thread continued to not waver. Now that they had arrived, she dismissed the thread. Her magic curled back into herself.

"Everyone converges on my mark," St. Dominic ordered into his hand, his hologram activated there, presumably transmitting. "No mistakes." He then turned to Rune, his eyes staring down on her haughtily.

"Sir," one of the men piped up, "shouldn't we wait for schematics of the building to come in—"

"I'm not waiting. They know we're here. We have to move now," St. Dominic snapped, activating the bracelet connected to his gun with an angry whine like a bee.

"Anything I should know before we go in?" he asked, directing the question at Rune.

"Like what?" she snapped, still trying to shake off the arm holding her and not succeeding.

"Layout? Boobie traps? I'm sure they don't have anything we haven't already guessed at but might as well ask."

"Wouldn't you know better than me? Didn't you escape from here or something?" Though as she asked the question, she realized that it would have been more likely that he escaped in transit with no clue where he was being taken.

He smiled at her instead of confirming anything and turned back to his controlled chaos. He snapped his holographic hand, and a sub-sound signal that Rune felt more than heard went out. The officers converged on the building as one mass. Rune found herself dragged along with the fast-moving tide.

The second she passed over the threshold, she truly regretted what she had done. The small contingency of guards were dead on the ground.

Zita. And Malachi. Maxamillion. What had she been thinking?

St. Dominic marched onto the service elevator, and Rune was hauled in after. Dully, she could hear thumps of gunfire and dull screams. It was like she was sinking into the bowels of hell.

The elevator arrested, but the doors did not open. St. Dominic flashed his hand over the controls and smirked. His fingers fiddled in his hologram, and then he snapped them.

The doors opened to a room of chaos.

Shots fired immediately.

All of the officers wore body armor, and sparks flew off them as they charged out of the elevator.

Rune did not have body armor. She didn't even have her coat to protect her or her belt to access her reserves of magic. Her captors barely had given her time to change into jeans and a sweater, nevermind allowing her to find her tools. She had her knee-high boots, but they weren't magical, just comfy.

Belatedly, she squealed as bullets hit the metal of the elevator's back wall behind her, narrowly missing her by inches. Her guard abandoned her, rushing out with their fellows.

St. Dominic stepped calmly from the elevator, unhurried by the gunfire, which also popped and sparked off of his armor, revealed as he dropped his trench coat. Before him, his people took cover behind a workstation with a flimsy partition that did little to absorb the gunfire and one of the large, abandoned crates that did more.

His eyes blazed orange like fire, and he lifted his gun, an extension of himself and fired with precise shots. There were still people shooting, but the suppressive fire at the elevator immediately lightened. St. Dominic strode forward like he was in a park.

"Move out!" one of his officers shouted, and the rest spread left and right, disappearing into the maze of the Old Praetorium.

Rune stood by the elevators, completely forgotten.

For one moment, she thought about going up the elevator, running away and never looking back.

But she couldn't. She'd never forgive herself.

Pushing off to force herself to move, Rune scurried along the wall until she was blocked by a tool cabinet. That forced her to move into the room. She ducked and wove her way through the improvised workstations, viewing the remnants left of the previous occupants: pens, headsets, coffee cups, and the occasional body, lying in a pool of their own blood.

This is my fault, her inner voice kept repeating. *What have I done? I have to save anyone I can.*

She had to. She had to make this right.

More shouts and firing burst to her left, and she ducked down, covering her head with her hands. When it stopped, she moved again, her heart pounding too fast to even feel anymore. She focused on trying to picture what she saw of the Old Praetorium in her head and navigate herself to the few rooms where she had left Jasmeen or where she might find the others.

She tried to scatter her magic, but she wanted too many things, and a useless network of threads appeared, shorting out as she lost the focus she never really had.

"St. Benedict! Where are you!?" St. Dominic shouted in the chaos.

Rune stopped, ducking behind a forklift as she saw St. Dominic move sideways like a panther, his gun held at shoulder height, searching for a target.

"This is it, St. Benedict. I've got you all surrounded. Your little side piece betrayed you," he howled manically.

Rune could see him through the wires and pipes of the forklift's guts. Though his eyes were blanked out, he seemed mad. Then he twitched toward her sharply and fired his gun. A yelp escaped her involuntarily, and she pressed her hands against her mouth. A body she hadn't seen fell down a few feet away from her, one of the techs she recognized but couldn't recall the name to. He didn't die right away but sucked in air in gasps, as if he were a slowly drowning fish seeking a final

breath. St. Dominic walked up to him with a cold, measured gaze, then put a bullet in the tech's head, silencing him forever.

"Kill everyone on sight!" St. Dominic shouted, reaching into his vest to pull out another clip of bullets, dropping the old one from his gun. "Bring me their Saints' heads!" More gunfire responded as he slapped the fresh clip home. Rune watched in horror as more bodies dropped from both sides.

St. Dominic moved on, but a trio of the officers took his place, automatics at the ready and locked to their shoulders as they moved methodically, looking in nooks and crannies for prey to be hiding in. Rune realized they were coming right for her and tried to back up the way she came but found another pair were moving along the wall where she had been. They hadn't seen her yet, but they would very soon.

I'm trapped, she realized with only a forklift between her and death.

So she turned the keys.

The rusted forklift burst to life, much to her surprise. They may have been rusted into the machine, but they still did their job. Not knowing what she was doing, Rune pulled on a lever. A brick that someone had left on what had to be the go pedal shifted down, compressing the pedal, and the machine jerked away from her into the three officers.

They scattered out of its way, one getting knocked straight down as the machine soldiered forward, unheeding of what it rolled over. The two officers coming up behind her appeared just as she ducked away and ran. She knew they would fire any minute, but the confusion and shadows distracted them.

"Rune, this way!" Malachi's voice shouted for her. She couldn't see him, but she went toward the sound.

Pulling magic roughly from herself, she flung it toward the voice. "Find me a path to safety!" she demanded of it, and at last the magic did what she expected it to, wove its way through with a gold thread in the direction she heard Malachi's voice.

More officers ducked out from where they hid behind shelters and fired in her direction. She flopped to the ground, lacking any clear hiding places to go. She felt hot liquid drop on her, and for a moment, she was certain she had been hit, and this was it. Then another person, another tech dropped to her knees beside Rune. She didn't completely collapse, however. With her weapon still raised, the tech fired just as the two officers moved forward, believing themselves safe to do so. Her shots took one in the leg, and the other one turned just in time to get a shot in an exposed portion of their neck where neither helmet nor vest completely covered.

With both targets dispatched, the woman looked down at Rune on the ground. They met eyes, and a terrible understanding passed between them. Blood trickled from the tech's lips.

"No, don't!" Rune tried to say, as if begging would stop the woman's life from leaving her.

More blood oozed from between the tech's fingers on her one hand. With the other hand, she held up her gun, bringing the bracelet to her lips. "Un-n-nlock f-f-for general ... use," she stuttered. The bracelet on her wrist turned from blue to green, and she held the gun out for Rune to take.

Before the Finder could, the woman collapsed, losing both her grip on the weapon and her life.

"No! no!" Rune heard herself say, but it meant nothing, even as she tried to turn the woman on her back to put pressure on the gut wound. "I need a healing crystal! I need a healing crystal!!" she called out recklessly, but her mind couldn't find a grip on the situation.

She didn't see St. Dominic until he pulled her back by her hair. Still on her knees, Rune grabbed at his hand, trying to wrestle away until a barrel pressed into her temple.

"St. Benedict! Give yourself up now, or I kill your little traitor here!" St. Dominic cried, forcing harder with the end of his gun, like he intended to drill it into her skull.

The heat from the barrel burned her skin, and she cried in pain. "Let me go!"

There was a blast.

Beside her, St. Dominic stiffened. His eyes blinked as if he couldn't comprehend what was going on. And he couldn't because someone had just put a bullet into the back of his head from close range.

Wordlessly, the light died in his eyes, and he dropped to the ground, releasing Rune's hair.

She dropped herself onto her hands, using the solid cement beneath to ground herself. There was no time for this, however, and she looked up to see St. Rachel leaning against a crate, a smoking gun in her hand. The beautiful, battered death angel panted as she held her pose for several beats.

Then her gaze and her gun barrel dropped to Rune kneeling on the ground.

"You *led* them to us," St. Rachel spat.

"No, I…" But that was a lie. Rune had. They had found the Old Praetorium because of her. "St. Rachel…"

The Saint didn't care. She kept her weapon focused on Rune. Pushing off the side of the crate, the injured woman wobbled and staggered toward her. "You did all this."

Rune stood up, her hands held out before her. There was no way she would get a strong enough shield out in time to stop a bullet. If she could even form a shield at all. "St. Rachel, please—"

The Saint fired.

CHAPTER 32

Rune stared at the bullet as it spun slowly inches from her eye. It was held suspended in the air inside a field of yellow light turning as if it had all the time in the world and making no headway. It took a second to realize she stared at that bullet over a shoulder. Everything had happened so fast, it was like she had blanked out.

Slowly, she became conscious of the body in front of her, heaving breaths. The arms around her waist held her close, with something rigid pressing into her side. She had a memory of feeling an impact, and the look of shock on St. Rachel's face as time seemed to slow down.

Then Rune's mind was able to put the pieces together. A person had managed to step in front of her just as St. Rachel fired. Rune also had managed to hold a shield strong enough to stop a bullet.

Recognizing that fact, she dropped the shield. The bullet dropped to the ground, pinging uselessly on the concrete.

"Are you alright?" a raspy voice rumbled. The body in front

of her pulled away to look at her.

St. Benedict... Justin... released his hand from around her middle to cup her face. "Rune? Are you alright?" he repeated, like it was the most important question in the world.

"Yeah," she whispered. She felt her head nod. "Yeah, I am."

It was.

It was alright now, though she had no idea why.

Relief poured down his face

"St. Benedict! What are you doing!?" St. Rachel screamed.

His face hardened. With one smooth motion, he turned. His arm lined up with his body and locked into a perfect determined shot straight at the other Saint. He shifted Rune back with one arm around her waist, using his own as both weapon and shield. That was when she realized he wore a kevlar vest over his shirt as the rough edge of it pressed against her cheek.

St. Rachel stumbled half a step back, her eyes widening. "Sh-she betrayed us!" she screamed, the weapon still in her hands shaking. "She's a traitor!"

Rune became aware of the quiet in the room. The fighting had stopped. Around her, she felt rather than saw people moving forward, staying back from the drama playing out.

St. Benedict didn't break from his locked stance. His face twisted into a cold, hateful mask. Rune knew with absolute certainty that he intended to kill St. Rachel.

"St. Benedict?" St. Rachel pleaded. Rage and hate for Rune boiled out of her. Still, she did not raise her own gun again at St. Benedict who threatened her. "Don't you see what she's done?! She's—"

"MY WIFE!!" St. Benedict roared, the words tearing out of him. They echoed harshly in the room.

St. Rachel stood there stunned. Utterly stunned, her eyes wide, her mouth hanging open.

Rune felt his body tighten against hers. "Justin, don't," she said, grabbing his weapon arm. Her touch stopped him. He didn't release the trigger, but the energy of her pull jerked his body a tiny bit. Enough for St. Rachel to subliminally see it and flinch, along with everyone else watching. Someone gasped and cried out while others grunted fearfully.

"Justin?"

Rune turned to the clear sound of Malachi's voice, now standing a few feet away from them. The fight was apparently over. Other techs stood around him, and they all looked battered with blood and bruises. Malachi stared, his eyes as wide as everyone else's, his gaze darting from Rune to St. Benedict to St. Rachel and back. Rune could hear his brain working a million miles a minute, putting pieces together.

"Oh my God. You're... You're Justin Masterson," he finally concluded, voice barely louder than a whisper yet echoing in the destroyed space.

St. Benedict didn't turn to acknowledge it. He kept his eyes completely trained on St. Rachel who couldn't even find the will anymore to lift her own gun. The other Saint looked broken and lost, no longer able to cope.

Rune slid her hand over his arm to press down on the top of the hot metal of the gun. "Put it down," she said.

Obediently, he yielded, letting Rune claim the gun entirely while never looking away from St. Rachel with that intent to kill in his eyes.

"St. Benedict. Justin," Rune said, coming around him to put herself between him and St. Rachel. At the sound of his true name, he finally met her eyes with his intensity, but Rune didn't fear it. She knew him. She knew him now. "We need to get out of here. Before more come."

A beat passed, but Rune could see him processing what she had just said behind his eyes.

"We've beaten them back, and they retreated when St. Dominic went down. We've lost a lot on both sides," Malachi reported. Rune looked to him as she listened to his report.

"Maxamillion?" she asked.

"He was away, lodging a formal lawsuit against SynthCorp. He's safe," Malachi confirmed.

Rune nodded. *The only way out is through.* Then, she

looked to St. Benedict... Justin, who hadn't looked away from her at all. "Where do we go that is safe?" she asked.

He blinked, his stiff face coming alive. He put an arm around her to pull her protectively close, and she let him. She wrapped her arms around his chest and held on, breathing in his sweat and scent.

They were both alive. They had saved each other. They could get through this together.

St. Benedict looked to everyone standing around them. "If you want to get out of here, follow me," he said.

He turned the both of them to go, but before he could take a step, one of the group surrounding them spoke up. "You've been Justin Masterson this whole time?"

"Yes," he answered unflinchingly, his voice carrying out to the entire group. "I have been Justin fucking Masterson this whole time. I lied to all of you. I even lied to myself. Any of you have a problem with that, you can go your own way, and I wouldn't blame you, but our work is only half finished, and I'm not done yet."

As they stepped away, heading to who knows where, the group of them stood staring at each other for answers or leadership. They got it in the form of Malachi, who moved to follow. It broke the spell around everyone, and the place was a bustle as everyone remaining grabbed tools, bags, computers, and who knows what else.

Justin never stopped to look at any of it but kept moving. He leaned his weight on Rune's shoulders, and she realized then he limped badly. Blood trailed in drips behind him.

"We need to stop—"

"We can take care of it when we're away from here," he said, his eyes fixed ahead.

This time Rune yielded, only kept her arm around... around her ex-husband's waist and steadied them both.

He did stop when they got to a far wall before a rusty pair of metal service doors chained together with a rusty chain. Instead of doing anything with the chain, he pressed his hand with his two fingers alit against the glass. A flash of green light passed over them, and the door popped open at what should have been the hinge to reveal a long sloping hallway. A light stuttered on overhead, followed by a series of them all the way down. Smells of moldy-wet and sewage hit them full in the face.

"This way," Justin breathed and grabbed the rail on the one side of the underground hall to pull them to the side. The remaining members of the Praetorium had filed into a sort of line three-people wide behind him, and he gestured them through, releasing Rune to do so. "Keep going. Down the hall until you can't go any farther. Stop there until I arrive."

Malachi nodded, grim-faced. Rune stopped him quickly with a hand. "Zita?" was all she said, since she couldn't really form a question.

"With Maxamillion. She went with to file her own complaints and make a witness statement," he assured her, then muttered, "She's going to be a mess until we contact her to tell her we're alive."

"It'll have to be later. It's not safe," Justin said.

Malachi nodded his understanding, but a dark look also colored his face as he eyed his friend. Rune interceded, setting a hand on Malachi's shoulder. "Thank you," she said. It seemed to be the right thing to say because Malachi flashed worried pity at her as he turned to take the lead.

Everyone walked past; none looked at them. Some couldn't as they were completely focused on helping each other move or moving themselves. Some of the wounded were suspended between others on field stretchers. But too many of them poignantly didn't look, too many for it to not be deliberate. And too many were being left behind forever.

At the last was St. Rachel, hobbling forward, her wheelchair lost, one arm slung around her middle, the other still holding her weapon, this time pointed at the ground.

"That's everyone who is still breathing. I think between you and me we took out thirty of them. They were too cocky. They

didn't expect this level of resistance," she said as if nothing had happened between them only a few minutes before.

But Rune knew that was the way of Saints.

St. Benedict nodded, and she moved on. A tech had lingered, and she allowed them to put an arm around her to help her move quicker down the sloping floor. Once they were through, he turned back and pulled the doors shut. A locking sound clicked hard, and he placed his lit hand over the glass. The scan appeared again.

Then he turned back to Rune. "Come on. We have ten minutes before this section blows itself and buries our escape route."

"That sounds urgent," she said, surprising herself with her own quip.

He couldn't laugh, but the corners of his mouth quirked, only to immediately die. "I promise. When we get to safety, I'll explain—"

"I know," she said and reached to grab his arm. "Come on. We only have ten minutes."

It took them only a few of those minutes to traverse the hall, which someone at some time had covered in various layers of graffiti: some vulgar, others pure art. They caught up with the group they were leading huddled together at the dead end, murmuring uneasily as they waited. As the Saint and the Finder approached, they parted to let them through. Justin gestured for the far wall and dug the chain that he always wore from around his neck. The one holding his Saint box. Holding out the engraved end, he leaned toward the wall and pressed it against a small cartouche image of the box. It sank into the wall, the fake smoothness giving way. There was large click.

"Password?" a disembodied voice asked.

"In mendacio verum video," St. Benedict said clearly.

"Accepted," the voice said. "Initiating Doomsday protocols."

A cracking noise boomed, and the ceiling and floor of the section the group stood on broke away. They all lurched as it dropped a couple of inches, and more than one person had to hurriedly press in, over and away from the suddenly appearing edge. Then the section of hallway and ceiling dropped slowly like a lift, swallowing them into darkness. Once the ceiling had sealed them completely in, more lights clicked on, this time into a rougher hallway. Like above, lights clicked on along the sides, encased in small metal cages leading in the direction they had been heading.

"Keep going and do not stop until we get there," St. Benedict ordered and quietly all obeyed. Rune continued to hold onto him, moving along with everyone else. After they had gone several feet, the ground shuddered and rumbled. Everyone hesitated for a moment and waited for it to pass.

"They can't follow us now," Justin called. Everyone took that in stride and kept moving.

The journey became about putting one foot in front of the other. Just covering the next few feet. Rune had no idea how long they had walked, but it was probably measured in miles. No one complained, and whenever anyone had trouble, someone else aided. Together, they kept moving.

"St. Benedict!" Malachi cried. The group stopped but again parted without being asked to let the Saint through to the front, helped by Rune. Malachi stood in front of a door, military grade metal set into the rock of the wall.

"This is it," St. Benedict assured him. He went to a small console set into the side and pressed his lit hand again into it. The cover popped open, and an eye scanner extended. St. Benedict triple-blinked, lighting his eyes, and leaned forward. His eyes flashed a sequence before he closed one and pressed the other into the scanner.

The door clicked open and swung inward. Everyone poured into a wide area also reminiscent of a military facility with industrial tiled floors and fluorescent lights coming alive in bars along the walls of smooth concrete. The space was shaped like a very large T-junction with words printed on each corner, and arrows giving directions. Malachi approached one of the corners and read what was written there.

"Okay, any and everyone needing medical facilities, go that way. Looks like we have food that way. Communications techs, if you are still alive?" He paused and received three "heys" in response. "Okay, go set up and get us outside communications. *Secure* communications. I have a feeling this place has equipment."

Once everyone was through, St. Benedict shut the door again. Rune thought she felt a pressure shift as it sealed.

CHAPTER 33

"**A**re we safe?" she asked softly.

"Yes," Justin said, moving to press on the door as if to tighten it more, but it didn't budge. "Nothing short of a tank can get in here, and if you haven't noticed, it's a bit tight out there for one of those."

Rune nodded, satisfied.

He turned then and went over to Malachi. "Can... Can I leave you in charge?" he asked, stuttering as he stumbled.

"Yes. Frankly, I would be more comfortable with that," Malachi agreed tersely.

St. Benedict nodded, accepting it, and moved down the central-most hallway, using the wall as a guide. He had only gone three steps before he turned back to Rune.

"You... You don't have to go with me. There are quarters for over a hundred people down that way." He pointed. She saw the word "Quarters" listed underneath "Kitchen" on the corner sign to the right.

"I think... I think I need to stay with you. We need to talk,

Justin," Rune said. The name still sounded wrong to her, but it was also the truth.

He nodded and gestured. "This way."

Rune passed a glance at Malachi, but his face was stony with anger directed at the Saint's back. This was hard for all of them.

She followed him as they approached another T-Junction, this one branching at slight angles to each other, like the fletching of a stylized arrow. The hallway he chose was unmarked.

"Where are we going?" Rune asked.

"My apartment," Justin answered.

Rune thought that she was too numb for surprise, but she was wrong. "Your apartment?"

"My real one, yes."

He led her down the hall and stopped at the only door, about midway. There didn't seem to be anything else at the end. He stopped just before it, his hand resting on the handle. Then he turned to her with haunted eyes. "I'm sorry."

She slightly turned her own head away from him warily. "For what?"

"For ... what you're about to see in here." He looked pained, but he dropped his eyes to the handle and turned it, as if he needed to witness his own bad decision himself.

The door opened easily and swung inward. A series of lights, much like the ones lining the walls of the halls, automatically came on, but with a warm yellow glow instead of an austere white one. It lit up a wide inviting space that could have easily encompassed two of her apartments within. It was filled with interesting objects, a few sculptures and items of interest lining the walls amongst green, fern-like plants. There were also bookshelves filled with books with a reading lounger positioned before them. A king-sized, four poster bed sat at the far end, butted up sideways against the rough-cut stone walls. There was also a nook with a computer system set up, but it was powered down and silent. Rune also spied a tree rack festooned with various colors of his signature fedora.

There was another click as Justin flipped another switch, and orbs of light hanging from the ceiling lit up, adding more comfortable light to the space.

That's when she saw it.

"Oh, my gods..." Rune breathed, her hand flying up to her lips as she took in the sight.

On the far-right wall was a shrine.

She felt overwhelmed as she approached it. There were a dozen images of her pasted to the wall, all of them from when she had still been Anna Masterson. On a small table before the pictures were several familiar books filled with even more pictures. The topmost one was of her and Justin's wedding.

Her fingers hovered over an image of her, slenderer and laughing in her wedding dress, barely holding her bouquet while her bridesmaids, friends, and family, long gone and forgotten, stood next to her laughing as well. It was magazine perfect.

Had she ever looked so happy? Ever looked so young?

She turned the page to see more pictures of Justin and his groomsmen, being just as silly but far more dangerous, some hanging from a tree, hanging off of the venue roof, and attempting a pyramid.

There were other things on the shrine table. Her favorite book as a child, *A Tree Grows In Brooklyn*, its tattered green leather cover barely holding the yellowed pages inside. She opened the inside of the cover to see her name "Anna Wainwright" written in a sloppy, child's hand with a pen. Her mother had been very upset at her daughter damaging a then-precious edition, but it was hers. Clearly marked as hers forever. Beside it was her teddy bear, its bead eyes scratched and roughed up from hard love and play. Her prom pictures and the corsage, dried in a small box. The pearl necklace Justin had given her on their first anniversary lay on a velvet stand. And more. So much more. Little pieces of her life before.

"These were lost. They were all gone after..." Rune could

barely breathe.

"It took a long time to find much of this," Justin said with St. Benedict's voice. She turned to look at him. Even now, looking at the man she had known for the past year, she couldn't believe she hadn't seen it before. The way he moved, slipping his hand over his head, through his hair, Justin had done the same thing too, once. Yet she had ignored that sign, dismissed it as her seeing things.

"What happened to your fedora?"

"Who the hell knows?" he said waspishly, then closed his eyes. "Sorry, sorry. I just..." He looked up at her. "This is all really hard. I never thought... I never thought you would see any of this. I... I didn't..."

He staggered then and looked down at his hands. They were covered in blood and dirt. In the better lighting, Rune could see how much the fight had marked him.

"I will explain. I will explain everything, answer any questions you have. Can I just..." He gestured to himself. "Can I take a shower and get all this off first?"

Rune nodded. It was only reasonable. "Do you need help?"

He waved her offer off. "No, it's not as bad as it seems."

He gestured to a sideboard right next to his computer alcove. She realized it was covered with various bottles of liquor. Beneath the sideboard was a small fridge. "Glasses are up above. Help yourself to whatever you want. I think I have cheeses in the fridge. They're vacuum packed so they still should be good."

Rune nodded and passed him to make herself a much-needed drink. "Are you sure you don't need help?"

"I'm fine. I've had worse."

"I know. I've been there for some of it," she said. Tension built up between them. So much more needed to be explained and gone over, but neither knew where to begin. Instead, Rune gestured at the bottles. "Do... Do you want anything?"

"Uh, yeah. Make whatever, you know what I like. Thank you," he said, turning to head to the only other door in the room.

And Rune realized she did. She did know what he liked.

"Gin and tonic coming up," she muttered to herself.

If she were honest, it was a relief for him to go into what she presumed was the bathroom. She needed a moment.

She grabbed the whiskey bottle and poured a generous amount into her glass. The liquid splashing inside flashed her back to a memory not too long ago of a night where St. Benedict came over and they drank like fish. His laughter rolled through her head, and she couldn't help but smile.

And he had kissed her. Or maybe she had kissed him.

Other times flashed through her mind, the times he was close to her, the times they had touched, the times he had held her close.

"You deserve to be loved."

"I love you."

"My life is yours."

All the things he had said to her. They all had different shades of meaning now.

"Why didn't he just tell me from the beginning?" she asked out loud.

Haunted by that question, Rune grabbed her glass and swallowed the whole thing down, letting it burn the memories and take up residence in her chest. She breathed in through her nose, then took up the gin bottle and slapped his together. Once it was finished, she stared at it.

"Well, now what?" she asked the glass. It didn't have an answer. But then drinks never really did, despite what people think. The drink would just be sitting there until he got out of his shower, however long that took.

She had a passing thought that she should bring it to him.

That she immediately dismissed.

Then immediately reconsidered. Because why not? He was her husband once. And... Well, she had seen him naked before, so what did it matter? Even if it was years ago.

She quickly refilled her own, then seized his glass so she had one in each hand before turning toward the bathroom door. She heard the sounds of water running through it. Taking a deep breath, she pushed inside. Steam hit her full in the face. At first, she didn't see much.

The bathroom was something out of one of her dreams. Wide and stone textured. A toilet and wide mirror were to one side and in the center of the room was a glass room opaqued by condensation. The only light came from above the shower filling the inside with a glow through the large-pebbled glass that distorted everything inside. Above, a large rain show-erhead poured water straight down, and as she stared, she could make out a skin-colored figure standing under it. Even without the details, her cheeks burned.

For a heartbeat, she almost turned right around, but the thought, *He's your husband,* stopped her.

He was Justin. Her Justin.

How many times had he said it? *"My life is yours."*

That declaration goaded her on.

She entered the rest of the way, letting the door fall behind her to announce her arrival.

Instead, it closed silently.

So she went up to the door of the shower, stepping over the abandoned kevlar vest on the ground as well as the other clothes also abandoned there. Lacking other options, she pulled the shower door open with her pinkie.

"St. Ben... Justin... I got your drink—" she started to say, and he screamed.

Jumping under the water, the fully naked man inside spun toward her, startled, then away from her as her eyebrow shot straight up.

Okay, so he physically *wasn't* how she remembered him. Considering she hadn't recognized his current physique with his broader shoulders and muscles prior to that of her skinny jeans wearing former mate, she guessed she shouldn't have been surprised.

"Rune!" he squealed, covering his front with his hands and turning left then right as if he too didn't know exactly what to do with himself. "What are you doing... What are you doing?"

Idiotically, she thrust out the gin and tonic. "I made you a drink... I..." She couldn't turn her head away from him, even as the voice inside her screamed that she should. *What the hell am I doing!?* she thought.

Releasing one hand from himself, he awkwardly stretched it out for the drink, and she bounced in a half-step to hand it to him. "Thank you..." he muttered and slipped the drink into an alcove cut into the stone side of the shower.

They stood that way for an eternal second, the shower water the only sound.

"Rune, don't take this the wrong way. But get the hell out of my shower..." He lifted his head, shocking her with the hunger and fear in his eyes with equal measure. "Or get the hell in it."

Her eyes widened even more. And then she shut the door too hard. She stared at him, not knowing what to do. Her heart beat rapidly against her ribs. Her stomach clenched. She could barely breathe. The opaque man, a rough smudge of him, seemed to continue to stare at the door for a pregnant moment. Then he turned away.

What was she doing?

What did she want?

What *did* she want?

What did she truly want, right then in that moment?

All of the questions clamoring in her head went silent and fell away. There was only the sound of shower water hitting the ground a mere few feet away.

What do I want?

To get the hell in it.

It took seconds to shed her clothes. They hit the ground silently. She took a fortifying breath as she gripped the handle of the shower. She wasn't the perfect skinny young thing she had been once. And now he would see her as she was. But it was too late for thoughts like that.

She opened the door.

Inside, she saw him, leaning forward with his hands braced

against the stone wall, banging his head against it. "Stupid, stupid, stupid, stupid..."

She couldn't help it.

It made her laugh.

At the sound of her laughter, he spun around and rushed her. She didn't know what to expect until his arms were around her, lifting her off the ground, pressing their bodies together. He buried his face into her shoulder. "I'm sorry, I'm sorry," he repeated, his face screwing up into an ugly cry.

It just made her laugh harder, and she gripped him tightly, wrapping her arms and legs around him.

He groaned, unable to bear her weight on his bad leg and set her back down. She tried to pull away, afraid she had hurt him, but he didn't let her, only tucked her head against him and held on. They remained that way, rocking and holding as hard as they both could. Then they were kissing, their mouths remembering, all the times denied, forgotten. Soon it was their hands sliding over their bodies, finding the secret places newly remembered that only a married couple could truly know, coaxing pleasure from each other through their pain. She wanted him and she had him. Together they consummated everything they had always been to each other, despite everything. In that moment, no matter what else happened or had happened before, that moment was all that she wanted.

She had found him. She had found her husband at last.

He had been beside her all along.

CHAPTER 34

"**W**hat is this?" Rune asked as she slid the cloth gently over Justin's back.

"I don't know. What does it look like?" he asked, attempting, and failing, to bend around so he could see it. The attempt made him groan in pain, and she nudged him with a hand to stop trying.

"It looks like it'll be a huge bruise in the morning," she said, washing away the crusted trickle of blood that came close to it.

"Right, that would be when I took that bullet St. Rachel so graciously tried to implant into your ample chest," he said in his usual dry, amused tone, before bringing his gin and tonic to his lips to sip, though it was half filled with shower water by now. They sat on the floor of the shower, the water still cascading beside them. The floor was where they had ended up, and the floor worked for Rune just fine.

She stared at the enormous red mark, already turning purple in places. "But ... I stopped the bullet with my shield."

"You stopped one of them, absolutely. Standard procedure,

two taps. One to the heart, one to the head. I stopped the one to your heart."

"I thought it was impossible for someone to actually jump in front of a bullet in time?"

"It is, usually. I was already moving toward you," he said.

Rune leaned forward to kiss his shoulder, then rest her chin there. "You were going to die for me?" she asked, not sure if she meant it as a tease or not.

"I would have failed," he said soberly. "If you hadn't blocked the second bullet with your shield, you would have died in my arms."

"Hey," Rune said, slipping her head under his arm, twisting around until she laid in his embrace, half over his lap. She set her fingers against his lips. "I did stop the bullet. I would have missed the first one."

"Yeah," he agreed and kissed the back of her fingers.

"So we both saved me," she said and rewet the cloth she was using in the stream of water. "Okay, my turn. I think we got everything off you."

He took the cloth and gingerly passed it over her face. "Oh, wow," he breathed.

"What?" she asked, cocking an eyebrow.

"I can't believe you're here. I can't believe you're with me."

She smiled bashfully despite herself. "You can't take it back now."

"I would never want to," he said solemnly, no trace of jest in his face.

"Hmm," she said, curling her body around his. "I've never seen you so serious."

He rested his forehead against hers. "I don't deserve you," he whispered and kissed her gently.

When they broke, she grinned. "I was sure you were going to run away when you saw the new model."

"Stop that," he said, practically barking it at her.

"What?" she said, furrowing her eyebrows.

"Stop..." he growled. "Stop tearing yourself down. You are

a fucking *goddess*. You are the most beautiful woman I have ever known in life... either life... and I..." He stopped then, and she could see the heart that had been so open only seconds ago start to close up.

She seized his face still hovering above her as he searched for words that wouldn't come. "Don't you dare," she warned.

He stopped at her warning, looking at her fearfully. "You must resent me. For all the women I had before when we..." He jutted his chin as if awaiting a firing squad. "When we were married."

"Must I?" she said.

"Rune, I want you to know, I have not been with anyone since ... that night ... when we were arrested. Not anyone." He closed his eyes again. "You see, there I go. I'm lying again. I can't stop fucking lying. I..."

"Justin," she said with a commanding tone. She sat up out of his arms. "Stop being a coward and making this all about you. Just tell me."

He took in a shuddering breath. "I mean. It's true, I haven't slept with anyone else since we parted—"

"Because of your Saint's vow," she filled in.

He double blinked, remembering that she knew that. "Yes, but... but there are other things I did. Kissing and some touching."

"Yes, Justin, I know."

His brows furrowed together. "Right. Right, you know that." He brushed a hand over his face and groaned down the scale. "You know about the vow."

"To remain faithful to your wife. Even though we aren't technically married anymore."

"And you aren't named Anna Masterson anymore. That was the problem. I couldn't be sure... I didn't know how much the wording of the vow played into the curse magic tied in the box."

Rune furrowed her brow at that. "Oh. So what you're saying... What..." This time she scrubbed her nose as she tried to put it together. "What happens if you break your vow?"

"The Saint box could have killed you and freed me from its control, which is how I weaponized it against my handlers. They couldn't force me to break the vow and risk losing their asset. And it was a vow I wanted to keep."

"So, with what we just did... if the box hadn't counted me as your wife?"

He held up the box, still on the chain around his neck. "We shouldn't have taken the risk. At least, I should have told you first."

Rune worked her lips. "It means this magic works by intention. You intended your words to mean me, and they did."

"Yes, they did," he agreed, "But—"

"Shut up. I just dodged three bullets today. Let's just call it a win." She grabbed his face and kissed him well, slipping her tongue into his willing mouth. Gods, she had forgotten how good he was at it. Unfortunately, they were both way too sore to go at it again.

"Okay, okay, we need to stop," Rune said, waving him away and putting the cloth back in his hand before offering her arms. "Come on. Hurry up."

Ease returned to his face, and he ran the cloth over her, washing away the pain and dirt from the last day. They washed each other's hair, Rune running her fingers along the scar at the top of his skull, all the pieces of him fitting together in her mind. He only sat with his eyes closed letting her, yet she wondered what it really felt like to him. Was he enduring pain because she wanted to touch him, or did it bring him comfort and pleasure to have someone accept it? Or would asking the question corrupt the answer?

Eventually, they both agreed by silent consensus to leave the shower. The stillness of the place echoed even louder when the rain sound disappeared. Justin pulled out a pair of towel sheets from another alcove, and they wrapped themselves up to pad out into the rest of his apartment. He led her to the opposite wall, to the left of the shrine to her, near the bed.

"Go ahead and sit down. I'll find us something to wear," he said and slid aside a large painting to reveal a secret room which turned out to be a walk-in closet filled with clothes.

Rune did as she was bid and sat down on the quilt atop the bed, wrapped warmly in her towel sheet. Looking down at the quilt, her whole self froze once again. Gently, she ran a hand over the surface as she recognized the pattern beneath. A few moments later, St. Benedict returned, now dressed in gray sweatpants and a dark blue t-shirt, bearing other similar clothes. It was his turn to stop as he realized she was examining the bed.

"You found our wedding quilt," she said softly.

"Your mother kept it in a storage locker," he said, setting the clothes next to her on the bed.

"You asked my mother for access to the storage locker?" she asked.

"No, I broke in and stole it from the storage locker," he said, taking the shirt and gathering it into his hands.

With a teasing smile, she recognized what he was doing and held her arms up like a child, letting the towel fall away.

He gratified her by swallowing and blushing as he pulled his shirt over her head. The sweatpants he brought her, she slipped on herself since it was just easier. He went back to the sideboard to fill fresh glasses, which she didn't mind. She let her gaze wash over the shrine of herself, which was when she noticed a new picture among the old ones. She went to the new framed image.

It was of herself and him, her using her shield crystal to create a protective barrier behind him while he had guns on either side of her body defending her.

"Marcus took this," she said, remembering seeing it as one of among many of his surveillance photos when he had been investigating her as a demonic practitioner, the charge that landed her in Corinthe custody in fact.

"Yes, I stole that from him too," Justin said, shaking the drink with ice from the little fridge.

"I can't believe I didn't realize it was you this whole time," she said, setting the picture down.

"No, you knew," he said, pouring out the drink. "You guessed it right from the first."

She remembered the moment he referred to. "When I told you who I was on the back of my porch. Gods, it must be almost a year ago now."

"Yes, you see. You got it right. You asked me if I was him."

"And you lied to me," she said flatly.

"No. Worse. I made you doubt yourself," he admitted as he poured, his hand clearly shaking, giving his feelings away. "I said, 'Well, if I said I wasn't, it would make it sound like I was.'"

"That wasn't exactly what you said," Rune corrected, knowing it didn't sound quite right.

"Close enough. And it was enough to make you lie to yourself for me and pretend you didn't know what you knew you did. And I've been sorry every day since that I did that. I just didn't know how to take it back, like a fucking coward."

She glanced over at him, studying his muscled shoulders. "To be fair, you've changed in more ways than one."

"Right, right," he said and scooped up the drinks, holding out the one that was clearly hers. It was her whiskey sour, this time with ice cubes floating in it. The tangy sweet on her tongue was delicious, but it also made her aware of how hungry she was.

"Can we get something to eat?" Rune asked before taking another sip. "I'm starving now."

He downed his whole glass. "Yeah, yeah. No problem. We just have to go to the kitchen, but there should be plenty of food, if you don't mind it reconstituted."

"I think I could eat cardboard right now," Rune said.

"Well, then you're in luck."

She laughed, and he led her out to the hallway. Walking hand in hand, they traced their way back and went down the hallway marked "Kitchen." Rune had no sense of time in that place, but it was quiet, as if it were night. The lights were bright enough to see but dim enough to give a sense of a late hour.

"Where do you think everyone else is?" Rune whispered.

Justin leaned in toward her. "Probably sleeping. We're safe here, and we've all been through a lot."

"It just seems so surreal," she commented.

Passing through a set of free-swinging, double doors, she found herself in what could only be described as a high-volume industrial kitchen. Everything was made of stainless steel from the appliances to the countertops, all empty and waiting to be used. A restaurant level dishwasher ran in the corner, humming away on a load, the only sign that the kitchen had already been used once.

Justin let go of Rune's hand to open the refrigerator, gazing in. "Right, I have eggs. Would you like eggs?" he asked.

Rune gave him a skeptical look. "How old are they?"

He pulled out the container and looked at the date stamped on the side. "Good for another week. It also looks like someone made soup earlier. There's leftovers in here if you'd rather have that."

"You know, the prospect of hot food, even if it is only scrambled eggs, is a lot more appealing right now," she answered honestly.

He nodded and gestured for a bar stool on the opposite side of the metallic central island. She sat and watched as the Saint pretended to be a chef and pulled out several metallic bowls. He expertly whisked the eggs into the bowl, and soon they were sizzling in two small pans on the range set into the middle of the island, instead of the one on the opposite counter where he would have had to turn his back. From another upper cupboard on that opposing side, however, he retrieved a few bottles, one of which had green flakes inside.

"I have cilantro, but it's only the dried stuff. I hope that's okay," he said, flipping the eggs over in with single flips each.

"Oh, the horrors," Rune quipped with a smile. They fell into a silence as he cooked, and she watched.

Propping her cheek on her hand, she wondered how many

times he had cooked for her in the past year.

"You never used to cook for me," she said out loud, more to herself.

The spatula paused before he could slide the newly made omelet onto a plate. "You mean, before when I was the world's biggest asshole?" He finished plating the omelet, laid a piece of cheese over it, and added a dusting of the cilantro.

"You're *not* anymore?" Rune quipped, then immediately wished she hadn't. It didn't come off as the joke she had intended.

As she feared, he didn't take it as funny, pretty much because it wasn't. "Rune. I know what I've done. I knew what I was doing when I did it, and I accept the consequences, whatever you deem them to be."

Rune picked up the fork, looking at the food before her, but her stomach had turned. "I don't know how to feel about all this," she admitted.

"You don't have to feel anything. I—"

She blew out a breath. "Justin, just calm down. Just ... tell me why you didn't tell me who you were then, back in the beginning?"

He swallowed. "At first..." He blew out a breath as he struggled, then slid his fingers through his hair, along his scar. "At first, I didn't recognize you. Not as my wife. I couldn't remember what she... what you looked like and then when you told me... I was in shock and I panicked. I did what I always do. I lied and got the hell out of there."

Rune took that in and compared it to her own memories of that time. "And that's why you stayed away for two months after and refused to see me when Maxamillion came to introduce himself to me that first time."

"Yeah. I thought, okay, the best thing I could do for you would be to stay out of your life and focus on protecting you. And I convinced myself that you had actually figured it out. Which I realize now was my wishful thinking." Justin glanced at his stove and realized he had forgotten to turn the burner off, so he flicked the switch.

Rune scoffed, this time cutting into her omelet and stabbing it with a fork. "When we saw the videos of your death. That would have been the opportune moment to come clean."

"I tried! I did." Justin turned away, pacing in a frustrated circle.

"How!?" Rune pushed. "How did you try?"

"I came to you after everything was done. I said I needed to tell you something. I intended to man up and you said, 'Let him be dead.'"

Her eyebrows popped up as the memory came back to her. He saw the look and took the point. "You told me, 'Let him be dead,' and I believed that you were telling me subtly that you knew who I was, but that he was the old me and to just let it go. Like you were Anna but now you're Rune. It's what I wanted to believe, and I did."

"But I *didn't* know. I didn't know that was what I was saying!" she snapped.

He held his hands up placating. "I realize! I did say it was what I wanted to believe. Okay? I was terrified of you finding out and having to face you as..." He gestured to himself. "I deserved everything that happened to me, but you didn't. You never did, and it was my fault you were there. And I didn't want to be him. The way you look at me, like I'm some goddamn hero, I didn't *want* to have been *him!*" He pressed his hand into his chest.

"But you love me," Rune said, finally getting it. Finally letting herself get it. "You love your wife. You love *me.*"

His face said yes.

She slid her own hands up her cheeks, holding her head at the temples like it might explode. "Dammit, this is so messed up." Then she laughed dryly. "And this whole time, I thought there was no way a guy like you could ever want..." Her hands gestured uselessly at herself now. She didn't know what she wanted to say; she just knew she wasn't saying it.

"I did," he growled in his throat. "I do want you. So

very much."

The intensity of his words made her pause, and her cheeks blushed, despite herself. "So that wasn't just ... emotions."

"I think I emoted a lot," he remarked.

"You know what I mean—all the tension ... and unfinished business between us."

He licked his lips. "You as Rune... you were the first person to tempt me to break my vow. Ever." Another pregnant pause stretched between them until at last more words dragged out of Justin, slow as a death knell. "And if we never do again, I will always be so grateful to you for one last memory. It was a mercy I didn't expect."

"I didn't do it as an act of mercy," Rune snapped.

"Then why did you do it?"

"Because I really, really wanted to sleep with you. I have since we met. Re-met," she confessed herself. "And I mean, why not, right? Everyone out there is going to want me dead in the morning, not just St. Rachel, so what the hell do I have to lose?"

"I will not let anyone out there harm you," he promised, his eyes glinting.

Rune swallowed the bile that rose in the back of her throat at the thought of everything she knew he could do. "It's not their fault. Nobody in the Praetorium did anything wrong. I led St. Dominic to you."

"He coerced you," Justin said resolutely.

"I..." She sighed, realizing she would be going over and over what happened for a while. "I didn't want anyone else to get hurt, but I was so angry."

"I shouldn't have left you there alone. I thought you would be safest there since who would think to find you at your old place?" he added.

"I figured as much. But find me they did." She pushed the empty plate away from her, suddenly aware that she had eaten the whole thing while they talked.

Hesitantly, he reached out his fingers to take her hand,

then stopped just short, waiting for permission, which she granted when she came the other ten percent.

"Okay. Maybe we..." She squeezed his hand. "Maybe, if we both survive tomorrow, we keep talking about this and not make any decisions about ... us ... until we get some distance from the current situation."

"If... if that's what you want," he accepted softly.

"Yes, I do," she said firmly. "I have a lot of questions. And you better tell me the truth, no matter what I ask because you're right. I don't owe you anything, but I owe myself the answers. If you don't think that you can do that, you better say right now."

He thumbed gently over the back of her hand, squeezing for all he was worth. "How can you trust me not to lie to you again?"

"I don't know. Maybe I won't." She leaned forward, forcing him to raise his downcast gaze to meet hers. "Do you intend to keep lying to me?"

He shook his head, not breaking eye contact. "No. No, I'll tell you anything you want to know. I swear. And if I don't," he dropped his gaze again, his voice growing thick, "my life is yours, Rune. You do whatever you want with it."

She withdrew her hand, recoiling. "Stop it. Stop offering ... for me to kill you. It's not going to happen, and honestly is not a great basis for rebuilding a healthy thing between us, so please cut it out!"

"Thing?" he asked, a hint of wryness in his voice.

"Yes. Thing because I don't think I can even attempt another label on this now. It's all too messed up."

"I couldn't agree more," Maxamillion said.

CHAPTER 35

His angry voice startled Rune off her stool, snapping her hand away from Justin. A stab of fresh guilt knifed through her guts.

The prince of the business world strolled in with his hands in his disheveled suit pockets. With his tie undone and an almost manic smile on his face, his movements seemed unusually dangerous. Gone was the charming jackrabbit, ready with a solution to every problem, and something more predatory and unrefined took its place.

Neither Rune nor Justin moved as he came to a stop at the end of the counter, nodding his head. "Yeah, yeah, that's the perfect two words for it. Messed. Up." He snapped off his perfect white teeth at each period.

When neither responded, he focused on Rune.

"You went *back* to him," he scoffed. It set him to sauntering again, moving past her like he gazed on a farm animal he had high hopes for but had disappointed him in the end. "The second you found out, you went running back to him without a second thought. And after everything he did to you."

The hairs on the back of Rune's neck rose straight, and she pulled away, standing up because it felt safer. Maxamillion chuckled and continued past her and the counter to stand face to face with his Saint. It was the first time Rune realized that Maxamillion stood several inches taller than St. Benedict as he stared down his nose at the person he owned. For once, their expressions were switched, one smiling, master of the room, and the other stone-faced.

"So how was she?" Maxamillion asked. "Everything you remembered ... Justin?"

The name rang out poignantly.

"You knew?" Rune asked, finding her voice and her own ire.

"Hell yeah I knew. I've known since I claimed this ... lucrative tool as mine. You told me yourself, didn't you? The whole story." Maxamillion moved off, brushing past St. Benedict, which shifted him a little but did not make him stumble. "He told me about how he had been the brilliant, new protégé, genius, extraordinary programmer who had unlocked the key to changing the world, but that he got greedy and stupid and dipped his hand in the cookie jar too deep and nearly had it slapped off. Got himself and his lovely young wife arrested."

Maxamillion turned to Rune.

"I know that he sold his secrets to get you out, Anna Masterson. All nobility at the very last second when it was more-or-less too late. Made a deal with your aunt or some bullshit to sell you off to her."

He continued to walk around the kitchen island, moving past Rune again.

"Kodiak kept him under their thumb, and he cracked it for his company. Managed to make a program spit out a magic spell, but during the procedure, something went wrong with the way he tried to jack himself into the system, fried part of his brain and essentially killed himself for a minute or two too long. But did he tell you what happened after that? Damn near a miracle. The company threw all their resources into saving him, preserving that special brain," Maxamillion shook his head in mock-sadness, tsking, "but too much damage messed him up."

Maxamillion stopped his recitation, pressing the side of his hand to cover up his smile, highlighting his angry eyes. "Did you tell her how you became a Saint, *Justin*? And all the terrible things you did? Oh. No? Really? You didn't tell her?" He slapped the side of his leg in mock outrage, dancing his feet back and forth as he shook his head. "Well, how do you like that? All those lies and omissions."

Now he spun back to Rune who glared hotly at him.

"All that and you still went, yeah, want me some of that," he sneered. "What do you think now? Want to go for a second round? Abusive assholes more your type?!"

Rune straightened her spine. "Why didn't *you* tell me?" she growled.

"It wasn't my secret to tell," he stated matter-of-factly, dropping the false merriment at last before turning back to St. Benedict. "Was it? Justin."

Justin's fist was already in motion, connecting with Maxamillion's jaw just in time with the other man's turn. His head snapped back, but it didn't stop him. Instead, he whirled and pummeled his fists rapidly into Justin's sides. Due to his injuries, Justin didn't react quickly and instead was forced to curl his elbows against himself, blocking them as Rune stepped up shouting.

"Stop it! Stop it, both of you!!"

As quickly as it started, both men backed off from each other, neither looking like they wanted to, but neither really being in any shape to continue.

Maxamillion panted, swinging his arms and dancing back and forth like a boxer as he calculated risk/reward. He then spun toward Rune, pointing his finger to the door. "I want you out of here," he said. "I want you gone and out of my... away from my people. Now."

Rune took a step back, recoiling from the force of that

command. "What? I—"

"My people are dead because of you! I've already seen the playback, Rune. You have to remember the Saints remember everything," Maxamillion growled, stabbing his finger at her.

And she knew he was right. She had seen it herself. All St. Rachel had to do was jack herself in, and her memories could be accessed using the tiny CPU in her brain. It would have shown everything that she saw, and she had witnessed St. Dominic exposing what she had done to the whole room.

She had no defense against something like that. Not in that moment anyway.

It also didn't change a few other facts. "I can't leave," she said softly, shaking her own head. "My sentence... My work order..."

"Fulfilled," Maxamillion said, and he reached into his inner pocket to pull out and slap an envelope onto the counter. "When I made you head of your own division, it allowed me to exploit a loophole in the corporate penal code. I was going to surprise you at dinner." He flicked his finger at it, making it jump an inch toward her. "You're a free woman. It's already done. Take it and get out."

"Maxx, you can't do that," Justin said, finally speaking up. "She'll have no protection now, and Kodiak will still want her..."

"Do I look like I care?!" He spun his manic eyes back to Justin. "They can burn her in a ditch, and it still wouldn't be justice."

Justin sneered. "You heartless mons—"

"Heartless!" Maxamillion exclaimed. "It's because I *have* a damn heart that I'm letting her *walk out that door alive!* She destroyed everything. The mission, the underground. We were at our most vulnerable, and she stabbed the knife in our back. I don't know if half of what we've got left is going to survive the night. Everything we've worked for has gone up in fucking smoke! Do you remember why we did this?"

"Do you remember?" Justin said, his voice menacingly low. "Your mission was your mission—" Maxamillion slapped his

Saint across the face. The other man's head whipped to the side and stayed there.

Expecting no retaliation, Maxamillion turned back to Rune, straightening his jacket. "And I *am* being *merciful* right now because *you*..." he pointed his finger straight at her nose, his voice low and menacing and precise, "get to walk out of here alive and free."

"She's not leaving here," Justin said. "You are."

"Excuse me?" Maxamillion snapped back.

"This place," the Saint gestured to kitchen but indicating the whole facility. "This is mine. Not yours. The only safe haven you have left for your underground belongs to me. I bought it. Not you. It's not a company asset, Maxx. It's mine. And *you* can get the hell out of my house!"

Maxamillion sniffed, jutting his chin as he crossed, coming up so close Rune was sure they would hit each other again. Instead, he grabbed at the Saint's neck, yanking the chain taut as he gripped the Saint Box.

"Yeah? And who owns your pretty ass?" Maxamillion growled softly through his teeth.

"I do," Rune said.

Both men turned toward Rune, finally shutting up.

This time, Rune pointed her finger at Justin. "He swore retainership to me. He belongs to me by his own choice."

Both men's eyes went wide as they realized the truth of that implication. She had a legal claim, set by case law as old as the city itself, copied from older still, before the Europeans came over the ocean.

And Justin's legal Saint status was ... untested at best. Saints weren't really supposed to exist at all.

Who had the higher claim?

"Well then, my *Lady*, you're going to have to take me to court." Maxamillion tugged on the Saint box, but the chain didn't snap since Justin used a double link necklace for strength, so he'd not lose the box. "Remove it," Maxamillion ordered.

Rune could see him trying to resist. The veins popped out

of St. Benedict's face and neck as he tried to force his muscles to not obey, but he was losing, his hands creeping up closer and closer to his neck. He struggled to breathe with the effort. Pain twisted his face.

"Justin, do as he says," Rune said urgently, unable to bear to watch him suffer.

Her retainer darted his eyes to her and taking in her expression relented, breathing heavily as his fingers struggled with the clasp. But too soon, it fell free and landed in his master's hand. Maxamillion looped the chain into his palm. "I will hold onto this for safekeeping," he said mockingly before stuffing it into his pocket.

Satisfied, Maxamillion turned and came around the island again to go to the door. "She can leave in the morning," he amended his orders. "Make sure of it, St. Benedict. Come see me when it's done."

Maxamillion had barely left when Justin came around the island and seized Rune by the arm, spinning her toward him. "He's wrong," he said urgently. "This is not your fault. You are not responsible for anyone who died tonight."

"St. Ben—Justin," Rune started, but he seized her other arm.

"No! You need to know this. You did not pull the trigger. You did not make the choice to order them to attack. You were under threat with a gun to your head—"

"Don't!" Rune slashed her hands at his chest, effectively pushing him away. He yielded his hands open, ready to seize her but terrified to hurt her. "Don't... Just leave it alone."

She wrapped her arms around him, resting her head against his chest. "I'm too tired to keep fighting right now," she murmured.

He nodded and pulled her away out of the kitchen. The door shut behind them, and a few minutes later, the lights went out as well, all on their own. They walked side by side quietly.

"What will happen if you don't throw me out tomorrow?" Rune asked, her voice soft.

His hand lifted to grab his Saint box, but it no longer hung around his neck. "It will kill me. But that is fine," he pronounced. "He can't actually make you leave. I will show you everything here. You will be able to drive them out and keep yourself safe, even after I'm—"

"No," she said, so simply and resolutely he flinched. "I'm leaving tomorrow."

He wanted to say no, to fight her on it, but he checked himself. "Where will you go?"

"Home. Though probably back to Maddie's house with Uncle Lucas. It's still magically fortified and will probably be safer anyway. The bar itself still needs a final integrity assessment before it will be deemed safe to actually stay in my apartment upstairs so best not to mess that up."

He wanted to tell her that if she left here, he would die. The pain would be too great; the guilt would finally crush him. In his mind's eye, he saw a vision of the future when he would find out she had been taken and killed by one of their enemies. It didn't even matter which one. He would end himself at the same moment.

Rob Maxamillion of his last triumph, he thought uncharitably. But he wouldn't say such a plan out loud. He would do what he should have done all along and protected her from himself.

Yet he said nothing, and when he didn't respond, she nodded, satisfied.

Leading her back to his room, every step was on high alert, waiting for someone seeking revenge around every corner, but no one came. He unlocked his door and held it open for her, and once she was inside, the tension left his shoulders.

She entered like a ghost and crossed to the bed, pulling the covers back before getting into it. He hovered by the lights, dimming them down to nothing as soon as she was safely within his bed.

She finally looked back to him, her eyes eternally unreadable.

He had no intention of attempting to climb into that bed with her, but before he could assure her of that, she asked, "Will you stay here tonight?"

"Don't worry," he said, nodding. "I'll keep you safe." He closed the door and gestured to lock it securely, the holographic failsafes responding to him alone. Then he gestured to his computer chair. "I've passed out in that hundreds of times, so we'll be—"

"No, I mean here." Rune scooted to the side closer to the wall, making space for him in the bed. "Just for tonight, would you be my husband again and hold me?"

His breath hitched in at her request, but how could he deny her? It was what he wanted more than anything.

He crossed the room slowly, searching for any sign that she would take it back, but she didn't. In fact, she moved even more so he could sit down, then slide into the bed, under their quilt, rescued from a tattered cardboard box with a rotting corner so many years ago. She wiggled up against him, and her head dropped into the nook of his shoulder while he curled to his side to bring his other hand protectively around the back of her head.

"Hmm, I remember this," she sighed into him, and he pressed his lips to her temple.

They lay there, listening and feeling with each other's breathing. He had never felt so sleepy and warm.

"Justin?"

"Hmm?" Her voice roused him from near sleep.

"Did I just get us wrong all these years?" Her fingers caressed his side, exploring lazily through the folds of his shirt.

He lay there so long trying to answer.

"Justin?" she whispered.

"I *knew* what I was doing back then, and I didn't care. I didn't care about you," he confessed. "I didn't care about our future or what could happen to us. I thought I was invincible,

and it destroyed everything."

His lip curled up as he sneered in hatred of himself, but she nuzzled him.

Obediently, he relaxed into her, his Rune, his lady and mistress, his whole reason for continuing on.

"Keep going," she whispered.

"And... And all I could do was blame it on everyone else. You, my parents, on society." He stopped and took a breath. This was so hard, but now was the time. "And everything that happened tonight is a result of *that*." He rubbed his hand up and down Rune's arm. "*You*," he breathed, saying the word tenderly. "You are innocent."

He could feel her shaking her head in his nook. "This doesn't make sense. You blamed me then, but you got me out?"

"I didn't love you until I realized..." He swallowed, "While they were torturing us, I watched. Waiting for the moment when you would turn on me. When you would confess that you didn't love me, that our marriage was just a contract that furthered both our social advances and that you had nothing to do with anything I did, for and then against the company. I waited for proof that you were just like everyone else in my life who said they loved me, when what they really meant was they were using me to get whatever they wanted out of me. My parents, every woman I ever..." He couldn't say the word, so he just moved on. "I waited for you to disavow me. I watched as they did so many horrible things to you."

Rune's whole body shuddered. He knew she had to be remembering, and the urge to tear his own guts out at having her brought her back to that pain lurched through him. "But I never did," she said softly, as sweet and innocent as a true saint, a holy and sacred woman who was never meant to be dragged through the darkness that he dwelled in.

"No." He shook his head. "No, you never did. You just ... loved me. Unwaveringly. No matter what happened. What they did to you. Proof. Undeniable, fucking *proof* that there *was* someone in this world who *genuinely* loved me. And by the time I figured that out, I also understood what I had done to you. How I had destroyed the only thing I really wanted but could not understand. I was a piece of shit narcissist, and something broke in me. And I'm still broken, Rune. I dare to love you, unbidden, unwanted, and all I can bring you is hell. I don't want you with me. I don't want you to love me back. I don't deserve it; you don't deserve it."

He couldn't find the right words. He could hear himself just ranting on and on, and he knew he would never be about to make her understand what he himself couldn't understand, only feel. He closed his eyes, living in the pain he had caused.

"What do you want me to say, St. Ben?" she whispered. "I've told you I forgive you, that I accept you, that I love you, and it's not enough for you."

She fell asleep like that, her breath evening out as her words faded away. Triple-blinking his eyes, his sight shifted to night vision. He studied her, asleep in his arms. Her heartbeat and breathing reported back to him that she was asleep, but even as his implants calculated the data, her fingers sought out his jawline, patting his cheek.

"You're mine," she muttered. "You can't give up."

He didn't mean to fall asleep as well, but even then, he held her close like it was the last day in the world.

CHAPTER 36

Getting herself back to her bar was surprisingly uneventful. The snow was finally melting away, and the wind blew warm. She hadn't even needed a coat, which was good because she didn't have one.

The lock had been changed on the door, as in, the lock had been replaced with a chain and padlock. While she could have gone around to the back and climbed the switchback stairs to her apartment, this was just as well. Cracking her knuckles, she laid her hand over the lock. She could feel the magic carved inside it, tied to the power of her Wizard's House.

"I'm home," she said softly.

The lock snapped open, and the chain fell away, spooling itself out of the door handle onto the concrete leading up to the door. She pulled it open like she had thousands of times before.

It looked exactly as it had when they had left Malachi inside, and even then, she only glanced at the destruction briefly.

And this was everything she had left.

Turning slowly, she ran her hand along the side of the bar in what had once been the Lounge. The bar itself was solid, but a thick layer of soot came away on her hand, greasy and cloying.

She wondered if she would have time to clean it before they came for her. Whoever "they" turned out to be.

She had no delusions that someone would be there for her soon. She had lost all her protection.

While her membership to the Magic Guild had not been entirely stripped from her, she had been put in the last category before expulsion. Her vote had been stripped, and her rights within the Guild both to its resources and representation were as jailed as she had been. It had been the only way the Guild could legally sell her to the Corinthe Corp once she had been found guilty of all charges.

Corinthe and, by extension, the Praetorium's protection were also thoroughly gone, and Rune couldn't argue with that. Despite what St. Ben— Justin thought, exile disguised as freedom had been the minimum of what she felt she deserved for her betrayal.

Maxamillion was right. He was being generous, she thought.

Other than that, what did she have? A Wizard House set into a burned-out bar that had not been in business for months. No resources, no money, no—

She finished her circle of the room, landing her eyes on a person who had not been there moments before.

He smiled at her, his hands in his pockets, his Hamburg hat pushed back on his forehead.

"Hey there, kid," the older, but still handsome, man said, smiling warmly to make a fan of wrinkles around his twinkling eyes.

"Oh, Uncle Lucas," she cried and ran to him, throwing herself into his arms like a child. He received her warmly, lifting her up in a tight bear hug.

"It's alright. It's alright now. We're here," he cooed at her, patting her back firmly while a sob hiccupped from her. It took

a moment for her to register what he had said.

"We?"

A clack and scrape from behind her made her turn, just in time to see Alf, her bar manager and the steward of her House, step up onto his old bench behind the bar. He set a clean bottle of liquor with a new red label on the side, a stencil outline of a white winking demon off the label's center. "Not a damn clean glass in the place," he declared.

"I got some," a teenager, almost a young woman, said, coming in from the Main bar.

"Ally?" Rune asked, unbelieving at how much her first retainer had changed in the few months Rune had been gone. She dropped the plastic glasses onto the counter in a flurry of hurry that annoyed Alf to no end. Ally didn't see nor care as she streaked across the bar to hug Rune like Rune had hugged Uncle Lucas.

"My lady!" Ally squealed. "You're already here!"

"What are *you* doing here?" Rune asked. "You should be in school—"

"I am, but when Alf called yesterday, I just had one class, so I told my professor I had a family emergency, and I'm so glad you're okay. I can't believe you're here," the kid said in one running sentence with no breaths.

"We're all coming," Uncle Lucas interjected. "Marcus and Ravinia went to pick up Margaret and Elias from Evanston of all places."

"What were they doing in Evanston?" Ally asked.

"Don't *know*, but knowing Elias, there will be a story behind it," Alf groused.

Uncle Lucas sighed and tried to pick up his explanation where it left off, "And Franklin will be—"

A clopping sound outside the front door interrupted the older man, and the once barfly centaur, a permanent fixture and the bar's actuary, trotted through. Instead of his usual business jacket and formal apron, he wore a hoodie with the Blackhawks icon of a hawk head profile with stylized feathers coming out of its crest and a long fleece apron that went down to his four knees. He still carried a briefcase. "It's actually getting hot out there," Franklin muttered, holding the door open. "Look, I swear we went from 35 to 70 degrees in 3 hours." Then he noticed Rune among the other retainers staring at him. "Oh! She's here already!" he said awkwardly.

Rune didn't hesitate a moment but rushed to her friend, who, like everyone else, scooped her into a hug.

"How did you all know I would be here?"

"Your Knight called us," Alf declared in his basso voice.

"He told us what happened," Uncle Lucas said more sedately.

"So of course, we came!" Ally interjected. "We're your retainers!"

"We're your family," Uncle Lucas stated.

"You can always find help at the Lucky Devil," Alf stated, coming up beside her with a full glass in both hands and offered her one. She took it, wiping a quiet tear that slipped from her eye. The gruff bar manager awkwardly patted her arm in a show of comfort that he was not used to giving. "Don't worry. It's going to be alright. Sometimes you have to let your friends carry you."

She laughed at that through her tears and brought the drink to her lips. It was sweet and sour and burned beautifully as she gulped it down. Warmth spread through her chest and calmed her frayed nerves. Alf passed around more glasses to everyone, though Ally's was mostly water with just a hint of the liquor potion in it since she was still underage.

Before the teen could drink it, he held a hand over the top. "We need to wait for the others," he warned.

"This is great. We're all going to be together again!" Ally crowed happily.

"No, we're not," Uncle Lucas interjected. It sobered the jovial mood as all eyes turned to him for an explanation. "One of us is still trapped."

"Who?" Ally asked innocently.

"The Knight," Alf said, shifting his gaze to his Lady. "The

last of us to swear fealty to the House Magdalene."

Rune realized that they were all looking to her for direction. He was right. Justin was... "But I don't know how..." she started to say, but the pain in her chest choked off the thought.

"We're going to figure it out," Uncle Lucas said, "together." Then he tilted his head. "If that is what you want," he added.

"Yes," she said softly, understanding the truth the moment she said it. "Yes, we have to get him back."

She looked to each of them, feeling her connection burn like a thread of light connecting her heart to theirs.

"Hello?"

The whole room turned to the foreign voice at the door. A bike messenger stood there, dressed in tight, workout clothes underneath loose fighting shorts and a windbreaker. The helmet sat on his head, but the straps weren't fastened. He held a box in both hands. "I'm, uh, looking for a..." He looked down at the package, reading the label. "Lady Leveau?"

"I'm Lady Leveau," Rune said, handing her glass to Franklin, who took it so she could step forward to take the package. Automatically, Uncle Lucas and Alf flanked either side of her and, giving the poor messenger threatening looks as he passed over his charge.

"Who's it from?" Ally asked as Rune examined the package.

"Uh, if that's all, then..." The messenger looked between the two aggressive men, holding his hands up, clearly wondering what he had walked into.

"Thank you," Rune said to the messenger directly, then to Alf, "Can you tip him, please? I don't have any cash."

Alf growled but complied as she tore open the end of the package to find another white box within.

She brought everything over to the bar and continued tearing the package. Ally popped up beside her to lean on the bar and watch. Once Rune cleared the white box from the brown, she tugged open the cover to find a mobile phone sitting inside. Staring at it, she didn't see the two envelopes that had static-ed themselves to the inside of the lid until they

fluttered out as well. Ally snatched one before Rune could set down the lid.

"Careful, kid. We don't know what that is," Alf tried to warn, but she already had it open, pulling out a small stack of sheets. Stamped across the top were the words, "Paid In Full."

"Isn't this the mortgage company for the bar?" Ally asked, pointing at the letterhead.

Rune furrowed her eyebrows and opened the other one. Folded inside a sheath of paper was an enormous check. Her eyes boggled out of her head at the amount.

"That's the bar's insurance company," Franklin said, leaning over Rune's head to look.

"I'll take that," Alf said, slipping it out of her hand and tucking it away.

That just left the mobile phone. Lifting it out, she saw it was sleek and silver. To Rune's unpracticed eye, it looked like a latest model. She turned it on.

"Are you sure that is safe?" Alf questioned, but it was too late. The screen booted on, and just as she started to look through the icons, it rang. She nearly dropped it. Everyone else startled about as much.

She answered it.

"Hello?"

"Anna!" the excited voice on the other side cried. The voice of Justin. The wrong Justin.

"What do you want?" she asked.

"Anna?"

"My name is not Anna, and you know that," she said in no uncertain terms.

There was a long pause. "I thought I would get a different response than this when I called you. You did get the envelopes in the box, right? There should be two of them."

"Yes, we found the envelopes," she confirmed, still holding firm.

"And what do you say?"

"They're mine," she stated.

"Really?" he said annoyed. "I had your mortgage paid off in full. The bar is all yours now, and I smoothed out you getting your insurance paid out. You can rebuild."

"You paid it off," she looked toward her accountant, who had picked up the mortgage letter to look it over. She flipped the mobile away and hit the speaker button, so all of her people could hear.

"Yes, my gift to you. I think it is the least I owe my wife after all."

"Ex-wife."

There was another long pause. "I see. No, you're right, absolutely. There's a lot we need to work through, together. Let... Let's consider what I'm sending you here as alimony owed."

She knew he wanted her to say "thank you." She had no intention of doing so.

"I need to get going, Justin," she said, looking around at her people. "I have a lot of work to do."

"I'll contact you again, soon," the fake Justin promised and then he hung up. Rune set the mobile phone back into the box and set the lid back over it.

"Who was that, my Lady?" Ally asked.

"Trouble. And there is more to come, I bet," Alf harrumphed.

"You have no idea," Rune said, leaning against the bar. "And first things first, we're going to bring my husband home."

BOOK CLUB QUESTIONS

1. How do you think the way Maxamillion and St. Benedict met has colored their relationship?

2. Why do you think Rune is so focused on helping Jasmeen?

3. Should Rune have accepted St. Benedict's help or not?

4. Who do you think would be better for Rune: Maxamillion or St. Benedict?

5. Has your opinion of St. Rachel changed at all during the course of the story?

6. How will St. Benedict dedicating himself as a retainer change his relationship to Rune?

7. How much do you hate the author now that you know St. Benedict's secret? (Sorry) Did you see it coming?

8. Did you agree or disagree with Maxamillion's reaction to Rune at the end? Is his perspective about what happened fair?

9. Knowing what you know, what or who do you think is the thing that is pretending to be Justin?

10. Where do you think the story goes from here?

AUTHOR BIO

Author Megan Mackie writes something for everyone—she's written cyberpunk, urban fantasy, paranormal demon romance, speculative fiction, post-post zombie apocalypse, steampunk, and mid-grade science fiction. She's also a contributing writer for RPGs Legendlore and Legendlore: Legacies by Onyx Path.

She's a popular figure at comic cons across the country, so if you come across her, ask about the Lucky Devil series and prepare to get your mind blown.

Whats the news, Barman?

Sign Up for Megan's Newsletter!
https://www.meganmackieauthor.com/newsletter

Also check out her free Wattpad novel!
https://www.wattpad.com/1423396171-i-can%27t-get-the-
vampire-rogue-to-romance-me

**It was all fun, until she got
sucked into the game.**

OTHER BOOKS BY MEGAN MACKIE

URBAN FANTASY/CYBERPUNK

THE LUCKY DEVIL SERIES
The Finder of the Lucky Devil
The Saint of Liars
The Devil's Day
The Digital Mage
Demonic Inc. – Coming Soon

THE SAINT CODE SERIES
The Lost
Constable – Coming Soon

MID-GRADE SCIENCE FICTION

THE ADVENTURES OF PAVLOV'S DOG AND
SCHRODINGER'S CAT
Maxwell's Demon
The Ship of Theseus - Coming Soon
Sniffy the Virtual Rat – Coming Soon

POST POST-ZOMBIE APOCALYPSE

DEAD WORLD
The Prisoner of the Dead
The Journey to Naraka – Coming Soon
The Damned Road – Coming Soon

SUPERHERO

WORKING MASKS
The Vilification of Aqua Marine
The Indemnification of Black Heart - Coming Soon

EPIC FANTASY

SILVERBLOOD SERIES
Silverblood Scion